A DEFENSE

FOR THE DEAD

FORGE BOOKS BY MICHAEL FREDRICKSON

A Cinderella Affidavit
Witness for the Dead
A Defense for the Dead

A DEFENSE
FOR THE DEAD

Michael Fredrickson

A TOM DOHERTY ASSOCIATES BOOK
NEW YORK

A DEFENSE FOR THE DEAD

Copyright © 2004 by Michael Fredrickson

All rights reserved, including the right to reproduce this book, or portions thereof, in any form.

This book is printed on acid-free paper.

A Forge Book
Published by Tom Doherty Associates, LLC
175 Fifth Avenue
New York, NY 10010

www.tor.com

Forge® is a registered trademark of Tom Doherty Associates, LLC.

Library of Congress Cataloging-in-Publication Data

Fredrickson, Michael.
    A defense for the dead / Michael Fredrickson.—1st ed.
        p.   cm.
    "A Tom Doherty Associates book."
    ISBN 0-312-87457-X (acid-free paper)
    EAN 978-0312-87457-5
    1. Serial murders—Fiction.   2. Boston (Mass.)—Fiction.   I. Title.

    PS3556.R3826D44   2004
    813'.54—dc22
                                                        2004040357

First Edition: May 2004

Printed in the United States of America

0   9   8   7   6   5   4   3   2   1

In memory of Jim Tyack

For Charlie Edwards-Hides and Kandi Kane–
reigning king and queen

A fetish is a story masquerading as an object.

−Robert J. Stoller, m.d.

If virtue is its own reward, then vice must be, well, versa.

−James A. Morrissey, Esq.

CONTENTS

A DEFENSE

FOR THE DEAD

CHAPTER ONE

THE SHEEP LIE

Jimmy Morrissey looked like a million bucks–in crumpled tens and twenties. With his feet up on his battered desk and the morning mail a drifting pile on his belly, he looked and felt like the very picture of rumpled repose.

He wielded a Bic ballpoint as a letter opener, clumsily ripping apart envelopes, some of creamy bond from other lawyers, others made of the cheap stock favored by the courts of the Commonwealth. He tore open requests for written interrogatories. Notice of a pretrial conference in his will contest. An adversary's threat to seek sanctions if certain documents were not produced with dispatch. Junk mail from a firm that found dubious expert witnesses for you. A hand-addressed envelope showing the Norfolk House of Corrections as its return address–from a prisoner, no doubt, demanding to know the status of his motion for a new trial. A stenographer's bill, third notice. And no checks whatsoever.

The pile included phone messages, too. Little needling pink slips, of sometimes ominous import. Like the one from an old client wanting to get "some property" returned to him–his file, perhaps? Never good news: the only reason that sprang to mind for requesting a dead file was to see if another lawyer could find fault with your handling of it. There was a call from Phyllis. One from his adversary in the will contest. A client wanted a status report on her slip-and-fall.

Jimmy sighed, papers still heaped helter-skelter across his swollen midsection. He had a dull day's work ahead of him. Documents to produce, some correspondence, a stubborn claims adjuster to badger. Plus trial prep for the will contest. He felt his stomach muscles clench against the stress that would seize him while gearing up and trying yet another bitter family dispute. And the lawyers he came up against just seemed to get younger and hungrier, as if they were in a competition to see who would prove the most mindlessly disputatious of the lot.

Maybe he could just blow it off for today and go home after lunch. Pick up Phyllis and take her for a drive or something. She'd like that, getting out and around for a change.

Thoughts of this wife's health ruffled what remained of his equanimity. Little snakes' tongues of depression flicked at him. He felt himself stepping into a swale of sadness and regret. As if bidden by some wistful pixie, he slipped into wishing for a major–no, make that tumultuous–change in his life. Away from his dull, drooping practice, from the tangled nets of a love turned terrifying. He pressed his eyes shut against the brutal certainty that nothing like that would befall him, no release would free him.

Then something filled the open doorway to his office.

It was Taffy, the office receptionist, bookkeeper, desultory secretary. Her short hair was an eggshell white this month, moussed into glistening spikes like a pomaded toilet brush.

"Jimmy," she said hesitantly. "There's some people here to see you."

Missing was the breezy disrespect she usually showed everyone in the office. Her altered aspect put him on edge.

"Do they have an appointment? Because I don't remember–"

"They're from the FBI. From Miami, they said."

He blinked back at her in confusion, but not for long. "Well," he said with a grunt as he lifted his feet off the desk, "show them in. We can't be having the federal government cooling their heels in a dump like this."

She disappeared. He gathered the clutch of papers with both hands and tossed them willy-nilly onto his pig's trough of a desk. He was wondering whether he should clear away some of the clutter when his doorway filled once again.

He had expected stocky guys in dark suits and shiny black shoes, champions of a Bureau still overcompensating for those gratifying stories of J. Edgar Hoover in a red tutu. What he got was a rangy, straw-haired man in a camel-hair blazer and knit tie, teamed with a good-looking woman under a blond China chop. Still, he felt J. Edgar's haunting presence, as if the old fruitcake were completing a hellish threesome.

"Attorney James Morrissey?" said the man, his badge wallet dangling open before him. The woman closed the office door softly.

"The sheep lie," Jimmy said earnestly, shaking the hand he was offered.

The man screwed up his face in puzzlement, mouth slightly open.

Jimmy took it another step. "You're not gonna take the word of a bunch of mangy sheep, are you? Over that of a sworn officer of the court? It was consensual, I swear."

Before the guy could respond, the woman said, "He's making a joke, Wallace." Her tone suggested this wasn't the first time she'd had to put him in the picture.

She stepped forward with a smile and offered her own hand. "Mr. Morrissey, I'm Special Agent Eleanor Butler. And this is Special Agent Ponsonby. Wallace. He's not much with jokes."

A quick glance at Agent Ponsonby confirmed this. He gave Jimmy a sour look, then turned away. He impassively took in the room and the disarray on the desk before him. Jimmy pushed aside a teetering stack of files so that he could view both of them at once from his chair.

The woman looked to be in her early forties. Button nose, freckles, pleasant manner. He liked her smile.

"Thank you for seeing us on such short notice," she said pleasantly.

"No notice at all, actually," he reminded her with a grin.

She gave him a propitiating dip of the head.

Jimmy gestured toward the oak chairs, and she sat down. Ponsonby followed suit a moment later, but he retained a sullen mien. Butler crossed her legs with an electric crackle of fabric and got briskly down to business.

"Well, let me explain why we're here. Mr. Morrissey, do you know a man named William Wolff?" She spelled the last name.

"William Wolff?" Jimmy rolled the name around in his mouth, giving the question more thought than it required. "No. I don't think I know anyone by that name."

"Does this help?" Ponsonby asked.

He handed him a photograph. It was a mug shot. The head-on view showed a heavy, nondescript young man with short brown hair, while the profile revealed a sharply receding chin beneath thin lips.

"Still no," he said after a moment.

Butler trotted out a bunch of other names, her eyes bobbing back and forth between Jimmy's face and a slip of paper in her hand. James Barry. Deon Chevalier. Edward Hyde. Godfrey Norton. Jimmy shook his head amiably at each.

The two agents exchanged glances. Ponsonby spoke up this time.

"What about Van Gogh?" he asked.

"The painter?" Jimmy's smile broadened. He pictured Kirk Douglas in the movie, standing desolate in a wheatfield.

"No," Ponsonby said flatly. "The killer. You heard of *him*?"

He had indeed. As a reader of the *Herald*, which wallowed in its crime stories, there was no way Jimmy could have missed the lurid coverage of the butcher the media had dubbed Van Gogh—so called because his signature was the harvesting of an ear from each of his victims. But that was about all he knew.

"Of course," he said. "But—"

"That's him," Ponsonby continued, which prompted Jimmy to examine the photograph again. "We sent a team to arrest him yesterday. Traced him to a small bungalow in Key West, Florida. He was shot while resisting arrest. Died on the operating table. His real name, we've learned, was William Wolff. The other names are aliases he's used in the past."

Butler said, "It's been a long haul for us. He's responsible for at least nine murders. In New York, Miami Beach, San Francisco, Washington, Key West—"

"And Boston," Jimmy threw in helpfully. That much he knew.

"*Two* in Massachusetts, actually," Butler corrected. "One here, in the South End. The other in Provincetown."

"My congratulations, I guess," Jimmy said as he handed back the photograph. "But what does this have to do with me?"

"Tying off loose ends," Ponsonby said, as if that explained anything. He slipped the photo into a vinyl briefcase perched on his lap, then dug around in it for a moment. "We found this on the nightstand beside Wolff's bed." He extracted a large gray envelope and emptied its contents into his hand. "Propped against a lamp. Like something he didn't want to forget to take with him." He leaned forward and handed it to Jimmy. "Do you recognize this woman?"

Intrigued, Jimmy took it from him. It was a photograph. Not a snapshot but a studio portrait, an eight-by-ten glossy in black and white. The subject was a young woman, in three-quarter profile, who smiled knowingly back at the camera over a bare left shoulder. A very attractive young woman. Soft blond hair and sparkling eyes of a washed-out hue that, even caught in black and white, you knew was blue or green.

But it was her expression that transfixed him. There was something uncanny about it. It was a look that insinuated—as if she knew things about you, about unspeakable desires you told no one.

"Mr. Morrissey?" Butler smiled at him from across the desk, interrupting his little *coup du portrait.*

"Uh, no," he said. "I've never seen her before. Was she one of his victims?"

He hoped not.

A look passed between the two agents before she answered. "No. All his victims were men. Gay men, actually."

"Homosexuals," Ponsonby added helpfully.

Jimmy smiled. "Tell me that's *not* why you came to me."

"Turn it over," Ponsonby commanded.

Jimmy obeyed. The writing was upside down, but as soon as he righted the photo and could make out what was written there, he froze. The blue ink appeared to swim on the white surface in sympathy with his bewilderment. Written in an almost childish hand on the back of the stiff paper was his name. James A. Morrissey. Followed by his business address, his home address on Vinal Avenue in Somerville, and his home and office telephone numbers.

He looked up at them with pop-eyed wonder. The two agents stared back at him, stolid and implacable, as if waiting to see whether this slack-jawed moron would give himself away.

"You sure you don't recognize the face?" asked Special Agent Ponsonby. "Turn it over and take another look."

As if to buff the rasp off her partner's rudeness, Special Agent Butler smiled encouragingly, with a faint nod at the photograph Jimmy held in his hand.

Jimmy turned it faceup again. Struggling to regain his composure, he tried to focus on the figure in the photograph. *Chilled,* he thought. That's how they described it in novels. *So call me tacky: I feel chilled.* As if he'd been groping in the dark, and his hand came to rest on a slab of raw meat. With a flaccid smile, he looked up at the agents again and shook his head.

"You have no idea how your name and address came to be found among Wolff's effects?"

"None whatsoever." A rankling edge of incredulity had crept into Ponsonby's voice. The adversarial turn made Jimmy snap to, forcing him to gather his wits about him once more. He laid the photo on the desktop and stared sulkily down at it. No one spoke for a moment.

"Is it his handwriting, do you know?"

"We believe so," Ponsonby said.

Butler weighed in again. "Have you ever been to Key West, Mr. Morrissey?"

He looked up at her and frowned. "Yes. Four, maybe five years ago. A vacation. But . . ." He shrugged again.

"But nothing sticks out about the trip?"

"Sticks out? In relation to what?"

"No odd encounters with strangers?"

"No."

She pressed her lips together. "I have to ask this, Mr. Morrissey. Please don't be offended."

"I'm not gay," he said, heading her off. "And I'm not offended." He cocked his head. "You think I should be?"

"No," she said quickly, wincing a little. "Of course not." They smiled tightly at one another.

"What about the newspapers?" Ponsonby asked. "Could he have read about you, maybe? You know, some high-profile case you were working on?"

Jimmy gave a little snort. "Look around you. And check out the view while you're at it." He tossed his head in the direction of his window, which looked out on an air shaft and the sooty bricks of the neighboring building. Butler looked; Ponsonby's eyes stayed on Jimmy. "Does this *look* like the office of a lawyer with a lot of high-profile cases? I got what you call a transom practice here. It comes over the transom, I take it. Believe me, he didn't get my name from the papers." Jimmy gave him a grin. "I had a gay sexual harassment case once, but I don't think that would do it. Do you?"

It was Ponsonby's turn to shrug. "Well," he said, "maybe we'll figure it all out someday. Like I said, it's just a loose end. We had the guy dead to rights anyway." He gave a little half smile. "Maybe I didn't put that right," he added.

Jimmy caught Butler's eye. "And you said he wasn't much for jokes."

She smiled at this and uncrossed her legs. She looked over at her partner, expectantly.

They were going to leave, Jimmy realized at once. He also knew they didn't much care if this loose end stayed untied. Dead to rights, indeed. They were just going through the motions. They were going to pick up this diversion, this . . . okay, release, and leave him in the same puddle they'd found him in.

"What about the names?" Jimmy asked quickly. "The aliases?

We could run them through the former client list and see if we get any hits. Just 'cause I don't recognize him doesn't mean he wasn't one of mine. I've had hundreds of clients. Thousands, even. I can check right now, in fact. It'll just take a couple minutes. You like some coffee?"

"No," said Ponsonby.

"I wouldn't mind," said Butler. "Extralight." Her partner shot her an irritated glare, but she ignored him. Jimmy returned her smile, then picked up the phone and punched in a three-digit number.

"Taffy," he said. "Can you come in here a second? And bring a cup of coffee for Agent Butler, wouldja? Lotsa milk." He hung up without waiting for a reply. Why leave her an opening? He was pushing it, he knew: Taffy didn't *do* coffee. But he was hoping the FBI's presence would bring her around—and keep her civil.

To Butler he said, "Can you let me see that piece of paper you read those names off of? I'll get Taffy to run them down."

She paused, looking down at the sheet, then turning it over to check the back. Apparently satisfied she wasn't giving away the store, she handed it to Jimmy. With obvious reluctance, he observed. He took his time reading them over, then looked up at his visitors.

"Let me write them down," he said as he scribbled on a note-pad, "and if—"

Taffy opened the door, sooner than he'd expected. As he turned abruptly in her direction, his arm collided with a stack of folders, which started to topple. He lurched clumsily after them, but that only made them tip over into his lap. The one on top slid out of his grasp and onto the floor, spilling papers at his feet. For a moment all four of them just stared at the mess. The sense of chaos was heightened by the nearly illegible doodles scribbled over the outsides of almost all of the folders—a bad habit that Jimmy seemed unable to break.

"Your coffee," he sighed, as if in explanation. He moved the armful of folders from his lap to the desk, where they wobbled pre-cariously. "No, please," he said to Butler, halting her before she reached her feet. "I've got it." He bent over to scoop up the spilled file. As he was tamping the edges of the reassembled file on his desktop, Taffy held out a paper coffee cup to see who would take it. Butler did and thanked her. Jimmy did, too.

"And Taffy?" he added, tearing off the sheet of names. "Would you please check these names against my old client list? See if any of them match up."

Taffy narrowed her eyes mutinously. He gave her his most beseeching smile. Relenting at last, she turned and moved silently in the direction of the door.

"Wait!" he added quickly. He grabbed the pad and jotted a rapid note, which he tore off and stuffed it into a manila folder he fished off his desk. "Give this to Vogelman and tell him I'll just be a minute. Okay?"

She frowned. "Vogelman?"

Jimmy fixed her with an earnest look. "Yes, Vogelman."

She gave him an odd look, but she took the folder. With a sullen nod she left the room.

"Now," he said as he directed his attention back to the agents and started squaring the pile on his desk. "What can you tell me about this Wolff fellow?"

Not much they were willing to share, he discovered. He soon tired of trying to chip information out of such obdurate rock and chose instead to make small talk with Butler. She was local, he learned, not from the Miami field office like Ponsonby. The two of them chatted about people Jimmy knew in the Boston office. Jimmy had just asked if she had any news of Ryan Butters, late of the Organized Crime Strike Force, when Ponsonby abruptly butted in.

"The photograph," he said peremptorily. "I need it back. It's evidence."

"Oh, of course," Jimmy said, snapping his fingers at his absent-mindedness. He looked down at his desk with his hands in the air, fingers waggling. "I had it right here in front of me before my little, ah, mishap with that stack of files." He shuffled papers and folders around on his desk for a few clammy moments.

The door opened, and Taffy strode in.

"Ah," said Jimmy, beaming at her. "Mercury's daughter." He reached out his hand for the manila folder she carried. "And what's the news?" He opened the folder like a menu in front of him.

"*Nada*," said Taffy. "No matches. We've got no record on any of these guys."

Looking up at his guests, Jimmy sighed audibly. "Sorry. It was worth a shot."

Butler stood up first. "Well, thank you for your time, Mr. Morrissey. If anything else comes to mind, just give us a tootle." She handed him her business card and took a last swallow of coffee. She set the paper cup on his desk.

"A tootle," he repeated doubtfully as he examined her card. She had added her direct line in neat cursive.

She nodded in the direction of his new cell phone, where it sat cradled in its charger on his desk. "You know," she said, working her fingers over the stops of an imaginary flute. "A tootle."

"Ah, yes. I will, I will indeed. Oh! And your photo!" He dug again, finding it this time, and handed it over to Ponsonby with a flourish. "That's one-good looking lady," he added with a smile.

Ponsonby grunted. He slid the photo into its big envelope, which he tucked into his briefcase.

Jimmy showed Special Agents Butler and Ponsonby—and the ghost of J. Edgar, who knows?—out his office door and shook hands again. As Taffy escorted them toward the lobby, he noticed that Ponsonby took strides a little too short for a man his size. They were gingerly, mincing steps, like those of an aging athlete with blown-out knees.

But I thought you said he took it with him?" Phyllis said that evening, when he showed her the photograph.

She was feeling pretty good for a change. The new drugs, she thought, and he had to admit her color was much improved. Maybe it was just a trick of the creamy light from the floor lamp. He'd helped her prop herself up in the daybed, the one in the living room, with the big reading pillow wedged in behind her. He sat facing her beside the bed in a straight-backed wooden chair.

"My little sleight of hand," he explained. "I was sure they'd never *let* me copy it. So I slipped it into the folder I gave to Taffy with a note to copy it–discreetly. Both sides. And not a bad job, don't you agree?"

She squinted at the high-quality copy Taffy had made of the photograph, then at the copy of the writing on the back. "Mmm," she said. "And what did Taffy have to say?"

"She wanted to know who the hell Vogelman was."

Phyllis smiled. "I'll bet she did." After a moment she added, "She's pretty, don't you think?"

"Taffy?" But he knew better.

"Don't be perverse. I mean the woman in the picture."

"I confess I had a few impure thoughts. Stirred the old dragon."

He regretted this flippancy at once. She said nothing, but she couldn't hide the tightening of the skin around her mouth. He cast about in search of a remark to divert her from one of those black spaces in which she lamented having become such a burden to him. Before her illness their silences had often been the hallmark of an easy intimacy. Now they were dark defiles in which their mutual terrors and inadequacies lurked, ready to spring up at the least misstep. Before he could think of what to say, she lowered the photocopies to her lap and looked down toward the foot of her bed.

She said, "It's kind of disturbing, don't you think? To know this . . . sicko made a point of finding out where you work and live? What does it all mean?"

Jimmy acknowledged that he didn't have a clue. In response to her question, he also admitted he couldn't fully explain why he had risked his little game of three-card monte with the FBI. "Maybe," he mused aloud, "it was because I knew it was the only chance I'd ever have to find out why Van Gogh had my name and address. Believe me, they don't much care. It was just a loose end, the guy said, and with the killer dead, they'll lose interest real fast in my little riddle."

"You mean," she said, "you plan to solve it yourself?" She wore a skeptical smile now. Laughing at him a little. A flash of the old scoffing irreverence with which she could keep him back on his heels.

"Well . . . maybe just poke around a little. See what I can dig up."

The two of them left it there, moved on to other things. Her day. What she was reading. How much better she was feeling. He realized he felt a little guilty for leaving out the questions that troubled him about his own day. Such as how he didn't know which side of the photo disturbed him more, the one with his name and address in a serial killer's hand, or the one showing that haunting woman with whom he apparently shared something he could not begin to fathom. Or the suspicion that he might have sneaked a copy of the photo because he felt protective, for some inarticulable reason, toward the young woman in the photograph. Or maybe, he was starting to wonder, maybe he was just suckered in by the intrigue of it all.

Because he knew someone or something had granted his foolish wish that morning. His diversion. His release. Running away from the drudgery and stress? Yes, he supposed so. And from the lurking terror and dread he felt every time he looked at Phyllis. But how could he tell her that?

So he buried qualms about his silence under the certainty that this diversion would be brief, a tiny respite from the aching pull of the traces. Just a few discreet inquiries. See what he could dig up, if anything. Then he'd give it up.

But of course he couldn't have known how it would send him dancing on the dizzy edge of things.

CHAPTER TWO

BRANDY PETE'S

I t wasn't as if Jimmy had to abandon his practice or neglect his wife to go out and do a lot of arcane research to learn about Van Gogh. All he had to do was read the local papers. Given the Massachusetts connection ("Two Bay State Victims!"), they feasted on the guy over the next two weeks. Readers were treated to a hastily mounted cavalcade festooned with lurid details: dramatic retellings of his last (failed) murder attempt, tales of FBI derring-do, grab bags of biography, instant psychiatric analysis. Stripped into the coverage were sidebar histories of his nine known victims flanked by photographs of their grim-faced survivors. Reporters descended on the killer's acquaintances: his bored Key West neighbors, who seemed not to know him, and the stunned ones in Felska, Minnesota, who had.

So Jimmy just read. Took notes. Clipped stories and photographs. He put together a little chronology, as best he could, just as he would have done if he were working his way into a new criminal case. He was trying to get a picture of the guy. He dug hard for some overlooked connection, some seemingly trivial bit of data that might summon a wisp of memory—anything at all, in other words, that might explain how he had ever wormed his way into the gnarled consciousness of a serial killer. There wasn't much.

Born William Allard Wolff in Enid, Oklahoma, in 1971, Van Gogh was the only child of Harris and Marjorie Wolff. He was an army brat, shifted from base to base seven times before reaching his teens. His father, a career boozer and ne'er-do-well who thrice reached—and lost—the rank of master sergeant, abandoned his wife and son within weeks after a general discharge was foisted on him in 1984. When the news broke, reporters tracked Harris Wolff to a sawmill outside of Medford, Oregon. He gave each one of them the finger, then returned to his silent watch over a woodchipper that turned the mill's bark trimmings into mulch.

Marjorie and her son had migrated to the Midwest, first to Ohio, where she had been born. After brief stints in Columbus and Dayton and Akron, they managed to sink shallow roots in Felska, Minnesota, a windswept town way up north on the worked-out Mesabi Iron Range. Marjorie had a saleable skill; she was a beautician. While William finished his last three years of high school in Felska, she supported them by giving permanents and manicures.

"And head," Eddie Felch added as he peered over the foam topping his schooner of draft beer. "But you won't read that anywhere,'cause who wants a libel action up his ass, right?" Eddie took a closed-eyed sip and smacked his lips, then twisted his slight frame about so he could scan the lunch tables for people he knew.

Eddie Felch was a distasteful, ferret-faced man in an unpressed chambray shirt and black Levis'. Eddie had covered the Van Gogh story for the *Globe* for the last year, and Jimmy needed a conduit to whatever might not have made it into the papers. The two of them were having lunch at the bar of Brandy Pete's, a watering hole favored by stockbrokers and lawyers on the northern edge of Boston's Financial District. Three lawyers, in fact, stood at the far end of the bar, where they were passing war stories around like a joint. A gigantic photograph of Pete himself, his splayed fingers reaching for the cigar in his mouth, hung right over the bar. The place had turned upmarket since moving into its new quarters a few years ago, and the menus no longer proclaimed Pete's longstanding motto: *Where the customer is always wrong.*

"Head?" Jimmy said, looking up sharply from his shepherd's pie. "She was a hooker?"

"That's what the cognoscenti say in downtown Felska. And in a town that size, nobody misses much."

"Isn't that a little too pat? I mean, the *mother*, for Christ's sake. A weekend Freudian could do a real number on this guy. It sounds like *Psycho* or something."

Eddie sucked in his cheeks to drag deeply on his cigarette—the reason they were teetering on high chairs at the bar instead of enjoying a comfortable booth upstairs. "I don't know from pat," he snorted through the smoke. "Or Freud. I do know that woman is one chilly drink of hooch. I met her last week—or tried to, anyway. Looks right through you with these ice-blue eyes that have seen everything. I sure wouldn't want to be a naughty little boy in *that* house. A real scrotum tightener, that one."

The two men lapsed into silence as Jimmy returned to his lunch. Eddie took another sip of his.

One thing Jimmy had been able to discern without Eddie's help: Van Gogh was no Hannibal Lecter. Even the guy's handwriting told you that—he wrote in a child's scrawl, not the copperplate calligraphy of the fictional demon. William Wolff was nobody's idea of a towering intellect. An undistinguished student, he'd received no education of any kind after receiving a mediocre high-school diploma. No trade, no skills to speak of. Leaving Felska right after graduating in 1989, he disappeared for several years before a leaving tracks in a series of arrests for minor offenses. Shoplifting in Des Moines. Possession of a Class B substance in Pittsburgh, followed quickly by an indecent exposure bust in Cleveland. An A & B in St. Louis. He dropped out of sight again.

Then, in 1996, he popped up in Boston, working as a busboy at the Howard Johnson on Commonwealth Avenue. After a few months in the hotel business, he drifted about town, taking a number of jobs, usually unskilled, for low pay. Fry cook. Cab driver. Accounts receivable clerk at one of the city's hospitals. Same thing for an optometrist. A gofer for a law firm. Kitchen prep. Stock man for a computer assembler. Another bust along the way, this time in Waltham for petty theft. Charges dismissed.

An anonymous drifter, in other words. Of interest to no one. Until March 7, 1999, that is. That was when complaints about the smell emanating from the South End apartment of Jonathan Ridley impelled the building superintendent to open the door. The young man's putrefying body, trussed up and missing his right ear, was found facedown in his own bed. Although no one knew it yet, Ridley was the first in a series, part of a pattern that was to be repeated with ritual rigor. Bloodstream full of sedatives. Bound hand and foot. Strangled. Raped.

"In that order, too," Eddie took pains to emphasize. "First he drugged them—something in their drinks, they figure. Then he'd tie 'em up before strangling them. And *then* he raped them."

Jimmy pushed his half-eaten lunch away.

"Didn't mean to put you off your native feed," Eddie said, without even the pretense of sincerity. "You said you wanted details. Stuff they didn't print."

"I never expected necrophilia."

"Hey, that way they don't talk back."

For six months Ridley's death remained just a South End curiosity, another bizarre urban horror story to titillate the straights in other, presumably safer, neighborhoods. Ridley became the stuff of smug op-ed pieces on how the seamy erotic life of gay men could turn deadly.

Then another killing, identical in every relevant detail, was reported in Minneapolis. Soon thereafter, it became apparent that Van Gogh, as he was now known, was a serial killer. A peripatetic one, too. From Minnesota he went on to San Francisco, then Los Angeles, New York, Washington, Miami, Provincetown ("HE'S BACK!" screamed the *Boston Herald*), Key West. He seemed to pick up the pace as time went on, the killings separated by shorter intervals—an indication, the shrinks opined after it was all over, that the internal pressures were becoming unmanageable, that he was about to self-destruct. Which he seemed to do, when he went after a second Key West victim less than two weeks after the first. And blew it.

Not really, Eddie explained. His luck ran out, was more like it. It was just that Number 10–a twenty-four-year-old recent arrival from Hoboken named Blake Siegel, who sold books at Flaming Maggie's–couldn't hold his liquor and knew it. So Siegel made it his clandestine habit, he would later explain to anyone who would listen, to pour out the lion's share of the drinks served to him. To keep himself from getting sloppy drunk, he said. As a consequence, he ingested a much smaller dose of Seconal than Van Gogh's previous victims. He got enough in him to knock him out like the others, but the pressure of the first knot being pulled tight about his wrist brought him back to his senses. Tearing himself away, Siegel ran screaming out the door of his apartment and into the startled arms of the local constabulary.

Van Gogh had fled, too, but in his haste he left behind what the reports called identifying forensic data.

"DNA?" Jimmy asked.

"Nothing so trendy," said Eddie. "No, it was the evidence formerly known as prints. Fingerprints. On the glass he'd slipped the mickey in."

Within twenty-four hours, the FBI had his photograph and address, and were deploying a SWAT team outside his dwelling, a rented bungalow around the corner from the Key West Alano Club. Agents fitted out in helmets and Kevlar vests stormed the place without risking a knock.

"Like it was Ruby Ridge," Eddie explained. "And he was waiting for them. But not the way you'd expect. He was just sitting there in the dark, in the only chair in his bedroom. So far as anybody could tell, he never budged–despite all the racket they made. When they reached the room, he just lifted his right hand and pointed something at them. So they shot him. You know what it was he pointed at them? A rolled umbrella. A fucking umbrella, they killed him for. Some heroes, huh?" Eddie guzzled beer.

"It sounds more like assisted suicide," Jimmy threw in.

Eddie shrugged. "Suicide by cop."

"And the photo was just leaning against the lamp beside him."

"So you tell me. With your name on the back."

"Like he'd put it there so they wouldn't miss it."

"Or so he wouldn't forget to take it with him when he left. Except there's no indication he was planning to leave."

Certainly not. One of the bedroom's walls was covered with press clippings detailing his exploits. In a beat-up highboy they found a stainless-steel tube, like the kind architects use to carry blueprints, only much shorter, two inches thick, with threaded discs capping each end. Inside the tube were ears, right ones only, each one as preserved as a dried chanterelle and nestled into the next, Eddie observed with glee, like Pringles potato chips.

They found his killing kit under a beach towel in the closet. It was a small, dark green backpack, like the ones students used for carrying books. Inside he kept a box of white latex gloves, a change of clothes, a bottle of Seconol, a boning knife made by Chicago Cutlery, plastic bags, and three rolls of heavy nylon cord, each a different color.

"Green for tying the feet," said Eddie. "Red for the hands. And white to go around the throat–for the strangling."

"Really?" Jimmy was intrigued. "Different colors? I didn't read about any of this."

"Of course not. This was part of his signature, the tricolors. Think of the Italian flag, if it helps. No, this was information the feds kept absolutely quiet. I only heard about it after they'd nailed the guy. The business with the ears they couldn't control: too sensational. But the rope, that's different. It was how they could be sure the killings were by the same guy. Same cords, same guy. And the same sequence of colors every time."

Jimmy frowned. "I don't see how you can rape somebody with his feet tied together."

Eddie lit another Salem and grinned. "That's because you have provincial notions about sex. What do you Irish do for foreplay–an Act of Contrition? It's simple, actually: you turn the guy on his belly and shove his knees up under his stomach. *Voilà!* You're ready to board the red eye."

Jimmy grimaced. "So far you haven't given me much I hadn't

already picked up from the papers. Except for the hooker business, anyway. And the necrophilia."

"And the tricolors. Don't forget the tricolors."

Jimmy nodded, then took a meditative hit of his own beer. "There's just nothing here that suggests why he was interested in me. Nothing at all. Why bring me into this?"

Eddie squared around to face his luncheon companion. "Listen, Jimmy," he said in his most urgent tone. "That's why you gotta let me run this story. It's a natural, man. Think about it. We got Van Gogh's farewell note: nothing but his lawyer's name and address—and on the back of some chick's picture. Why? Inquiring minds want to know, Jimmy—and desperately. The resulting publicity could generate the lead you need."

Jimmy shook his head. "I'm *not* his lawyer, damn it. And I told you: no story. Not yet, anyway. I may not know what this guy had in mind, but I do know he chose a pretty roundabout and low-key way of doing it. I gotta think he had a reason for doing it this way. A *Globe* story might shake the bushes too much. Frighten the natives and all that. No, Eddie. Let me be my own bwana for a while. If my hunt comes up empty, we'll try your way. In any event, I promise you the exclusive. Just not yet."

Eddie emptied his schooner and, holding the bottom against his eye like a telescope, ostentatiously swept the horizon on the other side of the bar. Taking the hint, the barman brought him another draft.

Eddie took a luxurious pull. Stifling a belch, he said, "My wife tells me I gotta do something about my drinking. I say, 'Are you kidding? I couldn't possibly drink any more.' She doesn't appreciate me, sometimes." He glanced up at the two television sets, one on each side of Pete's portrait, both with ribbons of stock prices sliding below muted talking heads.

"You may be right about one thing," Eddie said. "The low-key business, I mean. Van Gogh was a coy one. He liked to play it cute. After the killings in Miami and Key West, he took to calling up the homicide dicks and giving them coded clues. You know, taunting them, like. Revealing just enough to convince them they were talking to the right guy, then stringing them along. The guy liked to play games."

"Is that what he's doing now? Playing games with me?"

"That seems pretty obvious. The question is, what's the game? And why?"

The question stayed with him, even after he left Eddie in his seat beneath Pete's cigar, the reporter waving for the barman's attention. Jimmy stepped out of the restaurant and felt the late-August heat slap him in the face. Stepping between two cabs stalled in the traffic, he crossed Franklin Street in safety. He plodded north on Batterymarch, turned left on Milk Street, then walked almost all the way to Washington before he realized he had passed the entrance to his office building. Shaking his head, he turned and doubled back.

He was grateful to duck into the cool interior of the lobby to his building. The security guard, a pretty African-American woman named Evelyn, was bent over a copy of the *Improper Bostonian* spread before her on the desk. She looked up, her wavy black hair glistening in the harsh artificial light, and smiled at him. He smiled back, feeling a tiny erotic charge.

It wasn't until he was in the elevator, the little car chugging noisily upward, that he thought about something Eddie had said. *Hadn't* said, actually. The elevator opened on the seventh floor, and Jimmy hurried into his office suite. He was leaning over his desk, waiting for his shuffling fingers to find the number for Eddie's cell phone in his Rolodex.

"Yes?"

"Eddie, it's Jimmy. One more question."

"When you're not here to buy? No way."

"Listen. The guy's kit. That was everything in it? I mean, the stuff you mentioned? That was all?"

A pause. "I can't think of anything we missed. Why?"

"There should have been something else, Eddie."

"Oh?" The reporter sounded amused.

"Condoms, Eddie. Wouldn't he be sure to have condoms? Or maybe he carried them in his wallet?"

"Ah," Eddie said, satisfaction in his voice. "Nope. No condoms. Not in his wallet. Not anywhere. I hate to break it to you like this. But the truth is, our friend did not practice safe sex. We know that from the postmortems."

Jimmy was quiet on his end.

"Maybe it's like the umbrella business, Jimmy."

Jimmy frowned, waiting.

"Maybe," Eddie explained, "the guy had a death wish."

Maybe. Jimmy hung up and sank into his abused chair. It whimpered at him. Staring blankly out his window at the drab brick wall visible across the air shaft, he tried to think through what Eddie had told him. He got nowhere. The image of Evelyn's smile kept intruding, breaking his concentration. It only took him a minute or two to realize what it was about the smile that had snagged him. It was a little bit like the other one. The one in the photograph.

CHAPTER THREE

CHERCHEZ LA FEMME

I f you take the Red Line train from Harvard Station to Downtown Crossing, as Thaddeus Glendening did every weekday morning, you can choose between exiting directly into the gusting swill of Chauncy Street or taking an indoor route through the handsome lobby of 101 Arch Street. To opt for the latter, you just climb the first set of stairs, head down the T tunnel about fifteen yards, and enter the lower level of 101 through a set of heavy glass doors. From there you're fed onto a narrow escalator that deposits you alongside the lobby's sleek security desk. Aromas from a coffee kiosk trail you past a gift shop calling itself the Urban Survival Kit. You hang a right in front of the shoeshine stand and make a point of looking up at the intricately wrought fire escape, a circular marvel of dark green iron chased by a gleaming brass railing, all still bolted to the exposed brick of what was once the facade of the old Kennedy's Boys' and Men's Clothing Store. Angling past Lawyers Stationery, you descend three steps, then three more, before you reach the revolving door that opens into Arch Street.

Such was Thaddeus Glendening's route, on a fine April morning, to The Trained Eye, a smart little shop he owned in the lobby of 75–101 Federal Street, less than a block farther along. As he ascended the escalator, Thaddeus was engrossed in *The Portrait of a*

Lady. He kept on reading when he stepped onto the marble floor, so absorbed he didn't even look up at the fire escape. He resurfaced briefly so as not to lose his footing going down the two sets of steps past Lawyers Stationery, but he quickly submerged himself again. He was still devouring Henry James's overmasticated prose when he blindly entered the revolving door.

A soft collision telegraphed his mistake at once. He was not alone. He found himself sharing his quarter wedge of the doorway's enclosure with a woman who had entered just ahead of him. He struggled to keep his distance, but each time he hung back the force of the door behind him shoved him forward again. The result was an involuntary humping rumba against the woman's buttocks. She responded violently, with flying elbows and piercing shrieks. Their enforced intimacy was brief, but once outside she was not assuaged by his stammering apology.

"Asshole!" she spat at him. Though her neck was pulled back like a cobra, her face still seemed right in his. "You're a fucking pervert, you know that?"

"I . . . I didn't—"

"Bullshit!" He didn't really hear much of the rest of her tirade. He managed to observe that she seemed much younger than he was, in her midthirties at most, and she wore glasses with thick red plastic frames. A yellow silk scarf fluttered over her shoulder in the warm breeze. When she knocked him stumbling backward by driving the heel of her hand against his chest, he felt his humiliation was complete.

But not quite.

"What's the problem here?"

The voice belonged to a uniformed police officer, a crew-cut man even younger than she was. He seemed to have come out of nowhere. Then Thaddeus spotted the patrol car. Despite a half-hearted effort to pull off to the side, the cruiser was putting a kink in the flow of angry traffic on Arch Street. The driver was emerging from his side of the cruiser, looking for a break in the traffic to join his partner.

The policemen just collected names and addresses. Told the

woman where she could swear out a criminal complaint if she wished. Eventually she stalked off toward Franklin Street after shooting Thaddeus one last basilisk's glare. "Creep," she hissed. The driver of the patrol car winked at Thaddeus—which only upset him more.

A wreck by now, Thaddeus made his way to his store. He spent over an hour in the back, with the sliding glass doors closed, trying to regain some composure before opening for business. He called his wife, Susanna. She found his stumbling frottage as amusing as the policeman had, though of course she knew to a dead certainty that she had married no masher—a conviction, he sensed, not entirely lacking disappointment. He resolved to put the trauma behind him.

He was almost over it, too, when the summons came four days later. He was commanded to appear before a clerk-magistrate in the Boston Municipal Court. A hearing would take place to determine whether a criminal complaint should issue against him for indecent assault and battery.

Thaddeus was shattered. He had had no experience whatsoever with the criminal justice system. Worse, he had read newspaper stories about the Commonwealth's new registry for sex offenders. He recalled horrifying tales from other states of men trapped in its sticky web. A tipsy man was convicted of indecent exposure for peeing off the back deck of his suburban home in some mid-Atlantic state; he had been forced to register, then to call on all of his neighbors and identify himself as the sex offender living in their midst. Thaddeus knew he could not survive that.

What to do? The only lawyer he had ever dealt with was the sarcastic young woman who had negotiated the lease for his shop and handled the closing when he and Susanna purchased their home in Cambridge. How could he even *talk* to her about such a humiliating predicament?

Fortunately, his barber knew what to do. He referred him to Jimmy Morrissey. And Jimmy, God bless him, had saved Thaddeus Glendening. He angrily rebuffed an offer from the young woman's lawyer to drop the matter in exchange for a sum of money.

Are you sure? Thaddeus had asked tremulously.

You're not gonna pay her a dime, Jimmy insisted. It felt more like a command than a prediction, so Thaddeus obeyed.

Jimmy was as good as his word. He swaggered into the hearing room and explained that the woman was holding up his client for money. The clerk-magistrate denied the application. The problem went away. The only long-term fallout Thaddeus experienced was a newfound distaste for Henry James and an abiding aversion to taking the indoor route through 101 Arch.

Jimmy himself had no such aversion when, more than a year later, he, too, had occasion to detrain at Downtown Crossing—though from the Orange Line, in his case. So he took the lobby. Once through the infamous revolving door, Jimmy picked his way across Arch Street and strode briskly into a tiny cut-through called Winthrop Alley. The alley's cobblestones were interspersed with plates of cast brass, each a brick-sized bas-relief of a whimsical nature: lobsters, a recipe for navy bean soup, the steeple of the Old North Church, swans, a flute in three segments, Paul Revere on horseback, codfish, a racing scull, a set of keys trapped in congealed metal. There were others, but Jimmy didn't slow down to examine them.

Coming out the other end of the alley, he stopped to look up at the mixed marriage of 75 and 101 Federal Street. Seventy-five was a sixteen-story Art Deco masterpiece of tan brick inset with delicate scrollwork and hammered-brass panels burnished by the morning sun. One-oh-one Federal was much newer, built in the mid-1980s, but it alluded clumsily to the architectural style of its mate, with metallic ornaments like huge rivet heads studding the panels of gray stone that climbed fifty stories before giving way to improbable crenellations at the roofline. Even its doors were subtly aggressive, with square steel handles that looked sharp enough to cut flesh. Shackled at the ankles by a shared lobby, the two buildings brought to mind a still-attractive dowager escorted by a lanky Yuppie gigolo. Jimmy figured theirs must have been a shotgun union, forced on the couple by the Boston Redevelopment Authority.

He negotiated his way across the busy confluence of Otis and Devonshire Streets to enter the lobby. There was a Starbucks just inside the door, so he popped in for a cup of joltless joe. The woman who took his money told him The Trained Eye was located over in the 75 Federal end of the lobby, looking out on Franklin Street. It wasn't quite nine yet, but the shop was open when Jimmy got there. He stepped inside and looked around.

The Trained Eye sold film, developed photographs (Thaddeus did the custom work himself in a darkroom he maintained in the basement of his house), and brokered out framing and mounting jobs. A long countertop was fitted over a glass case displaying sample picture frames and matting materials. Photographic prints—original stuff, Thaddeus's own work, Jimmy surmised—were mounted all over the walls. Landscapes, mostly, in black and white, with delicate shadings and grainy textures. Jimmy was impressed with their quality, but he admitted he was easily impressed in such matters.

Thaddeus, dressed in festive grays, approached the counter with a bright, officious smile. When he recognized his visitor, his smile seemed to freeze momentarily, but then it broadened.

"Jimmy!" he said warmly as he rounded the counter, right hand outstretched, the other reaching for his guest's shoulder. The two men shook hands, Jimmy's eyes still taking in his surroundings on this, his first visit to his client's shop. Absently, he set his decaf down on the counter.

"Very nice, Thaddeus. Very nice indeed." He gestured toward the walls. "This your own work?"

"Yes, yes," said Thaddeus, with a wave of his hand, dismissing his life's work as an irksome interruption.

Jimmy nodded appreciatively. "Not bad. Really."

"How are you, Jimmy?" Thaddeus seemed to back off a little and examine his visitor. "You're not here with bad news, are you?"

"What?" Jimmy turned from a leafy autumnal glade to focus on the man. "Oh, no. Nothing like that. That business is over, Thaddeus. Trust me."

"I do." Thaddeus was beaming at him, but Jimmy knew his appearance had unsettled his client. He took a sip of his coffee.

"No," he said, "I'm here with a problem of my own. I was hoping you might be able to help me."

Thaddeus stood to attention. "Of course. Tell me how I can be of service." His voice took on the tooled precision he brought to his work.

From his inside jacket pocket Jimmy pulled out the photocopy. He unfolded it and smoothed it out on the counter before Thaddeus. Thaddeus peered down at it intently.

"It's this," Jimmy said. "I'm trying to track it down."

Thaddeus frowned. "Who is she?"

"I have no idea. But I need to find her."

Thaddeus looked blankly back at him.

"I need to find the photographer who took this picture," Jimmy explained. "Maybe he can lead me to her. Can you help?"

Thaddeus held his eye for a moment before examining to the photocopy again. "It's a Xerox copy," he said carefully, an edge of disapproval in his voice.

"It was the best I could do. I had a look at the original, but I don't have it now."

"Was there a stamp on the back, do you recall? A sticker, maybe? Or a copyright notice? Anything like that?"

"Nothing on the back," he said. Nothing that would help, anyway.

Thaddeus picked it up and held it up to the light. "Hmm. Well, it's a nice piece of work. Smartly executed."

"I thought so, too," Jimmy said, trying to sound encouraging.

"What you xeroxed," Thaddeus continued, "is a contact print. An eight-by-ten contact print made directly from an eight-by-ten negative. That's what gives it such sharp resolution: there's been no reduction and no enlargement." He pointed. "You can also see that the print was made edge to edge, completely uncropped. Hence the black border around it."

He stopped, turning the paper a quarter turn to examine the edges.

"What's all that mean?" Jimmy asked. "That it's a professional job?"

"Oh, yes. That's obvious. In fact, it's kind of a show-off print, if you know what I mean. A contact print lets you see the whole film, even the notch code—that's these three little Vs in the upper left corner. To make it look arty."

"Arty?"

"Yes. It gives it a rough-hewn look. Kind of like using a hand-held camera to make an art-house movie, if you know what I mean. You leave the markings in. This particular notch code indicates the photograph was shot on Tri-X—that's a black-and-white Kodak film, four hundred speed."

Jimmy pinched his chin and frowned. "I think you're losing me there, with this technical stuff. I just wanna find the guy. Does any of this help me do that?"

"I'm not sure," Thaddeus confessed. "You might be able to do something with these edge markings, over here on the right." He tapped the upper right corner with his forefinger. He paused. "Hold on a second."

Thaddeus sidled back around to his side of the counter and ducked down for a moment. When he reemerged, he was holding a black-rimmed magnifying glass. He turned the photocopy in his direction and bent over to examine it through the glass, shifting the paper slightly from time to time.

"And?" Jimmy prodded after waiting longer than he expected it to take.

"It's very interesting," Thaddeus said, spinning the page about and handing the glass to the lawyer. "Take a look for yourself. Can you read the edge markings?"

Jimmy moved the glass in and out, seeking an unblurred view. He could make out a salad of handwritten numbers and letters. He read them aloud.

"It looks like a one, then VP, a space, then two, one, one, nine, nine, six, K, four, nine, Z." He looked up at Thaddeus. "Is that what you got?"

"Just about. Though I think the first character is a letter, not a number. The letter *I.*"

Jimmy squinted through the glass again. "You might be right. It looks like the number one to me, but it could also be an *I.*" He fished in his shirt pocket and brought out a pen. Opening it, he jotted the alternative readings across the bottom of the photocopy:

1VP21199K49Z
IVP21199K49Z

"What's it mean?" he asked, as the two of them stared at what he had written. "Is it some industry code or something?"

Thaddeus slowly shook his head. "I doubt it. It's nothing I recognize. More likely it's an in-house code of some sort. A colophon, if you wish."

Jimmy cocked his head. "Color what?"

"A colophon. An inscription used by a printer or a publisher to identify his work. I use a Sharpie myself—a fine-point felt marker. This one's pretty obscure, though. Photographers usually want you to be able to read their name loud and clear, if you know what I mean. This fellow doesn't seem to care—which is what the pretentious ones sometimes do. Clarity would seem too, well, commercial."

"Just my luck," Jimmy grumped. "An arty-farty type who doesn't want people to know who he is."

Thaddeus smiled. "Oh, he wouldn't go *that* far. He may not want to parade his name in a crass fashion, like Yves St. Laurent or Valentino, but believe me: he wants to be identified. And he's pretty commercial anyway. Despite the border, this has the look of a publicity still, not an Annie Leibovitz portrait." He turned over the photograph and peered at the edges again. "The middle numbers look like a date," he said. "It could be February 11, 1999. Look here."

He turned the sheet over and, plucking Jimmy's pen from his fingers, drew parentheses around the numbers and slashes to separate them:

IVP (2/11/99) 6K49

"And the code segment after the date," Thaddeus continued, "assuming it *is* a date, might be a cataloging sequence of some kind.

So let's focus on the first group, the ones before the date. They seem promising."

"The One VP?"

"Or *I*VP. If it's the latter, they might be the photographer's initials. Or those of his business. You know: as in TTE–for The Trained Eye."

Jimmy looked hard at Thaddeus.

"You might give it a try," Thaddeus urged.

"How? Is there, like, a national directory of photographers? Or photographic shops?"

"National? Well, there's a trade association you could check out. The ASMP. I don't know how helpful that would be. I suppose you could just look under *I* for somebody with these initials. Assuming it *is* an *I* and not a one."

Jimmy's eyes popped wide open, and he started grinning. "Or the Yellow Pages. I could just look in the Yellow Pages."

Thaddeus frowned. "But I thought you needed a national directory. Is there such a thing as a national Yellow Pages?"

"No," said Jimmy, excited now. "Not that I know of, anyway. But I figure Boston's will do."

After all, the guy had picked a Boston lawyer. He must have had a reason. Yes, Boston would do, he thought.

But it wouldn't, he discovered as he riffled hurriedly through Thaddeus's phone book. There were no promising entries under Photo Finishing–Retail. The same held true for related categories, like Photo Offset Reproductions, Photo Retouching & Restoration, Photographers–Commercial, Photographers–Portrait, and–the big enchilada–Photographers. Jimmy even tried Photographers-Aerial. Zilch. Nothing likely to be abbreviated as IVP.

Thaddeus had moved on to other chores while Jimmy did his digging, but the client came over to him when he slapped the phone book shut. The cooling coffee slopped about in its paper cup.

"No luck?"

Jimmy shook his head. He had been so sure there, for a minute. The guy had picked him, a Boston lawyer. The guy had spent a lot of time in Boston. Why send the photo to a Boston lawyer if there was no Boston connection?

"I was thinking," Thaddeus said, his tone meditative. "There really are national Yellow Pages available."

Still lost in thought, Jimmy barely heard the words. He looked up at Thaddeus. "What?" he said.

"The Internet," Thaddeus continued. "You can do a Yellow Pages–like search online." He stopped, pursing his lips. "No, that won't work either, come to think of it. You have to have either a name or a city. You don't have a name, just these three letters, so you can't search that way. If you had the city, you could get a list by category, which is really what you were doing with the phone book. But it turns out you don't have the city either. So I don't know what to suggest."

Jimmy brightened again. "Phone books," he said. "*Other* phone books. I got a list of likely cities. If it's not Boston, it's probably one of those. Do you suppose Bell Atlantic stocks phone books from other cities?"

"Verizon," Thaddeus corrected. "Bell Atlantic calls itself Verizon now, but–"

"Okay, Verizon then."

"But Jimmy, you want the library, not the phone company."

"The library?" But Jimmy remembered as soon as the words left his mouth. Of course!

"Libraries," Thaddeus continued, "keep out-of-town telephone directories. They're reference materials. When I was in college I once had to–"

But Jimmy wasn't listening. He was flipping through the Yellow Pages again, stopping this time at Libraries–Public. Boston Public Library–536-5400.

"Can I use your phone?" he asked, interrupting Thaddeus in midremembrance. Thaddeus slid the console over to him.

Yes, he was told, the main branch of the Boston Public Library did stock volumes of the Yellow Pages for the major cities. Just ask at the information desk on the second floor of the Research Library.

Forty minutes later, after one more subway ride (on the Green

Line this time), Jimmy was paging purposefully through the Yellow Pages for Minneapolis, the site of Van Gogh's first murder after leaving Massachusetts. No luck. Jimmy had moved on from there to San Francisco and was looking for the Washington book–following in Van Gogh's footsteps, as it were–before he was struck stupid by the obvious.

Provincetown.

How could he have missed it? There were *two* murders in Massachusetts, and only one was in Boston. The other was in Provincetown. So maybe it wasn't a Boston lawyer but a *Massachusetts* lawyer Van Gogh wanted to pull into this thing. And the last time he looked, Provincetown was still in Massachusetts.

So was IVP. Or IP anyway. Right there in the Provincetown book, under Photographers–Portrait. And repeated under plain old Photographers. Iver Peairs–Fine Photography. 138 Commercial Street. With a sense of satisfaction, Jimmy carefully replaced the Provincetown phone book.

He was willing to bet Iver's middle name started with a *V.*

CHAPTER FOUR

NOBODY'S PERFECT

Holding a hand over the vent and feeling a stream of stale, tepid air, Jimmy cursed the air-conditioning in his nine-year-old Taurus. So he sat back and absently inched forward in the queue leading to Lopes Square, where Standish and Commercial Streets met to form the grinding hub of Provincetown. He wiped sweat off the back of his neck and watched the dancing cop do his shtick.

The cop was plump and elderly, a rubicund man behind dark glasses. Despite the ninety-degree heat he spun about with a skater's grace, effortlessly governing the flow of minivans and bicycles, underdressed pedestrians and overloaded SUVs outfitted for the Olduvai Gorge, all making their gravid way through the choked intersection. The cop pirouetted on one spit-polished toe, flicked imperative fingers, hectored stragglers, shouted crisp instructions, and generally played to the crowd of tourists, some of whom were catching his act on video for the folks back home.

Now nosed into the square, Jimmy saw his chance and fed gas to the Taurus. It squirted across Commercial like a melon seed. He nodded thanks to the policeman, who crooked an index finger to wave him on. Jimmy slowed to a crawl again, up the short spur to the Bay, past shops purveying knickknacks, ice cream and salt water taffy, costume jewelry, whale watch tours, T-shirts, ersatz tattoos, baseball caps. To his surprise, the parking lot at MacMillan Wharf was not full—a piece of almost unhoped-for good fortune on an August afternoon, even for a weekday. He paid the entry fee and circled in what seemed a vain search for an open space among the Volvos and Saabs and Explorers and Maximas—thinking, in the heat, *I am definitely undercarred.*

He found a slot at last, almost all the way to the pier. Berthed, he shut off the ignition and listened to the ticking of the cooling engine. After a moment he reached over to the passenger seat for his suit jacket, thought better of it, and instead slid his hand under it for the manila envelope. Opening it, he took out one of the copies he'd made of the photograph and folded it into his shirt pocket. He hauled himself out of the car. A smartening breeze off the Bay carried a welcoming coolness, like a wetted handkerchief on the brow. Breathing in the salt air, he peeled his sweated shirt away from his back. Then he slammed the car door and turned to make his way back toward the hubbub.

When he reached Commercial Street, he peered up at the Pilgrim Monument looming above him from the highest point in town. A curious memorial to the Pilgrims' brief sojourn there before moving on to Plymouth, the monument seemed anything but Puritan: an Old World campanile surmounted by battlements, as if plucked from a Tuscan hill town and heedlessly repotted in the sandy soil of Provincetown. A minaret on Coney Island. Jimmy asked the cop which way the numbers ran on Commercial and, following the guy's thumb, headed west. It surprised him a little; the serious galleries were congregated in the East End.

Apparently, the clear skies were keeping the beaches full and foot traffic down, for he was able to walk the north sidewalk of Commercial Street with minimal interference from oncoming pedestrians. He passed the town hall, the cinema, and untold bars and restaurants and erotic-toy stores and fudge outlets and card shops before the retail establishments began to thin out, giving way to guesthouses and even residences. And still number 138 lay ahead of him.

He almost walked past it, in fact, before he noticed the sign. It bore no number, just the name. Iver Peairs—Fine Photography. The sign hung from a metal lamppost near the front of a lawn surrounded by wrought-iron palings. Beyond the lawn crouched a bay-windowed bungalow in a state of some dilapidation, its white paint and red trim peeling like a dry scalp. The neglected siding didn't go with the garden, which was lovingly tended, the walk and borders rich with blossoms despite the heat. Cables of some bloomless ivy, wisteria perhaps, garlanded the fan window over the front door, its vertical glass panels ablaze with sunlight from the Bay. The building suggested a residence, not a place of business, but he pushed open the iron gate and took the flagstone path to the door. He was about to knock when he saw a notice to "Please Enter Quietly." He did his best to comply. A tiny bell jingled as he pushed the door inward.

He stepped into what looked for all the world like someone's empty living room. He took in a brocaded love seat flanked by two Mission-style floor lamps. A Windsor rocking chair. A pair of matched wing chairs with tatted antimacassars. Filling a corner to his right was a hutch crammed with bric-a-brac. If this was a business, it seemed more an antique store than a studio.

Except for the photographs. How could he have missed them when he first entered? They nearly obliterated the flocked wallpaper, climbing almost to the ceiling, each one mounted in the same black-metal frame with a discreet sticker in the bottom corner. Some were coastal landscapes, artfully done (perhaps too artfully?) and reminiscent of Glendening's work. Others were shots of collapsing rural structures, decaying barns and outbuildings and hutments, taken from unusual angles. There were also several studio portraits, all in black and white like the one in his shirt pocket. He advanced eagerly to look for black borders with the telltale edge markings that got him here.

There weren't any.

"May I help you?"

Startled, Jimmy spun about in the direction of the voice. It belonged to a woman, and she stood, backlit and self-consciously poised, in the very center of the triptych formed by the bay window. How did she get there?

"Uh, yes," he said, squinting at the woman, whose face he couldn't see clearly for the sun behind her and the shadow she made for herself. "I'm looking for Iver Peairs."

"I'm as close as you're likely to get," she said, her voice husky, smoky, he noticed. "And it rhymes with *spears*, not *spares*. It's not a fruit."

"Of course. Peairs." He corrected the pronunciation, but he remained puzzled. "Iver *V.* Peairs?"

"For Vincent. But he's moved on, I'm afraid. I bought the business from him six, no, make that seven years ago."

"And you kept the name." He spoke as if thinking aloud. It was becoming clearer now. And the initials were right. This had to be the right place.

She took a single step toward him, moving out of the gloom of her own shadow, and her features took form at last. A slight, round-faced woman in her early thirties, all dimples and creamy complexion, she didn't go with the Tallulah Bankhead voice. She wore khakis and a man's navy polo shirt above Birkenstock sandals. An olive beret sat on her head like a cow pie.

"My name is Jim Morrissey," he said with a grin. "I'm a lawyer from Boston, and I have this little problem."

She lifted her eyebrows a little. "Sounds like you've got two already." It was sexy, that wasted voice.

Jimmy frowned.

"You're a lawyer," she explained with a little tossing gesture, "and you live in Boston. QED."

"Good one," Jimmy said with a chuckle, pointing an appreciative finger at the woman. "But they're not the problems I mean. I represent this couple, you see. Middle-aged couple from Concord named Wilkins. Herb and Ruthie Wilkins. Nice people. They've asked me to find their daughter. They've been estranged for a while, parents and daughter, ever since Cheryl–that's her name, Cheryl–since she left college, three years ago. She did this against their wishes–wishes expressed a little too forcefully, perhaps, because they haven't seen her since. And they want to make up, you see."

He kept an eye on the woman, but she just stared back at him, with a look of sardonic amusement. Did a lot of kids run off to Provincetown? Jimmy pressed on.

"They have reason to believe she might be entertaining similar thoughts. Because she sent them letters, three in the last six months. Not much info in them. Straightforward stuff. Just, you know: doing fine, don't worry. And no address, of course. That's why they came to me."

"Instead of, like, a private eye?"

Her grin was bigger, so he met it. "Well . . . sometimes a lawyer has to be a whole bunch of things. I never thought of myself as a PI, but, hey, you got a point. But the thing is, see, in her last letter she sent them a photo of herself. Which they asked me to run it down, like. To see if I could maybe find her and who knows? Maybe Cheryl would agree to meet with them? So I did. I ran it down, the photo. And I *think* you took it."

As he spoke, he pulled the photocopy from his shirt pocket and unfolded it. There being no surface immediately before him, he spread it across his belly and held it there with thumbs and forefingers at the corners. His tie bunched up a little above it.

She stayed where she was and peered across the five or six feet that separated them, hairline cracks appearing on her cheeks from the effort. Then her face seemed to soften. She said nothing, just raised her gaze slowly from the photograph to his face. If anything, she looked more amused. Mocking, even.

She recognizes her.

He stumbled on. "I got here because of this." Looking down at the copy spread across his midsection, he stabbed his forefinger at the edge markings along the border. "The letters, you see? IVP. I figured: initials. Gotta be. And I found a photographer named Iver Peairs in the phone book. Which brought me to you."

When he looked up at her again, he caught her just as the black border registered for her—for the first time, it appeared, for the mirth fled from her face, its place usurped by something else altogether. A much more serious look. She straightened up, the physical space separating them seeming to expand as she did. As if taking his measure, she looked him over carefully before she spoke again.

"I'm sorry. I don't know her. This is not my work."

"But you can't even *see* the initials from way over there," he said, moving forward and extending the copy. "How can you know that?"

"I don't need to look," she answered, taking an involuntary step backward. "I don't put my initials on the borders of my work. So I don't need to see the markings."

Jimmy's face was screwed up, trying to read her.

"Check it out," she added, with a little toss of her head in the direction of a photo-crowded wall. "You'll see. I use a stamp on the back. It gives my name and phone number. My address, too. No borders."

She smiled again, but it wasn't like the earlier ones: this one took effort. It seemed hung there, like one of her prints. "You know, you can't make a living by advertising on edge markings. Most customers won't hire a shamus to track you down."

It wasn't until Jimmy was down the walk and opening the gate to reenter Commercial Street that he realized what it was that had replaced the mirth when she first saw that black border.

It was fear. He'd bet money on it.

Of course you should stay," she said. "It was the whole point of the trip. You've gotten this close, you can't give it up now."

Jimmy sat with his cell phone pressed to his ear and his butt in a chair facing the back hall of a restaurant called the Molly House. A waitress handed him a tasseled menu the size of a cupboard door. She smiled at him before moving toward the back hall and the toilets. He watched her disappear behind a door marked SETTERS. Jimmy looked from it to the other door, for POINTERS. *Provincetown,* he thought, then tightened his grip on the phone.

"I thought it would just be a day-trip," he explained. "I figured I'd either strike out or come away with some kind of lead. I didn't expect this."

Understatement of the year.

Phyllis chuckled a little. "I'll *bet* you didn't. But you go ahead and stay. Learn what you can. I'll be all right."

Jimmy wasn't convinced. He hadn't spent a night away from her since they first got the diagnosis, more than a year ago. He felt a tug of guilt. A little diversion was one thing. Overnights away from her hadn't figured in this fantasy.

She knew him too well, though. "Stop it, Jim," she said. "I will *not* let you turn me into some kind of burden. We used to joke about the Irish slavery, remember? How the children get saddled with taking care of their parents? Well, I won't have some twisted version of that for us. Hey, are you still there?"

He told her he was still there. He laid the menu on the table and opened it.

She said, "But it's just incredible, don't you think? You leave the shop thinking you have struck out, and then . . . well, I don't know what. Fate? Fortuity?"

"Happenchance?" he suggested, weakly.

"Indeed," she said.

Indeed, indeed. He hadn't walked five minutes, after leaving the photographer's bungalow and crossing over to the south side of Commercial Street, headed back for the car with the photograph refolded and tucked back into his shirt pocket, when it simply leapt out at him from the right. No doubt about it, either. It was the same bare shoulder, the same pale hair and pale eyes, the same knowing smile full of wicked promise. The very photograph—without the border. The jolt was like missing the bottom step while going down the stairs in the dark. He felt his thoughts massing for the calving of some icy realization.

The mystery face smiled out at him through the plate-glass window of a shop called the Cock and Bull. From a poster taped to the glass on the inside, where it blocked a full view of leather merchandise: vests with buckskin fringe, studded jackets and belts, piles of valises, purses, and wallets. The poster advertised a nightclub act, he grasped at last. Her face commanded the center of it, bracketed by smaller photos of two other women, one of them white, the other African-American. Except those two clearly were not women.

And neither—the certainty swooped in at him—was she.

Her stage name was Virginia Dentata, and their drag show, called Where the Boys Are, ran five nights a week at something called the Drooping Lizard.

"A transvestite," Phyllis said slowly. It was the first time either of them had used the word, and he pictured her shaking her head and smiling when she said it. "That's some cutie pie you've got there, Jim."

"No wonder the photographer gave me that smirk when she saw the photo."

"I guess she figured out it wasn't 'Cheryl.'"

"She knew it was a man. I should have guessed it long ago. I mean, *Provincetown*, for Christ's sake. 'Drag show' is the first thing that comes to mind for most people when you mention the place. You should see the other two. No way you'd mistake *them* for female. But her—well, you saw the photo. She was damned convincing."

"Him, you mean."

"I'm struggling with the pronouns here."

"No reason you shouldn't. I seem to recall you saying something about her stirring the old dragon."

"Oh, sure. Rub it in." His tone was one of mock savagery; he felt more on solid ground as the butt of a joke. "It's a little disconcerting, you know."

She chuffed at him. "Please. What is it with you guys, anyway? It's like the worst tragedy in the world to be fooled about somebody's gender. I mean, so what? Who *cares*?"

"Must be something primitive," he said, lamely.

"Like homophobia? *That's* pretty primitive, though probably not in the sense you mean."

"You didn't grow up with these stories, as an adolescent boy. The bait-and-switch stories."

"Like the Kinks song, you mean? 'Lola'? Get over it, Jim. Remember *Some Like It Hot*? Joe E. Lewis plays this guy who's got the hots for Jack Lemmon in drag. He finds out Jack is really a man, and you know what he says?"

"What?"

"He shrugs, and says, 'Nobody's perfect.' The best line in the movie. So give it up, Jim. Go to the show. Spend the night. See what you can find out. Like I said, I'll be just fine here. I've got my book and the TV and the telephone and I don't know what all. I'll be fine."

The waitress reappeared. Jimmy showed her a tiny space between his thumb and forefinger: just a wee minute. "I gotta order," he told Phyllis, scanning the menu as he spoke. "And I may have made a mistake here. I'm having this out-of-wallet experience just checking the specials."

"Go beyond the children's menu for a change, Jim. And remember what the doctor said."

"About getting more exercise? Hey, I bought a heavier fork. What more do you want?"

"I want you to lose the weight, like he said. It's too hard on the heart, Jim."

"Look," he said, "I have to eat to *preserve* weight. I'm a skin donor. I've got a card in my wallet, confirms this. I eat so that others might live!"

"Just don't hurry the harvest, that's all I ask. Fish, Jim. Eat the fish. Promise me. We can't have both of us being sick."

He winced, then promised. He had no defense against the big guns of her illness.

"And Mr. Detective?" she added. "Aren't you kind of missing the point here?"

"What do you mean?"

"I mean getting all hung up because you found out you had the hots for a man. Instead of considering what it *means* that he's a man. What it means for the mystery that sent you to the Cape in the first place. Think about it, Jim. Your dead murderer didn't put your name on the picture of some pretty girl. It was a man. A transvestite. Have you thought through the implications of this?"

He had not, and he felt himself color as it hit home. He'd let his disappointment (or whatever it was) befuddle him. Why was a transvestite's photo propped against Van Gogh's bedside lamp when the FBI burst in on him?

"Do you think the picture could be of *him*?" she asked, several stops ahead of his train of thought. "Of the killer, I mean?"

"You mean is it Van Gogh in drag?"

"Why isn't it worth considering? He preyed on gay men. Seduced them, went home with them. *Raped* them. He obviously harbored a powerful rage against them, no doubt driven by a measure of self-hatred, maybe over wanting them in the first place. It's got to be bound up with his own sexuality. I don't know much about why men dress up in women's clothes, but it could have had something to do with Van Gogh running from his own gender."

"Like it would be all right to be attracted to them if he could think of himself as a woman?"

"Something like that. I'm groping in the dark here, too, Jim."

"But he wasn't in drag when he picked up his victims. At least, the one who survived, Siegel, he never said anything about the guy being in drag. And anyway, Van Gogh's dead. And the person in the photograph isn't. At least, that's what the poster says. He—or she—is at the Drooping Lizard tonight."

"Or somebody who *looks* like the person in the photo."

He considered this. "No," he said at last. "It's not just a likeness. It's the same person. In fact, it's the same goddamn *photograph*. The poster used the identical photograph. It can't be of Van Gogh."

She was silent while she absorbed this. Then she said, "So maybe they knew each other. Or Van Gogh's trying to tell us something—tell *you* something."

"Me? Why me?"

"I don't know, Jim."

"The only thing I can figure is he thought I'd look for the connection. Because there's gotta be one. One between Van Gogh and this . . ."

"Transvestite."

"Yes. Between the two of them. And one between me and one of them. Or both of them. That's all I've got to go on."

"So, as I said, check it out, Jim. See what your drag queen has to say. I'll see you tomorrow night when you get back."

He said good night. He told her he loved her, as he made a point of doing lately.

"Love you, too," she said. And she was gone.

The sudden deadness from the cell phone whistled through him like a cold draft, and he felt scared and alone. He set the gadget down on the menu. Maybe it was the prospect of a night away from her. He was reminded of the early times, when he was newly hooked on her eyes, those chestnut brown eyes that made her so alive, so *present*, sizzling right into him, and her listening so hard he'd entertained the wild suspicion that he didn't exist outside her gaze. Leaving him terrified that she would go away. Of course, that was just the neurotic anxiety of a young man falling in love. Nothing like now, when it looked as if she really might.

He had been working in the clinical program at law school when he first met Phyllis Cronin. She was a social worker then, scrabbling hopelessly to keep their mutual client—a fire-hardened fifteen-year-old from Navillus Terrace in Dorchester—out of adult prison. She had ash-pale hair that brushed her shoulders and the tiny body of an adolescent: slim hips, a skinny butt with indented cheeks, a flat chest (like two fried eggs, she used to joke, but he knew she was proud of them). He had noticed the pointed chin that appeared to draw the flesh away from her cheeks, giving her an angular face, like a sour schoolmarm in a Western. But that illusion did not survive the lips quivering with suppressed mirth, or the big hoop earrings and thrift-shop clothes that suited her, fresh and campy at the same time. And, of course, the eyes. She had intrigued the project rat in him, this optometrist's daughter out of Secaucus, New Jersey, and Wellesley College, a bright, gaudy creature unlike anyone he'd ever met in his native Charlestown.

It was a lark at first, their going out together, a bit of exotica. Until their fourth date, that is. That was when he heard her sing, in an *a capella* group with three other women. She sang in a voice as country as tortured Appalachia, with a quicksilver melodic line broken by little catches and jumps in register, breaks that broke his heart every time he heard them. He was lost to her by then, lost to the voice and the eyes, to the intensity with which she listened to him.

Jimmy wrenched himself back to the mundane. He had to make seven calls before finally getting a room at the big Comfort Inn, halfway to Truro, judging from the map. He ordered fish chowder and the striped bass—and a Rolling Rock, damn it—then picked up the phone again. Should he call that FBI agent, what was her name? Give her a *tootle*, she'd called it, about his discovery? No, he thought not. Instead, he retrieved his phone messages.

The Middlesex clerk's office said he was being called for trial a week from Monday on the *Radigan* matter. Eddie Felch wanted to know if he was ready to run with the Van Gogh story. A man calling himself Tristan said he was a former client who needed help retrieving property from the Boston Police Department. Taffy would be in late tomorrow: dentist, she said, though it was just as likely she was going in for more body piercing.

The waitress brought his chowder and beer. Jimmy tore open the oyster crackers and shook them into the soup bowl.

Tristan. He knew he'd heard it before, and it was too odd a name to forget. But he couldn't place it. Who the hell was Tristan?

He blew on a spoonful of the thin chowder, then eased it back in the bowl untasted. He stared off into the middle distance, thinking about what Phyllis had said. He was unaccountably upset about the development. This bait-and-switch business. Unsettling, yes, and probably for the reasons Phyllis had touched on. Okay, he was what he was. Nobody's perfect, she said, and he wasn't either.

But there was something else, too. The hunt had lost much of its intrigue, its savor, he realized. Gone was the titillation of wondering why *his* name should be keeping company with the foxy young thing in the photograph. Instead, he was paired with some guy who called himself Virginia Dentata.

Jimmy figured he'd better find the sandbox before his striped bass arrived. He was still standing before the urinal when he heard the flush from the stall to his right. He focussed on the graffiti on the wall while the guy ran the faucets beside him. *Do homeless people get knock-knock jokes*, the writer wondered.

It was the humming that made him look over at the guy. Except it wasn't. A guy, that is. Or at least he wasn't dressed as a man. Whoever it was was busy straightening the seam in his nylon hose, while at the same time watching himself in the mirror as he pressed his lips together, as if to distribute the lipstick.

There's a Setter in the Pointers!

Reflexively, Jimmy leaned farther into the urinal.

CHAPTER FIVE

THE DROOPING LIZARD

H ello, hello, hellooooo!" she called out, then extended the microphone down toward the audience like a rapier over a fallen duelist, lest he rise again.

"Hello, hello, hellooooo!" they roared back as one.

"Oooh," she moaned, eyes closed, the microphone oscillating as she clutched it to her breast with both hands. "Such awesome, *puls*ing virility! I don't know if I can *stand* it."

She froze, cracked open one lid, and eyed her audience with suspicion. "You're not buying this, are you?" A shrug. She tossed her head, as if throwing her hair over her shoulder. "But enough about you. Let's talk about me." Presenting a profile now, she flicked her vermilion fingernails upward along the side of her neck, flouncing her hair in the process. "Be honest, now. What do you think of my new perm? Divine, don't you agree?"

Whistles and catcalls. Her hair was nothing like the silken tresses that fell to her shoulders in the photograph; standing on end in frightened spikes, hers was the hair of a cartoon character with his finger in a light socket—more Phyllis Diller than Veronica Lake. But no doubt about it, it was the woman in his photograph. (Man? Person? Jimmy gave up trying to sex this creature.) Luminous gray eyes, delicate nostrils. Full lips in that same witchy smile. She was dressed in a sequined turquoise evening gown—scoop-necked, hip-hugging, slinky—and she pranced about like a model on a runway, shoulders first, thoroughly convincing on three-inch heels.

Jimmy had reached the Drooping Lizard twenty minutes before showtime—and a good thing, too: the line threading up the outdoor stairs to the second-story entrance already reached the street. He had expected a crowd of gay and lesbian revelers—girding himself, in fact, for sticking out like a straight thumb—and they certainly predominated: short-haired women wearing silk-screened sweatshirts and, yes, sensible shoes; neatly trimmed young men with even shorter hair and tight T-shirts, some of them showing off exquisitely toned bodies with beef-jerky tans and shrink-wrapped biceps and muscle cuts so sharp they seemed embossed. But there were plenty of obviously straight tourists in line as well, including three corn-fed farm boys in University of Illinois billed caps, a nervous father dragged along by college-age daughters, a pair of pigeon-shaped matrons cooing over their summer places in Wellfleet. *Thank God for diversity*, Jimmy thought. He took his place in line.

When the doors opened, he hobbled up the stairs a step at a time as if ankle-chained to the rest of the crowd. He paid the twelve-dollar cover charge and entered a dark cavern that shuddered from the bass thump of recorded rock music. The noise sounded vaguely familiar—even a nonlistener like him couldn't miss *everything*. He gathered he was listening to one of those hot groups Taffy jabbered about to her friends when she was supposed to be working the phones. Gleet, perhaps. Or Smegma. Those, at least, were groups he'd heard of.

He picked his way past the bar in the earsplitting noise and semidarkness, getting the lay of the land. A few tables, already taken, were tucked just beneath the lip of the stage. The rest of the seating consisted of folding chairs lined up in rows as if for a lecture, with an aisle down the center. He settled for an aisle seat midway between the stage and the bar at the back—and still he was no more than fifteen feet from the stage. He sat down and peered about him.

Blue bunting over the proscenium arch (if that term had meaning in such a tiny theater) proclaimed the words SARASTRO'S VAULT. Two very fit-looking waiters in black were gliding through the audience, taking drink orders. The big farm boys from Illinois took seats right in front of him, which meant he'd have to lean to one side to peer around them. Looking behind him, he spotted a balcony over the bar, though nothing in the entryway had intimated a route up there. He bought one of the plastic cups of beer off the waiter's tray (were they afraid he'd throw bottles, like a long-suffering Fenway fan in the late innings?). He took a sip and waited for the show to begin.

By 9:10 the music was still throbbing. The crowd was packed in and growing restless. Responding to cheers behind him, he peeked up over his left shoulder. Two women were dancing in the balcony, gyrating wildly. Every so often one of them punctuated her maneuvers by raising her T-shirt to flash her breasts at the crowd below. Hence the cheering. The lighting was so dim Jimmy could not tell if her breasts were bare beneath the shirt. The carnival atmosphere, it occurred to him, was more like a frat house keg party than the chic gay culture he associated with, say, Boston's South End.

The two men who occupied the seats to his immediate right were holding hands. The far one, plump with pearl white stubble for a beard, leaned over to whisper something into the ear of his companion, whose smile broadened as he listened. Jimmy looked away lest the man catch his eye and think he was trying to listen in.

Suddenly, the voice of Connie Francis, whining into the title song from *Where the Boys Are*, superseded the edgy rock music, to scattered applause. Then a male voice over hers. "Ladies and gentlemen . . . WHERE THE BOYS ARE!"

The applause swelled and the curtains parted for a production number, three men in drag doing a Rockettes-like routine to a Latin beat. A cha-cha, perhaps. The performers wore Carmen Miranda hats and outfits, festooned with tropical fruits. The almost indecipherable lyrics appeared to tell the saga of a man picking up a woman who, it turns out, sports a pendulous penis. A lackluster number, Jimmy thought, of slight wit and eminently forgettable, but the audience loved it. They clapped and cheered whenever a kick revealed a gusset of colorful panties. Jimmy spent his time staring at the performer in the middle. The one in the photograph, her complexion turned yam orange in the stage lights. Jimmy was relieved when the number ended, the maroon curtain sweeping back to hide the stage.

Darkness fell on the applauding crowd, then the male voice again. "Ladies and gentlemen, please welcome, back from her triumphant, sell-out performance at Bob Jones University, P'town's own, the talented . . . the titillating . . . the toothsome"–whereupon, the audible clacking of teeth, twice–"Virginia Dentataaaaaa!"

More cheers and clapping for the hometown favorite. And out she had popped, through the still-drawn curtains, in her glittering turquoise gown. With her "Hello, hello, hellooooo!"

She batted her eyes as the crowd whistled its appreciation for her new hairdo. "You're such loves," she told them. "Citronella and Yvette and I are *so* excited to be home and–" Here she paused, her eyes sweeping the ceiling, then the arch above her head, as if taking it all in for the first time. Her left hand on her hip, she cocked her body to one side, Bette Davis–style. "What a dump!"

More cheers. Her voice, Jimmy noticed, was light, feminine, but with an edge, too. Not at all like the brassy contralto of the unconvincing female impersonator he had once heard at a nightclub in the Castro.

"Hey," she said, perking up. "Am I glad to be back! You know, we, Citronella and Yvette and I, we spend the winter down South. Honing the show down there on South Beach."

A few cheers.

"Amen to that," she said, nodding. "Nice spot. But the *rest* of Florida . . . ? How should I put this? Well, here. Did you hear about this? They got this Web site I read about? Where you can watch live-streaming video feed from a webcam that's trained on a piece of raw meat. This is true! I couldn't make this shit up. You log on, and you get to watch–in real time, now–you get to watch the meat . . . *rot.* Is this a fantastic country or what? Talk about postmodern? This is like post*digital.* Of course, if you aren't online, you can get the same effect by watching, like, C-Span. But, but." She shook a monitory finger at her laughing listeners. "I'm here to tell you: life in mainland Florida is *just* like that. Think about it. You live there, it means you're either old or a cracker. You can tell them apart because a cracker is somebody whose family tree has no fork in it. This is a place where the tedium is broken only by early-bird specials. I'm there—*the whole fucking winter*—and I get this epiphany. An insight out of the blue, boiling up out of the tedium. And it's this: the membrane separating boredom from violence is *thiiiis* thin. It's true! You suddenly under*stand* mass murderers. People who wade into a shopping mall with an AK-47. It begins to make *sense!*"

She tipped her head to one side and smiled sweetly. "But here. P'town. Ah, home. You just gotta sit on a bench in front of the town hall and watch the fruitcakes go by, and all that tight-sphincter boredom and torpor and poison just leaches out of you. You know what I mean? I'm standing there, the day I get back, and these two leatherman studs amble by. Lewd, screwed, and tattooed. Jingling with stainless steel and smelling like joss sticks, and they're holding hands and walking two Russian wolfhounds the size of yearling heifers, and I say to myself, *Ginny, dear, you're home.* Isn't that why we come here? Huh?"

The crowd clapped and stomped.

"What have we here?" She arched her eyebrows as she peered down at a foursome seated at a table to her right. "Hellooo, ladies." Then, in a stage whisper from her cupped hand to the crowd, "Bulldaggers out on the town." She descended three steps at the end of the stage, the microphone at her lips. "Jewish lesbians, don'tcha just love 'em? Still trying to figure out if a dildo is meat or dairy." She had reached their table now and leaned over toward them. "Sweetheart, it's *parve!*" she hollered. "A bicomestible. All sex is *parve!*" Spotting a straight couple in the second row, Virginia sidled quickly toward them. "The rock!" she called out. "Let me see the rock!" Reaching the startled but smiling young woman, she reached out and took her left hand, then lifted her ring finger to within an inch of her eye. "Oooh. Did he give you this?" she asked, looking up from the ring. "This good-looking stud here?" The bride nodded vigorously as her husband's shoulders shook with uneasy laughter. "That's *so* sweet." She let the woman's hand fall and cranked her head toward the crowd. "Slut," she hissed.

She whipped her head around to face the couple again. "You're newlyweds, aren't you? Am I right?"

Two enthusiastic nods told her she was right. "I knew it. You still have that new-marriage smell. And I *love* the smock. It's so . . . so après-detox. What's your name, dear?"

"Daphne."

"And where are you from?

"White Plains, New York."

"And you're . . ."

"Todd."

"Todd." She closed her eyes dreamily. "Todd of White Plains, you luscious brute. Make me a muscle. Come on, crank up the biceps for me."

He reluctantly complied, standing up and raising his right arm to flex it. She felt it, her knees buckling in ecstasy. "Oh, Todd. That's harder than the paste in Daphne's ring. Guys, can you imagine what his lipid profile is like? Daphne, honey, listen to Aunt Ginny, now. You watch this guy, you hear? He may look like a lover, baby, but he's a farmer."

Still massaging the groom's upper arm, she cocked her head and asked him in a simpering tone, "Tell me, Toddkins: how old were you when you first realized you were straight?"

The laughter ringing around him, the young man just stared down at her with a wooden smile of stupefaction. His head bobbed slightly, as if to some inner music.

"Don't go Trappist on me now, Todd. My act's depending on you." She leaned toward him, pouncing on his discomfiture. "You don't have to say it out loud," she whispered. "Just stamp your foot, and we'll count."

The man just laughed helplessly, his sweating tonsure gleaming in the half-light.

"You know," she confided to the crowd, "people are always asking me that." She rocked her head from side to side as she made the question sound melodic and perky, the voice of a morning talk-show hostess. "*When did you first know you were gay?* I don't know for sure. Somewhere about the third or fourth time I had a dick up my ass, I got the picture."

She moved on, her magpie's eye scanning for new victims. Jimmy found himself feeling grateful for his refuge behind the big college boys.

"Well, well," she said after the crowd had quieted down again. "What have we here?"

She had fixed her attention on a middle-aged couple seated two rows in front of Jimmy. The man, with a high, glossy forehead, nudged the shoulder of his companion, whose head was bent intently over her lap. She snapped her head up.

"You're taking notes!" Virginia exclaimed, with feigned shock. "What are you guys, vice cops? 'Cause there aren't any in this town. Or you're reporters, maybe, covering this for the *Banner*? Oh, I feel so . . . *dirty!*"

The woman laughed, shaking her head. "No," she said, though Jimmy had to read her lips.

"A joke thief, then? Is that it? Tell me you work for Jay Leno."

"No," the woman said, audible now. "I'm teach at Boston University. Gender studies."

"That's why the notes?"

She nodded. "A book."

Virginia looked up with astonishment, her eyes sweeping over the crowd. "You guys getting this? I could be *famous!* She's writing a book about gender and shit, and *I'm* in it." She spread her palm across her breast dramatically, her head turned coquettishly to the side. Then, glancing down at the woman, she added suspiciously, "I *am* in it, aren't I?"

The woman smiled at her. "If you want to be."

Virginia looked up again. Like a voice-over on *Candid Camera*, she whispered to her audience. "She's wondering, you know. She's trying to figure it out. *Hmm,* she wonders." And here she made a burlesque of pursing her lips. "*A drag queen. Is this a misogynistic put-*

down, a self-hating parody, or a high-spirited deconstruction of the contrivance of gender?"

Jimmy was caught short by the change of discourse. So was the professor, for she just stared back at her from the ruins of her smile.

"Hey!" Virginia growled, one hand hitching up her balls like a slugger at the plate. "Dig it. I'm a man. You got a problem with that?'

He voice had taken such a dip in register, more than an octave, and tapped a vein of such growling machismo, that the crowd took a long beat before dumping laughter on the professor, as if in relief.

"That," Virginia lectured the professor, "was a tell. I mean, God forbid you should think I really *am* a woman. Remember this, honey: status trumps gender bending. Does that work for you, Doc? After all, a queen can move as far as she wants in any direction. Unlike a king."

The professor played the good sport, pretending gravely to write down everything Virginia said—which evoked a pointing finger and an appreciative nod from Virginia, as well as another laugh from the audience—a laugh with the professor this time. Her male companion put his arm around her shoulder and whispered something to her.

Jimmy pulled back behind the man in front of him when Virginia looked away from the couple. Too late! He'd been seen. She tilted her torso to one side, squinting slyly around the shoulder of the beefy blind where Jimmy crouched.

"Peek-a-boo!" she called to him, as if to a child. "Aw, honey," she purred with mock reassurance, "you don't have to hide from lil' ol' Ginny. She doesn't bite. Well, not unless you ask *real* nice. You look like Pooh-bear, huddling back there. Come on, now: what's your name?"

The microphone was inches from his face. Jimmy smiled sheepishly and sat up straight.

"Jim." His voice broke a little and he cleared his throat.

"Well, Jimbo, where are you from?"

"Boston. Somerville, actually."

"Hmm." She brought a knuckle to her lips. "I'm a little confused here, Jimbo. Because I can see you're not with *this* fellow." She bobbed her head dismissively toward the couple holding hands to Jimmy's right. They grinned appreciatively. "And the seat on the other side of you is empty. So you're here all alone, have I got that right?"

Jimmy glanced idiotically at the vacant seat to his left before admitting she was right. He was by himself.

"Jim," she said, stepping up next to him and giving his shoulder an avuncular squeeze with her free hand. She slipped her hand under his tie, waggled it with her fingers. "You ever notice, by the way, how men's ties point down toward their genitals, like one-way signs? Interesting, huh? I prefer a bow tie myself: something more ambiguous, you know what I mean?"

Jimmy smiled uncertainly.

Virginia squeezed his shoulder again, and her voice turned grave. "Jim, we have to talk. A guy comes in here alone—and wearing a *tie*, even. Well, I gotta figure he's cruising, looking for a little action from one of these boys here."

Jimmy felt a redness enshroud him like a chrysalis.

"Because," she continued, "if you're straight and hoping to get lucky in a place like this, you're even sicker than we are."

Jimmy showed the laughing audience as much of a good-natured smile as he could muster.

"Just teasing, Jimbo, just teasing," she assured him, bearing down on his shoulder again. "So tell me: what do you do, Jimbo? You a professor, too?"

"No, I'm a lawyer," he said, and regretted it at once, for she jerked her hand back and pulled away, both hands raised theatrically.

"Frank!" she shouted toward the rear of the house. "Frank! Call my agent! Tell her to get onto legal right away. We may have us a problem here." Without moving her body, she tipped her head in Jimmy's direction again. "I haven't, like, libeled you or anything, have I? Or engaged in an offensive touching?"

He shook his head affably.

"'Cause I have no liquid assets to speak of. Cold cream, mascara, blusher—the usual body condiments. An open bottle of creme de menthe. A few dental dams. That's about it. And believe me, I have nothing against lawyers. It's just the ninety-nine percent that gives the rest of you a bad name. Hey! Did you hear about those prisoners who overpowered their guards and took over a courthouse? No? Well, they threatened to release a lawyer every hour until their demands were met."

She was moving away from him now. "No, really, Jim, you've been a great sport. You hunker back down behind that dreamboat again. And listen up, guys," she added as she skipped up the stairs to the stage. "We girls have put together a great show for you tonight. Citronella and Yvette and yours truly, Virginia Dentata." A curtsy. "And we have some very special guests. Beginning with . . . Celine Dion!"

As the lights dimmed, she backed away, out of sight, and the curtains parted. To recorded music, the other white member of her trio—Yvette Bimbeaux, Jimmy later learned—appeared in a blond wig and lip-synched her way through a pop song that Jimmy found vaguely familiar. The crowd lapped up the mugging and antics as Yvette artfully slipped in and out of character, but cross-dressed celebrity impersonation held little fascination for Jimmy. He sat through it waiting for Virginia to return.

Which she did, right after the song ended—instantly recognizable, and convincing, as Hillary Clinton in pantsuit and chopped hair, right down to the round cheeks and fake dimples and her voice crisp and brittle and bloodless and angry, boasting about her public image ("I'm a human frost pocket") and detailing the exquisite revenge she planned to take on the miserable lecher she was married to.

So the show progressed, with Virginia morphing into a new persona between each act while Yvette Bimbeaux and Citronella Snowdrift took turns mouthing pop lyrics and impersonating the likes of Barbra Streisand, Bette Midler, Bonnie Raitt, Carol Channing, Cher, and others Jimmy couldn't place. Virginia herself appeared in comic takeoffs on Judge Judy, Joan Rivers, Martha Stewart (who confessed she really lived in a trailer park—"It's a good thing"), Rosie O'Donnell, Sally Jessy Raphael. During one entr'acte, she played a foul-mouthed female magician whose seeming ineptitude masked a deft hand at prestidigitation, climaxed by Citronella's disappearance from a locked trunk and, after a blackout lasting no more than a few seconds, her improbable return, handcuffed and wearing a wholly different costume, upon the opening of another trunk at the other end of the stage.

But Jimmy had not come for magic acts or lip-synching or even Virginia's comedy, which he rather enjoyed once he was no longer its butt. The milieu, the raunchy content of the gags, did little to dispel the anxiety he felt ever since learning she was not the woman of his imaginings. Nor did the show offer any insights that might explain the mystery he and Phyllis had just discussed. He tried to strategize how he might approach her. Straight on, he thought. Just come out with the story of how he got to her. That seemed to be the best approach. And then again, how would he even go about contacting her? She, or her troupe, must have an agent. Was that the way?

The show ended not with Virginia, but with Citronella alone on stage. She sat before a mirror, where she removed her makeup and women's garments while mouthing the recorded lyrics of a song Jimmy had never heard before. It was a sad, haunting piece, composed in the French cabaret style and sung in a voice remarkably like Marlene Dietrich's. Apparently entitled "What Is a Man?" the song was a transvestite's lament about the mingling of image and essence. When it ended, with the cold cream wiped away and Citronella's blond wig on the vanity and her bustier perched atop her discarded hosiery on the floor of the stage, "Citronella" was no more. She was supplanted by a slight black man in shorts and a shaved head. As he stood to acknowledge enthusiastic applause, Virginia and Yvette joined him, one from each side of the stage— they, too, having shed their female trappings—to curtsy, hand in hand, with Citronella. Then the three of them rushed down the center aisle and out of sight through the entrance.

When the clapping ended and the house lights came up, Jimmy sat back and waited, expecting the crowd to thin out quickly. It did not, however, and when he realized the reason for the bottleneck at the door, Jimmy saw his chance. Pulling the photograph from his shirt pocket, he opened it on his lap and hastily scribbled a note on the back. By the time he finished folding it back up again, the room was almost empty. The staff were picking up plastic cups and folding the chairs. Jimmy fell in line behind those still making their way out the door.

On the landing outside the door, the three performers were still accepting congratulations from the departing theatergoers. Jimmy shook hands with each, Virginia last. She glanced down at his hand when she felt the folded paper Jimmy had slipped into it. Suspiciously, he thought. Her real hair, Jimmy noticed, was very short and very red. A deep, auburn red.

Just like my face, Jimmy thought as he tottered down the stairs.

The heat and humidity had been shushed away by a fresh breeze off the bay. Tomorrow promised to be more comfortable. A single cloud in the shape of a dagger bisected the arc of the crescent moon, a cents sign that fragmented as quickly as it formed.

The walk to his car, still berthed at MacMillan Wharf, was not a short one, but Jimmy felt grateful to be outdoors a while longer. He walked Commercial Street, a far busier thoroughfare now than when he had made his way to the photography studio in the afternoon. Tourists gaped at the wildlife from the safety of automobiles, while gays and lesbians, in couples and larger groups, strolled along in an exuberant *passeggiata.*

Mulling it over, Jimmy didn't begrudge them the sense of release they flaunted here. *Free at last, free at last,* and all that—and Lord knows it must be a horrible burden to have to keep something as powerful as your sexuality hidden from the world. But at some level, he just didn't buy it. There was, he felt, a hysterical edge to such flamboyance that made it suspect, as if protesting too much masked a corrosive ambivalence they could not openly acknowledge. And it fed, in turn, an uneasiness in Jimmy, too, something that kept him from experiencing a wholehearted solidarity with them.

Or was Phyllis right to peg him as homophobic? He'd never given it much thought before. He supported measures to ban discrimination based on sexual preference, didn't he? Surely she had misread him. This bunch was just too much in your face about it, was all.

Then he remembered how mortified he had felt when he saw the curious look on Virginia's face as she felt the note he had slipped into her hand. She would assume he was trying to hit on her, he was sure of it. (Even in mufti, she still seemed a "her" to him.) Such a misunderstanding on the part of a real woman would be embarrassing enough, but this? He had no framework, no context for this particular species of mortification.

The only corollary he could find in his own experience was an episode at Nini's Corner in Harvard Square, several years ago. He had popped in to buy a candy bar. The line for the register was long, so he wandered among the racks of magazines. Absently, he found himself in front of the gay beefcake periodicals, his interest piqued but careful to touch nothing. Then, glancing to his left, he caught the eye of a fleshy young man who was paging through something called *Mandate*. Jimmy had cut his eyes away quickly and left without his Butterfinger. This feeling now was something like that, but it had more . . . solidity this time.

Jimmy had looked away from Virginia, too, when she raised her head after noticing he had passed her a note. She would have read him at once, would she not, intuiting his obvious unease? First impressions meant a lot in Jimmy's business. Why not in hers, too? She would have had a lifetime of experience reading reactions like his. Even if she realized he wasn't making a pass at her, she'd dismiss him as a fat-assed homophobe with some neurotic agenda.

No, Jimmy held out little hope that she would respond to his message.

She did, though. She was already there on his voice mail when he got back to the Comfort Inn. Lunch at noon. Some place called Vaffanculo. Jimmy to buy.

CHAPTER SIX

NICKEL EPIPHANIES

He slept in. The clock radio read 9:36 when Jimmy finally slid out from under the covers and sat up on the side of the bed. Despite the extra sleep, he felt groggy and stiff. He rolled his head around as he massaged the back of his neck, all while arching his back. Then he caught his reflection in the full-length mirror mounted on the wall to his left.

The image that greeted him was jarringly at odds with the comfortable self-image he carried about with him. Here instead was a pasty-fleshed naked man, chubby, his sagging breasts furred over with grizzled hair. No six-pack abs here. More like a beer keg–or a wine sack, maybe. The bottom folds of his stomach lolled like spilled bread dough across his bare thighs. Muscle tone? Atonal was more like it. *Christ,* he mumbled to himself. *People my age don't need birth control. We got nudity.*

He heaved himself to his feet and turned to brave the mirror, ignoring the drooping haggis of a belly that hid most of his pubic hair. When he was nearly up to the glass, he rubbed his jaw in the webbing of his hand and examined the white stubble of his beard. He'd reached the point in the aging process, he realized, when the hair in his nose and on his ears grew faster than the thin stuff on top of his head. The prospect of shaving his ears made him feel like some kind of seedy elf. A misanthropic troll skulking beneath the Sagamore Bridge.

Best just to get it over with. He headed for the shower.

Twenty-five minutes later, unshaven but combed and decked out in the same soiled shirt and wrinkled suit he had worn on the drive up here the day before, he stepped out the front door of the Comfort Inn. But for some cantaloupe and wheat toast, his stomach was empty. He carried a paper cup of sweetened coffee. The air was fresh, almost cool after yesterday's beastly humidity. The desk clerk had promised him the walk back to the center of Provincetown was twenty, thirty minutes tops, and Jimmy intended to hoof it. Yes, Phyllis would be proud of him this morning. He set off purposefully up Route 6A.

His sense of purpose was beginning to wilt after fifteen minutes of trudging the dusty shoulder, the gravel crunching as he faced oncoming cars loaded with children and sand chairs and boogie boards. And no cabs to flag. His big wing tips felt hot and heavy. His tie had long since been folded away in the pocket of his jacket, which was now slung over his shoulder. At least the buildings seemed to be huddled closer together along Bradford Street, a hopeful sign that he was nearing the center. Time he took a breather.

He spotted an oblong chunk of granite beside the road up ahead on his left. Making for it, he noticed that the rock afforded a vantage from which to view the Bay to the west. He sank gratefully on his makeshift bench, scootching about for a comfortable roost, and laid his jacket across his lap. He peered out over the Bay.

Even with the sun approaching its zenith, the light was marvelous. It seemed to set fire to every color it touched. Several white lobster boats and a small catamaran, with crimson canvases taut in a shouldering wind, bobbed on the hammered surface of the water two hundred yards offshore. Painted boats on a painted sea. Jimmy felt the release he always experienced along a shoreline on a beautiful day—as if the world, wearing itself like a loose garment, had sloughed it off to give a privileged glimpse at the numinous energy beneath it all.

Not loose enough, however. Barging through his brief transcendence came a vision of Dr. Bergman's hangdog features. The oncologist's tight curls and oversized, glittering earrings did not go with her basset hound's physiognomy, but her diagnosis sure did. This, she explained as if to a child, was not the death sentence it had once been. While a radical mastectomy was indicated, there was no immediate evidence that the tumor had metastasized–and there was every reason to hope that chemo and radiation might force the cancer into remission.

Hope, she'd said. He'd glanced furtively at Phyllis. Why *hope*, he would have asked if he'd dared? What was wrong with *expect*? Or even *believe*? But he looked into the doctor's blandly reassuring smile and knew she had chosen her words with care. More than the blunt news itself, it was the doctor's verbal precision that had driven joy underground, and even its timorous resurfacing during his better moments, like these seaside nickel epiphanies, was defenseless against the memory.

As if to mock him, the first bars of an electronic rendition of "Ode to Joy" burst in upon him. It took him a moment to place it as an emanation from the cell phone clipped to his belt. A tootle–wasn't that what Agent Butler had called it? He unholstered the thing.

"Yes?"

"Jimmy. Where *are* you?"

Taffy.

"I'm sitting on a rock here in P'town, drinking in the sun. My business took longer than I expected, so I stayed over. Anything going on there I should know about?"

"Just your *law* practice. I mean, it's practically *noon* here, and nobody knows where you are. Don't you have like a *deposition* or something this aft?"

Sonically italicized words surfaced in Taffy's speech when she got worked up, like stepping-stones across the white water of her emotions.

"Oh, shit." He tilted his head back and shut his eyes, feeling the sun turn his eyelids into an orange scrim. It was a bullshit third-party depo, postponed twice already at his adversary's request. Time he claimed his turn. "Call Previtt for me, will you? Tell him . . . tell him I'm stuck in LaGuardia. Or I got a bad ice cube last night. Anything. Use your imagination."

"I thought that was why you got the cell phone."

"No, Taffy. That's why I've got *you*." Best to nip this insubordination in the bud—as if it hadn't already gone to seed and overrun the whole goddamn garden. "I thought you were going to be in late this morning. Dentist or something."

"Don't ask," she said. "Don't even go there."

He couldn't tell whether what darkened her voice was his snapping at her or the unmentionable something that had ruined her plans. Taffy's love life read like a rap sheet, and on occasion Jimmy had helped her obtain protective orders against fractious swains who resented being dumped. Not going there was the easiest decision he'd make all day.

"What else have you got?" he asked.

An audible sigh, then a pause. "Well, nothing I can't handle *for* you." He chose to let that one go. "There's this Tristan fella. Tristan . . . *Sliney* it is, wants his file back. Plus some stuff he says the police won't give him. You know, Jimmy? I had a name like that, I'd probably *slaughter* my parents. I mean, Tristan Sliney?"

Sliney! Of course. So he was using his given name now. He had been Desmond to Jimmy, with Tristan popping up only on court papers—of which there were bundles, no doubt gathering dust like bound newspapers in Pemberton Square. T. Desmond Sliney was a crafty, if small-time, con artist Jimmy had represented on several occasions over the previous decade. He'd dealt in bogus rare coins. Engineered the odd bust-out. Sold marina slip condominiums in Squantum that no harbormaster had never heard of. Nothing in the last couple years, of course, thanks to his incarceration in Concord for credit card fraud. So Des—Tristan—was back on the streets. And wanted what?

"His *property*, he says. Claims the police have it, from when he was arrested. He wants you to get it for him. And his file."

His file. Not good. Jimmy could think of only three reasons a client might want his file, none of them welcome news. He might want to contest a fee. He might have decided to fire you and take the case to a new lawyer. Or he could be planning to sue you for malpractice. But Sliney? Jimmy had expended many more hours than Sliney had ever paid him for in their last matter together, so it couldn't be a fee dispute, and there was no active case the guy could be shopping to someone else. That left only the malpractice option. But even that seemed doubtful. To sue for legal malpractice in Massachusetts, a criminal defendant had to prove he was not guilty of the charges his counsel allegedly bungled. This Sliney would have a hard time doing, since all his convictions had come on guilty pleas. They'd had him dead to rights.

"Jimmy? You still there?"

"Yes. Did you pull the file?"

"Looked. Not here. Must be stored 'off-site.'"

He smiled to hear the sarcasm. Jimmy's off-site storage depot was the crawl space above his garage. Other lawyers wrote checks to outfits like Iron Mountain to "archive" their inactive files. He kept his at home until he could safely put them out on the street with the garbage.

"In that case," he said, "it'll have to wait until I get back."

"This just in, Jimmy: we have, like, *fire* now. People are even doing things with something they're calling a 'wheel.' Get with it, will ya? You should be storing this stuff on disk. Like a *real* law office."

"Hey, I bought the damn cell phone, you badgering me all the time. That's about as high-tech as I can manage right now."

"*Which* you hardly use. Except to tell *me* to call people."

He snorted, as if to give her that one, too. "Enough," he said. "Please. I'll pull the file. You call . . . Tristan back and find out more about this property he wants. Meanwhile, I've got an appointment for lunch, which oughta be over by one or so, then I'll drive back. I'll check in on the way home. And call Previtt right away about that depo."

"I'll tell him you had to go give your random urine sample."

"I gave at the office."

You *must* be Morrissey."

The inquiry, if it was one, came from Jimmy's left as he stared fixedly at the Town Beach from a window-side table in Vaffanculo. The restaurant occupied an aged bungalow, which in its slumping *déshabillé* resembled nothing so much as a failed cake tricked out with pink icing–this last from the rosy paint slathered over its scalloped cedar shakes. The place was tucked between an erotic toy shop called Phallus in Wonderland and an antique store whose display window was dominated by a poster for something called a 3 DAY BREAST WALK. Jimmy had shaken off disturbing images evoked by the poster as he climbed the steps to the restaurant's gabled portico.

The air conditioner was set on meat locker, so he had pulled his jacket on over his clammy shirt. The maitre d' led him to a table. Jimmy ordered a Rolling Rock–no, make that an iced tea. Waiters scuttled in and out among the tables like the sandpipers working the beach out the window.

Jimmy glanced up toward the voice that had addressed him.

The man smiling down at him was tall and thin. His sleeveless shirt showed off sun-bronzed arms that looked as if they had been polished with a chamois. The man's most arresting feature, however, was his quilted complexion: his cheeks were pale, a white ground to a variegated field of inflamed splotches of pink and red and puce. Was he undergoing some kind of elaborate test for allergic reactions? And where the hell was Virginia Dentata?

"I'm Joseph," the man said, as if reading his confusion. "Ginny asked me to pop in and tell you he'd be a few minutes late."

Ginny. He.

The man gripped the back of the chair opposite Jimmy. "May I?" he asked, arching his eyebrows to form a circumflex over each eye.

Jimmy nodded, then sipped his tea. It needed sugar. While Joseph settled himself, Jimmy reached for the Sweet'N Low, shook a packet to settle the contents, then tore it open and poured the fine powder into his tumbler. Stirring now, he kept an eye on his table companion.

"Do you work with . . . Virginia?" Did she actually *call* herself that? Offstage, even?

Joseph found this very amusing, his laughter coming in staccato snorts, but sotto voce. "*Hardly.* I'm just a friend. *Someone* has to look after the dear thing, you know."

Jimmy didn't know. The remark seemed odd. Off a semitone, it seemed to him. He thought it best to nod knowingly.

Joseph said, "We all pitch in for support in any way we can. Which is why I agreed to come ahead and chat before Ginny gets here. I'm sure you can understand."

He couldn't, but he kept smiling. Encouragingly, he hoped.

Joseph lowered his fine eyebrows as he scrutinized Jimmy for a quiet moment, looking for something.

"Excuse me for being blunt. I don't know what you have in mind. But I will do everything in my power to protect Ginny from being harmed by some . . . some seedy effort to exploit his misfortune. I understand you're a lawyer. Okay. You should know that we have access to lawyers, too—some very fine ones, in fact. Am I making myself sufficiently clear?"

Jimmy waited to make sure the man had finished before responding.

"As a matter of fact, no. I don't have the faintest idea what you're talking about."

Joseph's face sagged with theatrical disappointment. "Well, then, suppose you lay out for me just what it is you want with Ginny. Then I'll be able to eliminate any confusion—on *both* our parts."

"No offense," Jimmy said, "but I'll give my nickel to the organ grinder myself."

Joseph's eyes widened in surprise, then anger, his lips twisting to shape a response. Before he could get it out, another voice intervened from over Jimmy's shoulder.

"I think you've just been called a monkey, Joseph." Virginia Dentata stepped into view and offered a hand to Jimmy, smiling warmly. "I'm sure Mr. Morrissey will be able to explain what he wants by himself. Be a doll, huh? Ask Derek to send over the usual brewage?"

Joseph waited long enough to glower at Jimmy once more, to nod a warning, then shoved back the chair and got to his feet. He walked away, head held high. With dignity, it seemed to Jimmy. A man who worked hard at seeing the world through a caul of indifference. Jimmy turned back. Virginia's eyes and smile were still on him, from Joseph's chair now. Checking him out.

Jimmy did the same, realizing this was the first time he'd had the leisure to observe Virginia in mufti. Slight, bare limbs poked out of a cranberry polo shirt. Matted red hair clung to the scalp like moss, above the fine features and small mouth. Sleepy gray irises beneath trimmed eyebrows that seemed—no, take that back. He was sure they were innocent of mascara. Call them well-defined, then. A young man, in his middle thirties, unprepossessing but decent-looking. He projected the seemingly ageless youth of the fit gay male. Nothing it would have occurred to him to call effeminate. Leaving to one side, of course, that this was someone who cross-dressed for a living.

Virginia said, "Winston Churchill said never to trust a man in brown suit."

"What's this, you're still performing? Are you always on?"

A pause. The eyes tight on Jimmy. Then they softened. "But, then, Churchill also told us the wogs start at Calais. So maybe we should view his snobbery as all of a piece with his racism. What do you think?"

"I think I don't know what the hell you're talking about." Jimmy craned his neck and made a show of peering about the room. "Maybe we should call Joseph back. He could be my interpreter in these . . . matters."

Virginia laughed. "Joseph with his face of many colors? No, I don't think we'll need him. That was my inelegant attempt at oblique apology, that's all. I was rude; I'm sorry. And besides, I'm the one who should be asking *you* what's going on. Your strange note and all."

The wrinkled photograph was now in Virginia's hand. Jimmy watched as it was smoothed out on the table between them.

Virginia said, "You're telling me the late William Wolff had this picture—*my* picture—in his possession when the cops came for him? Do I have that right?"

"More than 'in his possession.' He had it propped up right beside his bed. Like it was a portrait of his sweetheart or something. With my name written on the back."

Virginia frowned. "Why? What's your connection to this . . . character?" The tone was sour.

"I haven't a clue. Or I should say, that photo is my only clue. As I said in my note, I traced it to Provincetown, to that photo shop, and I discovered you."

Virginia nodded. "Iver Peairs."

"Right. Except the lady there, she claims to know nothing about it."

"Lee. Her name is Lee. She bought the business years ago from—"

"So she said. But me, I know she's lying. Not about buying the business, that I wouldn't know. But she sure as hell lied about the photo. Because she took it. I'm sure of it. The markings on the picture were right. And when she saw them, they'd like to scare the shit out of her. I mean, she was as smug as a State House lawyer 'til she saw them. Then she clammed right up."

Virginia said, "I know."

Jimmy blinked.

"I went to see her this morning," Virginia said. "Well, what did you expect? Your note said you'd got to me through her shop. She does some work for me, you see—publicity stills, stuff like that. And you're right: she took this picture. So I wanted to find out what she knew about you—you and your client Van Gogh—before I kept our luncheon appointment."

"He's *not* my client."

"Well, don't bark at *me*. You're a lawyer, after all. What am I supposed to think?"

"So why'd she lie to me—this Lee? And what's she so scared of?"

Virginia paused, as if deciding whether to answer. A waiter appeared. Derek? He placed a drink of some kind in front of Virginia, then looked brightly from one face to the other.

"We should order," Virginia translated. "I recommend the scallops. They come in a Hoison sauce. Very nice. You'll like, I promise."

Jimmy ordered the scallops. It made Derek disappear. "You were explaining."

Mind made up at last, Virginia said, "Lee *was* afraid. And feeling guilty, too. It was she, you understand, who sent the photo to Van Gogh–to Wolff, as he called himself. He called her up, claimed he was a theatrical agent who had seen some of her photos on my Web site. He was impressed, wanted his clients to use her. He had to have one, right away he said, and could she FedEx one to him in Key West? Something he could show around. Well, Lee didn't have any of the finished prints. I'd cleaned them out. So instead of making a new one, she sent him the contact print. Lazy, you ask? Maybe, but really, she said, the contact print showed off her work better."

Jimmy nodded. "With the markings."

"So she explained. At any rate, this was more than three weeks ago. Then Van Gogh gets shot by the FBI. Identified as William Wolff. Now, we are a tight-knit community, Mr. Morrissey, we of the homosexual persuasion. Like a small town in a lot of ways. A notorious butcher of gay men finally gets caught, people talk. People hear. So Lee hears. And lo and behold, his name turns out to be Wolff–and they find him at the very same address where she'd sent the picture."

"He used his real name?"

Virginia's brow wrinkled. "Yes, I suppose he did. And address. Is that significant?"

Jimmy shrugged and waited for Virginia to proceed.

"Anyway, this is bound to be upsetting for Lee, don't you agree? And then, out of the blue, *you* show up, some lawyer waving the picture in front of her, and spinning some bullshit about a missing coed–well, of course she was frightened. She doesn't want to get mixed up in all this."

Jimmy was quiet for a moment. It made sense, he figured. Except . . .

"Guilty?" he said. "Okay, so she'd be scared, but you said she felt guilty? Why should she feel guilty? Because you owned the copyright, or something like that?"

Virginia sat back in the chair, eyeing him skeptically. "You can't be that obtuse. What did you expect, she'd welcome me finding out she'd sent my picture to that . . . *creature* after . . . ?" The sentence went unfinished. "The woman has feelings, after all, and she knows I do, too. You, I'm not so sure about."

Something didn't add up here. Jimmy squinted across the table, as if the way out of his puzzlement could be found in Virginia's face. It was largely blank except for the upward tilt of one peevish eyebrow.

"Feelings I got," he said at last. "But–and I seem to be saying this a lot this morning–I don't know what you're talking about."

"I'm not speaking in argot here, Mr. Morrissey."

"Jim. Will you just tell me what's going on?"

Virginia's eyes widened with a look of dawning recognition. "You really *don't* know, do you?"

"Know what?"

"That Donald Gilfillen was my partner."

"Who?" Jimmy felt totally lost now.

Virginia's eyes were shining now. From brimming tears, Jimmy realized. "My significant other. Long-term companion. My lover." As if hoping to hit on a term Jimmy could grasp. "Six years we were together."

Jimmy lifted his hands, a gesture of embarrassed confusion. But the name . . . ? It was familiar somehow. Where had he heard it?

"Donald," Virginia said, straightening up, "was the man Van Gogh killed in Provincetown. I assumed you knew that. I figured that was what brought you to me. That and the photo."

Jimmy just shook his head as the odd atonalities of his luncheon meeting began to tumble into some coherence. Like why Lee should feel guilty. Virginia's lashing out at him for having no feelings. Joseph's strange remarks about people pitching in for support, or the man's suspicion that Jimmy was out to exploit Virginia's "misfortune"–which, like the ignorant square he was, Jimmy had taken as an allusion to homosexuality, or perhaps transvestitism. Even Joseph's silly threats about resorting to other lawyers made some sense now.

Jimmy said, "So that's where I heard the name."

"You're telling me you didn't know?" Virginia's incredulity had diminished, but it was still there. No wonder he and Joseph had come on so guarded and suspicious. They must have feared he was working some angle, looking to prey on Virginia in some way. They must have thought him callous and crude to barge in on her sorrow, to rake through the coals of her grief for some meretricious purpose.

Jimmy shook his head. "No, of course not. I just had the photo." He saw the pain shimmering in Virginia's eyes. He said, "I'm sorry." Feeling how lame it was. "I had no idea."

Virginia hesitated, eyes sharp on his, as if probing for falseness somewhere. "It never occurred to me that you might *not* know."

"Why would I? Even if your name appeared in the papers, it wouldn't mean anything to me." He frowned. "Did it, in fact? Appear, I mean?"

Virginia sat back a little in the cane chair. "Well, it did here, anyway—in Provincetown. Big-time. I guess I don't know about the Boston papers. I just assumed . . ." A slight wagging of fingers died out with the sentence.

"Well, if it did, it never registered," Jimmy said. "It wouldn't have seemed relevant, you know what I mean? Van Gogh picked up strangers. So I paid no attention to the names of the victims' families and . . . such."

Jimmy stopped short, cocking his head to one side as he watched Virginia. A single tear had escaped the pool filming the right eye and was sliding downward.

"Now that you mention it," Jimmy said, "what *is* your name? I mean, if they'd mentioned someone with a handle like Virginia Dentata, believe me, I'da noticed that. With a wife in the shrink business, I picked up that it was a pun on Freud's vagina with teeth. So I knew it wasn't for a for-real name."

Virginia's head was bent down, as if intent on the blue cockleshells stitched into the linen place mat. "It's Taub. Richard Taub."

Virginia—Richard—looked up at him now, patting the tears with a napkin as a small smile broke through. "A long way from Virginia Dentata, I admit."

"Ain't that the truth. Still, I never heard it before."

A silence wedged itself between their uncomfortable smiles. It was broken almost immediately by Derek's noisy arrival with their scallops. More silence as they ate, Jimmy trying to weigh this new information, not from Virginia's perspective this time, but from Van Gogh's. He got nowhere. Why would the guy want a photo of a victim's lover? Was he planning to make Virginia his next victim? To show that lightning could strike twice?

Or was this was the wrong answer to the wrong question? He looked across the table at Virginia, who was carefully quartering a caramelized sea scallop the size of a Ping-Pong ball.

Jimmy said, "It doesn't make any sense."

Just Virginia's eyes lifted, wearily, to meet his. "What does, in all this?"

Jimmy was staring out the window, but his eyes were focused on nothing at all. "I'm trying to figure. I mean, the guy sets this whole thing up, in a sense. Think it through for a minute. Just over two weeks before he's shot—have I got my dates right? He called your friend—what's her name, Lee?—about three weeks ago, you said?"

Virginia considered, then nodded. "August ninth, she said it was."

"Okay. The ninth, then. And the cops take him down on the nineteenth. So it's ten days before. That's when he arranges to get a photograph of the partner of one of his victims. Has to have it, he tells her. Can't wait. Doesn't take any precautions either. Uses his real name—this from a guy who comes up with a new alias everyplace he goes. Plus, he makes a point of having the photo shipped by overnight courier. Which tells us what—besides that he's in a hurry?"

Jimmy bobbed his head to cue his sluggish audience. A puzzled moment of silence preceded Virginia's tentative response.

"He wants to be identified?"

The answer startled Jimmy for a moment. Then he said, "I hadn't taken it quite that far. I'll need to think about that some more. All I meant was that, for such a careful guy, he's being awfully cavalier all of a sudden. You look back on what they know about his last few weeks, you get the picture of a guy in one hell of a hurry. Rushing things. Losing control, the shrinks tell us. Going after that last would-be victim so soon after the one before him. But consider, too, that asking Lee to use FedEx is like leaving tracks in wet cement. This is an outfit, keeps serious records. Tracking numbers and shit like that. Electronic stuff. They wanna, they can document everyplace their drivers stop to take a leak."

He squared around to look at Virginia, elbows on the table now. "And it gets worse. He doesn't just pick them, he even arranges to have them deliver to his house. Not to some post office box or a safe mail drop. Right to his goddamn house. Talk about your death wish."

"Death wish?"

"What else would you call it? The guy's been so careful for so long. He's got a little 'death kit' he carries with him when he's hunting, if that's the right word. Like a doctor's bag, I'm telling you. Careful planning, lots of precautions. He always moves on after a kill. Changes names everywhere he goes. A very careful, very organized guy. And then he starts all this, leaving tracks, getting sloppy chasing this last victim, not even lighting out when the guy gets away. Figure, he wasn't exactly packing for the road when the FBI showed up at his place. After the botched mickey, he goes home—he takes a shower, for Christ's sake. His hair was still wet when they hauled him out on the gurney. It's like he cleaned himself up just to wait for them. He positions that photo right next to his bed, settles into a chair with an umbrella on his lap. And waits. Points the umbrella at them like that—well, that's about as close as you can get to suicide. So what's going on here?"

Virginia shrugged. "We're not talking about a particularly stable individual."

"Can't argue with you there," Jimmy said through a mouthful of rice. "The guy was a few fries short of a Happy Meal. But there's method here, too. Some planning. He wanted the photo, he didn't care about leaving tracks. He refuses to run after he fucks up. He waits for them, almost makes them kill him. And he writes my name on the back of your picture, props it up beside him, and waits. You know what that sounds like to me?"

"You said it. He lost it."

Jimmy shook his head. "No. Like he's sending a message."

The two of them said nothing, Virginia staring at Jimmy.

"A message? To whom?"

Jimmy shrugged. "Who knows? The FBI? If so, they sure don't seem very interested in decoding it. That leaves you and me."

"Me?"

"Hey, you're the one in the picture."

"And you're the one on the back. So?"

"So doesn't it make sense he's trying to tell us something?"

"Tell us what?"

"Don't know what. That's probably the wrong place to start, anyway. Seems to me the first question isn't what he wants to say. It's why he picked us. Now you, you at least have a connection to the guy. Through your friend, I mean."

Virginia's eyes narrowed. "Donald."

"Yeah, Donald. What else have we got to go on?"

Virginia's eyes were slits now. " 'We'? What's this 'we' you're talking about?"

That stopped him. Jimmy noticed Virginia's tight glare, the air across the table between them now ionized by suspicion.

Jimmy said, "Fair enough. I shouldn't be jumping to conclusions. You don't want in, I can understand. I just figured, the guy went to a whole lot of trouble to seek out the two of us for this. Tied us together, like, putting us in the same picture and all. I think he wants us to dig–I don't know what for. For something, anyway."

"Dig?" Virginia responded as if Jimmy were alluding obliquely to something distasteful, like sewer work or maybe grave robbing. "Dig where?"

"Where? We have to start with the only common point of reference. With Donald . . . Gilfillen, was it?"

Virginia's eyes widened now.

Jimmy said, "Maybe you could tell me about him. Anything you can think of. It's the only place I know to start."

After a heavy silence, Virginia raised both arms and looked from one to the other. "Jim." Using his name for the first time. "Look at me. Will you look at me?"

Jimmy looked. For a long few seconds the gray eyes held his own above a trembling lower lip.

"Okay, I'm looking. What's your point?"

"My point, Jim, is that whatever you may think of me, I am human. You with me here?"

"Yeah. I see that. I'm not some homophobe thinks you guys are, like, aliens or something. I know you're human, like the rest of us."

"Well, I suppose I should take some small comfort in that," Virginia said. "But what if it was your wife—you married?"

Jimmy nodded, warily.

"So, if it was your wife who was killed by an animal like this, and I came to you, say, and suggested you . . . 'fill me in' on the details of her life so I could figure out why a dead man was scribbling my name on pictures, how would you react?"

Virginia let the question hang there while Jimmy gawked back and saw nothing at all for a moment. He was working hard to quell his initial flush of anger at the allusion to Phyllis, at the presumptuous pairing of the two, before the feeling dovetailed into a flickering terror that he might lose her—an intimate terror that had no place here, no place at all, in this frou-frou eatery with this drag queen mourning his . . . whatever. Then he caught the look of angry composure, of bleak loss on Virginia's face, and he felt himself blush. Confused, he waited a moment before trusting himself to speak.

"Look," he said at last. "I'm sorry. I didn't come here to stir up your misery. I didn't even know you had any. Far as I knew, you had some connection to Van Gogh, and I wanted to find out how I fit in. It was just a riddle, a puzzle to be worked out. You know what I mean?"

Virginia nodded slowly. "Yes. I can see how it would have seemed that way. It's just that it's a whole lot more than a puzzle to me."

Jimmy sighed. "Frankly, the whole thing had a lot more zing to it when I thought you were a woman."

Virginia's gravity was eroded first by a twitching around the mouth. Then it gave way completely to a rush of loud, ringing laughter that pealed through the room. Jimmy peeked about to see if anyone was noticing.

CHAPTER SEVEN

YOUR MOTHER'S MAIDEN NAME

Neil Leifer was hurrying through some last-minute paper-work in an effort to get away early for the weekend bike trip he'd promised to take with his son. Forces seemed to be colluding against him, led by his project manager, who kept demanding to see a timetable for the proposed patches now that the beta test results were in. Neil didn't have any yet, and wouldn't have any (as he'd explained to Brown at least four times already) until the pro-grammers got back to him, and they didn't report to him but to Rudnick. He pecked out another email to that effect–to Brown, copy to Rudnick–taking care to keep his exasperation out of it. His phone rang, for the umpteenth time, and he let it. He spell-checked his message (Brown was too anal for words), then clicked on the send icon.

"Neil?" The voice belonged to Millicent, the receptionist. Her auburn bangs hung out from the side of her face as she tipped her head around the wall of her cubicle. "You might want to take this one. It's about your credit card."

Neil screwed up his face, still staring at his computer screen. "My credit card?"

"That's what she said."

Queer. He sighed and reached for the phone. Goddamn Brown.

"Hello." He wedged the handset between cheek and collarbone as he started shoving papers into a vinyl-fabric briefcase on his lap.

"Mr. Leifer?" A woman's voice. Crisp, professional.

"Yes."

"Neil T. Leifer?"

"Yes." With less patience this time.

"This is Valerie Perugi from Agrobank, in Sioux Falls, South Dakota."

"You're not telling me we're over limit." He felt the guns of his annoyance wheeling about as Brown slipped out of their sights. "Because we mailed the last—"

"Oh, no. Nothing like that. You see, my department monitors unusual activity in our customers' accounts. And we've had a rather, well, unusual request to charge your account. So I'm calling to verify the purchase."

It's Janet, he thought, as his irritation switched targets once again. Neil pictured his wife breasting the clutter in one of those restoration hardware stores. Old brass door strikes and mirrored sconces. Not again. He'd like to torch that overturreted Victorian she'd bamboozled him into buying.

The woman said, "Did you authorize a wire transfer of twenty-five hundred dollars to a vendor in Worcester called Triple-A Bail Bonds?"

Neil sat up straight. "Bail bonds?" Then, smiling in spite of himself, he added, "I could ask my wife, but it seems a bit of stretch, even for her."

"You might want to listen to this, then," she said, apparently in no mood for levity. "See if you recognize the voice. Just listen, please. Okay?"

"Uh, okay."

"Hold on just a sec."

The phone seemed to go dead for a moment, then the woman was back on the line, still crisp and professional. "I'm so sorry to keep you waiting, Mr. Leifer. I have now accessed your account."

Neil was about to respond when a man's voice beat him to it. "No problem."

"Is that a wire transfer?"

"That's what I said."

"Just to verify, for your protection, could you give me your billing address again?"

"Look, I already told that other girl. She—"

"I'm sure you did, Mr. Leifer, but please, it got kicked over to me, and I'm the one who has to approve the charge. So please bear with me."

Neil heard the man expel his breath noisily, his exasperation genuine. "One-oh-nine East Wyoming. Newton, Mass. Oh-two-four-two-seven."

"And your daytime phone, area code first?"

"Six-one-seven, two-two-seven, eight-three-nine-five." The man had a wheedling, querulous tone that radiated entitlement.

"Home phone next?"

Neil listened in stark amazement as the man reeled off, surely from memory, his telephone numbers, date of birth, social security number, the names of his wife and children, even his mother's maiden name. Where did the guy get this stuff? He'd read magazine articles about identity thieves going through your garbage looking for old bills and such, but his mother's maiden name, for crying out loud?

The man was now protesting, and vociferously, the woman's intention to put him on hold once again (the chutzpah, the nerve of the guy!). Then she was back, one on one with Neil again.

"Do you recognize him at all?"

"No. I don't know him."

"Of course, we'll shut down the card at once. I'll have a new one sent to you in a few days. Should I have it delivered it to your home or office?"

"Office. But what about the guy?"

"Oh, he's already hung up. I can see that from looking at my screen."

"That surprises me, actually. He sounded like he'd never give up. But, no, that's not what I mean. I mean what happens to him now?"

"We'll report the incident to the police, of course. But, well, you know how it goes . . ."

"Yeah. I guess I do," he said, feeling very much the urban veteran resigned to the fecklessness of law enforcement. "That's the last we'll hear of him."

He couldn't have been more wrong. Because almost four weeks later his replacement card still hadn't come, and he was back on the phone to customer service, feeling himself grow increasingly truculent with Cindy, a perky clone of the first woman he had dealt with. Cindy spoke with the same Midwestern accent, a singsong lilt that suggested Scandinavia.

"But it's right here, Mr. Leifer," she said, as if he should be able to see the screen in front of her. "Our records show that we shipped your new card on the eighth, nine days ago. And–"

"Where?" he demanded, in a mood to cross-examine. "To what address? And who signed for it?"

"You did, Mr. Leifer. And the card went to your home address— at your insistence, I might add. It says here . . . where was that? Oh, yeah. You called on the fifth, and you asked why the card was not being honored. When our representative explained that the card had been cancelled the day before because of unauthorized use and that a new one would be shipped to your office address in a day or two, you instructed us to ship it to your home address instead. Which we did, on the eighth, as I said."

It was him! It had to be. Who else would have known to call? But why? Yet even as he asked the question, the obvious answer settled over him like a damp mantle.

"Where did you send it to, exactly?"

"Where you said. To your home address. Two seventy-three Brewer. Chelsea, Massachusetts."

Neil squeezed his eyes shut. "I don't live in Chelsea." He enunciated the words carefully, as if to a slow child. "Never have, never will. I live in Newton. Which is miles–worlds–away from Chelsea, believe me. I've been living here for seventeen years."

"But you said—"

"No, I didn't say. The man who called you said that. The same one, I'll bet you dollars to donuts, who was using my card number in the first place. And it looks like you people just sent him another one."

That shut her up. But not for long.

"Gosh, then, it's sure been getting a lot of use over the last week."

"I can't tell you how gratifying that is."

"Now, there's no need to get sarcastic, Mr. Leifer."

Oh, but there was. The guy had begun to exist for him, to take on flesh and blood, the living embodiment of his frustration. Neil could picture him, too, slouching against a wall beside the pay phone in some sawdust bar under the Tobin Bridge up in Chelsea, inspecting his nails as he schmoozed Cindy or Valerie or whomever into giving away the store. Neil's store. He'd be a small, sharp-featured little man, with a scraggly beard, maybe, and he'd be wearing an imitation silk shirt. Smoking, too. Guys like him would be smoking constantly.

Neil's mental portrait of the man seemed consistent with his purchases—the ones that kept showing up on Neil's bill despite abject vows that no further consequences of the bank's ineptitude would be visited upon him. The guy had splurged on what passed for luxury in Chelsea, at least as Neil perceived it. (But then, Neil always used to say, what was Chelsea but Everett without the glitter?) The man had spent three nights at the Holiday Inn on Cambridge Street. Ran up a bar tab at Jillian's that would have done Dean Martin proud. Clothes from the Men's Wearhouse (no genuine silk here, if price was any indication). Bruins tickets. A portable CD player from Tweeter. Three dinners, on successive nights, at the Hilltop Steak House up in Saugus. All of them in the Boston area. It made Neil grind his teeth to read the bill. Granted he'd never have to pay it, but he knew he'd be months, years even, cleaning up his credit history.

And still his new card didn't arrive.

Customer service was ready for him this time. Melanie (where did they get these people?) cheerfully documented through UPS that the card had indeed been delivered to his office. As they had advised him over two weeks ago, when he called to check on its status, it had been signed for by someone named Millicent Swanson. Did not such a person work in his office?

She did indeed, a bit of information that only fed his confusion, for he also knew that he had made no such call. He was not the Neil Leifer who had called to find out where the card was? No, that would be Augie, the name Neil had chosen for his identity stalker. Augie had found out when it shipped and where it was headed. And somehow he had intercepted it.

"Let me guess," he said. "I've been spending a lot lately, haven't I?"

"Well, yes, as a matter of—"

"Wait a minute!" he said, when it sank in. "When you get a new card in the mail, don't you have to, like, call in and activate it somehow? I mean, you can't just go out and start using it, right?"

"Oh, absolutely. We put a removable decal on the card with a twenty-four-hour eight hundred number to call for activation. And the call must be made from the telephone number at the cardholder's billing address. Even then, the customer must be able to supply special personal identifying information before the card will be activated. No, sir. No way."

"Wait a minute. What billing address did he call from?"

"Brewer Street in Chelsea, Massachusetts."

Neil closed his eyes. "And the personal identifying information." These words bore not a hint of interrogatory inflection.

But he knew what was coming and, slave to destiny that he apparently was, he mouthed it in unison when she answered.

"Your mother's maiden name."

Neil spent a few brisk but satisfying minutes telling the woman what her South Dakota bank could do with its card. Assured, finally, that his account there was closed forever and that no card bearing his name would ever again be issued to anyone, anywhere, he gently laid the handset back in its cradle. Sweetly, he called out to the receptionist.

"Oh, Millicent?"

"Yes, Neil?"

"Could I see you a second?"

"You betcha."

God, don't tell me she's from South Dakota, too.

A package from UPS had arrived, she confirmed, but it was a mistake.

"A mistake?"

Millicent's features reconfigured themselves as she frowned. "Yes, that's what the other Neil said. He said–"

"Whoa. Wait a minute. What 'other Neil'?"

"The one who called, like I was saying. To explain the mistake. He called and said his name was Neil Leifer and was there another Neil Leifer who worked here. Small world, huh? I said there sure is, and wasn't that weird and all. I guess this isn't the first time you two have gotten mixed up like this. He's explaining this, and I go, what do you mean mixed up. Anyway, the long and the short of it is he's been expecting to get a package from UPS and when it didn't arrive when they said it would, he called them up, and they said they'd delivered it here, to the other Neil Leifer. That was you."

"Me."

"Right. And he wanted to know for sure, did it come. I had it right in front of me, so of course I said yes. So he called UPS and they came and got it."

"Somebody from UPS showed up here and took my package?"

"Not yours," she said, with bountiful patience. "I explained that. It was the other Neil's."

"How did you know he was from UPS?"

"Well, who else would it be? I mean, the guy was wearing a uniform and everything. You know, brown–you've seen their guys. And he had a clipboard, I remember that."

Millicent paused as she seemed to pick up, for the first time, the storm gathering all over Neil's countenance.

"Did I do something wrong?"

"Millicent, you never worked for a credit card company, did you?"

She crinkled her cheeks into a quizzical grimace, as if sniffing out a trick question. "No," she said at last.

"Well, I think it would be an ideal match, given your skills and talents. When you're looking for your next job—which will be as soon as humanly possible, if I have anything to say about it—I hope you'll give it serious consideration. Because believe me: there's a place for you in South Dakota."

"South Dakota?" She looked close to tears. "But I've never even *been* west of the Rockies!"

A police detective dispatched to Neil's office the next day learned what he could, but a red-eyed Millicent could describe the other Neil only as wearing brown, of medium height, and "kind of cute." Still smoldering, Neil watched as the cop, a skinny man in his early fifties named Rampino, solemnly entered these clues in a notebook from a chair beside her cubicle.

Neil said, "You gonna to put all that in the APB?"

Rampino looked up at him over drugstore reading glasses. "Oh, yeah. For a manhunt like this, we're gonna stick fliers on every lamppost in the city."

Neil stared back at the stone-faced cop in disbelief.

Rampino said, "Look. You're upset. I take that into account. Who wouldn't be? I'll let you in on a little secret, though. This guy? We'll get him. His balls are too big for his brain, you know what I mean?"

Neil didn't, but he said nothing.

Rampino said, "When we got your call yesterday, I got right on to the credit card people, to that number you gave us, the one for—what was it?" He flipped a page in his note book. "Niagara Bank?"

"Agrobank. Think farmers."

"Yeah, whatever. So they faxed me the records of your account. And you know what?"

Neil just stared, waiting.

"You rented a car out of Logan yesterday morning—or your pal did, anyway. He's probably tooling around in it right now. And the plates are on the hot sheet in every cruiser in the city. Odds are, we'll pick him up. So spare me the wise-ass remarks, okay?"

The two of them locked eyes while Neil considered this. It made no sense.

Neil said, "How did he do that? You have to show a driver's license to rent a car. You telling me he's got more fake ID?"

The prospect had not occurred to him before. It made him feel even more vulnerable.

There was something a little malicious in Rampino's smile. "No, he found a way around that little problem. Listen to this." He crossed his legs and squared around to face Neil. "Guy goes to Logan, to the Massport police station there, and he tells them he's Neil Leifer, just got off the Delta Shuttle from New York. His wallet's been stolen. Stolen, now; not lost. They shrug. What are they supposed to do, anyway? And he says, well, can you at least make out a police report so I can give it to my insurance company? Which they do. And this, this here's the best part. He goes to Cumberland Car Rental farther down in the same terminal. Shows them the police report and your credit card. And guess what?"

"They gave him a car."

"An Olds Cutlass. Dark green. Plate numbers went out over the radio late yesterday afternoon, right after your call. I figure we'll pick him up."

They did, too. Less than twenty-four hours after Rampino gave Neil a wink and left the office. They spotted the car in Jamaica Plain, around the corner from Doyle's, a long way from Chelsea. Three stereo receivers, still in their original packing, were stacked in the backseat. The officers just waited in a sub shop across the street until the other Neil—Augie—showed up.

Of course, Augie wasn't the name on his birth certificate. Or on his rap sheet. Augie's real name was Tristan Desmond Sliney. Whose file an overheated Jimmy Morrissey finally managed to retrieve from the rafters of his garage the day he got back from Provincetown—while still feeling some regret that his Van Gogh diversion was behind him now.

CHAPTER EIGHT

A MOUTHFUL

Fingering the valet parking stub in his coat pocket that evening, Jimmy smiled across the table at Phyllis. She smiled back. Her hands absently smoothed the white linen of the table-cloth. There was delight in her eyes, a glint of silver throwing back the soft lighting of the table lamps. He put it down to their being out on the town for the first time since the surgery in the spring. Jimmy had pressed her, right after he got back from Provincetown three days ago, to pounce on the break in the chemotherapy. She *was* feeling better, she had acknowledged, and she had even recovered enough appetite to make dinner a conceivable option.

So here they were, tricked out in their finery—Phyllis in a white skirt and lavender silk blouse, Jimmy in his beige tropical worsted—at their usual table at La Vucciria. Jimmy figured patronizing a familiar place—one owned by friends, in fact—would make the outing more relaxed, more convivial, and less tiring for her. Its intensely Sicilian fare, a look at the menu brought home once again, was more to her liking than his. She had once described her dining experience here as a "culinary summit." He fixed a weather eye on the entrees in search of safe crevasses and familiar toeholds for his own, less precipitous ascent.

"I bet the porterhouse is good," he said. It was more plea than prediction.

She didn't even look up. "Forget it. You're supposed to be cutting back on the red meat. No more suicide by lifestyle, remember?"

"Oh, great. Now I'm getting medical advice from the ill."

She twisted her mouth in appreciation. He sighed noiselessly and returned to the menu. He surveyed the fish and seafood offerings for something that might actually satisfy. Sepia? What the hell was that? Wasn't it that grayish brown color in old photographs?

"Jimmy! Phyllis!"

The call, more a stage whisper than a shout, came from the direction of the kitchen. They both looked up as a beaming Arthur Patch, one of the owners and Jimmy's former client, strode toward them. Arthur hugged Phyllis from the side, gave her a loud smooch on the cheek, then turned to shake his lawyer's hand.

"Joanne told me you were coming." He pulled a chair over from an adjacent table and, turning it backward, straddled it to face them. Pinched by the chair back, the bib of his starched white apron filled like a sail above it. "Great to see you. It's been . . . well, too long. How are you both?"

"We're doing fine, Arthur," Phyllis said. "It's my first night out in a while, and I'm quite enjoying myself." She spread her hand to take in the room. "And I'm so *pleased* to see that business is good."

"Me too," Arthur said. "But not as much as Joanne. I try to leave that side of things to her, you know."

Jimmy smiled wryly to hear this. The first time he had met Arthur, the cook was in the federal lockup for refusing to answer questions before a grand jury investigating the loan shark who'd been supplying him with working capital. Yes, better to confine Arthur to the kitchen and leave the finances to his partner, Joanne Balzer, a no-nonsense businesswoman who gave no quarter.

"And Danielle?" Phyllis asked. "How's she doing?"

"Fine," Arthur said, giving nothing away—if he had anything to hide. "In fact, she said she might stop by later. To see you guys, she said."

This time Jimmy made a point of not smiling, wryly or otherwise.

He knew more than he had ever wanted to know about Arthur's on-again, off-again affair with Danielle Gautreau, a talented lawyer who had once been with the US Attorney's Office and now persecuted lawyers for a living. She worked for the Board of Bar Overseers, the state agency that could pull a lawyer's ticket for unethical conduct. Taking out the trash, she called it. As one who'd nearly ended up in the garbage bag himself on a couple of occasions, Jimmy preferred to keep her at a wary distance, despite his affection for Arthur.

He waited for a break in the exchange of pleasantries, then said, "Artie, tell me: what's this sepia stuff? Would I like it?"

Arthur paused to consider this. "I don't know, Jimmy. Sepia is cuttlefish. Much like squid. It's stewed in its ink. So you tell me. *Would* you like it?"

"In your dreams." Jimmy shuddered for show. "I don't eat filter feeders."

"Cuttlefish aren't actually filter feeders. Not like clams or mussels. They—"

"Save it, Artie. You'll be pushing tadpoles and slugs next. A lecture's not gonna convince me here." He cocked his head to one side. "You got cuttlefish on that blotter of yours? You still write 'em down like that?" He looked over at Phyllis. "Used to be, every time he came across a new word, he'd write it on his desk blotter."

She smiled uncertainly in Arthur's direction.

"So I can look them up later," he explained. "And yes, I still do it. But not cuttlefish. No need to look that one up. It goes with my *other* obsession. The food one."

"Well, then, maybe you can tell me," Jimmy said. "What's another word for synonym?"

Arthur bit long enough to set Jimmy laughing. Arthur and Phyllis soon joined him.

"Really," Jimmy said to Phyllis, solemnly shaking his head. "When I first met Artie, he was on his way to becoming the Wordman of Alcatraz."

Arthur laughed. "And all because I wouldn't sing." He used the chair back as a fulcrum to pry himself up. "Jimmy, try the couscous. It's got fish and chicken, it won't blow your diet, and you'll like it.

No surprises, I promise." Smoothing the apron, he turned toward the kitchen. "I'll catch you later, when we close. Maybe Dani will be here by then. And Joanne, of course."

So Jimmy tried the couscous. He took a timid bite, then fell on it like a condemned building. Which was more than he could say for the *cassata* he chose for dessert. He was busy, some time later when theirs was one of the last tables still occupied, picking distasteful bits of candied fruit out of this oversweetened sponge cake, when Phyllis returned to the subject of his sagging interest in Virginia Dentata.

"You must admit it was nice of Richard to invite you to his birthday party, after all that."

Using his knife as a grader, Jimmy scraped another piece of candied citron toward the shoulder of his dessert plate. "Richard, indeed. He, she—whatever. I guess so. Still not offering any help, though."

She expertly quartered a medlar. "Oh, I'm not so sure. I doubt he invited you out of a sense of social duty." She tasted a section of the fruit, meditatively rolling it about in her mouth. "Umm, nice. Anyway, you don't usually do that for a near stranger, particularly one who's just blundered into your private grief like you did. He just might be more interested than he's letting on."

This was a possibility Jimmy hadn't considered. He had left Vaffanculo convinced that Virginia wanted no part in any "investigation" into the strange business of Van Gogh's annotated photograph. And Virginia's resentment had been palpable when Jimmy refused, as politely as he could, to leave the ghost of Donald Gilfillen in peace. Not that Jimmy didn't understand. He did. But Van Gogh had cast him in this dumb show, and Jimmy had felt he was just playing out his part—trying to discover what his part was. And for the moment, Virginia's dead lover held scant interest for him. Just some bizarre joke at his expense. An embarrassing one, at that. Downright humiliating, if truth were told. So he shook it off.

And yet. He'd been invited to the party. When Jimmy showed astonishment at this, Virginia had gone mysterious on him.

"Maybe seeing me in context will help you understand."

What the hell was *that* supposed to mean? It certainly was no indication, as Phyllis was now suggesting, that assistance was in the offing.

"That makes no sense at all," he said to Phyllis as he abandoned his fork for good. "At best, it was just a way to keep tabs on me. Anyway, I'm out of it now. No reason to go. What good could possibly come of it?"

"At the same time, what would you have to lose—besides enduring a little social discomfort in an alien environment? I doubt it would be much like a meeting of the Charlestown Elks Club."

"Ain't that the truth, now." Jimmy sipped his coffee. He wished he hadn't passed on the sugar.

Phyllis shook her head. "Men can be such babies. You're accustomed to distinguishing gender with unhesitating certainty. When you can't, it hooks something in you. This is just men, too, by the way. It doesn't bother women. Maybe because we've been female impersonators all our lives—Gloria Steinem said something like that once. But then, men have a harder time with homosexuality, too. It's always the men who get the most bent out of shape over it."

Jimmy frowned. "What do you mean, female impersonators?"

"Women have been socialized to accept artificial conceptions of what it means to be feminine. Which often means you feel like you're faking it."

"Faking?" he said, in mock outrage. "You fake it?"

She grimaced. "You know what I'm talking about. Have you never felt like you were playing a role when you were doing something expected of you just because you're a man? A he-man, maybe?"

"You mean like John Wayne or something?"

"Or something. Yes."

"Yeah, I guess so."

"Well, it's the same thing with women. Only more so."

"Now wait a minute. I thought your point was that it was more so for *men*. That men have a harder time getting away from being impersonators. Which is why, if I understand your point here, we're supposed to have such a harder time with guys who, well, step out of role. Like cross-dressers and gays."

That seemed to stump her for a minute—not the most common of events in their marriage. Teach *her* to take on a trained advocate. Jimmy rewarded himself with another sip of coffee.

"You're right, in a way," Phyllis said. "Maybe it's that men are more emotionally hemmed in by their roles than women, while women have less room to be different socially. A woman has a much narrower range of acceptable behavior. She has to walk a thin line between too Barbie Doll on the one hand, and too bitchy on the other."

"Oh, right," he said, feeling himself on a roll. "You should just *watch* what happens to a man, *socially* now, if he experiments with dressing the least bit . . . effeminately—on the job, say. Or flaunts being gay. It'll do you in a lot faster than a woman coming on as a frosty bitch in a pantsuit. Believe me."

"My point," she said with some asperity, "is that gender isn't innate, it's . . . well, engendered. And whatever the relative social consequences of breaking the rules, men have a whole lot harder time *handling* it. Emo-tion-al-ly." She smiled. "Hence your obvious discomfort."

"What discomfort?"

"Whatever it is that has you twisting your napkin when you talk about these things."

Jimmy glanced down at his lap. He had indeed torqued his napkin up into a tight wad of linen—the way he used to make a rat-tail out of a wet towel for snapping at asses in the shower after gym class. When he looked up again, she was wearing her gotcha smile. It was a look that only love could distinguish from a smirk.

"Whatever," Jimmy said, hoping to pull things back on track. "I don't care. The guy wants to wear women's clothes, fine. No skin off my nose. And I don't care if he talks with his mouth full either. I just want—"

"Talks with his *mouth* full?" said Phyllis, her eyes narrowing. "Is that allusion what I think it is?"

"Well, yeah, I guess so." Jimmy could feel the high ground crumbling beneath him. "Sort of like saying a guy's light in his loafers. A little more explicit, perhaps."

"It's a little more *ugly*, is what it is. Where have you been the last twenty years?"

Jimmy looked away sharply, trying to deflect her anger through a show of his own. "Come on, Phyllis. It's just an expression. More of a joke than serious. I'm trying to explain what it's like for men."

"So I've noticed. You know, I could abide the homophobia, I suppose, if you guys were at least consistent. You want to insult somebody you call him a cocksucker, but you all work awfully hard to get a *woman* to be one."

Jimmy raised both hands in surrender. "Okay, okay. So call me politically incorrect. I didn't mean to step–"

"Oh, no," she broke in. "You weren't being 'incorrect.' You were being crude. Distastefully so."

Her remark hung there in an accusing silence for a moment. It stung. A reminder of old tensions, of class differences between them. Jimmy watched her lower lip tremble, whether from anger or upset, he couldn't tell. Maybe both. It was the trembling that confirmed it for him, and he felt a painful bit of self-realization seat itself inside him like a ball in its socket. He gave it up.

"You're right," he said, looking straight at her, "I'm sorry. Just put it down to where I come from. And ignorance."

"Horsewhippable ignorance," she said. But her tone was softer, and Jimmy detected an accompanying slackening in her jaw muscles.

"Horsewhips? Somebody needs horsewhips, I've probably got one."

The remark came from Joanne Balzer, who was suddenly standing beside their table, apparently having abandoned her hostess station at the front of the restaurant. She said, "You kids fight in my restaurant, I'm gonna take away snack."

Joanne was tall and solidly put together, what Jane Russell used to call a full-figured woman. Her dark hair was cut casually short, as if she'd hacked it off herself at home, but Jimmy seriously doubted that. She just stood there in front of their table, legs slightly apart, arms akimbo, and grinned broadly.

Jimmy's eye found Phyllis's across the table. She gave him a slight smile, and they both laughed.

"No fight," Phyllis said. "An exchange of opinion, is all." She stood up to greet Joanne. Jimmy followed. He held the woman by her square shoulders and administered a chaste peck on the cheek.

"Joanne," he said, "you keeping Arthur in line?"

"Arthur?" Joanne raised one dismissive eyebrow. "These days he doesn't order *celery* without clearing it with me first."

The three of them settled in around the table, by then the only one still occupied. A few minutes later they watched as Arthur backed out into the dining room, shielding from collision a tray of some sort. As the door swung back to its rest position, it muffled the kitchen clatter. No longer in livery, Arthur wore a green T-shirt with writing Jimmy couldn't make out for the tray. The tray was laden with a bottle and several tiny glasses. Arthur set his burden down on the Morrisseys' table.

"*Grappa?*" he said.

"Cool T-shirt," Jimmy said.

Arthur tucked in his chin to peer down at his chest while using both hands to stretch the shirt taut from the bottom. Its lettering asked: IS THERE A HYPHEN IN ANAL RETENTIVE?

"A gift from Joanne. But I bet you figured that out."

Jimmy sat back as the brandy was poured. When Arthur held out a glass, he shook his head. He listened as the conversation drifted in desultory fashion from topic to topic. The success of the restaurant. Danielle's new job. Phyllis's health. Even recent films.

"Oh, I've given up," said Joanne. "There's nothing I want to watch coming out now. The choice seems to be between *Shrek* and dreck—as in *Charlie's Angels*. I'm telling you, I've been renting nothing but old classics. *Bringing Up Baby*, stuff like that."

"That's funny, because we are, too," said Phyllis. "Last week we watched *Rear Window*. I liked it so much I want to get that other one of his. I forget the title. The one about the guy with the imaginary rabbit. What's it called?"

"*Hare?*" Jimmy offered.

"*Hair?*" Phyllis stared at him. "You mean that play about hippies? 'The Age of Aquarius'? I'm talking about the movie with Jimmy Stewart. He was in *Rear Window*, remember?"

"It was *Harvey*," Joanne said. "And I think Jim was misspelling the other one."

"Deliberately, no doubt." Phyllis said.

Jimmy grinned. "You *said* Jimmy Stewart."

"*That's* not why we rent old movies," said Arthur. "There are lots of new films I'd like to watch. Dani, too. What's hard is finding one the two of us can agree on. She always wants to see some chick flick."

"And you," Phyllis said to him, while shooting an accusatory glance in Jimmy's direction, "want to watch one of those high-tech thrillers. Or some hack-'em-up. No wonder we're driven to films from the forties."

"Ah," Joanne said, "that's my new market niche. All you straight couples having nasty fights in video stores? We should be selling movies that can woo *both* men and women. Hence my cinematic amalgams. Think about it. Films like *When Dirty Harry Met Sally*. No, seriously, don't laugh. Or *The Sixth Sense and Sensibility*."

"What if the couple isn't straight?" Jimmy asked. "What happens then?"

"*Then*," said Joanne, in a pitying tone, "you've got no break along gender lines to hassle about. Of course, you'll still fight about other things. Trust me."

Phyllis said, "You'll have to excuse Jim. He's been getting a crash course in the gay culture lately. It's left him a bit . . . befuddled, I guess you'd say. Wouldn't you, Jim?"

"No," he said shortly. He realized he was twisting his napkin again.

"Why don't you tell them about your . . . mystery. Your adventure."

Irritation flared in him. He wasn't sure he wanted to share this with them. Then he spotted Danielle Gautreau approaching from the restaurant's rear entrance. Her appearance settled the matter for him. Maybe, he thought, it was just a reflex, knowing where she worked. He wasn't sure that everything he'd done since the FBI had beaten a path to his door–or that he might be tempted to do in the future—would pass inspection by the Board of Bar Overseers. He used her arrival as cover to change the subject. As the first to see her, he stood up and smiled.

Danielle Gautreau was a blond, striking woman whose beauty was so far outside his everyday experience he felt a tiny thump of erotic desolation every time he saw her. "Hi, Dani," he said to the side of her face as he hugged her hello. "Good to see you again."

"How are you, Jimmy. I was sorry to see the Alvarez trial didn't work out for you, but I suspect the public is better off."

She referred to Jimmy's failed efforts on behalf of an MBTA bus driver who had shot his wife's lover as the man lay in a bed at Newton-Wellesley Hospital. The wife had been present to witness the carnage.

"Hey, I consider second degree a victory. It's not easy to make a case for self-defense when your client reloads."

Arthur brandished the bottle. "Any takers?" Discovering a sudden thirst, Jimmy extended his glass. Arthur filled it. The tinkle of glass was the only noise for the next few minutes. Joanne was soon announcing other titles for her hybrid videos. *The Long Goodbye Columbus. Snake Eyes Wide Shut. Prince of the City Slickers. Terminator of Endearment.*

Phyllis, Jimmy noticed, seemed to shine in the company of her friends, and her face was crinkled with pleasure. He sought out her hand under the table. When he found it, she squeezed him back. Then she methodically unlaced his fingers and pressed his open palm against the top of her thigh. It was an intimate gesture, but chaste—and all the more erotic on that account. The two of them exchanged tiny, secret smiles, a spider's thread of complicity taut between them.

CHAPTER NINE

STOCK

J immy held the *Boston Phoenix* out at arm's length, as much to keep her personal ad at a safe distance as to squint at the tiny print.

"Taffy," he said, "you gotta understand. Most people my age have zero experience with this kind of thing."

"Most people your age are dead." She snapped her gum, then tongued the wad over to the other cheek. "Well, I'm not, and I gotta live. So . . ."

When he was sure she wasn't going to finish the thought, Jimmy read her personal again.

> ### FRESH KILL
> Still warm. Wretched wench wants
> churlish rogue for intense chemistry
> and intellectual sparring.
> No husbands, boyfriends or convicts.
> Nonsmokers and ax-wielding homicidal
> maniacs preferred.

"Who did you expect would answer this? Alan Alda?"

"Who?" She held up a hand to stop him. "I don't want to know. Hey, look. I always expect the worst. I think death and work back from there. I knew this might put me behind the wheel of the wrong hearse, but at least I'd be driving for a change. And say what you want, that ad got results."

Jimmy smiled. "Any convicts?"

Taffy shrugged. "Of course. And every *one* of 'em wasn't like what I was thinking of when I wrote the ad. Just ask them. But like I said, it got results."

"Your friend who kept bees, what's his name–Darryl? Did he answer the ad?"

She rolled her eyes. "Darren. Darren Odlum. Yes, that's how we met. A *total* drone. I mean, I kept asking myself: how did a guy like this ever beat out a million other sperm?"

He pictured Darren, a slight fellow with deep-set, wounded eyes and a look of wondering perplexity, as if he'd just been stung by his own swarm. Where Taffy was involved, that probably wasn't far from the truth. The guy only lasted two or three weeks, then he was gone before he knew what hit him. Jimmy imagined him standing in a field of clover, his broken heart deafening him to the buzzing of bees all around him.

"He seemed like a nice guy to me."

"He just showed up and fogged the mirror. Come to think of it, he didn't even fog the mirror."

"Didn't you ever worry about Mr. Goodbar?"

Taffy just cocked her head and looked at him sideways, as if he were speaking Urdu.

"*Looking for Mr. Goodbar,*" he prodded. "The movie. With Diane Keaton?"

"Who?"

"She plays this single woman, picks up strange guys and takes them home. Hoping to find the good one. Mr. Goodbar, she calls him."

"I'd settle for Milk Duds."

"It doesn't have a happy ending, you know."

"You talkin' about the movie or this thing we're discussing? Because I–"

"The movie. Or maybe both, who knows? I worry about you, Taffy."

"Well, you're gonna have to take a number. My *parents* aren't even at the head of *that* line." She finally flopped down, in the wooden chair just to the right of his desk, swinging her right leg over the arm to flatten an expanse of black leotard above the knee.

"Thing is," she said, "I gotta do something about this one. It's gonna be ugly, Jimmy, if something doesn't get done about it. He calls me at night and hangs up. Like I don't *know* it's him. And yesterday I saw him hanging in a doorway to the Dunkin' Donuts across the street from my bus stop, like I'm supposed to think it's an accident or something. Not to mention *this*."

Jimmy winced to see the bruising on the skinny wrist she thrust under his nose. When she figured he'd seen enough, she sloughed it back under her sweatshirt.

"That's just from trying to pull away from him. The bus driver hadn't hollered, there's no telling what might have happened."

"Okay," he said. "It's ugly, like you say. You need a court order. But you of *all* people should know how to swear out a two-oh-nine-A. You just go see the clerk and–"

Taffy's face went immobile. "You don't get this, Jimmy. A restraining order won't do it with this guy. He is *serious* trouble. I need to have somebody talk to him he'll, like, listen to. 'Cause a court order he'll just ram up my you-know-what."

Jimmy paused, thinking this through. "How long did it take you to figure that out?"

"What? That he had a head full of loose change? Too long, obviously. I mean, at first I thought he was just another hard-hat bowling type. You know, a six-pack every Thursday for his date with the reset button? Oh, I knew he had a violent streak and all. You could tell by how he reacted to other guys when we were out together. But it was kind of flattering, too, you know? Then? After a while? Well, I figured out that what separates him from the rest of us is only one, maybe two *million years of evolution!*"

She wound up with such ferocity, Jimmy held up both hands to calm her down. "Okay, okay. We all make mistakes. Somebody to talk to him?"

"Yeah, I thought maybe you knew somebody who's . . . *persuasive*, if you follow my drift. Somebody close to Peetie Coniglio, maybe. One of those heavies from the North End. Somebody Reb will listen to."

Have I come to this? He addressed her in what he hoped was a mournful tone. "Is that what you think I am? Someone who can find you a hard guy to scare off your ex-boyfriend?"

"It's not what I *think*, Jimmy. It's what I *hope*. This is a guy, broke a baseball bat over the hood of his buddy's pickup because he got it into his head that the guy was trying to look up my skirt."

This being Taffy, the guy must have gone through more bats than Ricky Henderson.

Jimmy sighed. "Okay. Rebstock, you say? What's his first name?"

"Willard. He prefers Will."

"Willard Rebstock, then. Jimmy wrote down the data she supplied. Rebstock's address. The Department of Public Works site where he had been working the last couple of weeks. Then the two of them sank into silence, Taffy staring morosely off toward the air shaft.

"Let me think about this for a bit," he said at last. "I'm sure we'll be able to come up with something."

Taffy didn't look up. She said, "You know, I think about this guy, and I keep wondering how I was ever attracted to him." She turned to face him, her eyes narrowed. "Because he was a code-six wing nut. I mean, he expected me to like hang out and wait for him to call. Do something homey, maybe. Like *what*, I'd like to know? Knit him a dick cozy or something?"

Jimmy shrugged. "Maybe you should reconsider the ad. But let me work on it, okay? And if it's that scary, stay with one of your girlfriends for a couple of days."

When he was alone at last, he pried the lid off his cup of coffee and took a sip. It was lukewarm, but what the hell. He took another. With his free hand he sorted through his message slips like a blackjack dealer distributing cards from a shoe. They sorted naturally into three piles: not urgent, who cares, and discard.

He set the cup down and bent over to reach in between the gaping jaws of the open briefcase on the floor. He fished out Sliney's file. If the two of them were to meet later on, he figured he'd better go through the file beforehand. It wasn't very thick, a manila folder with notes scribbled all over the cover like most of his files, crumpled at the corners and still a little dusty from its sojourn with the starlings and spiders up in the crawl space above his garage. He laid it on his desk and slipped off the rubber band he had put around it after descending from the rafters. He opened the folder to see what could suddenly be of so much interest to an ex-client four months after getting out of M.C.I. Concord.

Not much there of interest to *anyone*, he concluded. A docket sheet. A copy of the indictment. The carbon copy of a receipt for $2,500, in cash, to cover Jimmy's fee. His appearance slip. Discovery materials from the DA's office, which consisted principally of police reports, a rental car contract, and signed statements given by five complaining witnesses. Some notes he had taken while visiting Sliney right after his arrest. Not much else. There were no notes of interviews with witnesses because he hadn't done any. Sliney had been brought upstairs for the pretrial, listened to the deal offered by the DA, conferred with Jimmy back in the holding area, and–to Jimmy's mild surprise–took the deal. Twenty-six months in Concord.

Jimmy's surprise had been mild because Sliney had not had much of a defense. They had arrested him, Jimmy reminded his client, in a car rented on Neil Leifer's credit card, which was still tucked in Sliney's wallet, and the swag in the backseat–"the electronics," as Sliney called it–had been purchased with a credit card in yet another name and also found in Sliney's possession. And the rental guy from the airport had had no trouble picking Sliney's picture out of an array of mug shots.

They also liked him for transactions made on three other credit cards–because of similarities in purchases, vendors, and timing–

and the indictment included charges based on those purchases. But because Sliney had not been apprehended with those cards in his possession, the additional charges were more problematical. The DA would have to rely almost exclusively on eyewitness identifications from shopkeepers and desk clerks–fodder for effective cross-examination. This, the DA admitted, weakened the case. Hence the offer of twenty-six months on the two cards in Sliney's possession and a dismissal on the other three counts.

Sliney was unimpressed at first. "Don't tell me I'm hooked," he had lectured. "You're a technical loophole lawyer. You can get me out of this. The law is an ass, like the fella says. You just gotta prove it to them."

Jimmy had shaken his head at such misplaced hubris. "This time, Des, it's *your* ass. I'm telling you, it's bad."

"But you're fucking *Houdini*, man." Then he repeated himself, softer, with less bravado this time. "You can get me out of this."

"The *exorcist* couldn't get you out of the first two charges. Look-it." He ticked the points off on his fingers. "The arrest was lawful because the car was hot, and you were in it. The search of the car was valid as incident to the arrest, and the car itself was evidence anyway. I've looked at the mug shots they showed to the rental clerk, and there's people in the array that look enough like you to knock out any claim it was too suggestive. You're not gonna skate on this one, Des. And twenty-six months is a lot less than what Judge Melick is gonna throw at you after trial even if I *can* take out the other three. You could pull ten hard. So you gotta start your thinking from the inevitable here. The first two charges are gonna stick. Which, with your record, makes twenty-six months look like a decent deal."

Sliney had gone silent on hearing this, and Jimmy let him sit with it for a minute before broaching the hard part. "The only way I know to improve your situation is to give them something."

Sliney lifted just his eyes to Jimmy's, waiting for the shoe to drop.

"Denyce–that's Denyce Acuff, the DA on this case–she's convinced there's got to be somebody else involved. Makes sense, too.

She's got five solid citizens who apparently have nothing in common, and certainly nothing in common with the likes of you, no offense. And yet, somehow, you come up with their card numbers and some *very* deep credit data on all of them. So she figures there's got to be somebody else, some insider somewhere, who's feeding you all this stuff. Odds are, by searching for common vendors patronized by the five victims, she's gonna be able to figure out where that person works. Of course, convicting that person—shit, even *identifying* him—is something else altogether. You with me here, Desmond?"

Sliney nodded, but gave nothing away.

"Now, if you were to give her this guy," Jimmy said, "*that* could change the entire calculation. 'Cause that's what they want. The source."

Some inner turmoil scrambled Sliney's features, but not for long. "I don't trade," he said. His voice was clear, proud even. "I don't give up my friends."

A good scam artist can even con himself.

"I appreciate that, Des. And so do your friends, I'm sure. I just want you to know all your options here. 'Cause the opportunity is there for a very pretty deal. A nice little package. *Maybe* one with no time inside at all."

Sliney had just shaken his head. And true to his word, he stood up. He took the deal that same afternoon.

Swave," said Tristan Desmond Sliney an hour later, as he sauntered into Jimmy's office, hands in pockets, eyes sweeping the room. He leaned theatrically to one side to peer out the window at the air shaft. "Real chick, Jimmy. Not quite the view I was used to seeing from the farm in Concord, but *definitely* chick."

Jimmy let the man's sarcasm roll off him. This was, after all, his client's first visit to his office. Their previous meetings had all taken place in courtroom lobbies or lockups, once in a bar in Brighton. If Sliney was not the kind of client who graced the anterooms of fancy law firms, he was making it equally evident that this wasn't one of those places either.

Not that Sliney looked anything like the rail-thin carny of Neil Leifer's imagination—except for the hair, perhaps, which was raked back in cords before curling up at the collar. Sliney was otherwise a plump sea lion of a man, turned out in gray slacks and a yellow sport coat of some indeterminate fabric vaguely suggestive of silk. His puffy head appeared to have extruded from his buttoned collar like icing from a pastry tube. A tiny cedilla of a scar hung off one corner of his smirk.

Sliney pulled a pack of cigarettes and a Bic lighter from his shirt pocket. He tapped the pack against his wrist to coax out a butt and put it to his lips. He raised an eyebrow by way of seeking permission. Jimmy shook his head.

"Taffy would be all over me," he explained. "You want to ask her?"

"No way," Sliney said. "We already met, outside. What is she, in some kind of Goth coven?" He started a wheezing laugh that soon broke up into a rasping cough.

Jimmy flinched to hear him. "Jesus, Des. There's enough tar in that cough to resurface my driveway. What's going on? You didn't use to smoke."

"Tristan," Sliney croaked when his hacking subsided. "It's Tristan now, Jimmy." He wiped a tear from his eye with the side of his thumb. "You'd be surprised what you'll pick up again when you're inside. It's different when you're on the outside, your pockets jingling with talking-back money."

He shook the change in his pocket to make his point.

"But inside? Well, whatever it takes, you do it. A smoke might maybe settle your nerves? You do one. Because if you're not careful, it can really turn your head around. I know. Some guys it really fucks up. They start out mumbling to themselves, pretty soon they got pedestrians comin' out from under the bunks. And I don't mean the long-timers, lifers and such. Guys that know they're in Everever Land, they learn how to cope. It's the short-timers I'm talking. The ones that think they just gotta wait it out. Well, the waiting can eat you up."

Sliney lowered himself indolently into one of the chairs across the desk. He laced the fingers of both hands behind his head and rocked back in the chair. Waiting. Through some synaptic detour Jimmy couldn't begin to understand, he looked into the pasty visage of his client and remembered hearing how longtime dog owners came to look like their pets. Could it be true of lawyer and client?

"How come you're changing names?" Jimmy asked, to shake off the thought. "After all those years as Des, I mean?"

Sliney didn't answer right away. He seemed to be massaging the back of his neck. Then he let the chair tip forward, its front legs finding the carpet again.

"Same thing," he said. "What I was saying before, about being inside. How it can turn your head around, you're not real careful. 'Cause that was no ninety-day county stretch. You know what I'm saying?"

Jimmy nodded. "I think so. It's a lot of time to think."

"Think, shit. It's a lot of time, *period*."

He looked off toward the air shaft. Like Taffy before him, he seemed to be pouting over the injustice of it all. Jimmy waited. Then Sliney turned back to his lawyer.

"*And* to think. A lot of thinking. A lot of taking stock, seems like. Like how my life's gotta change. So I start with the name. I mean, it *is* my name, after all."

An unexceptionable proposition, and Jimmy nodded his agreement.

"That business with the credit cards?" Sliney said. "I been thinking about that, too. Tell you a story?"

Jimmy smiled encouragingly.

"When I was fourteen," Sliney began, "my mom—you remember my mom?"

Jimmy remembered his mom.

"Well, she sent me to visit my cousins, their folks lived on a chicken farm in Jersey. Toms River, New Jersey. Now, you tell a kid from St. Gregory's parish he's gonna spend a summer on a chicken farm in Jersey, he's not gonna like the idea. And I didn't. But—"

"Hatchery," Jimmy interrupted.

Sliney frowned.

Jimmy said, "I don't think they call 'em farms when it's chickens."

"Hatchery, farm, *corral* for fuck's sake. Who gives a shit?"

"I just—"

"And who's screwin' this cat, anyway? Jesus, Jimmy, *you* wanna tell the story?"

"Sorry," Jimmy said, waving him off. "You were saying. Chicken farm. Kid from St. Gregory's."

Sliney scowled a bit longer, then proceeded. "Where the legal drinking age was fourteen—which it's not in Toms River, let me tell you. But that's not the story. The story is these cousins, Saul and George. Both about my age. They had this weird game they played. Hypnotizing chickens. I shit you not. They would pick up a chicken and rub its neck like, and the thing would fall into some fuckin' trance or something. Then they'd plop 'em down and the birds'd just sit there like they were asleep. Not for long, though. In a little while they'd wake up. The game, George and Saul's game, was to see how many you could get in a line before the first one woke up."

Sliney paused for the setup.

"You know what these chickens remind me of, Jimmy?"

Jimmy shrugged. "Sounds sort of like a jury trial to me."

"Reminds me," Sliney went on, ignoring him, "of that credit card business I was into. I was too fucking cocky, you know? No pun intended. I went on too long. I let one of the chickens wake up."

He sat back to let it take.

Jimmy thought it over. He shook his head. "No, Tristan. You just kept working the same chicken—and a few too many times."

Sliney stared at him with billowing disappointment—as if beholding the ruins of his carefully wrought parable, deconstructed before his very eyes in a matter of seconds. Then he blinked it off.

"Whatever," he said shortly. "Point is I need to change my tack.

Start over. Something legit, this time. Maybe more like those slips I was selling there in Squantum, that time. You think about it, I was actually ahead of the curve there. Nobody thought to condo-ize marina slips before I came along. Slip condos was a big-ticket idea."

Recalling the man's narrow escape on that one, Jimmy had to conceal his incredulity. "But you never *owned* any slips, Desm—I mean Tristan. They weren't real."

"But they *coulda* been, Jimmy. That's the point. Don't you see? The *point* is I can think this shit up. I just need the right hookup, is all. A little fresh-up money and the right gig. You know, suck 'em in and suck 'em off—but legit this time." He stopped to make sure he had Jimmy's attention. "How much you know about penny stocks, Jimmy?"

Jimmy had to suppress an urge to look over his shoulder; the man *had* to be talking to someone else.

"Not much. Securities are not my thing. I'm told penny stock scams are all mobbed up these days—greed being the unwed mother of invention, after all. But I can tell you this: securities is federal. Diddle with stocks and you're up against the SEC and the US Attorney. And there's the federal sentencing guidelines: they measure out inflexible penalties in months. You can end up with a sentence that looks like a goddamn phone number. So if you go into penny stocks, you make dead sure it's legit."

"Hey, I told you. This is different. I met this guy inside, knows the stock business. It's all gonna be legit, like I said. I swear on my mother's grave."

"She died? I thought—"

"Well, no. But it's the same thing, right?"

The two men said nothing, staring at one another in the little office.

"I retrieved your file," Jimmy said at last, turning it 180 degrees and pushing it across the desk to his client. "What do you want with it, anyway?"

Sliney held his position for a moment, then leaned forward and draped his right arm over the folder and pulled it a little closer. Not once, Jimmy noticed, did he so much as glance at the file.

"Nothing, really." Sliney said. "I'm just taking stock of myself, like I said."

"Stock."

"Yeah. But what I *really* need is that stuff the cops are still holding, from right after the bust. You know what I'm talking about? A whole bunch of stuff. I call 'em up, I even *go* there, to Berkeley Street, and they just give me the runaround."

"What stuff?" Jimmy was mystified now.

"Oh, personal stuff they took. A cell phone. My pager. My appointment book. There's some papers, too. Personal papers which are, well, *personal,* like I said. That's the most important thing."

Sliney flashed a toothy smile of seraphic innocence. It was one, Jimmy knew from experience, the man could pull off and on like a glove. It also meant that the truth did not sit on Sliney's lips, but Jimmy let it go. He just took out a pen and clicked it into readiness.

"Who did you talk to about your property?"

He shrugged. "Some witless deputy."

Sliney started the story of his misadventures with the BPD, and Jimmy took notes. They were several minutes into this when something caught Jimmy's eye among the graffiti on the manila cover of Sliney's file. The messy surface of Jimmy's file folders reflected his bad habit, usually indulged while waiting in courtrooms, of scribbling on whatever folder was at hand. Jotting down expenses or points to make in argument, drawing stick figures, just plain doodling. This, Taffy was wont to remind him, made the folders unsightly while preserving nothing of value. So he had paid his scrawls no mind when going through the file earlier. But spun about and viewed from a different angle now, the chaos gave up a legible bit that seemed to beckon to him from across the desk. There, hedged in a sloppy trapezoid drawn with a Number 2 pencil, he deciphered a single word in his own handwriting.

Deon.

Jimmy blinked, Tristan's monologue lost to him for a moment. Why did the word arrest him like that, he wondered. No, not a word. A *name.* That's what it was. A name he'd heard before.

Wasn't he a singer? No, that was Dion. Dion and the Belmonts. Wrong spelling. Wrong, too, for that football player who had retired recently. A defensive back, used to play for Dallas. Deion Sanders.

But Deon?

"Hey, Jimmy. You listening?"

"What?" Jimmy looked up.

"Come on, Jim. I got a hangover here, could kill a fucking *woodpecker*. Can we get this done?"

Jimmy made eye contact with his client. "Tristan," he said sharply. "Who's Deon?"

Sliney froze. Jimmy could have taken it as a look of ignorant wonder at such a wild non sequitur, but that wasn't how he read the man. No, Sliney froze. In something akin to shock. Or fright, maybe.

"Who?" Sliney said after the briefest of pauses.

"Deon," Jimmy said, tugging the file out from under Sliney's reluctant arm. He turned it so the other man could read where he pointed. "It's right here on the outside of the folder. A name. Deon. You see it?"

Beholding it now, Sliney nodded without looking up.

Jimmy said, "That's my handwriting. I wrote it there, for some reason. And I would have done it in the courthouse, most likely while waiting with you. Did I meet him with you? Waiting for a hearing or conference or something? Who is he?"

Sliney cocked his head, his smirk back now. "You wrote it down, and you're asking *me* who it is? How come *you* don't remember?"

"This was over two years ago. I don't have the vaguest recollection."

"And *I* should?"

"I don't know. That's why I'm asking. Does it mean anything to you?"

Sliney held his gaze and shook his head gravely. "Not to me. Don't know no Deons. Do you?"

Jimmy stared at the folder again. "Apparently, I do. Or did. And there's something . . . familiar about the name." He looked up at his client. "But not to you?"

"Nope. Not to me."

And with that Sliney carefully extracted the folder from under Jimmy's hand and stood up. "But you'll get on that stuff I want back from Berkeley Street, right?"

Jimmy promised he would. Sliney nodded his thanks.

"Until then, as they say in Ethiopia—Abyssinia."

And with that Sliney took his leave. Once Jimmy saw him disappear behind the door to the stairwell—Sliney seemed to have some phobia of elevators—he turned on his heel and walked directly to Taffy's cubicle.

She was doing precisely nothing. Headset in place, no calls, no typing, nothing. The gum didn't even move in her mouth. Jimmy smiled at her. "Deon," he said. He spelled it for her. "Ring any bells? We ever have a client named Deon?"

She regarded him without any change of expression. "What is this? You getting a head start on that memory loss thing?"

"Huh?"

"This is the second time you asked, Jimmy. And no, we *still* don't have a client named Deon."

"Second time?"

She looked away to her left in disgust, as if appealing to a visage beside her: *You see what I have to put up with?*

"The list." She enunciated the word so slowly and deliberately her tongue made a brief appearance between her teeth. "From the FBI lady. Remember? You wanted to know if any of them were clients? I got it right here." She rustled about and pulled a sheet of notepaper out from under her Rolodex. "One of the names was Deon. There, see? Deon Che . . ."

"Chevalier," he finished for her.

"Whatever."

"As in Maurice."

"Who?"

But Jimmy wasn't listening. He had locked on the name. Deon Chevalier. It was one of the aliases used by William Wolff. Along with James Barry, Edward Hyde, and Godfrey Norton.

Deon Chevalier. Otherwise known as Van Gogh.

Jimmy sat back in his chair as the implications of this discovery began to hit home. He had abandoned the frolic occasioned by Virginia's photograph–his trip to Provincetown and the Drooping Lizard–because it had hit a dead end at the feet of a grieving drag queen. And he'd come back to the mundane.

Only to see the same name come back at him from another direction altogether.

That could mean, he supposed, that Deon Chevalier's reappearance in his life was nothing but a remarkable coincidence. A *very* remarkable one. But Jimmy didn't think so.

If the guy was coming at him from two different directions–in a pincer action, you might say–Jimmy figured he was more than the plaything of coincidence.

Coincidence, hell. This was personal now. Jimmy felt targeted.

And he intended to find out why.

CHAPTER TEN

THE GRAIN EXCHANGE

I t was just a short walk from his office, due east down Milk
Street toward the Harbor. Jimmy stopped when he reached
India Street and peered up at the Custom House Tower. He tried to
imagine what the city was like when that absurd structure was still
the tallest building in Boston—thirty stories of offices rising with pri-
apic presumption from the dome of an older, granite structure gir-
dled by Doric columns. These days the tower was known mostly for
the huge, perpetually inaccurate clock face just below the pyramid
at its apex—and as home to a pair of nesting peregrine falcons who
supped on unsuspecting pigeons around Post Office Square.

Directly across the street from the tower was a wedge of land
formed by Milk and India Streets on two sides and on the other by
the peeling girders of the Fitzgerald Expressway. On the wedge
squatted a curious construction called the Flour and Grain
Exchange Building. This was a bulbous, sandy-colored structure
of rock-faced masonry, surmounted by a mammoth dunce cap of
a roof that was itself hedged about at the cornice by spired dorm-
ers. Resembling nothing so much as the castle of a mad Bavarian
duke, the building clashed exuberantly with its surroundings,
Romanesque excess hunkered down among curtain-wall high-rises.
Jimmy had always thought it would be a splendid place to have an

office–beautiful in its way, yet offbeat enough to make it a funky address.

It housed only two law firms, however. Its anchor tenant was a property management company so prominent it was a household name in the city. The Grain Exchange was also home to a pair of ad agencies, a software company, and three architectural firms, including the big one that had given the building a makeover in the late seventies before moving in. Jimmy was here to visit one of smaller ones. McChesney/Seiberlich Associates, as a brass plaque in the columned hallway announced, occupied the second floor. He took the wide stairway at the far end of the hallway.

By the time the massive glass door to the offices of McChesney/Seiberlich was silently closing behind him, Jimmy cashiered for good the fantasy of working there. The Darwinian traffic on the Expressway, which rumbled by at eye level right outside the big picture window to his left, laid down an omnipresent drone he could not shake from the foreground of his awareness. Even when designing space for themselves, the architects had been unable to muffle the sound of cars and semis barreling by right under their noses, a scant thirty feet away.

A receptionist in thick glasses and mahogany curls asked him to take a seat while she buzzed Ms. Shagoury for him. He did, on a long leather couch dyed an unnatural burgundy. The leather squeaked. He picked through a firm brochure as he waited. The buildings it featured were unknown to him: suburban office park stuff, generic design-build structures suited to high-tech start-ups and mail-order houses and data storage centers. It occurred to him that McChesney/Seiberlich was the architectural analog of the third-rate, middle-sized law firms on Court Street he did battle with every day. He tried to picture Donald Gilfillen coming to work here every day, cranking out shop drawings and change orders and spec sheets, all with the hum of I-93 boring insidiously into his marrow.

"Mr. Morrissey?"

The smiling young woman extending her hand to him was pretty and plump. Her glistening face expressed a timid pleasure to see him. Her hand was soft and damp. "I'm Anna Shagoury. So you're Eddie's friend?"

"Guilty as charged," he said. "Nice to meet you. I'm Jimmy Morrissey. So Eddie Felch told you about me?"

She sank into a seat at the other end of the couch, her baby blue skirt blousing up a bit along the hips. "Yes. Excuse my rudeness for not inviting you inside, but I don't exactly have an office we could talk in, not privately. You know what I mean?" She laid her arm along the back of the couch. "Eddie said you weren't a reporter or anything."

"No, no," Jimmy said, shooting her his most disarming smile. "I'm a lawyer. It's our business to be discreet. I've just been asked to look into this business about Donald Gilfillen. For family. You understand."

Her brown eyes widened. "*Sarah* hired you? She's *such* a sweetie. And what a sad case! I mean, to lose a son like that. I met her at the memorial service. I didn't know–"

"No, not his mother." Roll the tarp out over *that* puddle, he told himself. "Not actual family. More what you might call de facto family. His community, really. In Provincetown."

"Oh," she said, nodding sagely. "Yes, I understand. It must be so hard. When people don't treat you like family even if you're close like one. You know, sometimes I just *hate* this country."

This last was uttered with such sudden vehemence, and preceded a silence that so plainly begged a response, that Jimmy had to suppress the urge to supply one. *Don't go there,* he told himself.

"What can you tell me about Donald? From your perspective as a workmate, I mean. What was he like?"

Her eyes were solemn, sad. "Donald was the nicest, sweetest man I knew. Quiet, and cheerful. Always a kind word and a good morning for you. For *every*body."

"That's what I've been hearing as well," Jimmy said. "You're an architect, too?"

"Yes, though I'm only four years out of school, so I'm–I *was*– Donald's junior in that sense. He'd been here almost seven years, you know. A good, steady worker."

Jimmy tried to envision the career path of an architect. Viewing it through the lens of the familiar, he imagined the pecking order of law firms. "Was he a partner or whatever?"

"A principal, you mean? That's what you become here if you're invited to join the firm. If you're lucky and all."

"After how long?"

"Usually five or six years. And no, Donald wasn't a principal. I gather–this is very confidential, now, okay?"

Jimmy raised his right hand like a man swearing an oath. It seemed to be all the reassurance she needed.

"Well, Donald was what we call a contract employee. A permanent associate. Non-tenure track, if you follow me. Don't get me wrong. He was a very capable guy, an architect with real flair, especially for the details. He just didn't have much of a head for business. It's a sad commentary, really. To make it in this profession you have to be a salesman, not an artist. That's what the principals are, salesmen. If you can't sell a design to a bunch of Philistine developers and zoning board officials–now *there's* a bright lot for you–well, you don't get the business. And, frankly, that wasn't Donald's strong suit. So he and management agreed a couple years ago that he would remain a salaried employee, working at what he did best."

"Which was . . . ?"

"Design and drafting, mostly. I mean, he was a bust even at contract administration, the grunt work most of us have to put in. Going out on the job site, checking on construction progress. Answer questions from the subs and stuff. They're a rough lot, you know, contractors and their ilk. I don't think Donald liked all that head-butting stuff. So he gravitated toward drafting, like I said. And models. Lord, he could build the most *exquisite* scale models. Of proposed projects for sales pitches and the like. And if you needed an elevation that would win people over with its grace, with panache, you went to Donald. He was really good. An artist, not just a draftsman."

"He struck you as pretty stable, did he?"

"Oh, yes. That's why all this was so hard, so painful for all of us. After all his personal progress, then to lose it like this."

Jimmy frowned. "Lose it?"

Anna looked about suspiciously, then eased closer to him. "He used to drink, you see. Then, a few years ago, he started going to that AA thing? He didn't talk about it much, but he told some of us. I mean, when you stop going out for an afternoon pop with the gang, people notice. You know what I mean?"

"Uh-huh."

"After a while he told me. About joining Alcoholics Anonymous and all. And how hard he worked at his recovery." She stopped, looking stricken all of a sudden. "Do you think I'm just *horrible*, telling you like this? Because it's supposed to be anonymous. I mean, I realize he's dead and all, but . . ."

Jimmy smiled encouragingly. "Who'd know but the two of us?"

"But it's like . . . *out* there now. In the universe. You know what I mean?"

He paused, then said, "Anna, if he's up there looking down at us, I'm sure he'd be smiling to hear you say that."

She lit up and smiled at him. "You're so right! That's exactly what he'd be doing. Smiling." She caught herself short, and a sadness took her. "Like he always did." She stared off into the space in front of her.

"But you said he 'lost it'? What do you mean? Lost what?"

She sniffed and turned her head to look at him. "He went out—that's what they call it when an AA member starts drinking again."

"That must have been hard. To watch somebody fall off the wagon like that."

"Oh, he never let any of *us* see that. He was very secretive about it, I guess. In fact, we didn't even know until after he was dead. We were all as crushed as could be to find out that he'd gone back to drinking. And then . . . to die like that? Such a horrible death. Mutilated and everything."

She looked down now, at the hands in her lap. "It's not how I want to remember him, but I can't shake the image. Tied up like that. And his ear . . ."

She absently raised a hand toward her own, then let it drop. A tear rolled down her cheek. It came to a rest just at the curve of her jaw.

"Well, *don't* remember him that way," Jimmy said. "You can't give in like that. Think of him coming into work, first thing in the morning, with a smile for everybody. Putting together one of those beautiful models."

She looked out at him from between teary eyelashes, ferns glistening with dew. "You know, I'm going to do that. Dammit, I really *am*."

That evening, when he told Phyllis what he'd learned from the architect about Donald Gilfillen, Jimmy mused aloud over the irony that Gilfillen had fallen off the wagon, after years of sobriety, only to end up in the bar where Van Gogh happened to be hunting. And poof—no more Donald.

"If you think about it," Phyllis said, "that might go a long way toward explaining why Richard is so defensive about him. Not only has he, she—now you've got *me* doing it. Not only does *he* suffer the trauma of losing a longtime partner to a brutal murder, he makes the further discovery that it happened because of an episode of casual infidelity. He cheats on him with a total stranger. Then *you* come along and want to dig it all up again. Asking him to help you find out all you can about his dead lover. How would you expect her to react?"

"Just about the way she did, when you put it that way."

And where did that leave him? Well, he thought, with another trip to Provincetown. Maybe he could find out where Gilfillen liked to drink once he got back in the game. Might even get lucky and stumble into the very place where Van Gogh had picked him up. Meanwhile, though, he had a law practice to catch up with. Taffy was about to pluck his arms out of their sockets if he didn't get his nose back into the business.

And then there was Phyllis's other curious suggestion, that night at the restaurant. If Virginia was so harrowed by the idea of his pawing through Donald's . . . remains, why invite him to the birthday party?

He might have to show up after all.

CHAPTER ELEVEN

THERE ARE NO COINCIDENCES

D enyce Acuff was not an easy person to reach. She was in
and out of courtrooms, lobby conferences, hallway arguments, sit-downs with criminal defendants and lawyers and proba-
tion officers. So Jimmy wasn't all that annoyed about spending a lot
of dead time hanging on the phone while legal assistants hunted
fruitlessly for the senior prosecutor. It was what he'd expected. His
luck changed on the fourth call. Denyce was actually in her office.
Eating lunch, from the sound of it.

"Deon?" she said through a mouthful of food. He couldn't have
deciphered the name if he hadn't just used it himself. "Are you kidding? This has got to be what, a year ago?"

"Two, actually."

"Come *on*. You expect me to remember some guy who *might*
have been with Desmond Sliney the day he pled out?"

"Tristan," Jimmy said. "He goes by Tristan now."

"*Tristan?*" she sputtered. "You're killing me here. He was a
brother now, I could see it—maybe. What's he think, he's the great
lover all of a sudden?" She barked a monosyllabic laugh—Ha!—and
Jimmy imagined bits of food being spat across her desk.

"I don't think he looks at it that way," he said.

"You ever actually *see Tristan*? The opera, I mean? I had this boyfriend, a couple years ago? White dude. Dragged me to the Metro-pol-itan Opera to see the great lovers in action. *Tristan and Isolde.* Jim, I swear: between the two of them, there must have been like seven hundred pounds of beef on the stage. Not a pretty sight, believe me."

Jimmy believed her. "But you don't remember any Deon?"

"Listen, the only reason I even remember *Sliney* is because he shoulda won some kind of award, for chutzpah or something, the way he kept going back for that credit card after it got canceled. That's some nerve, boy. No, the only Deon I know is a singer."

"Dion and the Belmonts. I thought of him, but he spelled it different. With an *i* instead of an *e*."

"You must be talking some white-boy group from way back. The dude I'm thinking of, the black dude now, he spells it with an *e*. No last name. And he's still the only Deon I know. Sorry. Can't help you."

"What about the property?"

"His personal effects? He try the arresting officer?"

"Yes, but you know the drill. They could give a shit. He got the runaround."

"So he needs a big-time lawyer to shake the tree for him, is that it? So why can't you go shake the tree?"

"You know damn well why. I go over there, they'll make me sit around for half a day just because I *am* a lawyer. A phone call from you could grease it."

Jimmy could almost see the cocoa-colored ridges form on her forehead as she weighed his request. He heard the slurp of a straw drawing air from the bottom of a plastic soda cup.

"All right," she said finally. "I'll do it. But you're gonna owe me."

"So I'll owe you."

"And you see your man *Tristan,* you ask him something for me."

"What's that?" Feeling wary now.

"It bugged me at the time, and you bringin' him up makes it bug me all over again. *Where'd he get the maiden names?* For all those guys! I mean, the other information I can understand. Social security numbers and addresses and shit, sure. But your *mother's* maiden name? That's pretty heavy."

"You think so?"

"Who else but a bank or a credit card company would have that kind of information?"

She was gone, and Jimmy was left to wonder. Not for long, though. He had been wondering overtime about a lot of things—none of them having anything to do with maiden names. Like who was Sliney's Deon? Was he the same as Van Gogh's Deon? Should he go to Virginia Dentata's birthday party? And what the hell was he supposed to do about Taffy?

Deon. Of course, as he'd admitted to Phyllis the night before when he told her about the name scribbled on Sliney's file, it could be just a coincidence. Deon was an odd name, but as Denyce had just demonstrated, it wasn't *that* odd. Some one-named singer answered to it. And he remembered there was another football player, a guy named Dyer on the Miami Dolphins, who did spell his first name the same way.

"Some people," Phyllis had said over her Chinese takeout, "claim there are no coincidences." Smiling at him in that teasing way, as she dumped Hunan eggplant from the carton and onto her plate. She licked sauce off the webbing of her thumb.

"Of *course* there are coincidences," he said. "That's why we have a *name* for it, for crying out loud. Don't give me that New Age crap. Coincidences happen all the time."

"Why don't you ask Taffy," she said, still smiling. "I'll bet she'd disagree with you."

"Taffy? You're talking about a woman leaves hunks of ginger on my desk to ward off who knows what. Bad vibes, negative energies, who knows? This from someone who never heard of Maurice Chevalier. Or Alan Alda, for that matter."

"I think you're just mad at her because she asked you to do something about her ex-boyfriend."

"No, I'm mad because of *what* she asked me to do about her ex-boyfriend."

That stopped her for a few seconds, chopsticks in midair. "What does she want you to do—besides going to court, I mean?"

"Find some thug to 'reason' with him."

Phyllis's eyes widened in disbelief. "To beat him up?"

"No, she didn't say that. Just scare the shit out of him, I suppose."

She set the chopsticks down on her plate. "Well, of *course*. You can't be going around dealing with . . . gangsters."

"Phyllis, I deal with gangsters all the time. I defend them, remember? It's not—"

"That's different. You of *all* people know that. Defending is what you do. It's not the same as . . . well, doing business with them."

For a moment Jimmy wondered if he had lost sight of the distinction she was drawing. It was, after all, the central moral premise of his profession. Had he been working too close to the bull all these years? She held his gaze while he mulled all this. She picked up the chopsticks again.

"You're not actually thinking of doing it, are you? Consorting with gangsters to . . ." She trailed off in search of the right verb.

"Strong-arm? Terrorize?"

She nodded uncertainly.

"No," he said. "Of course not. I have *some* self-respect left. There's got to be another way."

"Why can't you just file the papers and get a whatchamacallit, that court order thing?"

"A protective order. A stay-away. I could. Thing is, she's convinced it'll just make him madder. Apparently, he has a hard-on about authority."

"So explain that to the police. Won't they take care of her?"

Jimmy snorted. "They'll just tell her to go to a shelter or something. She's already staying with a girlfriend so she won't have to go home."

She picked up a limp slab of eggplant. It drooped from her chopsticks. "It's too bad the *police* won't go and scare the shit out of him."

Jimmy had grunted. He grunted again to recall it now, but come to think of it, it didn't sound that far off the mark. What if . . . ?

The ringing phone prevented him from landing the thought. He picked up the receiver. It was Denyce, true to her word.

"Okay, here's the scoop. They got his stuff. He's not gonna get it all back, though. The cell phone, for example? An instrumentality of the crime. His account records showed he used it to buy stuff with the credit cards. So that's forfeit. He doesn't get it."

"He said there was some cash. A couple hundred bucks, he thought."

"Jimmy," she said with exaggerated patience. "Cash? You think there's cash?"

Of course not, he thought.

"Of course not," he said. "Where do I go?"

"Send him to Cambridge Street. Berkeley Street doesn't have it. Tell him to ask for the property cage. They'll have it ready."

Send Tristan? The hell he would. He'd go himself.

But he didn't share that with Denyce. He just thanked her. She reminded him that he owed her.

CHAPTER TWELVE

BODY BY FISHER

The property cage was aptly named: a dank, windowless enclosure surrounded by hurricane fencing. It was tucked into the subbasement of the big North Station precinct house. As Denyce had promised, the cop at the window didn't make him wait. He had already retrieved Sliney's effects, which were stuffed in a white-plastic bag bearing a Borders Bookstore logo. Jimmy signed to acknowledge receipt and took the bag by its reinforced handles. As he neared the elevator he pulled it open to peek inside. He spotted a pager and a brown appointment book. A couple of pens. It dawned on him that a uniformed officer was holding the elevator for him, so he pulled his nose out of the bag and entered the car.

"What floor?" the cop asked.

"Second," Jimmy said. "Thanks."

The cop got off on the first, and Jimmy was pushed to the back by the noisy quartet of plainclothes who took the guy's place. One floor up, he let them all pile out ahead of him before exiting.

From the moment he got off the elevator, Jimmy was struck by how much quieter things were in Homicide than in the rest of the building. Must help, he thought, when your customers are dead. He walked by four glass-walled offices before it registered that he had just passed a vending machine. He paused and considered, then turned back to it. Freeing two dollar bills from the jumbo paper clip in his pocket, he fed one of them into the machine. He punched the buttons for his coffee, a regular with two sugars. As the cup dropped and was filling with muddy liquid, he fed in the second bill. He paused before punching the buttons for the second cup, struggling to remember how Bivens took his. He gave up and selected one just like the first. With a cup in each hand and the plastic bag swinging by its handles from his right wrist, he toddled carefully up the hallway.

He passed four offices, three of them with closed doors, before reaching his destination. It was the last interior office before a line of larger, window offices reserved for higher-ranking detectives. Jimmy poked his head around the corner of the open door. A thin black man with slicked-back hair and a gray sweatshirt sat hunched over his desk. Jimmy, his hands full, tapped the door with his toe, twice. The man looked up at him, then tipped his head back and flared his nostrils, as if in search of fresh air. If he was pleased to see Jimmy, he hid it well.

"Leevonn, I forget," Jimmy said, holding the cups aloft as he stepped inside. "How do you like your coffee?"

"Alone."

"Well, I messed up then," he said, deliberately reframing the answer, as Phyllis might have put it. "It's regular and sweetened. Can you choke it down?" Jimmy extended the cup.

Pausing long enough to keep the hard look bearing down on Jimmy, Detective Leevonn Bivens finally accepted the offering. He said, "You put on weight, I see."

"Good of you to notice," Jimmy said.

Bivens sipped. He grimaced.

"Hey," Jimmy said. "It's your coffee machine, not mine. So how are you, Leevonn?"

"I'm holding my own."

"Well, let *go* of it, will you? Jesus, give the poor thing a rest. Try a little self-control here. You might actually get some work done.

Case you hadn't noticed, you guys aren't giving me a lot of business lately." Jimmy sat down in one of the chairs in front of the desk. He put Tristan's bag on the floor beside him. Its handles lolled across his shoe.

"Yeah?" Bivens was smiling slyly now. "You still writing solicitation letters to guys we pick up for driving under?" He swung his feet up on the desk. Black denim jeans, so oversize they hung off his skinny legs like wash on a line, were rucked up past the laces of his white high-tops. His pants showed an inch of turned-up cuff, but it seemed a pathetic gesture, given inseams at least eight inches longer than the man's legs.

Jimmy sipped some of his own coffee. He returned the grimace, then held the cup out from him and regarded it with distaste. "I see what you mean. You want I should pour 'em out? No? I didn't think so." He set the cup down on the desk. "What were you saying? Oh, yeah. OUIs. Nah, I gave that up. No money in it. At the moment I'm negotiating with Fisher Body to have my ad stamped on every airbag in America. Listen. This is pure genius, Leevonn. First thing anybody'll see, they get in an accident, is my name and number staring at them. In big, bold colors. Might even have it embossed, so it'll leave an imprint on your forehead. Good, huh? Plus I'm gonna put posters up on the ceiling of ICUs. I'll need banks of telephone operators 'standing by,' as they say."

Bivens actually laughed. "Okay. So why the coffee?"

Jimmy pulled his head back and put on his hurt look. "I couldn't have other business over here and just be popping in to say hi to an old friend?"

"Do you?"

"Matter of fact, I do. Picking up a client's personal effects, if you must know." He held up the Borders bag and shook it.

"That means you don't want nothin' from me, I suppose." The voice was dry.

Jimmy gave him a dip of the head. "Ah, well, yes, I do. Guilty. A little information, I was hoping for."

"What about?" Bivens drank more coffee. No faces this time.

"William Wolff. AKA Van Gogh. Didn't I read where you were the guy that caught the first homicide? Jonathan Ridley, over there in the South End?"

"That one's closed, Jimmy. Didn't you hear?"

"I *know* that. Christ, even people live in *Lincoln* know that. Makes me optimistic, in fact. The constabulary doing its job and all. Also makes me think maybe I could get a peek at the autopsy report. What do *you* think, Leevonn?"

Bivens shook his head slowly. "Forget it. The Fibbies are all over that one. I don't even know if *I* could get at the report."

Jimmy chewed his lip and frowned. "Still? The guy's dead."

"Still. What's your interest, anyway. You bringin' a wrongful death action against Ridley's landlord or something?"

Jimmy brightened. "Now *that's* a thought. *Had* to be poor building security. But no, nothing so cutting edge, I'm afraid. My real interest is the *other* local victim, the one in Provincetown. I've, ah . . . been asked to look into it."

He beamed at the cop, as if daring him to ask who by, but Bivens didn't bite. He just said, "That one's a little different."

Jimmy cocked his head. "Different?"

Bivens nodded.

"How so?"

Bivens regarded him. The man wondering if he was squandering valuable capital here. "Guy'd been knocked around. Death by blunt trauma to the side of the head. Never did find out what with."

Jimmy fought to keep from rushing into the silence that followed this revelation. When it became clear Bivens was volunteering nothing further, Jimmy prodded. "Anything else? Different, I mean?"

Bivens seemed to be taking a five count before each response. "No Seconal. All the other victims had enough Seconal in them to fell an ox. Not this guy, what's his name."

"Gilfillen." Jimmy's excitement would have overcome him if his confusion hadn't gotten there first. "Donald Gilfillen. None of this was in the papers."

Bivens just shrugged.

"So how could you be certain it was Van Gogh?"

Bivens opened his mouth, but he checked himself, for no sound came out at first. "On account of there was other . . . *characteristics* only Van Gogh coulda known about. So we knew it had to be him."

"Ah," Jimmy said with a broadening smile. "You're turning cryptic on me. It's not the colored ropes you'd be alluding to now, would it?"

Bivens raised his eyebrows respectfully, nothing more.

Jimmy said, "I'm not completely without resources of my own, you know. So the killer on the Cape knew stuff he wasn't supposed to. That still doesn't explain the discrepancies, does it? I mean, the others were all drugged and strangled."

Bivens made a give-a-shit shrug, to greet a moot question about a dead file. "You gotta see it in context, 's all I'm saying. Just like that last guy, the one in Key West? That got away? For some reason the guy on the Cape didn't take the Seconal, and Van Gogh had to get rough. That's what happened in Key West, right? Guy woke up and put up a fight. Besides, there was other stuff. The ear thing. And he was raped the same way. Go marinade on it for a while, you want. You come up with a better theory, I'd like to hear it."

Jimmy thought about it, as the man suggested. And yes, it made sense. Enough sense, at the very least, for the FBI to pounce on the Gilfillen murder, treat it as one more bead on Van Gogh's long string. He wondered what Agent Butler would have to say about the discrepancies. Then he remembered how unforthcoming she had been when she and Ponsonby had dropped this whole thing in his lap that first day.

Jimmy said, "All this would make the autopsy report awfully good reading."

"Which one?" Bivens said with a smile. "Ours or the one from Provincetown?"

"Both of them, I guess. Kinda makes 'em a matched set, don't you think?"

"Wouldn't know. On account of I don't have either one of 'em. Like I said, try the FBI."

Jimmy pictured Butler's perky face and smiled to himself. He said, "I forget, Leevonn. Which way's the men's room?"

"First door on the right after the elevator. One for the road?"

"One for the prostate," Jimmy said as he got to his feet. "When you get my age, there's three things you never do. You never pass a toilet, you never waste a hard-on, and you *never* trust a fart."

CHAPTER THIRTEEN

ST. THERESA-LUTHERAN

Once outside the police station, Jimmy waded through the frozen traffic that filled Cambridge Street and made his way toward City Hall Plaza. He tried to digest what Bivens had told him about Gilfillen's murder. The discrepancies troubled him, but the tricolor ropes and other details seemed an unassailable link to Van Gogh. Maybe Bivens's explanation was right: somehow Gilfillen hadn't taken the Seconal, and the killer got rough. Discordances, was the word for it. Disharmonies he'd have to tolerate unless new information led him elsewhere.

It wasn't until he was halfway across the Plaza that he remembered Sliney's effects. They reminded *him*, actually. He felt a sharp pain as the Borders bag swung into his knee. He winced. The pager. His curiosity returned. What was it that Sliney wanted back so bad?

He made for a cement bench off to his right. He sat down and lodged the bag between his knees. He thrust his hand inside it and retrieved the pager. He turned it over in his hand. He'd never handled one before, but it looked like others he had seen clipped to the belts of his more fashionably wired acquaintances. The battery seemed to be dead, since none of the buttons responded. He set it on the bench beside him and reached in the bag again.

A pen. Fat, heavy, black. A Meisterstück, according to the logo.

Which meant it was either a knockoff or the fruits of a crime, knowing Sliney. He unscrewed the cap and touched the ballpoint's bared nib to the end of his finger. It appeared to be dry. After two years, what should he expect? Well, if it were a genuine Mont Blanc product, wouldn't it still write? He replaced the cap and laid the pen beside the pager. He dug in again.

A matching mechanical pencil. He took it apart, carefully laying out the parts on the cement surface of the bench. He found nothing. He put it back together and set it down with the others.

He fished out a money clip. Empty. He wondered if it was when it was seized. Real silver, from the look of it, but what did he know? He used a paper clip for his folding money. This one was engraved with initials: T.D.S.

A set of keys. Six of them. Could it be a key Sliney wanted back so bad? If so, Jimmy was getting nowhere: none of them had any obvious purpose or origin. No car keys. No safe deposit or locker keys, as far as his untrained eye could detect. Maybe he could take them to a locksmith, somebody who could tell him more about the kind of locks they might fit? Save that thought. He laid them down.

The appointment book. Brown leather. Small, about the size of a playing card. Bound pages, not loose-leaf. No, he amended, not an appointment book. It was an address book. With letter tabs.

Jimmy felt a little tingle of excitement as he fingered the tabs. He flipped to the entries under "D."

No luck. Three names, in a surprisingly neat hand. None of them Deon.

He flicked back one letter, to *C.* He almost jumped up. There it was.

> Deon Chevalier
> 84 Strathmore Road, # 3
> Brighton, MA 02135
> 482-9600 (W)
> 426-9444 (H)

Jimmy just stared at the page and felt his pulse race. And completely confused. It confirmed his suspicions about Sliney's evasions when the name was pointed out to him, but it explained nothing. And nothing came to him now that might help—except that he was going to have to have another sit-down with his client.

Looking at the entry, Jimmy felt something else, too. An itch he couldn't help but scratch. To keep the pages from riffling in the gusting breezes that eddied in the Plaza, he laid the pager across the address book. It held his place. Then he plucked his cell phone off his belt and punched in Deon's home phone number. After a short wait, he got the annoying tone he knew would be followed by—yes, there it was. A woman's prerecorded voice.

"The number you have reached is not in service. If you believe you have reached this message in error—"

He cut her off. What did he expect? Van Gogh had pitched camp in half a dozen different cities since Sliney was arrested and the address book was seized.

He called the other number Tristan had listed for Deon. It was picked up on the second ring.

"Patient Accounts. Jessica speaking."

Jimmy was dumbfounded for a moment. He hadn't really planned to reach anyone. To the extent he'd had any "plan" at all, it was just to see if anyone answered.

"Hel-lo," Jessica insisted. "Anybody there?"

"Uh, I'm sorry," he managed at last. "Who have I reached?"

"This is Jessica Smith in Patient Accounts. Did you have a question about your account?"

"Patient Accounts? Where? I mean, what company?"

"Ah," Jessica said, a smile in her voice now. "This is St. Theresa-Lutheran."

"The hospital?"

"Yes. Isn't that what you wanted?"

"Yes," Jimmy said, a smile breaking across his face like sunlight escaping cloud cover. "Yes, it is indeed. Thank you, and have a nice day."

He ended the call and closed his eyes. St. Theresa-Lutheran. The name made Jimmy reflect briefly on the multicultural effects of the rush toward consolidation in Boston's hospitals. St. Theresa-Lutheran. Beth Israel-Deaconess. What next, Intifada-Shalom? And could Catholics and Jews ever put aside theological differences long enough to dispense health care? Where would they start to compromise? No abortions during Lent?

Van Gogh, he recalled from his earliest research just after the FBI had descended on him, had worked for the hospital in question. In accounts receivable. Right after his stint at the law firm and before moving to some chain of optometrists. Jimmy was willing to bet that once he consulted the chrono he had put together, he'd find that Van Gogh was working there about the time Sliney got picked up in the rental car.

But what could Sliney possibly have to do with Van Gogh? And by what loopy train of circumstances was he learning this now, so soon after the FBI had posed the riddle of Virginia's portrait and Donald Gilfillen's murder?

One thing he knew for sure, though. He didn't need any theological baggage to reject the notion that this was a coincidence. There had to be a connection between Virginia's photograph and Sliney's sudden interest, more than four months after his release from prison, in recovering his address book. The connection was obvious. It was a serial killer named Van Gogh.

Jimmy made another call, this one to the office. To ask Taffy to look up Tristan Sliney's cell phone number. Still on hold while she checked, he stood up and made his way across the Plaza. There was Staples Express over on Court Street. There was no point, he figured, in returning the address book without keeping a copy for himself.

CHAPTER FOURTEEN

LIVING WITH A STRANGER

The joint was a squat cement cube, the corners seemingly staked to its tiny lot by the girders supporting the elevated Green Line trolley. Most of the letters in its name sputtered blue in the half-dead neon sign on the roof. An oversize electronic clock, incongruously mounted to darken the building's only window, told him it was 4:03 and time for a Bud Light.

Wrong on both counts.

Jimmy pushed open a dark green metal door and entered the Barley Mow. His nostrils contracted involuntarily against the first whiff of stale beer and urine. Even for a gloomy North Station dive, the place seemed underpopulated at this, the noon hour. Of the five booths to Jimmy's left, only two were occupied, and a lone man at the bar was trying to make conversation with a blank-faced bartender.

Tristan Sliney was lounging large in the third booth, both arms spread out along the Naugahyde banquette, his head tipped back. The puffiness of his face seemed to have been reconfigured somehow, and the yellow jacket he had worn to Jimmy's office was wrinkled and shabby-looking. After a long night of gaying? So Jimmy wondered, reviving a hunch drawn from Tristan's talk of prison life. Then again, Jimmy seemed to have gays too much on his mind these days. Maybe he was jumping to conclusions. The guy could just be hungover again. The bleak look on Tristan's face was a further clue, and the half-empty pitcher of flat beer seemed to clinch it.

"Another hangover, Tristan? The wrath of grapes, my daddy used to call it."

Tristan lifted his reddened sclera to take in his tormentor. "Don't ask. How you doin', Jimmy?"

"Can't complain," he said as he slid into the seat across from him. "And it doesn't help if I do." There was no fight left in the seat cushion, and Jimmy sank to an unnaturally low level relative to the tabletop. He considered resting his chin on it. Instead, he nodded toward the pitcher. "Rushing the growler, I see."

Tristan frowned.

"The pitcher," Jimmy said, nodding again. "It's a Navy Yard expression. When a guy ordered a pitcher in Charlestown, we'd say he was rushing the growler. Don't ask me why, though."

Tristan gave something of a snort. "I forgot you were a Yardie. You gonna order? Don't let the place fool you. Food's not bad."

As if on cue, a waiter appeared with an enormous platter and a cup of coffee. Something Jimmy couldn't identify poked out from his armpit.

"Eggs on a raft?" he asked, looking from one man to the other.

Tristan tapped the table with a fingernail, twice. The platter slid into place, a huge waffle with three underpoached eggs quivering in the center. The thing under his arm turned out to be a bottle of Log Cabin syrup, which he set down beside the plate.

"How about you, Jimmy?" Tristan asked again. "You usually go for the full English."

"For *breakfast*, Tristan. It's almost one o'clock, for Christ's sake." He glanced up at the bartender. "Just a Diet Coke."

The bartender walked away.

"Not even a sandwich?" Tristan persisted like a man ashamed of eating alone.

Jimmy looked about him. "The air in here would take the tang off the Miracle Whip."

Tristan shrugged. He started in, sawing away at the waffle with the side of his fork. As he sectioned the waffle, the yolks and whites intermingled while filling the potholes in the waffle. Tristan sprinkled salt and pepper and poured syrup over the whole. When the man started scooping food with his fork, Jimmy looked away.

"You said you got my stuff?" Tristan asked through a mouthful of breakfast.

"I don't want to put you off your eggs, Tristan, but I gotta ask you again. Who's Deon?"

Tristan let his shoulders sag, a here-we-go-again gesture followed by a theatrical rolling of the eyes. Jimmy cut it short by sliding the address book, face up and open to the entry, toward Tristan's platter of food.

"Deon Chevalier, Tristan. Van Gogh to his enemies. He's right there, in your address book, so don't act like I'm torturing you. You knew him."

Shoulders still caught in mid-droop, Tristan stared at him. Jimmy could almost see the hamster in the man's head, kicking the little wheel into overdrive as he clamored for a way out. In the end he smiled tightly and gave it up. But how much?

"Guy's a killer, Jimmy." He abandoned his silverware and leaned back in the booth. "You can't hardly blame me for wanting to keep our . . . association to myself. Hey, that's just Self-Preservation 101, right?"

Jimmy shook his head. "Van Gogh is dead, Tristan. Don't give me that."

"*Is* he?" Tristan snapped into an erect position, his face tight and his jaw set. "Then how come he's sending me letters, huh? Tell me that."

"What are you talking, letters?"

"Yes, dammit! I'm talking letters!" Then he seemed as taken aback by his sudden vehemence as Jimmy was. He composed himself and sat back again. "Well, one letter, anyway. And dated August twenty-sixth—the day *after* the FBI says they took him down. How could he do that, Jimmy? Him being dead and all?"

Jimmy raised both hands. "Whoa. Back it up here, will you? You got a letter from Van Gogh—"

"From Deon, actually, but I see your point. In the letter he even *admitted* he was Van Gogh."

"But he signed it 'Deon'?"

Tristan nodded.

"And it was dated the twenty-sixth? You're sure?"

Tristan nodded again, vigorously. Then he stopped and tipped his head to one side and peered off into the middle distance, as if conjuring an image of the letter. "No," he said. "I'm talking about the postmark. The postmark was the twenty-sixth. I don't think the paper itself had a date on it, come to think of it."

Jimmy considered this in silence for a moment. He said, "He could have left it with someone to mail. For that matter, he could have dropped it in a mailbox before the Feds showed up. Depending on the pickup schedule, it might not get postmarked 'til the next day."

"Coulda happened that way, I suppose." Tristan didn't sound all that convinced.

"You still have it?" Hoping.

Tristan narrowed his eyes in disbelief. "Are you kidding? I'm gonna hang on to evidence could link me to this guy? For what—a souvenir? No way. I burned it over the toilet bowl. Then I flushed the fucking ashes."

Jimmy fought his disappointment. "Why was he writing to you?"

"You think I know? The guy was always playing games, like. Came at everything sideways. I don't have the foggiest."

"But what did it *say*." Jimmy felt he was getting nowhere. "What did he talk about in the letter?"

"About you, far as that goes."

"*Me*? He mentioned me?"

"Not by name, no. Don't think he ever knew your name."

You never saw the photograph.

Tristan said, "But he did talk about my lawyer, the one he saw in court that time."

"What time?"

"When I copped the plea."

"You mean on the credit card charges?"

"Right. He was there, for support. I pointed him out to you in the crowd, across the railing there, in the courtroom."

"And I must have jotted the name down on the folder," Jimmy said, more to himself than to hold up his end of the conversation.

"I don't know that. Makes sense, I s'pose. Anyway, he wrote in the letter that he was the guy did those killings. Said he figured he was about to go down for them—in the 'near future,' was how he put it—and he wanted to warn me so I could stay out of it. He said if they learned about our connection, I could get caught up in it—the police activity and publicity, the whole shitstorm. So I should get busy cutting ties. He mentioned you, how he'd understand if I might of told you about him and our little business together. Which, of course, I didn't. He told me I should get my file back—get rid of anything else that might tie him and me together. So I did. I tried to get my stuff back from the BPD, too. And I called you. I got busy, like he said."

"Covering your tracks, you mean?"

"That's exactly what I mean."

"So you got hold of me. To get your file, your effects. Remove all traces of your connection. Is that it?"

"Damn straight. And why not? I'm still on parole, you know. The last thing I need is to give the BPD a reason to roust me. No sir, I want completely shut of him." He tapped the appointment book. "Guy's listed in my book. His number's stored in my cell phone. Plus, you met him, sort of, so how do I know he isn't written down in your file on me?"

It made sense, Jimmy figured. Sort of. It would not have been difficult to set Tristan off with a letter like that. If so, it also meant that Van Gogh had taken two distinct avenues to Jimmy himself: first setting him up by putting his name on the back of Virginia's photograph, then siccing a former client whose own ties to the killer would likely come out in the wash. For reasons that were still unfathomable, Van Gogh hadn't just teased Jimmy with a photograph. He had deliberatedly targeted him. He apparently meant to set him in motion to some end.

Well, whatever the reason, it had worked.

He focused on Tristan again. The man had lost all interest in his breakfast and seemed to be watching Jimmy's face for clues to his own riddle.

Jimmy said, "Well, first off, the cell phone is history. You won't get it back."

"Shit."

"It's not that bad. Nobody's gonna go through it looking for phone numbers. Some assistant DA is probably carrying it with him right now—assuming it's not obsolete already, which I understand it happens pretty fast with these things. Anyway, the first thing anybody'd do is wipe all the numbers from its memory. I'd put it out of my mind."

Tristan didn't look like he'd managed to do that yet.

"Tristan," Jimmy said, "tell me about Deon. He was your source for credit data, wasn't he? From the billing department at St. Theresa-Lutheran, right?"

If Tristan was surprised that Jimmy had figured out Deon's role in his credit card racket, he didn't let on. He just stared back at him, as if making up his mind how to handle this new wrinkle.

"Lighten up, Tristan. If the fraud boys were interested, they would have figured it out on their own by now. They'd have picked up that all six victims had been in St. Theresa's before their cards got hijacked. Besides, those other charges were nolle prossed when you took the plea. They're as dead as Deon."

Tristan gave a little snort. "*Assuming* he's dead."

"Well, dead-*er*, then. So tell me if I've got this straight. He would get information on patients from the hospital—card numbers and other credit information. Then he'd feed it to you. Right so far?"

Tristan waited just long enough not to seem easy. "Yeah. He did a lot of billing for a surgeon group there. Some kind of thing with eyes and lasers, I think it was."

"Cataract surgery?"

"Whatever. I don't know." Tristan's interest in his breakfast seemed to have revived, for he picked up his fork again. "Point is, a lot of it was elective surgery, the kind that isn't covered by insurance, and people paid by credit card. Which meant their patients were in the bucks, 'cause who else could afford to pay for these procedures on their own? And *that* means their cards would have high credit limits. So Deon would dish it off to me, being as I'm the one knew how to make use of it."

Jimmy thought of Denyce's query and smiled to himself. "What about the mothers' maiden names? How the hell did he get those? I never heard of a hospital asking for them."

Tristan smirked as he dispatched a forkful of waffle and eggs. He made a sour face. "Cold," he said. He dropped his fork and pushed the plate away.

"Mothers' maiden names?" Jimmy prodded.

The smirk resurfaced. "Jimmy, where you been? That stuff is public information. A guy's born in Massachusetts, you can get his birth records from the Registry. Vital Records and Statistics. Where you go to get a birth certificate. Down in Dorchester there, Mount Vernon Street."

Jimmy frowned. "But don't you need ID to get a birth certificate?"

"Beats me. Didn't need one. I just needed to look at it to see who the guy's mother was. Don't need ID for that. In fact, these days you don't even have to make the trip. You can get it all off the Internet."

Jimmy thought it through, looking for problems. "How did you know if the cardholder was born here?"

"Didn't need to. You give 'em the guy's name and birth date. They don't have a birth record that matches, you don't use his card. Deon had plenty to pick from."

Denyce, Jimmy thought, *is going to love this.*

Jimmy said, "So Deon was the guy you wouldn't give up for a better deal."

Tristan stiffened. "I don't give up my friends."

"So tell me about him, your good friend. What was he like?"

If the look on Tristan's face was any guide, the conversation had just taken an unwelcome turn. "What do you mean 'like'? He was a business partner. I didn't pay much attention to his private life."

"Sure," Jimmy said. "That would explain why you had a key to his apartment."

Tristan's eyes widened. Jimmy was capable of surprising him after all.

"I checked," Jimmy said. "It was on your key ring." He held it up and jiggled the keys in the air between them. "There seemed to be two different sets that looked like house keys. See?" He separated them out for him, but Tristan's eyes remained on his. "A locksmith agreed with me. So I went to Brighton, to the address you had for Deon, and I tried them. Of course, the locks had been changed for the new tenants, but not enough. Same group of locks, I guess. Anyway, one of the keys slipped right in the slot for apartment number three. Wouldn't turn, but it fit. And I said to myself, 'Self,' I said, 'what are the odds ol' Tristan would have a key that just happens to slide so smooth into Deon Chevalier's door lock?' For support, you said. That's why he came to court that day? Okay. Makes sense. Unless it was so he could see that you went through with the deal and kept your mouth shut."

Tristan's expression looked troubled. "What're you talking, see I'd go through with it?"

"Well, I keep getting these conflicting signals here, Tristan. He's there for you–for support, you say–but you don't know him all that well. Though you're willing to spend extra time in Concord instead of turning in someone you don't know all that well. But well enough to have a key to his place. So which is it, Tristan? Did you care for him or were you just scared of him?

Tristan looked straight ahead but at nothing in his immediate environment. "Maybe both," he said at last. "Yes, I cared and yes, sometimes he scared the living shit out of me."

Jimmy let him sit with that for a moment before pushing him again. "He was more than a friend, you mean."

Tristan's eyes flashed with anger. "Deon and I had a thing for a while, okay? Is that what you wanted to hear?"

"Well, it's what I figured. The key to his place. Him showing up in court. But the scared part? That would be . . . ?"

The unfinished question sat there between them for a time, like a third person in the booth. Tristan's unfocused gaze seemed directed over Jimmy's right shoulder.

"He was way weird. Eerie, like. I mean, getting a letter postmarked after he was dead? Well, it kinda fits him, you know? He used to get off on weirding you out. Like, if somebody crossed him? He'd be smoked, muttering for days about how he was gonna cut the guy. I never took it all that serious, but it could get under your skin anyway, you know what I mean? And now . . . now I find out he really *was* cutting people. Worse, in fact."

Tristan dug a cigarette out of his shirt pocket and looked at Jimmy with raised eyebrows.

"Go ahead," Jimmy said. Tristan lit up.

"Clears the chest," he explained, as smoke streamed out of his nostrils. "Deon was always hinting at secrets he could never tell. Wild shit. It would put me in danger to even know this stuff, he said. I figured it was bullshit, just smart talk, but like I said, it could creep you out, too."

"When did you figure out he was Van Gogh?"

Tristan cut his eyes sharply at Jimmy's, as if hearing an accusation in the question. "When he told me. In the letter."

"The thought never occurred to you before then?"

Tristan took another drag and flicked ashes onto his congealed eggs. "I wondered, yeah. When I read about the killings. 'Cause he had this doll, like. Life-sized. He was pretty weird about it."

"They make *male* inflatable sex toys?"

"No, no. I mean, I wouldn't know. Do I look like a guy who'd know about shit like that?"

"Now that you mention it . . ."

"Ha. Very funny. No. It wasn't like that. It was made of hard plastic. No usable orifices, if you take my meaning."

"A mannequin, then? Like a department store dummy, in the windows?"

Tristan screwed up his features. "Kind of, I guess. Anyhow, Deon kept it in his closet. Dressed it up sometimes. He even had a name for it. Anders, he called it, him, whatever. A beat-up piece of crap is what it was, all banged up and everything. Face scuffed. One of the legs would keep coming off at the knee. I asked him once, how come you don't get a new one, instead of keeping that sorry thing around. You know what he said?"

Jimmy shook his head.

"He said he didn't want to live with a stranger. Can you believe it? A stranger, for Christ's sake? Is that weird or what?"

Jimmy shook his head again, more to himself now. For the first time, he noticed that the bartender had delivered his Diet Coke. He drank from it. "We're getting off track here, aren't we? You were telling me you had your suspicions about the killings."

"That's what I'm trying to tell you," Tristan said, an edge of exasperation in his voice now. "It was the *doll.*"

"Wait a minute." Jimmy smiled. "Let me guess. It was missing an ear, right?"

"Yes!" Then he picked up the look of amusement on Jimmy's face. He expression turned wintry. "If you looked," he said, "you could tell it was cut off. This wasn't just 'cause it like fell off that rattletrap piece of shit. The ear had been fucking *cut* off. With a knife. You could see where the paint and the plastic was shaved off when he did it. With a lot of force, too. Like a guy really bearing down on the blade."

Jimmy wasn't grinning anymore. "The right ear?"

"The right ear."

"Did he ever tie up this, uh . . . Anders? Like Van Gogh's victims?"

Tristan's head slowly bobbed up and down in assent.

"In three different colors? The ropes, I mean?"

Tristan sat up sharply. "How did you know that?"

Jimmy paused. "Just a wild guess."

The two of them sat in silence. Tristan sipped cold coffee. Jimmy had more Diet Coke.

"When was last time you heard from him? Before getting this letter, that is?"

"That day, when I copped the plea. When I made the call."

"What call?"

"When we made the deal with the DA, there. I said I'd do it and all, but I needed to make a call. You don't remember?"

Jimmy shook his head.

"Well, I said I'd do it if I could make a call first. They were gonna take me back to the lockup 'til the afternoon, when that judge would be back on the bench. That's when I would take the plea. And the DA agreed I could use the pay phone in the hall outside the courtroom there. This coming back to you now?"

"No." Was this why he'd written down the name?

"I called Deon. Told him what was going down. That I'd be pleading out that afternoon. I told him what you'd said, about how they'd be matching credit charges to see what the marks had in common, and maybe they'd come looking for somebody at the hospital there. How maybe he should look for another job."

"What'd he say to that?"

"He said not to worry. Somebody there would see to it he landed on his feet."

"What does *that* mean?"

"Oh, I don't know." Tristan's store of patience seemed to have run out. "He was always talking about some connection he had at the hospital, some guy who looked out for him. Said the guy knew better than to make him unhappy. I never paid it much mind, you know. I figured it was another one of those 'deep secrets' I wasn't supposed to know—for my sake. More bullshit, you asked me. You gotta keep in mind, him and me had already broke up a couple months before this. The call was a courtesy, like. A word to the wise from an old friend."

"But the sense was he knew somebody at the hospital who would grease his way to another job? Is that it?"

Tristan shrugged. "I guess."

"And that was your last contact with him?"

"Except for him showing up, like he promised, when I got sentenced."

"That same afternoon."

"Yeah. He said he'd be there, in the audience. And he was."

"For support or to see you kept your mouth shut?"

"You tell me."

Tristan doused his cigarette, savagely, in one of the congealed potholes of his waffle.

CHAPTER FIFTEEN

INCOMING!

Moonlight polished the ceiling of the bedroom. Jimmy stared up at it, waiting for sleep to take him at last. He rolled over on his side to face the edge of the bed. The green readout on his alarm clock seemed to mock him—2:13 A.M. He considered whether to turn on his light and try once again to read himself to sleep. Then he felt Phyllis stir beside him.

"Are you awake?" she whispered.

"Yes." He lay on his back again. "You too, huh?"

"Me too."

He heard a rustling of covers and felt her hand seeking his. Lying side by side now, fingers interlaced.

"Jim?"

"What?"

"I'm scared."

He tightened his fingers around hers. A reflex he hoped she misread as an encouraging squeeze. "You're scared?"

"Yes. That's why I can't sleep."

"What are you scared of?"

She took a deep breath and let it out slowly. "Of the cancer, dummy. Of dying."

"Of course you are," he said, as if it were the most natural thing in the world.

"At first, the shock and the numbness got me through. Then the focus on doctors and treatment protocols—that kept me occupied. Followed by the treatments themselves, and the surgery. By then I was too sick to think about much of anything. It was all so . . . so all-consuming, I guess. And exhausting. I never really had time to let myself experience the terror of it."

"That's my job," he said, in a hushed voice. "I do that for you."

She turned toward him, on her side now. He followed suit. Their faces were inches apart, noses almost touching, and he could see the faint light reflected in the whites of her eyes. One further remove: sun to moon to ceiling, then a glinting in her eyes.

She said, "You do? You go around feeling terrified?"

"Sometimes. Total terror."

"Oh, babe," she whispered.

"It's not the same as yours, though. Mine's totally self-centered. I'm just scared of losing you."

She was silent for a moment. She said, "You know what it's called, don't you? When you experience your concern for another person as a 'self-centered' fear?"

"What?"

Incoming! Jimmy felt himself hunch against the rain of psychiatric jargon. But she surprised him.

"It's called love, Jim. Just love. Nothing selfish in that. So don't beat yourself up, okay?"

Jimmy waited to make sure of his voice before responding. "Feels selfish, though. Even now, for instance. How you start out telling me you can't sleep 'cause you're afraid, and here we are, talking about *my* fear instead."

She smiled, the moonlight jumping to the flash of her teeth, but just briefly. "Okay, have it your way. Back to mine, then. I'm scared. And not, I'm ashamed to say, of losing you."

"That's because you won't," he said. Saying it like a promise.

"I know that, Jim."

They looked at one another in silence again, before Jimmy

said, "You were saying you're afraid. Of dying. Which you're not gonna do."

"Not just dying," she said. "I'm even scared to talk to you about it. That's what feels really shameful."

"Don't," he said. "Jesus, I count on you for that. If *you* feel too ashamed to talk, we're both lost."

She smiled again, but it disappeared even faster this time. "I'm scared of dying, yes, but I'm even more scared of dying without having lived enough. Living fully, anyway. You know what I mean?"

"I'm not sure. You mean, like not getting a chance to do certain things—go to India, jump out of an airplane? 'Cause we could fix that, I think."

"No. I'm talking about . . . *authenticity* is the word that comes to mind. If I sound like a sophomore waxing existential, I'm sorry. All that dorm-room talk seems pretty real to me right now. You live your life, stumbling along day by day. Things come and go, you deal with them, new things come along. You're so busy keeping up with it all, you don't take the time to look at it whole. To see it as something purposeful . . . integrated."

"Authentic," he said.

"Yes." There was an urgency to her speech now. "Something to give it meaning beyond just . . . bopping along from day to day."

"Phyl, you don't 'bop.' You have to be the most authentic person I know. You spend your life helping people, making their lives better. That's not a useful purpose?"

"I guess. As far as it goes. It's not a perfect shield against regret, though. I'm afraid of ending with regrets—and the bitterness they bring."

"What regrets?" he asked, bracing himself.

"Nothing new, Jim. Nothing about us, really. It's an old one."

"It's kids again, isn't it."

"I can't get past it. I'm afraid of dying a childless woman. It just eats me up. I know we've been all over this, again and again, and sometimes I can fool myself into thinking it's behind me. After all those fertility tests and procedures and . . . everything. But it just lies there, way down in the quick, where I live. And the more I think about dying, the more it burns. Like a coal you blow on, whether you want to or not. Just by breathing."

She paused, and he let himself breathe.

"Is this making any sense?"

"Sure," he said. "I think so. Like maybe we should have adopted after all?"

"Maybe that would have helped." Her voice sounded smaller.

"Well, *that's* easy to fix. You get better, we'll adopt."

"Come on, Jim." She raised up, supporting her cheek in the palm of her hand. "Get serious. I'm forty-eight years old."

"And your point would be . . . ? I'm fifty-one, remember. So what?"

"I have breast cancer—and only one breast. *If* I can keep it."

"I don't know how to break this to you, Phyl, but if your baby's adopted, you can't breast-feed it no matter *how* many breasts you have."

Her smile had more staying power this time. "What are you trying to do here, jolly me out of my funk? Is that it?"

"No," he said, dead serious now. "I'm dead serious. You get better, we'll adopt. I don't care how old you are or many breasts you have, I'll find a way. From China, Guatemala, *Uzbekistan,* I don't care. Someplace. I'm a lawyer, after all. I can do it."

She said nothing, so he kept heaping it on. "You just get better. Do your part, and I'll do mine. I'll take care of everything else. Deal?"

Her voice was husky when she answered. "Deal."

They were quiet again, facing one another, and he listened to her breathing. She said, "What about you?"

"Me?"

"Yes. Why couldn't you sleep?"

"Oh." Thinking fast. "I'm just trying to figure out what a straight guy wears to a drag queen's birthday party. You think I should stop at my barber's, maybe thumb through *GQ?*"

"You're a bizarre person, Jim Morrissey." She let go of his hand and snuggled up against his side.

"I thought maybe I'd start off with my glen-plaid boxer shorts. A good foundation. Build from there, like."

"Sure, Jim." He could hear the yawn in her voice. "Work up from the foundation garments."

As she drifted off to sleep nestled in the crook of his arm, Jimmy stared up at the pale surface of the ceiling.

CHAPTER SIXTEEN

VIDI, VICI, VENI

W elcome to my yurt." Virginia Dentata showed a neutral smile while appraising Jimmy's tan chinos, their stressed pleats gaping, and the blue dress shirt open at the neck. At least the boxers weren't visible. Nothing that would call unwanted attention to him as long as he kept his pants on. Virginia, he noticed, wore carefully ironed blue jeans and a black turtleneck sweater. At least it wasn't a costume party.

Moments before, Jimmy had stepped timorously through the open front door of the side-entrance bungalow, into a smallish hall-way with a steep wooden staircase on the left, an arched opening to the living room just afterward, and a clean shot to a sunlit kitchen straight ahead. Spotting Virginia across the living room, Jimmy entered it. The room was almost filled with guests already, and none of them paid him any mind. When their eyes met, Virginia slipped out of a foursome and moved to greet him.

"Don't you leave. Stick around 'til people go home."

"I planned to," Jimmy said. "We got things to talk to about."

Virginia lifted an eyelid, as if to acknowledge a promise of secret possibilities. Virginia told him drinks and food were being served in the backyard, then scurried off toward the kitchen and a beckoning wave from a woman in an apron. The caterer?

The living room was tiny and crowded, and Jimmy felt ill at ease among so many strangers. There was no empty corner to slink off to. He noticed that every available bit of wall space in the living room was hung with watercolors and charcoal sketches, most signed in bold cursive by Virginia—by Richard Taub, actually. Making way for an enormous man draped in a pinto serape, Jimmy found himself in front of the dominant structure in the room: an enormous fireplace with a fieldstone chimney breast and a mantel carved crudely from a single slab of mahogany. He reached out to touch the surface of the wood, its edges so roughly scalloped they looked gouged.

"Victor Hugo," said a voice behind him.

Jimmy turned toward the voice. It belonged to Joseph, Virginia's protector from the restaurant. The splotches on his face were still much in evidence. Without removing his eyes from the mantelpiece, Joseph shook a cashew into his mouth from his cupped left hand.

"Oh, hi," Jimmy said. The man seemed completely absorbed in the mantelpiece. With his empty hand now resting on the top of his head, he absently smoothed an eyebrow with the tip of his ring finger. He chewed.

"Every time I look at it," Joseph continued, "I think of Victor Hugo. In his senescence Hugo took up carving furniture—with his teeth, believe it or not. I always imagined he would have produced objects like this. Doesn't it look gnawed to you?"

As a matter of fact it did, and Jimmy nodded his agreement. *Victor Hugo?*

"Sad, really," Joseph said. "How the mighty fall." He dropped his arm and turned to face Jimmy. "So, we meet again. Without the tasteless brusqueries this time, I hope." He arched a trim eyebrow. "Ginny tells me you're actually *not* some sleazebag out to prey on him, so I'll try not to be such a bitch. And here you are. Ginny's asked me to serve as your cicerone for the evening."

"Sissy what?"

Joseph vouchsafed a small, wry smile. "Are we being droll? No? Well, I'm not referring to some special edition of Rice-a-Roni for queers. But then again," and the smile broadened as he picked up the cadence of the old jingle, "talk about your 'San Francisco treat'!"

In full smile, with the eyes crinkling, the splotches on the man's face seemed magically to recede. Jimmy gave him a blank stare of incomprehension.

"A cicerone is a guide," Joseph translated, in an exhausted tone. "Usually one of those glib pansies who show you around museums. The term derives from the Roman orator Cicero—for his long-windedness, no doubt. Get it? Cicero—add a syllable—cicerone? You savvy?"

Jimmy frowned. "Cicero," he said.

Joseph shrugged. "Okay. Think of me as your Virgil, then. He led Dante through the underworld in the *Divina Comedia.*"

Jimmy smiled. "Is that what this is supposed to be, then? The Inferno?"

"Well, if beauty really *is* a painted hell, you may have a point. But it's all a matter of perspective. Call it Purgatory for now, and let's see where we end up. Come." The man tapped Jimmy's elbow. "Let's rustle you up a libation."

Jimmy followed the man's slim hips as he picked his way toward the back of the room, through an open pocket door to cross the flagstone floor of an equally crowded kitchen, then down a set of slate steps to the back garden.

The late-September air had a nip to it already, and Jimmy buttoned his sport coat against it. No one else in the crowded garden seemed to pay any attention to the chill. Joseph led him to a long table laden with drinks. A languid bartender behind the table leaned against a stone wall bright with moss like green velvet. A small crate of lemons and limes sat at his feet.

Joseph sipped his Pinot Grigio and the bartender waited for the head to subside on Jimmy's glass of Sam Adams before topping it off from the bottle. Jimmy looked about the grounds. Most of the revelers were men, though a few women were interspersed among them. He recognized no one. No, check that. There was a judge plucking boiled shrimp from a convex bowl of ice on another table a little farther along the stone wall. A tall, phlegmatic man who lorded over the Waltham District Court. He was gay? Then Jimmy remembered that *he* was there, so maybe he was jumping to conclusions again.

Joseph said, "You behold here those who choose to live lives of noisy desperation. We're a shrill bunch. You see that man there, with the angry curls and the blousy sleeves?"

Jimmy looked where Joseph's chin indicated. At a dark-haired man in a white Errol Flynn shirt who was conversing animatedly with two younger men.

"Jason Brady. A novelist who enjoyed some renown in the late eighties. Remember *Whither Love?*"

Jimmy shook his head.

"Well, I'm afraid his fifteen minutes of fame went to commercial years ago. And would you *look* at that blouse. I mean, really. Jimi Hendrix wouldn't have been caught dead in something like that. Even alive, for that matter. We have to hope he stays clear of the grill. Some of those synthetic fibers turn into napalm when ignited."

Two young men waved to Joseph as they passed on their way to the food. "Hello, girls!" Joseph called. Then, from the side of his mouth, he said to Jimmy, "A long-term couple. Something of a rarity in this town of promiscuous *boulevardiers*. And over *there . . .*"

Joseph nodded in the direction of a phalanx of rosebushes at the rear of the property, where three men and a tiny woman were laughing, apparently at something a fourth man had said. "The unlaughing center of that little klatch is Darryl the Daunted. Darryl Michaels, to his public. He's a Broadway producer of modest note. He's the one who launched that musical adaptation of *Krapp's Last Tape*—what was it, two, maybe three years ago? Well, *Krapp!* didn't exactly take off, but then maybe Beckett and musicals weren't meant for each other. Anyhoo, Darryl summers in Wellfleet, with all the shrinks and literati and other cerebral sharecroppers. Though his presence tonight suggests that his idea of what constitutes 'summer' has become a little more capacious—perhaps as demand for his services falls off. Here he is, anyway, forgotten but not gone, swapping fatuities with anyone who'll trade. Oh, come."

Joseph pinched the cuff of Jimmy's jacket and, like a tug with an oil tanker, deftly towed him through a shifting archipelago of conversations. They were headed toward the door to the garden shed, Jimmy vaguely realized. Along the way he picked up disembodied snippets of conversation.

". . . called Isotopes of Shiva. The drummer used to . . ."

". . . but Andrew Sullivan is *such* a whore . . ."

". . . only if I can go as Bea Arthur—in a big, floppy hat and my own . . ."

". . . I'm serious, Rosie really wants . . ."

He observed peculiarities of dress and grooming never encountered at dinner meetings of the Fourth Middlesex County Bar Association. A young, finely featured black man wore a flowing, rose-colored silk shirt whose slits, running from armpit to just below the waist, afforded glimpses of skin like waxed mahogany. He saw a seemingly ageless man whose prematurely orange hair and a matching beard had been cut short to resemble prepubescent peach fuzz. A dreamy-eyed woman with long, dark tresses looked like a dead ringer for Joan Baez until he noticed her bracelet was a single gold-plated handcuff, three inches of chain dangling from it; she brought to mind Virginia's magic trick, the one where Citronella Snowdrift emerged from a different trunk, in different garb and handcuffed. How did they do that, anyway? Then he realized the black man in the slit shirt *was* Citronella Snowdrift.

Jimmy thought of male baboons or gibbons or whatever they were, some kind of ape anyway, strutting with bright red butts to attract suitors. He remembered a cartoon he'd seen years ago, of a resplendent peacock in full feather lording over a tiny, bedraggled peahen, and saying, "What do you mean, *no?*" Then it dawned on him that the guests he was noticing were anomalies: the provocatively got-up were sprinkled sparsely through a crowd of conventionally dressed partygoers, people whose plainness allowed the wild ones to catch your eye like coruscating bits of quartz embedded in gray concrete. Even Virginia Dentata—his drag queen hostess, after all—had greeted him in conventional garb. He was still considering all this when Joseph's downward tug on his sleeve brought him to a halt and snapped him back into focus.

They had joined a foursome standing just outside the entrance to the garden shed at the back of the property. A tall man with angular features and close-cropped red hair was frowning down at the others. "So that's the question," he was saying. "Do I tell him to go fuck himself or choose to be more discreet?"

"Discretion has to learn its place," said a much shorter man to the speaker's left. The man had drawn a perfectly symmetrical smile across a perfectly round head that seemed to float like a balloon above his square shoulders.

"Its *fucking* place," said the first man. "I mean, who does he think he is, telling me how to run my love life? Talk about your unmitigated gall."

Joseph intervened. "Is there such a thing as *mitigated* gall?"

All three men turned toward him and smiled. The tall man said, "When it comes to my love life, all gall is divided into three parts. Vidi, vici, and veni."

Jimmy flinched as he fought back the urge to put the components of Caesar's boast back in their proper sequence. Then the man translated.

"I saw, I conquered, I came."

The others laughed. They took turns greeting Joseph, one with a hug, the others with quick kisses on the mouth. Joseph introduced them all to his charge. Except for Martin, the tall man, Jimmy forgot their names as fast as they were given.

Martin waggled his fingers at Jimmy. "Hi, sailor."

"You have to forgive Martin," Joseph explained to Jimmy. "He's a throwback, really, an oversexed devotee of the circuit parties up and down the coast. Still trying to fuck the Unknown Soldier, is my theory."

"Ignore him," Martin said, with great dignity. "And my little joke. He's just reminding me that you're straight. I *mean*. As if I didn't know."

Jimmy lifted his hands, palms up, and looked down at himself. "It shows?" he asked.

They laughed. A pudgy young man emerged from the open shed door with three folded lawn chairs under each arm. "Pardon me," he said. The men eased to their left to let him by. Through the open door Jimmy caught a quick glimpse into the shed. Sunlight streaming in through a side window set fire to the dust motes that swam in its interior. Rakes, hoes, spades lined up against the back wall. A couple dozen scavenged buoys, their faded colors in sharp contrast to the still-brilliant colors of their nylon lines, were hung like hams from the rafters. A blue wheelbarrow leaned against the back wall with its handles pointing up at the roof, the wheel suspended.

Martin stayed on him. "Huh. A lawyer. What brings you to us?"

Jimmy wondered if he was being asked what a straight man was doing here. If that was the subtext, he ignored it. "I was invited. I've been . . . looking into something for Virg—Richard."

"Really? Anything juicy? Embezzlement? A morals charge?"

Jimmy smiled tightly and shook his head. "Sorry. Can't say. Attorney-client privilege and all."

Martin nodded knowingly.

"Maybe," said the round-headed man through his beatific smile, "Mr. Morrison is here from the network."

"It's Morrissey," said Jimmy.

"Network?" said Martin, peering down at the other man.

"CBS. You mean you haven't heard?"

"Heard what?" said Joseph. Martin nodded again, as if seconding the question.

"Rosie. Ginny's been contacted about going on the *Rosie O'Donnell Show*." He turned to look at Jimmy. "So I thought maybe . . ."

The others stared at Jimmy, too.

"You thought *I* . . . ?" Jimmy smiled and shook his head. "No, no. Nothing like that. What I know about television isn't enough to get around on my remote."

Martin said, "Virginia's gonna be on *Rosie O'Donnell*?"

"Well, that's what I'm told, that they called, anyway," said the round-faced man. "They're trying to set something up, 's what I hear."

Martin nodded again. "Could be the big break. A national audience and everything. Just Ginny, or do they want the whole act?"

Jimmy started. He had been assuming Virginia had been asked to appear on the show as a sufferer, a transvestite mourning the loss of a partner to a serial killer. Wasn't that how these daytime talk shows worked? Rapists say the darnedest things, that kind of slant. But to appear as a performer?

Joseph put Jimmy's question for him. "Rosie O'Donnell is going put a drag show on daytime television? Have any of these people actually *seen* a performance of Where the Boys Are? We're not talking family fare here."

"No, no," said the round-faced man. "Not the whole show. Just Ginny's Rosie O'Donnell impersonation. It's a great bit, you know. They say Rosie saw a video of it, and she absolutely loves it. And you're right, Martin," he said to the tall man. "The exposure could be big, a very big break."

All four men nodded. When they moved on to discuss a friend's opening at a gallery in the East End, Jimmy found himself lost in thought. It had never occurred to him that Virginia might leave town, even temporarily. Given the direction his inquiries had taken him, Jimmy was counting on working with Virginia to solve the riddles Van Gogh had posed for them. But if Virginia weren't around, how could he ever get anywhere on the Provincetown end of it?

A woman passed him with a plate of food, and Jimmy realized he was hungry. There were no waiters, just the long table laden with food he had seen earlier, so he took his leave of Joseph and company and made for it. He had made two trips to the table, and several more to the bartender, before he noticed that most of the party, already beginning to thin out, had moved inside. Jimmy joined them. From a living-room window he watched the bartender hump the carton of citrus halves, all pulped out now, toward the front of the house.

Jimmy felt a little high from the beers, then realized with a jolt that he seemed to be in the minority in that regard. He wasn't sure just how he'd expected the party to end: in a decadent, Gatsbyesque manner, he supposed, with some debauched grotesquery to close out the millennium: fender benders and sobbing inebriates, the garden strewn with coke spoons and used condoms like failed O-rings, the whole extravaganza captured in a concluding tableau with an effeminate young man sitting alone on the front stoop and snarling "Bitch!" at the departing guests.

But it was nothing like that. People wished Virginia a happy birthday, exchanged hugs, sometimes kissed one another on the mouth. Left. Drove Volvos. Jimmy had actually found an empty chair beneath the Victor Hugo mantel, where he had settled in with just one more beer to stare into the dying fire, when he realized he was the last remaining guest. He could tell because Virginia was back in the living room, standing before him, arms akimbo and grinning with anticipation.

"So," Virginia said. "It's down to just the two of us. And you interest me."

Jimmy blinked back in tipsy surprise, both hands clutching the bottle of Sam Adams propped up on his lap.

"Oh, relax, for Pete's sake," said Virginia. "If a woman said that, would you take it as a come-on?"

"Absolutely," said Jimmy.

Virginia's smile now looked greedy to him, a little malicious even. He realized he was squeezing the neck of his beer bottle.

CHAPTER SEVENTEEN

DOLPHINS AND ASHES

W hat first struck him during Virginia's guided tour of the
bungalow was the huge framed photograph that filled the
steep wall to his left as he climbed the stairs. Jimmy leaned back
against the railing to get perspective on the man pictured there.

"That's Donald," Virginia said, stopping behind him on the
stairs. "A few weeks after he died, Lee gave it to me. You remember Lee? From the photo shop?"

Jimmy nodded without taking his eyes off the photograph.
"I. V. Peairs. I remember."

"Lee blew it up from a snapshot I took that summer. I bawled
like a baby when she brought it to me."

It was enormous, as photographs go, about three-quarters life-
sized, and it showed Virginia's dead partner in a carefree pose. As
pictured, Donald Gilfillen was a thin, gangly young man in knee-
length shorts and an unbuttoned Hawaiian shirt. Smiling back at
the camera, he rested his tailbone and the heels of both hands on a
split-rail fence. A sand dune, choked with tufts of long yellow grass
bent by the wind, rose gently in the background. The man showed
the camera a big, open smile on a handsome face, his long sandy
hair swept back. An errant quiff drooped across his forehead.

"I can see why," Jimmy said. "He's very handsome." What do you say in situations like these?

"He was beautiful," Virginia said with abstracted conviction, as if correcting someone who wasn't there.

"Mm," Jimmy said, less in agreement than to fill a painful silence. He could not help imagining how this man must have looked in the police photographs, naked and pale and trussed up with nylon cords. Minus an ear.

Virginia continued climbing the stairs; Jimmy followed.

At the top was a small hallway crowded with photographs and prints and more of Virginia's sketches. Jimmy looked them over without ever quite stopping and made approving noises over Virginia's own work. The sketches were portraits mostly, freely drawn, as if at great speed. Each face was deftly rendered, a mood or character neatly captured.

"You ever have a mind to leave showbiz, you could do this stuff full-time, don't you think?"

Virginia chuffed at this. "Now he's an art connoisseur. All this, and law, too?"

Jimmy smiled. "No, just photographs. Ones with my name on the back, anyway."

They moved on. Virginia stood aside to let him into a large bedroom with a bay window that overlooked the walled back garden, still spangled with party lights. A patchwork quilt covered an old four-poster bed, which was positioned to give its occupants a clear view out the window. The room was tidy, impeccably kept, aside from some wrinkling of the quilt, where guests had been invited to pile their coats. A single, bright orange rested on a square dish on the top of the dresser. With one hand clinging to the doorjamb, Virginia leaned in just far enough to tug the quilt smooth with the other.

"This is where I sleep when I'm married," Virginia said. "These days I sleep in here." And led the way to an adjacent, smaller bedroom that bore the marks of everyday habitation. Books and several issues of *The New Yorker* and a half-empty water glass crowding the surface of the nightstand. The toe of a brown sock poking out from a closed bureau drawer. Shoes neatly lined up at the foot of the bed. Vitamin jars and prescription vials on the dresser.

"And the last bedroom," Virginia said, leading the way across the hall. "It does duty as my office."

An office it was. The smallest of the upstairs rooms was taken up by two ill-matched pieces of furniture. One was an open rolltop desk, exquisitely made and in perfect condition, with books and heaps of paper bound in rubber bands and torn-open overnight mailers spilling out every which way. The desk's clashing companion was a computer workstation. It was a white, functional piece built from cheap materials, like something right out of Home Depot, with a couple of drawers, an alcove that harbored a printer, and a slide-out tray for the keyboard. This desk, too, was chockablock with stacks of paper. The computer, he noticed, was on—its screen saver was visible, anyway. Jimmy watched as images of all three cast members from Where the Boys Are materialized and decayed, crossfading one into another. Virginia's was the same portrait the FBI had dropped in his lap.

"This," Virginia said, "is where I work."

Jimmy was surprised. "You have a job? I mean, beside . . . performing?"

Virginia's smile seemed to mock him. "A day job, you mean? You think I need one?"

"No." Jimmy felt himself backtracking. "I mean, I don't know about these things. I just never gave it much thought."

Virginia continued to smile at him in silence, letting him squirm.

Jimmy said, "Do you, like, write your . . . *material* up here?"

"Oh, sometimes," Virginia said at last, glancing disdainfully at the clutter on the rolltop. "Pumping irony, you might say. It's very difficult to make a decent living as a performer. It's like what Mario Puzo said about writing. It's almost impossible to make a living, but if you're extremely lucky you can make a killing. Well, I haven't made a killing, obviously. So, yes, I have a day job."

"What do you do?" Thinking, antiques. An art gallery, maybe.

"I'm an editor. Freelance. I do a lot of work for a New York house you probably never heard of."

"Really?" Okay.

"Yes. Science fiction, mostly. Thrillers. A lot of Westerns."

"*Westerns?*"

Virginia's smile vanished. "You got a problem with that, Pilgrim?" The voice had slowed, and its cadence, like the rolling of Virginia's shoulders, was John Wayne's.

Jimmy grinned. "No, sir. It's just not what I expected, is all."

"You thought maybe romance novels, did you? Or English country house mysteries–cozies, as they're known in the business?"

Jimmy gave a little shrug of surrender, but Virginia refused to accept it.

"You figure I'm not butch enough, is that it? A squeamish little fairy who'd faint if I saw a blood spatter on my antimacassar? Couldn't handle all that machismo and violence?"

Jimmy's smile evaporated as he watched what started out as needling turn to something more . . . More what? Malicious, maybe. Certainly more personal.

Virginia glared at him. "It would help if you left your preconceptions at the door. You come into this expecting nothing but stereotypes, that's what you'll see. But enough," Virginia said. "You've seen where I lurk. Let's go downstairs and get you something to drink."

Back in the living room, Jimmy reclaimed his chair as Virginia coaxed the fire back to life. Once it was blazing again, Virginia reached up to pull off the turtleneck, the T-shirt riding up with it to bare a flat midriff. Poised to step into the kitchen, Virginia asked Jimmy what he wanted to drink.

"I was thinking of having another beer," Jimmy said, "but I'm gonna have to drive after. How about you? What are you having?"

"I don't drink," Virginia said, tugging the T-shirt back into place with one hand and tossing the sweater on the couch with the other.

"Like Donald?" Jimmy said.

Virginia stopped, eyes narrowed.

Jimmy said, "Yes, I know about Donald. It's part of what I wanted to talk to you about."

"I see you've been doing that digging you discussed."

Jimmy shrugged. "Like I said. Plus which, I've discovered some interesting things."

"Hmm." Virginia's head cocked to one side. "How about I make coffee? Could you drink some?"

"Great idea," Jimmy said, starting to push himself up from his chair. "Let me come and help"

"No, sit." Virginia waved him back down. "I'll just be a minute."

Sitting alone and listening to the growl of the coffee grinder in the kitchen, Jimmy eyed Virginia's artwork from his chair. "I was serious about your pictures," he called out. "I really like them. Especially the charcoal sketches. Did you ever go to art school or anything like that?"

"I did, actually. For about six months, after I finished college. Then I had an unhappy love affair and it spoiled it for me. I was twenty-three, you see, and tragically in love. Turned out he was a shit. Or maybe *I* was, I don't know. We both took pleasure in flaunting our dueling infidelities. Whatever, it was too painful to stay there. So I went on. To other things. What do you take in your coffee?"

"A lot of everything. So you were always drawn to the arts. Drawing, acting, writing."

Virginia filled the doorway, holding two mugs of coffee. "When I was growing up, I was short, no good with girls or sports, but very good at school. In my neighborhood, that made me oh for four. So I figured what the hell, why not add a fifth?"

Jimmy took his coffee. "What neighborhood was that?"

"Davenport, Iowa." Virginia handed him a mug and settled into a creaking Windsor rocker on the other side of the fireplace. "But it could have been almost anywhere. Wouldn't that make you oh for four in most neighborhoods?"

Jimmy dipped his head in assent. "It would do it in Charlestown, yes. I escaped the shutout, though. I wasn't particularly good in school either."

"You were truly blessed."

They both sipped coffee. Virginia stared into the fire.

"So what other dirt did you dig up about Donald? I mean, how bad could it be? We used to do things they don't even *talk* about in Iowa."

"Nothing you'd call dirt," Jimmy said. "Unless you count the drinking thing–which I don't. Otherwise, it seems he was a model citizen. A good worker. Well liked by his colleagues. Seems everybody was shocked when he died."

"Tell me about it."

Jimmy said, "My point is I didn't find anything about Donald that led me anywhere. Nothing that helps explain what's going on with the photo anyway."

Virginia turned to look at him. "You mean you struck out?"

"Oh for four?" He smiled. "No, more like one for two. You see, I found out why *I* got picked this."

Virginia stared at him.

"Turns out," Jimmy said, "I'm not the only person Van Gogh got in touch with before he went down. I mean, besides your photographer friend, there." Jimmy bobbed his head to indicate the stairway. "Lee, that mailed him the photograph. Because he also sent a letter to a former client of mine. A guy named Tristan. Tristan Sliney. Ever hear of him?"

"No."

"Also went by Desmond."

Another head shake.

"Well, that makes you even,'cause Tristan never heard of you, either. Or of Donald Gilfillen. But Tristan is a guy that Van Gogh used to hang with. A boyfriend, actually. Back when Van Gogh was living in Boston, before he started collecting ears. Called himself Deon Chevalier then. The two of them ran a little credit card scam together 'til Tristan took a fall for it–which is how I got involved, defending him."

Jimmy took Virginia through the business with Tristan, his dealings with Deon, the letter postmarked the day after his death, how Jimmy had spotted the name on the file jacket, then found the entry in Tristan's address book. About the plea bargain and Deon's presence at the hearing. And how Jimmy had concluded that Van Gogh had set Tristan on him, with the expectation that the lawyer would put it together.

"Put what together?" Virginia asked. "And how could you know what Van Gogh *expected?*"

"I don't *know.* I'm just trying to piece it together, is all. Look, the guy knew who I was. Tristan told him about me. Guy even showed up when Tristan took the plea. Apparently, I actually *saw* the guy, 'cause Tristan says he pointed him out to me in the courtroom there. The point is he sicced Tristan on me with that letter. Told him to get his file back, remove all traces of any connection to Van Gogh.

"Mind you, it didn't take a lot of deep thinking to figure Tristan would do just that. A guy like him, on parole and all? He'd be scared shitless he'd get dragged into all that Van Gogh business. The devious part is Van Gogh knew how *I'd* react when Tristan called me. Or correctly guessed I would, anyway. Figure, Van Gogh once worked in a law firm. One of his jobs in Boston was with some small insurance defense shop. So he knew a little bit about how lawyers think. Like how when a lawyer gets a call from an ex-client who wants his dead file, the lawyer's gonna want to know why. Now, I'm probably not the guy should say it, but we live in a litigious world here. People sue a lot. Even their lawyers, the ingrates. So when I get Tristan's call, wants his file, my antennas are gonna be up. I'm gonna be suspicious. This much Van Gogh knew.

"Figure, too," Jimmy said, "he doesn't know that Tristan never told his lawyer who his partner was in the scam the lawyer's been hired to get him out of. So he's hoping I'm gonna find out, one way or another, that the guy Tristan pointed out to me in court that day was a certain famous serial killer. Maybe I'd figure it out, maybe Tristan wouldn't be able to keep himself from telling me—and Deon made sure, in the letter, that Tristan knew exactly who his former boyfriend was. The point is, he set it up so I'd find out."

Jimmy sipped coffee again, as Virginia watched him. "And I did. All of which tells me a lot. We got a guy going to a whole lot of trouble, and in a really sideways fashion, to hook me into all this.

From two directions, he comes at me. First with the photo, hoping I'm gonna hunt it down and find you. Then through Tristan, in case he didn't really set the hook the first time. I tell you, there's got to be a method to his madness. Or a message, like I told you before. A purpose."

"A purpose." Virginia's tone was bitter, hard. "I'll give you a purpose that doesn't require a lot of . . . what did you call it? Deep thinking? Did you ever consider the man just wants to *torture* me some more? From the grave, even?"

Jimmy thought he detected a false note, a performance just a tad over the top, but he went with it. "No, I confess it never occurred to me. The sadism, I mean. I've tried my best not to make this too hard for you."

"*Hard?*" Virginia looked at him as if examining some alien thing. "You have no idea what you're talking about. What I went through. How–"

Virginia turned sharply away, chin slightly elevated. Claudette Colbert turning away from Clark Gable? Jimmy cast about for something to say, but he came up empty. When Virginia spoke again, still not looking at him, it was with a small voice, as if from far away.

"I was the one who found him, you know. That Sunday. I didn't even know he was in town, for Christ's sake. He wasn't supposed to show up that weekend. I walked up the stairs there, into our bedroom, and . . . I didn't even recognize him at first, lying facedown like that."

Virginia stopped and looked at him. "You know what my first thought was–my first *coherent* thought, after I realized it was Donald?"

Jimmy just held Virginia's gaze and said nothing.

"I wondered how he could have *betrayed* me. Do you understand me here? Because I knew he had to have invited someone in, taken him to the, to our bedroom, knowing I wouldn't be there. For an 'assignation.' Isn't that a loving, magnanimous thought? My partner, my *lover* for over six years, lies murdered on my bed, mutilated even, and my first thoughts are of betrayal."

There were unshed tears in Virginia's eyes, Jimmy noticed. Were they held there by surface tension or virtuoso control? "I'm sorry," Jimmy said.

Neither of them said anything for a few moments. The fire popped. A car went by on the street.

Virginia said, "I haven't been able to force myself to enter that bedroom since. It's like a stain on a floor or a carpet that I have to walk around. My cleaning person looks after it. That room is closed off to me. And that part of my life that was closed off with it. Jesus, I miss his very bitchery."

Jimmy flashed on the orange, glowing in the lamplight from its dish on the dresser.

Virginia looked up at him with an odd look he couldn't decipher. A look of distaste? Was that it? "I'll tell you a dirty little secret, since dirt seems to be what you're so all-fired interested in. It's something I haven't told anyone before. I mean *nobody*."

Jimmy waited.

"When the police finally . . . finished with him, released the body to his family? Well, he was cremated at a funeral home here in Provincetown. His mother claimed his ashes. Which I didn't begrudge her, mind you. I mean, she was his mother, right? I was just his fag lover. No legitimate claims there. But the mortician was a friend of mine. He made me a gift of a small portion of Donald's ashes. Enough to fill a small vial. Would you like to know what I did with them?"

Jimmy's imagination ran wild, but he just nodded.

"I asked a friend with a sailboat to take me out on the Bay one evening. When he was occupied with doing something nautical, I sprinkled Donald's ashes on the water. I shook them out of the vial like salt from a shaker."

Jimmy said, "That strikes me as kind of nice, actually."

"Oh, but you haven't heard the best part. You see, when I first opened the vial, I put my finger over the top and turned it upside down." Virginia mimed this for him. "When I righted it and took my finger away, there was a little circle of ashes stuck to the pad of my finger. And you know what I did?"

Jimmy's eyes were riveted to the fingertip Virginia was holding up. Images from the Ash Wednesdays of his youth scrolled before him.

"I licked it. I tasted his ashes. Donald's remains. Is that sick or what?"

The two of them locked eyes for several uncomfortable seconds. "Oh, I don't know," Jimmy said at last, expelling tension with his breath. "People need something to help them deal with grief. A ritual, I guess. You made up your own, is all. I wouldn't dwell on it."

"It was a kind of unholy communion, you mean? *Take ye and eat of this, for this is my body.* Something like that?"

"I don't know. I'm no shrink. I just try to think what a loss that heavy would do to me, and—"

"You've had such a loss?"

It stopped him dead. "No," he said. "Not yet. But I can imagine it, dimly. And when I imagine a loss that great, I realize I'm not able to pass judgment on somebody else's response to it. Because the mind would have to find some way to deal with it. Maybe this was yours."

Virginia rubbed both eyes dry with the thumb and forefinger of one hand, and breathed deeply. The two of them sat in silence for a while. Jimmy finished his coffee.

"You make me think of dolphins, Mr. Morrissey."

"Come again?"

"Come to think of it, maybe it was porpoises. One or the other. You see, there was this scientist named Bateson. Gregory Bateson. Well, he wasn't so much a scientist as an anthropologist—a philosopher, really. Anyway, Bateson was doing experiments with, let's just say dolphins, keep it simple, on what he called meta-learning. Learning about learning. He wanted to see if any animals besides humans had the capacity for such learning."

"You lost me already," Jimmy said.

"Just listen to the experiment, see if it doesn't make sense. Bateson instructs his assistants to reward a dolphin with a fish for doing a new trick. The point is to reward the animal only for doing something *new*. A dolphin would do a body roll and the assistant would give it a fish. The dolphin would do it again. No fish. Again, and no fish. Finally, in frustration the dolphin would splash the guy. Who gives him a fish. Which provokes another splash. And no fish. You with me?"

"Yes."

"Well, the dolphin is having some kind of nervous breakdown over this. It can't figure out what it's supposed to do. It's swimming around like crazy, getting all bent out of shape, apparently trying to make sense of all this. The animal is in crisis, as Bateson sees it. In all this random activity, it does something the assistant identifies as new, and he gets a fish.

"And then–the dolphin gets it. Do something *new*! And the dolphin does about eight or nine new things in a row, one after another, collecting a fish each time. *Dolphins have the capacity for meta-learning.*"

Virginia was sitting straight up now, looking oddly calm. The eyes were red, but the tears were gone.

"Now this happens to dovetail with what Bateson has been thinking about the nature of meta-learning in humans. It takes a crisis, he believed, an emotional or intellectual clash of competing and apparently valid responses, to jolt the brain into making that kind of leap. To jump up one category of thinking or feeling. To see and feel anew."

Jimmy thought about this, hard, as Virginia rose to poke at the fire. If there was some connection between this story and Virginia's strange ritual with the ashes–if that's what it was–it had gone right over his head. So he said the first thing that popped into his head.

"Are you telling me that eating the ashes was some kind of transforming experience? Meta-learning?"

"Why not? Oh, I don't know. I'm not sure where I'm going with this. It's more like when you suddenly see a pattern in your own conduct. You've been stuck in individual actions that once made sense as separate events or responses. Or maybe they didn't. Once you see the pattern, though, that sense dissolves into the larger picture, which shows you how self-defeating they were, and you're able to move on. To go beyond that to something new. Something hopefully better."

Jimmy smiled now. "That's your dirty little secret? That you licked some ashes and moved to some new plateau of . . . what? Thinking? Feeling?"

"Spirituality?" Virginia was smiling with him. "Or maybe I'm just jerking off–and *that's* what makes it a dirty little secret."

Jimmy laughed. "Fair enough," he said, shifting about in his chair as a prelude to changing the subject. He leaned forward toward Virginia. "Now, do you want to hear *my* dirty little secret? I warn you, though. You may not like it."

"I suppose it's only fair. Shall I gird myself?"

"It's about the photograph again."

"I guess I'd better, then. That picture's become a fetish for you, I see."

Jimmy paused for a second. "Not once I learned you weren't a woman."

Virginia raised an index finger and smiled. "Good one. Though I suspect you're naïve about fetishes. So tell me your *other* dirty little secret."

"It's about the message Van Gogh is sending us."

"You've decoded it?" The tone was mocking.

"I think so. I think, in his roundabout way, he's trying to tell us he didn't kill Donald."

The mockery left Virginia's face.

"That's not all," Jimmy said. "I think he wants us–well, me, anyway–to find out who did. What other reason could there be to involve me in all this?"

"That's . . . that's . . ."

"Wild? Insane? Or is just too horrible to contemplate?"

"All of the above. And the perverse way he's going about it is vile. Just vile. That he would really leave this . . . this business behind him. Like some hideous legacy. A headless snake that won't die."

"Could be," Jimmy said. "All the same, I think there's a very good chance he didn't kill Donald."

"I'm not sure I'm ready for this."

"I'm not sure I am either. But I'm the guy he sent the photo to, and I'm the guy who has to figure out why. And right now, it all seems to be pointing to the possibility that Van Gogh didn't do this one."

"And you're going to make me listen to why you think this?"

Jimmy frowned. "Nobody said you had to. You invited *me* to the party, remember? I figure you must have *some* interest in this stuff. Not to mention the possibility, however remote, that Donald's killer might be getting away with it."

Virginia sat back in the chair, appraising him. "Okay. Tell me why you think that."

"There are some things that just don't jibe with the other murders. For example, this cop I know who was in on the first killing, the one in Boston? He tells me Donald had no Seconal in his system. All the others did. Why not Donald? Plus which, he wasn't strangled like the others. He was coshed with something. This just doesn't fit Van Gogh's MO."

Virginia said, "I didn't know about the Seconal, but obviously I knew he was clubbed. I saw him, after all. He bled all over the pillow. But what about the police? What does your cop friend say about these . . . discrepancies?"

"Well, I haven't exactly laid everything out for him," Jimmy said. "But he–like any good cop–says there are always little unexplained things in the most open-and-shut case. Little differences, things like these, they just show the best-laid plans don't always go the way killers expect, even ones as methodical as Van Gogh. And he points out that the last guy, the one in Key West that got away? He didn't fit the mold either. 'Cause here was a guy who managed not to ingest a full dose of Seconal, and when it turned out he wasn't as far under as he looked, Van Gogh tried to bang him around."

"That couldn't have happened here?"

"Sure, it could have. But *did* it? That's the question. Because we've got other discrepancies. Like the sequence of the killings. Take Donald out of the picture, and there's not a single instance of Van Gogh doubling back to a state he'd already left after doing a killing. He liked to drift from place to place, spend some time in a city, do some guy, then move on. But never back. Uh-uh. Always on to someplace new.

"Yet he comes back to Massachusetts," Jimmy said. "Not only does he come back, he does so at considerable inconvenience. He did Donald after the guy in Miami and–"

"Do you think you could pick a different *verb*?"

"Huh? Oh, sorry. Okay, he kills the guy in Miami and moves on to Key West, but in between them he flies or drives or whatever up to Massachusetts to do a random killing in Provincetown? Plus the timing is awfully tight. Why, you have to ask yourself. What's his motivation?"

"What's his motivation for any of this?"

"Fair enough. That we'll never know. All I'm asking is why a guy whose routine is so tight it's like some kind of ritual, why would he break it like this? And figure this, too: he's no commuter killer. He moves into a town–Boston, Minneapolis, whatever–he gets a job, hangs for a while, months, weeks at least, before he kills somebody. Then he moves on. But this one, he had to make a special trip to kill Donald from Key West, where he had just moved to at the time, from Miami about ten days earlier. And then he goes south again before killing the next one–in Key West. It doesn't make any sense."

"Unless," Jimmy said, then paused. "Unless we assume he had some particular reason to target Donald. There's no reason to think that. Far as we can tell, all his victims were strangers he picked up."

"Which, by the way," Jimmy continued, "brings up another point nobody has explained to me. There's no evidence he was ever in Provincetown. No job, no apartment, nothing. That's also different from all the other killings."

"There *is* evidence he was here," Virginia said. "The way Donald was found. Tied up, the ear. The rape."

"Most of that the killer could have got from the newspapers. Which makes it equivocal evidence. It supports two different theories with equal force: that it was Van Gogh did it or it was somebody who wanted it to *look* like Van Gogh did it. And everything else I've mentioned points away from Van Gogh."

"But what about . . ."

"What?"

Virginia paused, thinking, then gave a shake of the head. "Nothing."

Jimmy waited, but Virginia was silent.

Jimmy moved on. "Don't forget some of the stuff we discussed the day we met. He launched this whole post-mortem inquiry of ours by–"

Virginia winced.

"Okay," Jimmy said. "Of mine, then. Van Gogh engineered it all–a complicated piece of business, I might add–and at not-inconsiderable risk to himself. Remember, he's down in Key West there, and he calls up Lee to get the photograph so he can inscribe it for me. In the process, he uses his real name, William Wolff, which he apparently hadn't used in years. And he has it shipped straight to his actual residence there when a box number would have been infinitely safer. By FedEx, too–the foolishness of which we already went into. Why?"

"He wants to get caught?"

"No, no, no! No offense, but that's psychobabble, you ask me. Oh, maybe at the end, after he botched the last guy, and he knew they were gonna have him cornered, maybe then he gave it up. But I don't think that's what *this* was about. No, when he called Lee, he didn't want to be caught. He wanted to be *traced.*"

"Traced?"

"Yes. Afterwards. By me. Or you and me. If and when he was caught–and it must have seemed more and more like *when*, not *if*, as the end neared–when he was caught, he would leave the photo to be found and arrange somehow to get the letter sent to Tristan. Coulda just dropped in a mailbox on the corner about the same time he propped your photograph up on his nightstand. And why? To pique our interest and then to permit us to retrace his steps. So we could sit here tonight and try to piece it together."

Virginia was quiet now, gazing off into the dying fire. Jimmy watched carefully to see if he had hit his mark or not.

"So what next?" Virginia asked at last. "How do you test your theory?"

"Good question. It's not like I'm overstocked with leads here. I figure I should try to get my hands on police reports, the autopsy report, if I can, though the FBI isn't one to cooperate with amateur inquiries. Especially into a cleared case. You need to understand the institutional inertia that keeps a dead case dead. Pretty hard to budge. But I'll run it down. Meantime, I was hoping you might be able to give me some helpful hints about stuff that went on here."

Virginia said nothing.

"Assuming," Jimmy said, hurrying to fill up the silence, "you're not leaving town soon. Going to New York or LA or whatever, be on that Rosie O'Donnell show."

At this Virginia smiled. "So you heard. No, nothing very soon. What did you have in mind?"

"Well, I was hoping maybe you could give some thought to where Donald might have gone that night. Where he picked up the guy he brought home. Some bar, maybe?"

The gaze Virginia fixed on him was focused and hot. Jimmy thinking, *A person could spot weld with a glare like that.* He pushed on.

"I know he went off the wagon. I figure that's probably what made him so reckless. But couldn't you just give it some thought? Maybe ask around, people who might know something?"

"You want me to ask my friends and acquaintances if they'd seen my dead lover catting around? Maybe check out some bars, is that it? I could try Chain Drive, that biker bar in the West End."

Virginia's tone was scathing, and Jimmy fought off the urge to wince. "That's not exactly what I meant."

"What *did* you mean?"

Jimmy realized he didn't know, exactly. "Just a thought," he said. "Maybe if you just gave it some thought yourself, is all I'm asking. I'm kind of a babe in the woods here, in case you hadn't noticed. This is a long way from Monument Square."

Virginia looked away, unmollified.

Jimmy said, "I do have one other angle to pursue, though."

"Does it involve me?" Still looking into the fire.

"No. It's something Tristan told me. He said Deon told him not to worry about him leaving his job at the hospital there because somebody who owed him would see to it he got another one. It kind of intrigued me at the time. A person of some influence who's beholden to a nobody like Deon Chevalier? Who? And beholden for what reason?"

Virginia said, "Maybe Deon was just a blowhard."

"That's what Tristan said," Jimmy said. "Doesn't mean I shouldn't run it down, though."

"Do you think it occurred to Van Gogh that you would be asking these very questions?"

Jimmy grinned. "There, you see? You have a devious mind, too. And yes, I think it might have. Which makes it even more important to check it out."

"How? Where would you start?"

"That might not be as difficult as it sounds. Deon said this person could find him a job. Let's assume he did. We know where Van Gogh worked after he left the hospital. He went to some optometrist's office. I figure it's just a question of finding something in common between the hospital and the new place."

"There is already," Virginia said.

Jimmy cocked his head to one side.

"Didn't you tell me," Virginia said, "that Tristan was stealing credit card information from people who had eye operations?"

Jimmy felt his eyes widen, and he grinned.

"You're right! It's *eyes*. There's got to be a connection. See? We might make a team here, after all."

"Don't you think," Virginia said, "you might be overlooking the obvious here?"

Jimmy frowned. "Like what?"

"Think about it. If you were a policeman, and there was no handy serial killer to blame for Donald's murder, who would be your first suspect?"

A tiny, tight smile had taken control of Virginia's expression. Despite its economy, the smile managed to convey something vaguely wolfish, and its effect was riveting. Jimmy felt the ground of their relationship shifting subtly in some alarming way.

"Of course," he said, mustering a smile of his own. "I'd suspect his old lady. So tell me: you got an alibi?"

CHAPTER EIGHTEEN

MINE EYES . . .

W as it a *good* alibi?" Phyllis asked him the next morning, after he had checked out of the Comfort Inn and was back on Route 6, struggling to keep the cell phone in place between his left ear and shoulder while wedging his coffee cup between the front seats. He blinked bleary-eyed at the traffic that was already choking both westbound lanes out of Provincetown.

"I can't tell yet. Nothing as good as being on stage at the Drooping Lizard, mind you. Went with Joseph and another guy to an opening, some gallery called Shivers in the East End. Then dinner with other friends at a house just a couple blocks from home, over on Windsor there. Leaves dinner early, feeling sick or something. Goes home and discovers the body, comes running right back, all hysterical. So it all depends on just when the guy was killed, which I don't know yet when it was, plus how long you could prove they stayed at the gallery. Point is, we can't exactly rule ol' Ginny out. Not yet anyway."

"How horrible," Phyllis said. "Imagine coming home to something like that."

"I'd rather not, thanks. But I tell you, that question about who'd be the primary if Van Gogh was eliminated? It came with a look that'd like to scare the shit out of me. For a minute there, anyway. You know what I'm saying?"

"The face of horror, like a head on a pike?"

"No, not like that. Just a cold jolt, is all. Enough to keep you from eliminating anybody, that's for sure—not unless their alibi's a whole lot tighter than what we got here. The whole night was weird, in fact. Kept me off-balance, you know? I could never tell what was performance and what was real. 'Cause some of that grief and stuff, it was just too over the top to take at face value."

"Maybe," Phyllis said, "it's hard for performers to stop performing, even when the feelings are genuine. Even people who don't act for a living can feel like they're playing a part during real events and with real feelings—especially momentous events, when they're keenly aware of how people expect them to act or talk."

Jimmy weighed the possibility. "Makes sense, I guess. It's just, it seemed there was more to it than that. Like this business about never going into the room where the guy was found? Well, who the hell put that orange in there? 'Cause there was one in there, a nice big fresh one, set out on a dish. Like for someone to eat. Who did that? The housekeeper? Why? Why would anybody put an orange, of all things, in a bedroom nobody was using—or even intending to use?"

Phyllis paused before responding. "You mean you think Virginia might have invented that business about not being able to go into the room?"

"It's a distinct possibility. And if so, you gotta wonder why. What's the point—unless it's to exaggerate the grief?"

"Maybe it's a way to cover feelings of guilt."

"Just my point."

"No, I don't mean guilt as in guilty of a crime. I'm talking about more subtle feelings. Survivor guilt, say. Things like, if I'd only come home earlier. Or been nicer the last time I saw him. Those kinds of feelings, Jim. They can be hard to bear in a such circumstances. Some people make things up to keep them from surfacing. And the feelings can *certainly* distort how it all comes across to others. That may be all that's going on here."

Jimmy allowed as how she might be right. He went on to tell her about the party itself, how much tamer it was than he had expected.

Phyllis said, "You wanted everybody to dress like Imelda Marcos, is that it? Twenty years ago, maybe. When the community was more into making a point. It's a different world now, Jim."

"So you and Taffy keep telling me. She asked me the other day if the World Wide Web was black and white when I was young. The little snot."

"How's she getting on?"

"Like a running blender with the top off. She spent the last couple nights with a girlfriend in Quincy."

"You figure out what to do about her nasty boyfriend?"

Jimmy spotted a line of brake lights ahead of him and slowed up. "I'm working on it," he said. "Jesus, what's the holdup here?" The traffic in his lane was stopped completely.

"Well, let me go," Phyllis said. "I got things to do, and I don't want to be the cause of an accident, you on the cell phone while you're driving."

"You really were okay last night? Leaving you alone and–"

"Yes, Jim. I wouldn't have told you to stay if it wasn't okay. It was so late. I didn't want you driving back then. Especially after all those beers."

"Yeah, but the night before you were pretty, well–"

"Scared, I know. But just talking about it helped. *You* helped. So lighten up, okay? See you tonight. Love you."

"Love you, too."

Jimmy dropped the phone on the passenger seat and raised his butt off the cushion to see if he could tell what was obstructing the traffic. He couldn't. The line of stalled cars stretched about five hundred yards before disappearing around a curve. He reached over for the phone again. Punched in the number.

"Law offices."

"You think you could sound a *little* less annoyed at having to answer the phone? We like our clients to think we actually *welcome* their business."

"*There* he is," Taffy said, as if finally pulling a missing comb from a jumbled purse. "What is it, you stayed over again? You're spending a lot of unscheduled overnights in P'town, Jimmy. With all those gays? People gonna start to talk."

"Well, don't you be the one to start it."

"Hey, I'm not the one sleeping alone–he *says*–in some cheesy motel in Sodom by the Sea."

"You're nobody to talk, Miz Fresh Kill. And Comfort Inns are not cheesy. Midrange, more like."

"What's high-end, then? Red Barn?"

"Taffy, for crying–"

"Which reminds me. You making any headway on my galoot problem? I mean, how long do I gotta stay at Darvonne's place?"

"*Darvon?*" Jimmy couldn't help raising his voice. "You have a friend named Darvon?"

"She doesn't spell it that way, smartie. Two *n*s, and an *e* on the end. And quit tryin' to change the subject."

"Yeah, I might be onto something there. Write up an affidavit for a restraining order. The two-oh-nine-A. You know how to fill out the form. Have the paperwork ready when I get in."

"Jimmy, I told you. An RO won't do it here. Reb is not–"

"I'm *on* it, Taffy. I got a plan, okay? Now, what else is going on there."

She laid down a brief, petulant silence before responding. "Not much. Coupla calls. No interesting mail. When you gonna be in?"

"Noonish, I hope. I'm stuck in traffic at the moment. Wait a minute. It looks like we might move." Jimmy eased forward with the other cars. "Who called?"

"Previtt. Wants to reschedule the depo. Some guy named Mook returned your call. You want the number?"

"Yeah. Hold on." He plucked a pen from his shirt pocket and, blindly so he could keep his eyes on the car he was tailgating, jotted the number on the scratch pad stuck to the dashboard. "Taffy, wait!" he called before she could ring off. "One more thing. Go into the top drawer of my desk and get a folder in there. There should just be the one. It says 'VG' on the cover."

"VG? What the hell's—no wait, I got it. It's a code for Viagra, isn't it?"

"Yeah, right. Just get it. I'll wait."

Taffy sighed audibly, then put him on hold.

The traffic picked up speed. As Jimmy finally rounded the curve, he spotted two parked cars on the right shoulder, separated by a crushed aluminum canoe, curled up at the toes like an old shoe. Two men were standing over the canoe and arguing. Jimmy surmised that it had slid off one vehicle and under the other. Hence the jam, and the argument. One of the men delivered a measured kick at the side of the ruined canoe. Jimmy checked the rearview mirror to see how the other man would react, but a big RV behind him blocked his view. He was sailing along at fifty again when Taffy came back on the line.

"Okay, I'm at your desk. And here's the file. Let's see now . . . *Jesus*, Jimmy! What's all this? All these clippings and shit. You studying up to be like this Van Gogh guy?"

"Something like that. Just flip to—"

"Jimmy, I'm serious! Jeez, is this like some secret life you're living here? Maybe explains why you keep making these trips to the Cape?"

Jimmy squeezed his eyes shut. "No, Taffy. It's just a case, okay? I've got a little piece of this business, is all. And it's very confidential, so keep it that way. Right now I need you to go to the back of the file and find something. A chrono I put together. Handwritten. You find it?"

"A chrono? You mean like—oh, here. Has 'Chronology' written across the top."

Jimmy smiled. "Can't fool you, can I?"

"Watch it."

"That's why you make the big bucks, Taffy. Just run your finger down the column to the right of the date until you find a reference to St. Theresa-Lutheran Hospital. Okay?"

"Uhhhhh . . . got it. St. Theresa-Lutheran. Accounts . . . something. Can't read your chicken scratches. When are you gonna learn how to write?"

"That's all right. I want to know what the *next* item is. Can you see it?"

"Next? Oh, you mean the one that starts with 'Mine Eyes'?"

Of course. Mine Eyes . . . How could he have forgotten the name? Followed by three dots just in case you missed its coy allusion to the song. "That's the one. Read the rest of it, okay? The whole entry, out loud."

" 'Mine Eyes. Optometrists. Thirty-seven Clarendon Street. Bookkeeping. Gofer.' That's all there is."

"Okay. Here's what I need you to do. I need you to get onto the City, find the DBA registration for Mine Eyes. If it's registered to do business for an individual, see what you can find out about him. You know how to do this stuff. And if it's a corporation, get up to the Secretary of State's office and—"

"Don't need to anymore, Old Folks. State's on the Net now. You want the articles of incorporation, right? Names of officers and directors. That what you want?"

Jimmy smiled again. "Now that really *is* why you make the big bucks."

" *Watch* it, I said."

Jimmy said, "Don't forget the names of the incorporators. And copies of annual filings."

"Your swish is my command."

Connie Mook's machine picked up on the fourth ring, but Jimmy pushed the disconnect. The guy would be in the shop anyway, and it was just off the Expressway on the way into town. Simpler to stop by.

CHAPTER NINETEEN

THE TICKER

Connor Mook's shop was in back of the sales office out of which his brother-in-law sold used cars. The cars filled the open spaces of a lot fronting on Old Colony Road in South Boston. There Mook doctored up the heaps Myron Grabowski tried to pass off as cheap but reliable transportation to first-time customers from the nearby projects–first-time because repeat business at Grabowski's Quality Preowned Cars was almost unheard of.

Jimmy pulled up in front of the glass door to the sales office. Myron Grabowski was out of the office and on him before he had a chance to shut the car door.

"Oh, it's you," Grabowski said, pulling up in evident disappointment. He was a soft butterball of a man in his fifties, turned out in wire-rimmed glasses, a wrinkled short-sleeved shirt, and a blue club tie that ran out of polyester several inches above his drooping belt buckle.

"Contain your enthusiasm, Myron," Jimmy said. "For all you know, I might be here to unload the Taurus."

Jimmy gave the car's roof an affectionate slap. Grabowski took in the Taurus and looked more disappointed. Worried even.

Jimmy lifted his eyes to the sign over the office. "I've always wondered, Myron. This business of calling used cars *preowned.*

Where's that come from—and who do you guys think you're kidding?"

Grabowski shrugged. "Beats me. It's marketing, is all. I just follow the industry."

"Well, figure. Here I am, standing in a lot full of *preowned* cars that backs onto Flanagan's Funeral Home there. I gotta wonder, Myron. Should Flanagan be referring to his stiffs as *postalive*?"

Grabowski harrumphed.

No sense of humor.

Jimmy bobbed his head. "Connie in back?"

"Last time I looked."

Jimmy let his right hand trail along the fender of the Taurus as he started toward the front of the car. "Don't accept any offers without checking with me." But Myron was already disappearing through the door to the sales office. As Jimmy rounded the building, he could hear the pennants snapping in the wind despite the whoosh of heavy traffic on Old Colony.

Connie's unlaced work boots, scuffed and spotted with grease, were sticking out from under the raised rear end of a beat-up Chevy Blazer.

Jimmy said, "I'd tie your shoes if I wasn't afraid you'd try to sit up in surprise. Probably knock yourself out on the axle."

Connie Mook slid out on the creeper, clutching a ratchet wrench and a handful of sockets against his massive sternum. He eyed Jimmy wordlessly for a moment, then used the heel of one foot to propel the creeper back under the Blazer.

"How come," Jimmy said, "everybody here's so happy to see me? First Myron, now you."

"Pieces of shit, these SUVs," Connie muttered. Jimmy heard the ticking of the ratchet and a light clink each time the wrench handle fetched up against metal. "Assholes run 'em in four-wheel drive on the blacktop and wonder why the rear ends go. Got no slippage on pavement, you end up overtorquing the whole fuckin' drivetrain. Somethin's gotta give, you know what I mean?"

Jimmy pulled a wooden barstool away from the workbench

and positioned it at the rear of the Blazer. He settled down on the stool.

"How come," he said, "a man with your obvious mechanical talents isn't applying them at the BPD motor pool? The force'd have to pay better than what you make offa Myron."

"On account of," said the grunting voice under the Blazer, "I'm totally disabled."

"So I see."

"That's what it says on my discharge, and the Department ain't about to go rehiring a cop's got a total disability pension. Even for the motor pool. Bad politics, something like that makes the papers."

Jimmy smiled to himself as he imagined the fun Eddie Felch would have with a story like that. "And you were disabled because of what again?"

Connie worked in silence for a minute before wheeling out from under. He let the tools lie on his chest as he fished a reddish orange rag from his hip pocket and wiped first his hands, then the tools. He gathered the tools in one hand and heaved himself to his feet. On the way up he used the empty hand to pick up the creeper.

"The ticker," he said as he walked over to the toolbox on the bench. "I took a heart attack."

He hung the creeper on a hook at the end of the bench. He laid the wrench in the toolbox, then, like a postal worker sorting mail, dropped each socket carefully in its place. He wiped his hands again on the rag, which he stuffed back in his pocket. He turned to face Jimmy.

Connie Mook was a large man, well over six feet and going two-fifty, easy. His shoulders seemed to bulge upward unnaturally, pulling his naked head into something of a declivity between them so that it looked even smaller than it was. The general effect brought the word *hulking* to mind.

Connie said, "I'm sitting there in the cruiser, and I get this achin' in my left arm, like. I never told you this?"

Jimmy shook his head.

"And Dropo, he's my partner at the time, Dropo looks over at me, and he says, 'D'ja hear me, Connie?' Which I realize I ain't heard nothin' for the last few minutes. The fingers on that hand are feeling tingly, like, and pretty soon I don't feel nothin' at all down there." As he talked Connie absently shook the fingers of his left hand. "I didn't think nothin' of it then. I mean, you figure a heart attack, hey, you're grabbin' your chest and feelin' this heavy-duty charley horse or something, you know? But a sore arm? No way."

"Happens that way, I hear," Jimmy said.

"*Now* they tell me. Anyway, Dropo, he's saying I look gray and there's sweat all over my face, so he hauls off to Emergency at BCH. Next thing I know they got wires and suction cups stuck all over me and I'm holed up there for most of a week. And the Department? They wanted me on a desk job. That asshole Harris, I'm talking. Jesus, *me*, on a desk job. Can you picture it? Me sittin' there, peckin' at one of them fuckin' computers? With these hams? So I get onto the union rep there, Leccese his name was, and finally, after going through I don't know how many goddamn hoops, they let me have the disability."

Connie leaned back against the workbench and dug a crushed pack of Salems out of the vest pocket of his coveralls.

"And here you are," Jimmy said as he watched Connie strike a wooden match on the zipper of his coveralls, "pulling down the full pension plus whatever extra you get from Myron. Taking home as much as when you were in uniform."

Connie scowled at him through the smoke. "No way. Not without the overtime on the detail work."

"Well, I might have a little detail pay of my own here. Let me ask you a question, Connie. What's orange and black and sleeps three?"

Connie blinked back at him, then shrugged.

"A DPW truck!" Jimmy laughed, but alone. "My girl Friday's got this problem with an ex-boyfriend works for Public Works. Name of Rebstock. Spent the last couple weeks smoothing out potholes over on Dot Ave. Up Savin Hill, last I heard."

Jimmy told him Taffy's story, how the guy was stalking her and how scared she was. "Thing is, the guy's got an all-over hard-on for authority or something, and the girl thinks getting served with a restraining order will just rile him up more."

"You want me to handle him?" Connie seemed indifferent to the suggestion.

"No, no, no. That's what *she* wants, maybe. I'm not in the business of brokering rough stuff. I just want you to serve the papers on him."

Connie's expression soured. "You want a fuckin' process server. A constable."

"No, I want a fucking *cop*. Maybe two cops. You must still have a shield somewhere, right? Something that looks enough like one anyway?"

"Still got the cookie cutter."

"Okay, then. What I want is I want this guy served by a couple burly cops who can bring it home to him that he's gonna be in the deep shit, he goes anywhere near her. No muscle. Just bring a little gravitas to the situation."

The strange word wrinkled Connie's brow like a rug, way up past his missing hairline.

"Seriousness," Jimmy translated. "Weight. A sense of presence, you know what I'm saying? We want him to appreciate as fully as possible the real-world consequences of violating that order. Convince him to give her a good leaving alone. You think you could handle that? *Without* getting rough, I mean?"

Connie shrugged. "Piece of cake. What's it pay?"

"I thought two hundred. And you take care of the second guy out of your end."

Connie shook his bald head. "Uh-uh. That's gonna cost me at least a hundred. I gotta have three-fifty."

"Three, then. Best I can do. I'm springing for this myself." Taking up the slack left by the man's silence, Jimmy pressed. "Who you like for the other guy?"

Connie's eyes were hooded in thought. "How about Harney, he okay?"

"Phil Harney? He still working security for Edison?"

"Nah, he fucked that up. Had a run-in with a super, some broad works there. Got wrapped around the axle's what I hear. He's servin' up phlegm-cutters, some bar in the Market. Prolly could use the work."

"Phil always had way too much mouth on him. I don't want him fucking this up."

"He won't. Where do I find this guy, what's his name?"

"Rebstock. Soon as I get the order signed, I'll get the papers to you and let you know his address."

Jimmy slid off the stool and hauled it back to the workbench. "Always a pleasure, Connie," he said with a smile.

"Haven't seen you in the Cork in a while, Jimmy. You oughta stop in. Have a few bumps with the lads."

Jimmy pointed a finger at him, like a pistol. "I'm gonna do that, Connie. Save me a seat."

Ah yes, he thought on his way back to the car. *When the heart attack didn't do it, Connie enlisted his liver in the battle.*

He got back on the Expressway, northbound toward the office. Maybe he could make some headway with whatever Taffy found out about Mine Eyes. Dot, dot, dot. It might be a long shot, but he figured it couldn't be as difficult as getting into the Government Center garage this time of day.

CHAPTER TWENTY

LIGHT TYPING

The parking boded ill. The Government Center garage was full, and Jimmy was left to seek refuge in the expensive lot beneath Center Plaza, where the prices were so high they probably took chattel mortgages. In this city, it occurred to him, and not for the first time, a really good, free parking spot can move you to tears.

By the time he'd threaded his way through the Big Dig chaos, slid the Taurus into a slot reserved for compact cars, and made his way to the office, it was one-forty. At least, he figured, Taffy would have had time to make some progress on Mine Eyes.

"Read 'em and weep," she said, after noting the inquiring lift of his eyebrow and hoisting a sheaf of papers above her head. Jimmy snatched them. Taffy's eyes remained fixed on the telephone console before her. "No, not you," she said into the dangling mouthpiece. "I was talking to somebody else. No, Mr. Palmer did not tell me what time he'd be in. Sometimes he doesn't come in at all. You want his voice mail?"

Jimmy squeezed his eyes shut. Someone was going to have to talk to her. Her phone courtesy had always been a slave to her moods, but this "galoot problem," as she termed it, seemed to have handed them a whip.

Trudging into his office, he flipped through the papers Taffy had given him. Some handwritten notes. Pages printed off the Internet. He sat down at his desk and started jotting names down on a yellow pad.

Taffy's handwritten notes indicated that Mine Eyes . . . was a DBA for Mine Eyes . . . Inc., a professional corporation established, according to its articles of incorporation, by one Isaac C. Quirk in 1996. Quirk was also listed as the corporation's clerk. Lawyer, Jimmy decided. A quick thumb-through the list of attorneys in his Lawyers Diary confirmed that assumption. Quirk worked at one of the city's biggest law firms, which lolled sumptuously over several floors of Exchange Place, an office tower barely a block away. Its proximity was tantalizing but unhelpful. There was no point even calling him. The guy would tell him nothing.

The past and present directors and officers named in the articles, as supplemented by annual filings, ran to nine names, total. All followed by the letters *R.D.O.* Something doctor of optometry, he translated. *R* for *registered?* None of the names was familiar, but he had expected that. He just wanted to find a connection to St. Theresa-Lutheran, and he thought he knew a way to trace it.

From his bottom right desk drawer he pulled out a chubby, paperbound book the size and shape of a small city's telephone directory. Its pale blue cover bore the logo for his Blue Cross health plan. Inside, as he knew from distressing recent experience, was a complete directory of the plan's preferred medical providers. The directory was broken down first by town, then subdivided further into medical specialties. Jimmy riffled right past them to the general alphabetical listing of providers at the back of the book. He began with the corporation's president.

Nothing. The same for other officers. He had run five names before a glance at the Mine Eyes home page, which Taffy had printed out for him, showed him where he had gone wrong. Mine Eyes was a chain of optometry offices, with seven outlets in the greater Boston area. This Jimmy had known, but it wasn't until he saw the home page's proud reference to the American College of Optometry that he realized his mistake. By statute, all the directors and principal officers of a professional corporation providing services in optometry had to be licensed optometrists. No one but optometrists could even hold stock in such a corporation. It followed that no medical doctors' names would appear here. And because optometrists were not medical doctors, it was equally unlikely that any of the listed individuals would have staff privileges at St. Theresa-Lutheran. You had to be a doctor for that. All of which told him he could expect no overlap between the names of those who ran Mine Eyes and those in his Blue Cross directory.

Where, then, was the connection between the hospital, where Deon's friend (protector? patron?) held a position of some influence, and Mine Eyes, where Deon landed his next job after leaving the hospital? Virginia had made the intriguing suggestion that the link might have something to do with eye care, but there was no direct, organizational link between Van Gogh's two consecutive employers. Where did that leave him?

Sitting back, he picked up the three-page printout of the home page for Mine Eyes. Looking for what, he didn't know. Designer brand names for frames? DKNY, Sophia Loren, Gucci Eyewear, Calvin Klein, Giorgio Armani, Eddie Bauer . . .

Eddie Bauer? What are we talking here, rustic horn rims? Flannel temples? He read on.

The site supplied information about contact lenses. Offered testing for glaucoma and cataracts. Q and A on issues of insurance coverage. There was a hyperlink to something called a virtual eye examination—Jimmy decided he didn't want to know.

Then he saw the notice to "click here" to learn about the company's "Consulting Ophthalmologists." He frowned. Why not? He remembered going in for an eye exam a couple of years ago, when he needed new reading glasses. His optometrist had suggested she refer him to an opthamologist—just routine, she assured him, given his age. Vaguely offended, he had passed on the suggestion, but the memory confirmed the obvious: ophthalmologists would have consulting arrangements with retail optometrists. And ophthalmologists were real doctors. Van Gogh's patron might have such a connection to Mine Eyes.

Jimmy reached under his desk and booted up his computer. Taffy had printed only the home page of the Mine Eyes site. If he wanted to "click here," he'd need to visit the site himself.

Old Folks, my ass. He wasn't *totally* clueless when it came to technology.

But the results were bewildering. Each of the seven Mine Eyes outlets had its own list of consultants, apparently driven by their proximity to the outlet. Jimmy began the laborious process of listing each doctor, taking particular note whenever one of them mentioned some affiliation with St. Theresa-Lutheran. By the time he had finished, he had twenty-nine names and writer's cramp. Seventeen of them boasted some connection to St. Theresa-Lutheran—which was not so surprising, given the hospital's reputation as a leader in treating eye and ear afflictions. Jimmy was stumped as to how he might reduce that number further.

As he read the credentials of these doctors, his bewilderment multiplied. He knew nothing of the terms and acronyms they tossed around. Refractive surgery. Astigmatic keratotomy. Corneal transplants. Adult strabismus. PRK. LASIK.

LASIK? Laser? Jimmy clicked on LASIK and started reading.

LASIK or Laser in-Situ Keratornileusis treats refractive errors by removing corneal tissue beneath the surface of the cornea. This procedure combines the accuracy of the excimer laser with the benefits of Lamellar Keratoplasty . . .

It seemed total gibberish, but there was also something familiar about it. Laser surgery. The golfer Tiger Woods came to mind. Jimmy had read about him, how his vision had been transformed by some kind of laser surgery. And how he claimed just about anybody could have it done. In fact, hadn't Taffy talked about it recently? Some friend of hers had gone through it, thrown away her glasses. Leaving Taffy to moan about how much it cost. Unlike her friend, she had to suffer the indignity of contact lenses because the office's health insurance didn't cover the surgery.

Which tripped a memory of something Tristan had told him.

"Taffy!" he called as he began to click back through the lists of consulting doctors and their credentials. "Can you come in here for a second?"

He busied himself with determining which consultants claimed an expertise in LASIK surgery. He succeeded in narrowing the possibles from seventeen to five by the time Taffy showed herself in the doorway.

Today she wore her hair black, which comported with her dark T-shirt, heavy eye shadow, and sepia lipstick. Her squarish earrings, he noticed, were fashioned from tiny printed circuit boards that refracted the cheap office lighting into dangling glints of verdigris and deep orange.

"Yeah?" The gum was back, rolling freely as her jaw moved.

"Tell me about this laser surgery. Your friend had it or something?"

Her arms went limp as she rolled her eyes. "Oh, Jesus. Now it's a makeover. A couple more trips to P'town, and he'll want a tummy tuck."

"Didn't you tell me that? About your friend?"

She sank with a sigh into a chair in front of his desk. "Yes. Darvonne did."

"With two *n*'s, and an *e* on the end."

"Hey. Short-term memory coming back and everything."

"Don't I also remember she had to pay it out of pocket? Because her insurance wouldn't cover it?"

"Right. 'Cause it's only *cosmetic*, they say. What a load of crap that is! Sexist, you ask me. If laser surgery is cosmetic, what does that make glasses–jewelry? A man now, a man can be hobbling along with a cane. Does anybody tell him the cane makes knee surgery 'cosmetic'?"

"Women don't use canes?"

"Canes? What are you talking, canes? You're missing the point here, Jimmy. It's–"

Jimmy swept his left hand, palm out, across his body from his right shoulder, as if brushing the thought away. "I agree a hundred percent," he said, which stopped her dead. "It's unjust. What's it cost, do you know?"

She eyed him warily now. "I'm not sure. Two, maybe three thousand an eye. You really considering this?"

He shook his head. "No. Too expensive. I didn't realize it cost so much. I mean, that's a lot of money for, well . . ."

"Cosmetics?" She was beginning to bridle.

"Visual perfection. I mean, I only need glasses to read."

"Count yourself lucky, then. You ever try swimming with glasses? Or worse, *without* glasses when you need 'em to see? It takes a lot of the fun out of it, 's all I'm saying."

"What about prescription goggles?"

"That steam up on you? *If* they haven't filled with water anyway?"

"I see your point."

"That's why you called me in here? Away from the phone?"

"Which," he pointed out, "hasn't made a peep since you left it. And by the way, give poor Palmer a break. You *don't* go telling a guy's clients he just doesn't show up some days. What are they supposed to think?"

"What am *I* supposed to think, he doesn't show up some days?"

"You're not *paid* to think. At least not about George Palmer's private life. His clients aren't complaining, he's not in here all the time. He's got a transactional business—closings and such. And he gets 'em done. Your job is to man—excuse me—to *person* the phones, do light typing and filing, and whatever else we can think of that might make you break a nail. So be nice to the clients and say nice things about your bosses."

She was studiously examining the cuticles of her left hand. "You want fries with that?"

"Yes, as a matter of fact, I *do*. Just like you want help—sometimes—when your own private life gets outa whack. Okay?"

She straightened her fingers and, waggling them before her, she pulled herself to her feet. She was almost out the door before he reminded her.

"So did you do up the papers for the two-oh-nine-A?"

"You've got 'em," she said without looking back. "They're in there with the rest of the 'light typing.'"

He looked. They were. He just hadn't reached the bottom of the pile yet.

But he was making progress anyway. Tristan had said the care group where Deon worked did some kind of eye surgery that wasn't covered by insurance. That, Tristan had explained, was what gave Deon access to cards with high credit limits. If so, it ruled out cataract surgery; both of Jimmy's parents had had cataracts removed, and he knew the procedure was covered. And LASIK usually was not. Hence a new working hypothesis: the guy did LASIK.

Jimmy finished running down his lists of consultants. He found one more laser surgeon in the bunch, bringing to five the number of ophthalmologists who consulted to Mine Eyes, had some affiliation with St. Theresa-Lutheran, *and* specialized in performing LASIK surgery. Graham Benoit. Douglas O. Nickles. Rudolph G. Brynolfson. Michael Feiler. Agnars Svalbe. Van Gogh's patron was one of the five, he could smell it. But how to narrow it down?

He printed out the blurb-bios on all five so he could read them over at his leisure, and with more care. While slipping them in his *VG* file, he remembered Tristan's address book. He stopped.

Was it possible? After all, he assumed Deon's patron was gay. Maybe he made an appearance in Tristan's little book.

He didn't. Jimmy looked up all five doctors in the photocopy he had made of Tristan's book. He tried both first and last names. He even tried looking under *D* for doctor, but no luck. If the guy was in there, he wasn't using his own name.

Okay. He would have to do it on the basis of the timing—and nature—of the man's affiliation with St. Theresa-Lutheran. He knew from the chrono just when the guy had to have been at the hospital. It also seemed reasonable to infer that he was an established surgeon at the time of Tristan's bust; no student or trainee, or even resident, would have had the kind of grease needed to slide Deon into Mine Eyes. So the trick, Jimmy calculated, was to find out which one was there then and already established in the LASIK racket.

He pored over their resumes, first as printed out from the Mine Eyes site, then under "Find a Doctor" on the St. Teresa-Lutheran Medical Center Web site. Three of the surgeons had Web sites of their own. They were all prominent-sounding fellows, after all: lavishly credentialed, board certified, official examiners for the American Board of Ophthalmology. Four of the five had served as president of the Massachusetts Society of Eye Physicians and Surgeons. But two of them, Jimmy determined after an hour of cross-referencing, had moved on from St. Theresa-Lutheran before Deon ever got there. Jimmy crossed Drs. Brynolfson and Benoit off his list.

That left three. He jumped to the *Boston Globe* site and accessed its archives. He picked up hits on two of them. Dr. Svalbe was quoted twice in a *Globe* Sunday magazine article on laser surgery in the midnineties. Dr. Nickles popped up twice. He surfaced as a disgruntled practitioner complaining about the turmoil wrought by the recent rage for consolidation among area hospitals. A second article, from the Living section scarcely a year ago, came with a picture of Dr. Nickles accepting an award for work done on behalf of Catholic Charities. Jimmy studied the handsome face for a long, curious moment before noticing that the woman beside him, according to the caption beneath the photograph, was his wife. No, the guy he wanted was most likely gay. What else could attract a high-powered doctor to an unremarkable drifter like Deon? Jimmy figured he should at least start by assuming his doctor would not be married. First pass, anyway.

Without Nickles, Jimmy was down to Svalbe and Feiler. The picture of Nickles's wife gave him another idea. *Find out if they were married.* Loading the Ultimate White Pages, a national online telephone directory, he entered Agnars Svalbe's name and hit search. He was not surprised to get just one Massachusetts hit on a name like that. An A. Svalbe in Brookline. The phone number was actually listed—but then, once you thought about it, how many eye surgeons had to worry about getting calls at home from their patients?

Well, it was time this one started. Jimmy punched in Dr. Svalbe's number. A woman answered on the third ring.

"Hello."

"Uh, yes," Jimmy said. "Is this Mrs. Svalbe?"

"There is no Mrs. Svalbe," the woman said coldly.

"Oh, jeez, you gotta forgive me," Jimmy said, ad libbing now and talking fast. "It's this call sheet they give me? Just says Dr. and Mrs. Svalbe. It makes no allowances for modern marriages, you know what I mean? I mean, my wife never took *my* name either."

"Okay, you're forgiven." He could hear a hint of thaw in the voice. "And it's Dr. Jorgenson. But this better not be a sales call."

"Ah, then," Jimmy said. "I'm afraid it is."

"Sorry then. No sale." And she hung up.

No sale indeed. Dr. Svalbe, too, had a wife, and a doc at that. Jimmy started to worry. He was down to one.

Finding a phone number for Dr. Michael Feiler proved a little harder. Jimmy found four possible entries. He thought he could safely eliminate the one in East Boston—not exactly a dream community for wealthy, successful surgeons. M. V. Feiler in Cambridge might be a woman, so he called that number first. A machine, a woman's voice, "I'm sorry I can't come to the–" First-person singular. Jimmy struck her off his list as well. The third number yielded a message telling him that Michael and Louise were not in at the moment. And there was no answer at all when he called the fourth number.

Frustrated now, Jimmy dug further into the Web site for Feiler's LASIK practice group, Feiler & Scheinerman Eye Associates. Brought up the guy's CV. Michael Feiler, MD, FACS. Completed his ophthalmology residency at blah, blah . . .

Ah, there it was.

"Lives in Wellesley with his wife, Louise, and their two daughters . . ."

Jimmy pushed the computer mouse away in disgust. He sat back in his desk chair, rubbing the back of his neck. Both Feiler and Svalbe were married. Which, of course, put Nickles was back in the running as well. He was stymied.

Okay, he thought, still massaging his neck. So the guy could be married. Not what he expected, but hey. First pass, right? Bisexual, maybe. It happens. Or the wife's his beard, allowing him to stay in the closet. All the more reason to stay in the background. But he still had no way to determine which of the three was Deon's benefactor. Unless, of course, this whole line of inquiry was wrongheaded.

No. Jimmy was unwilling to abandon it. Not yet, anyway. After all, he had found three prominent ophthalmologists who could have known Deon at the relevant time and who had an association of sorts with the place Deon worked after leaving the hospital. Maybe the fact that he was able to find as *many* as three cast doubt over the whole enterprise, but he wasn't about to give it up until he had some reason to eliminate all of them. Other than their marital status, that is.

Oh, it could be done. He was sure of that. He'd need to hire a professional, a real investigator. Someone who could get out there and do a full background check on his eye doctors. Talk to people who knew them. Look for somebody holding both information and a grudge. If one of the good doctors had a secret sex life, especially a gay one, it could be prised out sooner or later. It was the "later" that bothered him—that and the cost. He didn't know an investigator who was likely to handle a job like this on the cuff. Plus it would have to be someone who could nose about unobtrusively in the gay community. Nobody sprang to mind.

But wait. Jimmy himself was not entirely without entrée to that community. Maybe . . . ?

Jimmy opened the *VG* file again. Folded the cover back smartly, hearing the snap of the cardboard. The telephone number was written on the inside cover.

"You want *what?*"

"Help," he explained. "Just to ask a few of your friends. Put the word out in the Boston community. See if there were any rumors about one of my doctors. I mean, I could do it myself. No doubt whatever. Just a matter of time—and a little money I'd rather not lay out. But I'll run it down. I just thought, maybe, you know . . ."

"You want me to circulate these names to my friends. Ask them to poke around, see if anybody's heard anything about what might be under their fingernails. Is that it?"

"Well, that's kind of a distasteful way to think of it. More like–"

"What way *should* I think of it? The whole point here, as I understand it, is that you think this doctor is a killer. Or am I missing something?"

"No, you're not missing anything. Remember, this was your theory in the first place, going with the eye care thing. I took it this far. I'm just asking you to pooch it along a bit, is all."

"Imagine my joy."

A long silence. Jimmy let it fester.

Virginia said, "I'll think about it. It's the best I can do right now."

"Let me at least give you the names, then." Taking silence for assent, Jimmy read from his pad. "Douglas O. Nickles, Michael Feiler, and Agnars Svalbe. I'll spell the last names for you."

Virginia's silence lingered for several long seconds after Jimmy had finished spelling them out. Too long, he understood at last.

"You still there? I mean, did you get it all?"

"I know him," Virginia said, in a voice that sounded oddly far away.

Jimmy noticed a dull throbbing in the receiver.

"Nickles," Virginia said. "Jesus, I know him."

Jimmy realized the thumping was the beat of his own quickened pulse.

CHAPTER TWENTY-ONE

THE LAW IS NOT AN ASS

By ten the next morning, Jimmy was humping it to catch up with Taffy as she flounced angrily out of the clerk's office and down the dingy, marbled hallway of the post office. The Boston Municipal Court had made the eighth floor its bivouac while awaiting renovation of the old courthouse at Pemberton Square.

"Taffy, wait!" he called, just as she was about to round the corner and disappear on him. She stopped in her tracks but did not turn around or look back. He saw her shoulders sag.

"Jeez," he gasped, pulling up beside her. "We got the order and everything, just like we wanted. What the hell's wrong with you?"

She turned her head toward him in slow motion and gave him a dark look, then snapped back to face front.

Jimmy said, "Am I missing something or what?"

"Oh, yeah, Jimmy. You're 'missing' something all right. You got no idea how fucking *humiliating* it is to go in there and tell that Mother Superior behind the counter what's been going on with your love life like that. So she can make sure you haven't missed a goddamn comma or something on the form, it's gonna make her day if you do. And then, then go tell your story—under *oath*, like I'd make this shit *up*, for Christ's sake—tell my story to that retard judge."

"McFeeterson? He's maybe not the sharpest tool in the shed, but he's–"

"Sharp? Jimmy, he was a knife, he couldn't saw through soup."

She resumed walking. Jimmy hurried after her.

"It's not like this is a new experience for you, Taffy. You've been here before. And women do lie sometimes, to get a two-oh-nine-A. I've had–"

She wheeled on him. "I don't *give* a shit if people lie. It's *still* humiliating. Every time. Christ! They make you feel like you're . . . like you're dog shit on their shoe or something–and they get off on it, too, you can just see 'em gettin' wet. All those fucking little hoops you gotta jump through just to get a piece of paper, tell some galoot he's s'posed to not beat the living shit of me. Which he's just gonna use to blow his nose with and that's about all. The law's not an ass, Jimmy, it's an *asshole.*"

She came to an abrupt halt before the elevator bank. As if sensing her mood, an elevator opened its doors at once.

Wise elevator.

She stepped into the empty car and turned to face front. Jimmy joined her.

"I thought I explained this to you," he said, as he pressed the button for the ground floor. "We're not just relying on the paper alone. I lined up a couple guys to impress on him the seriousness of this business. We'll get the papers to them and–"

"And when is *that* s'posed to happen?"

"Uh, good question." Jimmy looked at his watch. "Shit. I gotta–wait, wait a minute here." He rubbed his temples with his thumb and middle finger, still staring at the watch. "Look, you're stayin' in Quincy now, right? With what's-her-name, Darvonne, still?"

"Yeah." Her tone sullen, suspicious.

"Guy's right on your way, Taffy. On the Red Line. His name's Mook, Connie Mook. You took his call, remember? Big dude, used to be a cop. He's the guy's gonna handle this, him and another ex-cop. You just hop off at Andrew Square, it's maybe two blocks, tops, to Grabowski's, a used-car lot over on Old Colony. Leave the papers with Mook, he'll be in the back, in the garage there. I'll call and tell 'em you're coming." He tapped the cell phone clipped to his belt.

She was glaring at him again.

He shrugged. "Hey, it's the quickest way to get it done." Suddenly, he felt his own anger flare. "You seem to forget I'm the one doing the favor here. You think I don't have a whole shitload of other stuff I should be doing? For paying clients, I might add— the ones you're always telling me I'm neglecting. It's not like I'm getting some fat retainer for this, you know. I'm helping *you* out."

She sighed and flipped out her hand, palm up. He slapped the court papers on it.

"Usually," he said, "my clients express a little gratitude, I do 'em a favor."

"Huh." It sounded like a hiccup, a scornful grunt. Jimmy shook his head once and turned away, facing the doors again. A moment later he felt her hand on his forearm. He glanced over at her in surprise.

"I know," she said, her voice all of a sudden like a little girl's, far away. "I'm not ungrateful. It's just . . ."

She shook her head. Jimmy watched her eyes fill up as she stared straight ahead and chewed her bottom lip. He tried to remember if he'd ever seen her like this.

"It's okay, Taffy. It's all gonna be okay."

She shook her head again. "It's not just Reb. It's like—"

The car floated to a halt at the lobby level, and the doors opened on a small crowd. She looked down at her feet and hurried out of the elevator. Jimmy followed her down the steps toward the exit, past security with the X-ray machines and conveyor belts, out onto the windy sidewalk along Congress Street. She paused to look back at him.

"You going back to the office?" she asked, her composure apparently restored.

"Uh, no, not right away. A couple hours maybe. Look, Taffy, if you wanna talk—"

She shook her head.

"Well, anytime," he said. Meaning it and wishing he didn't.

"Thanks, though," she said with a nod. Then she took off.

Jimmy watched her chugging up Congress Street. Followed the short skirt, the skinny legs in their black leotards disappearing into high-top Kombat boots, also black. All by herself she seemed so small, tiny even. He felt a soft ping of sadness for her. For all the fragility back of her sexiness and that quick lip of hers.

All pluck and vulnerability, Taffy.

CHAPTER TWENTY-TWO

TASSELS

After you pass City Hall and Center Plaza, Cambridge Street hooks hard to the left. Jimmy followed it, heading in the direction of Massachusetts General Hospital and the river. He crossed over to the north side near the brand-new courthouse on New Chardon Street and stayed on Cambridge until he reached Staniford, where he turned right. The Lindeman Center loomed above him to his right. The most user-hostile of all state office buildings, Lindeman was a massive, precast edifice, charcoal in color and grooved in texture, which presented a gloomy facade nicked only by a few forbidding passages. They led, one could only hope, to an entrance somewhere. No, wait. Yes, there was an entrance, a real one facing the street, with glass doors and everything.

Jimmy turned away to cross over to the west side of Staniford. A tiny strip of retail shops fronted the curtain wall of his destination, a copper-glassed, twelve-story office tower of recent construction. One of the shops was a busy deli. Better get something, he thought. No telling how long he'd have to wait.

He stood in line, got a large regular, two sugars, then made his way to the cramped foyer of the office tower. He checked the plaque on the wall. Sixth floor. He walked up to the two narrow elevator doors, pushed the call button, and listened to the soft hum of responding machinery. When the door opened, he moved aside to allow an elderly couple to exit. The man had a beige patch taped over one eye and his arm in both of his wife's, who was making sure he didn't stumble getting off. Jimmy stepped inside and pushed the button for six. The machinery hummed again, and the elevator began its slow, whining ascent.

Once inside the waiting room, he was surprised by its diminutive proportions and unkempt appearance. The furniture was nubbly and shabby, the magazines dog-eared and months old—just like his doctor's office. Just like his own office, for that matter. He strode up to the reception counter. Behind it sat a tall blonde with a lantern jaw and large breasts. She looked up from her computer screen to bestow a perfunctory smile.

"Uh, I'm here to see Dr. Nickles?" He set the coffee on the counter.

"You been here before?"

"No, but—"

She slapped a clipboard on the counter and laid a ballpoint pen on top of it. "You need to fill this out, then. Name?" Her eyes were back on the screen now, and she made a couple taps on the keyboard.

"It's Jim Morrissey," he said, picking up the clipboard and pen and holding them out for her. "But you won't find me in there. I don't have an appointment."

He had her full attention now, and she gave him a wondering look. "Dr. Nickles is booked three, four months out. He couldn't *possibly* see another patient today."

She finally noticed the clipboard in his hand and took it from him. She missed the pen, which slid off, dropped to her desk, and rolled toward her. She caught it in her lap, reflexively squeezing her knees together to do so. She picked it up, hunted for ink markings on the starched white fabric of her smock. Apparently finding none, she looked up at him again.

"Do you have a referral from your PCP?"

Jimmy frowned his confusion. Angel dust?

"Primary care provider," she translated. "I could put you on our cancellation list if–"

"Ah, no." Jimmy smiled and shook his head. "I'm not a patient, you see. I'm a lawyer–a lawyer who needs only a few minutes of Dr. Nickles's very precious time. If you could just tell him I'm here . . . ?"

She frowned. "He knows you?"

He broadened the smile. "Not yet. But I know he'll want to talk to me. Could you tell him that for me?"

Leaning over, he reached down and plucked the handset from the telephone console in front of her. She watched this maneuver as if hypnotized, and when he handed it to her, she tipped her head back slightly, her eyes flicking to his. He smiled. Their eyes stayed locked as she slowly took the handset from him, her movements guarded. Then she straightened up, looked down at the console, and punched in a three-digit number. She peeked up at him again and, smiling uncertainly, pressed the receiver to her ear. Waited. When she got an answer, she lowered her head.

"June? Yeah, hi. Look, is he in with somebody right now? Mm-hmm. No, no, I mean . . . Yeah, well, look. Tell him there's this guy here, a lawyer? Name's–"

She lifted her eyebrows to cue him.

"James Morrissey." He took a sip of coffee, then set the cup down again.

"James Morrissey. And he wants to see him. No. I know . . . Uh-huh. Okay, I'll tell him."

She hung up. "Dr. Nickles is with a patient at the moment. His nurse will give him the message as soon as she gets a chance. You might wanna have a seat."

Jimmy picked up his coffee. "I think I will, thanks."

He chose the chair near the exit because it was also the farthest from the other patients. Other? He shook off the thought. Leaning to his right, he picked up a handful of magazines piled on a round table that resembled an upended plastic wastebasket. He laid them on his lap, idly tipping them toward him, one at a time, to lean against his stomach. A *Newsweek,* six weeks old. *Redbook.* Two issues of *Country Living.* Some boating magazine without a cover. *US. Yankee.* He slapped them back down on the table.

Remembering the cell phone, he left a message for Mook. That Taffy would drop off the papers he was to serve. That Rebstock's home address was on them. He couldn't think of anything else to say, so he hung up.

He realized he hadn't actually formulated a plan for approaching the doctor. The further research he'd done, in the *Globe* archives again and on the doctor's own Web site, confirmed his impression that Dr. Douglas Origen Nickles was much more than successful. He was a certified big shot. Out of Johns Hopkins and Harvard Medical School. Did his chief residency at the Yale Eye Center, Yale School of Medicine. Won a Heed Fellowship in Corneal Surgery at the Massachusetts Eye and Ear Infirmary. Past Deputy Director of the Novatec Laser Surgery Program for Nearsightedness at the Massachusetts Eye and Ear Infirmary. Clinical instructor at Tufts School of Medicine. Research associate at the Massachusetts Institute of Technology. Chief of staff at St. Theresa-Lutheran. Invented a whole bunch of the machines used to perform LASIK surgery all across the country. Featured as one of *Boston Magazine*'s "Top Doctors." Active in many high-profile charitable endeavors—not Catholic Charities, as it turned out. Greek Orthodox. Was that why Origen showed up as his middle name?

Virginia had said the guy popped up from time to time in Provincetown, especially at arts events. Didn't know him except to say hello, thought he might have a summer place on the outer Cape somewhere. Loaded, too. "If the man has a family crest, it's a dollar sign." It was Virginia's impression that Nickles was not out, which people respected—"and I'd appreciate it if you did, too." Jimmy had pointed out that, if his suspicions went anywhere, getting outed would be the least of the doctor's problems. Virginia had advised him not to get ahead of himself.

Jimmy was twiddling his thumbs—literally, first in one direction, then the other—when he heard the receptionist call out.

"James Morrissey?"

Like he was a patient, his turn at last. Which sent a little shiver of the old fear through him. He stood up and smiled at the woman, who was standing up and pressing the telephone against her hip.

"Dr. Nickles wants to know what this is about," she said when he had closed the space between them.

Jimmy pointed to the phone. "He on the line there?"

She pulled it behind her, her eyes darting about as if assessing the adequacy of the space that separated them.

Jimmy raised both hands, palms facing her, to show he intended no harm.

"Just tell him," he said, "that Deon Chevalier referred me, okay? Deon Chevalier. You got that?"

She nodded, the phone still stowed behind her back.

He turned around and walked back to his chair, where he thumbed ostentatiously through one of the magazines. Then another, with nothing registering as he flipped the pages. He deliberately did not look back toward the counter.

It took much longer than he'd expected—so long, in fact, that he'd begun to doubt the whole chain of reasoning that had brought him here. Because if the name Deon Chevalier had no effect—

"Mr. Morrissey?"

The voice was soft, and just over his right shoulder. He craned around to take in another woman in white, this one tiny, with a brown bun and bangs.

"Dr. Nickles can see you now."

"Splendid."

The doctor was facing away from the door, intent on his computer terminal. When the nurse announced Jimmy's arrival, Nickles twisted around and leaned back on the leather-padded arm of his chair as if it were the cantle of a saddle. He even looked like a cowboy, despite the white coat, what with a square chin you could rappel down and tanned, strop-leather skin crinkle-creased around the eyes. His hair was full, the color of sooty snow, combed straight back. Rugged, handsome guy, and very fit from the look of him.

His wife wasn't half-bad either, judging from the framed photograph propped up on the windowsill. No room for her on the walls, apparently. They were filled, not with the usual framed diplomas and board certificates, but with original artwork. Interesting modern stuff that Jimmy found himself examining in spite of himself. The doctor brought him back.

"Mr. Morrissey, you've got five minutes."

He spoke in a clean baritone, with machined edges. No welcoming smile, no encouraging cadence. Delivered with a look of entomological detachment. Jimmy decided not to risk a handshake.

"That ought to do it," Jimmy said, with a smile and a little dip of the head. He slipped into a wooden chair across the desk from the man. A clean desk. The only paper product on it was a folded copy of today's *Boston Globe.* "I want to thank you for fitting me into your busy schedule."

"I'd prefer some nonvacuous explanation." Distrust was tooled into the man's visage.

So that's how it's gonna be.

"Fair enough. I'll get right to it. I'm a lawyer downtown here." With a snap he laid his business card on the desk and pushed it forward. Nickles ignored it. "I've been looking into the death of Donald Gilfillen."

Jimmy paused just long enough to see if the name registered, but Nickles gave not the slightest sign of recognition. Of course, he didn't say, "Who?" either, but the guy seemed to have taken an unresponsive tack, a give-'em-nuthin'-but-ice-in-the-wintertime attitude, so Jimmy withheld judgment.

Jimmy said, "Mr. Gilfillen was one of the victims of the late William Wolff. Better known as Van Gogh."

Still nothing.

"You knew him as Deon Chevalier."

Ah. That got him. Color invaded the good doctor's cheeks, and his eyes narrowed.

Jimmy lifted his hands. "Hey, come on. It was the *name* got you to see me. So you don't have to look at me like I'm a fresh box of kitty litter."

"Oh, for Christ's sake! Of *course* I know the name. Why the hell else would I let you intrude into my day like this? Look, I have patients backed up out there. I've got to be a good hour and a half behind already. What I don't need is you trying to play these pathetic little mind games, supposed to make me quake in my boots and tell you everything I know. You watch too much television, is that it? Well, don't insult my intelligence. I know you didn't come here for your *eyes.*"

"Actually, it's my nose, when you put it that way."

Nickles wrinkled his own.

"Yeah, my nose," Jimmy said. "My nose is open, 's what I'm sayin', and I'm smellin' all kinds of things here. Like these odd connections between you and Van Gogh—excuse me, Deon. Going way back, to before he was . . . is *active* the word I want?"

"I don't know what word you want, Mr. Morrissey, and I have no idea what you mean by 'odd.' Deon Chevalier once worked in my department at St. Theresa-Lutheran. And of course I have since learned what he . . . became. That's about all I know of him. But none of this explains why you came to me. Or what assistance I could possibly be to—what did you say his name was again, the victim?"

"Donald Gilfillen. Okay, odd. Let me tell you what's odd. It's *not* so odd that Deon should have worked for you. I mean, he had to work *somewhere*, right?"

"I didn't say he worked *for* me. I said he worked for my care unit. In accounting, someplace. He was not someone I supervised, or even knew, for that matter, except as a face, a name. It's an unusual name, and when the papers identified him as this killer, his memory recrudesced."

Jimmy frowned. "As in . . . ?"

"Reappeared. Broke out again. Like a suppurating lesion."

"Ah, yes. Have to look that up when I get home. But that's not the odd part, Doctor. What's odd, now, is that when he leaves the hospital there, he goes to work for this optometrist outfit. Mine Eyes, dot, dot, dot. You heard of them?"

Nickles nodded shortly. "Yes."

"I'm not surprised," Jimmy said. "Lot of those shops around. Point is, I got a witness says Deon told him he—that's Deon, I mean, not the witness—that Deon had a friend in the hospital, a big shot, and this guy had enough torque to find him a new job when he left the hospital. Which he was about to do, and fast, so he needed the help, you know what I mean?"

"Not in the slightest."

"No? Well, it doesn't matter. Point is, first I'm hearing Deon works in a ward full of eye doctors. Then he shows up in an office full of optometrists. And hearing this, now, I'm all ears. All eyes, actually." Jimmy cocked his head and smiled. "Hey, will you listen to me? Eyes, ears, nose? That's three of the senses right there. Gonna be hard to work in the other two, but what the hell."

Dr. Nickles did not seem taken by the whimsy of it.

Jimmy chuckled at himself and shook his head. "Sorry about that. Sometimes I just . . ." *Focus, Jimmy, focus.* "Oh, yeah. Eyes. All eyes. That's what struck me. 'Cause it's not like the guy—we're still talkin' Deon here, right? It's not like he has any particular expertise when it comes to eyes. He was a bookkeeper at the hospital, became not much more than a gofer for Mine Eyes. So the connection between the two jobs isn't, like, overlapping skills, you know what I mean? No, the connection is another *guy*. A guy who's into eyes. Just like my witness said. You with me so far?"

"Did your 'witness' descend to any details?"

"Nope." Jimmy shook his head once, slowly. "Don't think he knew any. All he heard from Deon was he had a friend in high places that could find him a job. And all *I* knew was the two jobs had eyes in common. Now, a coincidence like that? It eats at you. So I start looking for somebody, a big shot, with connections in both places. And who do you think should pop up as a consulting ophthalmologist for Mine Eyes? Well, you're the one doesn't like playing games here. Why don't you tell me?"

Nickles seemed less furious now. More like amused, in fact, at his visitor's naïveté. "I imagine you stumbled on my name–along with a couple dozen others. Mine Eyes is a big chain. It has many consulting physicians. An understandably large proportion of them would have links to my care unit at St. Theresa-Lutheran, given its reputation in the field."

"A care unit," Jimmy said, lifting his index finger, "*you* were the chief of."

Nickles shrugged. "Which means what, I'm a big shot? So it must have been me? Pretty weak stuff, even for a lawyer. I'm sorry, Mr. Morrissey, but I don't see where this takes you."

"Not me, Doc. You. It takes *you* to Provincetown."

Dr. Nickles's expression did not change in any way Jimmy could have described, but the amusement had left his features.

Jimmy said, "I like to think of myself as fairly enlightened on questions of sexual preference. My wife now, she'd give me an argument. But for your average nun-haunted Irishman? Hey, I've come a long way. So I intend no judgment when I report this. But the word down there, in P'town now, is you've got a whole 'nother lifestyle. One that doesn't exactly go with the one you live up here, with the missus and all."

Jimmy nodded in the direction of the photograph on the window ledge.

Phyllis will kill me when she hears about this.

Nickles was on his feet, and fast. Jimmy was surprised that he was as big as he now appeared. Red-faced now, he glowered down at his seated intruder.

"Your five minutes are up, pal. And just who the *fuck* do you think you are? Some cheesy . . . *shyster* is the word for you. In your ratty suit and that . . . that, what is it?" His hands moved about in search of the mot juste. "That *reversible* tie."

Jimmy dropped his chin, slid his right hand between his shirt and his tie, and used the backs of his knuckles to lift it slightly for examination. Paisley. A little purple, a little green. Went with the suit, sort of. He lifted his head in perplexity.

Nickles leaned forward, the pads of his fingers resting on the desk to take his weight. "If this is some kind of extortion here, you've picked the *wrong* guy. You try blackmailing me, and I'll have you disbarred. They'll . . . they'll strip the tassels off your fucking loafers. Now, if you've got anything else to say, you can say it to my lawyer. And trust me, he's not a bottom-feeder like you."

Jimmy shook his head gravely. "There you go, now, calling me names and everything. By all means, you wanna talk to your lawyer, you go ahead. Hey, that's how the adversary system works. 'Cause we got a name for people like you, too—for people that withhold material information about a crime? We call 'em *defendants.* Be sure to ask your lawyer. Next thing you know you get hit with a subpoena, for a look at your records. For correspondence and such, see if there's a letter of recommendation for Deon in there. Or your phone records. Most people have no *idea* how dangerous it can be just to use the telephone, you know what I mean? Then, too, maybe somebody fires off another subpoena, this time to Mine Eyes. To get Deon's personnel file. Would your name pop up there too? Then there's depositions under oath, unpleasant stuff like that."

Jimmy watched the doctor's head dip down toward the surface of his desk. At the *Boston Globe* before him.

"Jeez, you're right," Jimmy said. "I hadn't thought of that. If the press got a whiff? Whoa, boy! They're as sleepy as an overfed pack of wolves now, since the story of Van Gogh's death maxed out a couple weeks ago. But give 'em a sniff of a connection like this? To a big shot who's supposed to be living a respectable life, neat and tidy like, with hospital corners?"

Dr. Nickles raised his head to meet his gaze.

Jimmy said, "They whom the gods would destroy, they first put in Eddie Felch's column."

Jimmy noticed that the pressure on the pads of the doctor's fingers had driven the color from his cuticles.

"Doctor, please. Sit down, will ya? Just relax. Neither one of us wants any of that. And I didn't come her to rattle subpoenas—any more than you expected to be threatening some stranger with disbarment." He smiled. "I gotta admit, though, I liked that bit about the tassels. Made me think of those old movies, you know? Where they tear the guy's epaulets off when they drum him out of the French Foreign Legion or whatever."

Dr. Nickles stood up straight. Smiling almost. As if rethinking how to handle this intruder.

"It was pretty good, wasn't it?"

"Top-notch, Doc."

"It's not that I have it in for lawyers. It's just that you go around messing things up without generating any social benefit. Like a surgeon who does nothing but appendix transplants."

Jimmy grinned. "Or spleens? Good one, Doc. Now please. Sit down, okay? Another minute or two and I'm outa your life."

He did, but his face hardened again. Doing still more rethinking, apparently. He laid his forearms on the desk and laced his fingers before him. Eyes still on Jimmy, the doctor started bumping the pads of his thumbs against one another.

"All right," Nickles said briskly. "I knew him. Briefly. At some point he gave me some story about how he had to leave the hospital, that he needed a new job. Wouldn't say why. I didn't particularly want to know. I wanted him out of my life anyway."

"Any particular reason?"

"No, not really. He was . . . what's the word I want? Edgy, maybe? Too much so. Anyway, he needed help, and I made a couple calls."

"To Mine Eyes?"

"Among others, yes." The thumbs were still moving.

"He ever mention a guy named Sliney?"

"Who?"

"Sliney. Tristan Sliney. Actually, he went by Desmond back then."

Dr. Nickles shook his head. "No. Come to think of it, I don't think he ever mentioned anybody. He was a loner."

"You mean, except for the guy who lived with him."

The doctor wrinkled his brow. "What? A roommate?" He pulled his head back slightly, incredulous. "Nah. Are you sure?"

"Well, sort of a roommate. Named Anders. You don't remember him?"

Dr. Nickles seemed to freeze for a second, the thumbs suspended in a quarter inch apart.

"Anders," Jimmy pressed, "was a doll. A mannequin. Deon never introduced you?"

The doctor maintained an uncomfortable silence. Then he shook his head. "I don't believe so."

"No? 'Cause Deon kept it tied up in his closet. In his apartment, there. It was missing an ear, just like the bodies he would soon be leaving behind him. And he tied up Anders the same way, too. Remember?"

Dr. Nickles waited again before flattening his hands to let them rest on the surface of the desk. His eyes never left Jimmy's. "I'm afraid I don't know what you're talking about. I know nothing about any . . . doll, tied up or otherwise."

But his voice lacked snap. Lacked the authority it had borne earlier in the conversation. Jimmy watched the man closely.

"Now," Dr. Nickles said, his finished courtesy regrouping, "you're going to have to excuse me." He bobbed his head toward the door. "My patients. I think you and I have finished our business."

Jimmy didn't agree, but he just nodded his thanks and took his leave.

CHAPTER TWENTY-THREE

FETISH

Phyllis didn't kill him. She claimed she wasn't even angry.

"Just disappointed," she said, and Jimmy could hear it in her voice. He was hugging the cell phone to his left ear while he bulled the Taurus into the left lane. He stayed with Route 3 when it sheered off the Southeast Expressway to cut through the sandy woodlands on the way to the Sagamore Bridge and Cape Cod.

"Why is it," she asked, "that it's always an angle with you?"

"Angle? What do you mean, angle?"

"I mean, why can't you do it straight up? Without some kind of con or . . . veiled threat?"

"Oh, right. I should just come right out and ask him—like, 'Hey, Doc, are you the one that killed Donald Gilfillen?' *That* would work. Jeez, Phil. You *gotta* come at him from an angle."

"That's not what I mean, and you know it. I mean that you held his secret over him. Jim, you practically blackmailed him into revealing himself, the way you played on his vulnerability like that. It's . . . it just leaves a bad taste, is all."

"You tell me. How am I supposed to get it out of him?"

She sighed. "Oh, I don't know, Jim. Investigate . . . something. You don't . . ."

Her voice trailed off. Nowhere to go.

"Look-it," Jimmy said. "Maybe it's the training–as a lawyer, I mean. You're taught to look for the leverage in a situation. A point of purchase to pry your way in. You find the weakness in the case, and you exploit it. That's all I did here."

She was quiet now, but he knew he hadn't won her over. Hell, he hadn't even convinced himself.

"Are you telling me," she said at last, "that all lawyers operate this way? They bully or scam their way to getting what they want?"

"Scam? What scam?" Diverting her attention from that reference to bullying. "I just–"

"What scam? How about the one you ran on Mavis Riley when you went after the reward? How you conned her into thinking she might inherit a fortune if she contacted you. *That* wasn't a scam?"

She referred to the hoax he had once perpetrated to trick a gangster's girlfriend into revealing her–and her fugitive boyfriend's–whereabouts. The guy had had a price on his head, and Jimmy had figured out how to track her down and claim the reward.

"Phyl, how else was I supposed to find her? The FBI was getting nowhere. And *I* found her, for Pete's sake. Which the FBI couldn't do. Plus which, we collected a pisspot full of money when I did. I don't remember you complaining about the money."

"Money you needed so desperately," she reminded him, "because you'd been 'borrowing' from escrow funds you were supposed to be holding for your clients."

That stung. Never before had she raised the issue of his nearly ruinous raids on his client's funds–all behind him now, he fought the urge to point out. When he had fessed up to the problem, after the funds had been restored with his share of the reward, she had been supportive and forgiving. And now . . . ?

"Jeez, Phil," he said, hoping she heard a little disappointment of his own now. "You make me sorry I ever told you. About the money, I mean. I didn't expect to have it thrown in my face. This from somebody who's always telling me I need to 'share' more?"

In the ensuing silence he could picture her face, the lipline awry as she considered her response. Choosing her words carefully.

She said, "I never promised you immunity when you share. Just an honest exchange. That's the whole point, Jim. To be honest on both sides. And sometimes honest means I tell you when you piss me off."

"Ah," Jimmy pounced. "So you *admit* you're mad."

"No, no. Well, yes. Oh, Jesus, I don't know. The *point* is I'm trying to be straight with you, that's all. And part of being straight is to react honestly when you act like . . . like this."

"Like what? Go ahead, *Ms.* Authentic. You can say it."

"Okay, then. Sleazy. Like an asshole, with that poor doctor."

Jimmy vented his aggravation by honking at a florist's van that had just lurched into his lane ahead of him without signaling. The driver languidly raised his middle finger out the window and rocked his arm back and forth.

"Phyl," he said. "There's a better than even shot that this 'poor,' shit-upon doctor is a murderer. That he raped and killed a man in Provincetown. If the only way I—"

"You're getting all this from that photo? The one you swiped from the FBI? Jim, you need to consider whether you're getting a bit . . . overinvested in that little piece of paper."

He smiled in spite of himself. "You mean like it's a fetish or something? You sound like my transvestite. Virginia said something like that—she said I was naive about fetishes. Believe me, Phyl, I got no erotic attachment to any of this."

"Then you *are* naive. You're thinking of fetishes in terms of women's feet or underwear or something."

Jimmy frowned. "Well, yeah, I guess I am. So I don't know my R. D. Laing from my k.d. lang. So what?"

"So let me give you a famous definition—and it's not Laing's, by the way. Or even Freud's. *A fetish is a story masquerading as an object.*"

Jimmy thought about that for a minute. He didn't get anywhere. As if sensing his confusion, Phyllis picked up the thread.

"Think of it as a chain of psychic events—a trauma history, say—that gets locked in and submerged. Too suppressed to be consciously accessible. It then gets projected onto an object. Which, naturally enough, then takes on a special, neurotic significance. You with me here, Counselor?"

"Hmm." Jimmy chewed his lip. "And what's the story behind the neurotic significance I attach to my photo?"

"Oh, Jesus, who knows? I'm not your shrink, Jim. I'm just—"

"Thank God for that."

"Amen, indeed. You'll have to unravel this one for yourself. Like how you were so attracted to the woman when you first got the picture. When you thought she *was* a woman. Who knows what it tripped in you when she turned out to be a man? All I'm saying, Jim, is you have an awful lot more invested in all this than idle curiosity about why you showed up on the back of the picture. Idle, hell. *Consuming* is more like it."

But Jimmy was no longer thinking about the photograph. In his mind's eye he saw Van Gogh's doll. Anders, he'd named it. Trussed up with the nylon cords in three colors, like all his future victims. He had thought of the color-coding of the ropes only as a signature before. Now, building on what Phyllis was telling him, he wondered if he should view the colored ropes as a fetish. Was that what she meant?

He asked her.

"I suppose," she said after a short pause. "There's definitely something ritualized about the ropes. Which suggests they carry fetishistic significance. They may represent a story for Van Gogh. But he's dead. It's unlikely anyone will ever know their significance. The story died with him."

Jimmy found himself smiling as a wild thought struck him. "Well, he left a noisy coffin. And maybe," he added, "just maybe, they'll tell a story for someone else, too. A disturbing story."

"What are you talking about?"

His mind was racing, the beginnings of a plan taking shape.

"Just an idea," he said. "A way to find the answers."

"A con, you mean?"

He actually considered her question. "Not exactly, no. A play, more like. On the stage. I mean, everybody knows what happens onstage isn't real, right?"

She took a beat. "What are you up to, Jim?"

"Nothing even you would disapprove of. Just a little charade onstage to see if I can spook the good doctor into revealing a bit more of himself."

"Spook him? How?"

"I'll just waggle the fetish, that's all. See what shakes out. That's why I gotta make this trip to Provincetown. You sure you'll be okay if I'm back late tonight?"

"Of course–don't start with that again. And why P'town?"

"I have to pitch my script to the talent. Make sure the show goes on."

"The talent?"

"Virginia Dentata. I want a new wrinkle in the act. For Dr. Nickles."

CHAPTER TWENTY-FOUR

THE DIVINE PLAN

Despite losing almost an hour in Barnstable, where he made a stop at the registry of deeds, Jimmy still made it to Provincetown before five. He found Virginia squatting in the back garden, deadheading roses with a pair of long-handled pruning shears. The two of them went into the kitchen. There Jimmy followed directions for filling the kettle and putting it on to boil (*duh*), while Virginia washed off the garden tools in the kitchen sink and set them to dry. Over tea in the kitchen, Jimmy pitched his script. Virginia remained completely silent until he had finished.

"You really think it was Nickles? How can you be sure?"

"Sure? Nobody's sure. Right now, it's just a scenario that fits what I know. Put yourself in Van Gogh's place for a minute. You're a famous killer. You take pride in your work, and in your hard-won fame. All of a sudden you learn that somebody else has appropriated your persona. You're being accused of a killing you had nothing to do with. You'd be curious, right?"

"I doubt I can put myself in such a mind, but yes, I suppose I'd be curious."

"Okay, then. Just indulge me here. Obviously, you know you didn't do it. But the police think you did. You also know, from following the newspaper coverage of all your killings, that the police have not gone public with your little hang-up about the ropes. How they're always the same, the same sequence of colors. You can appreciate why they haven't. It's a way they can be sure it's your work. It establishes its provenance, so to speak. And yet they make this *huge* mistake about Donald, declaring him one of your victims. Now, what runs through your mind when you hear this?"

Virginia shrugged. "That they're incompetent. Cops in P'town ride around on bicycles and keep the tourists moving. What do they know about crime scenes?"

"Fair enough. But the FBI is on this, too, and they take the same position. That Van Gogh killed Donald. Now I admit stories of FBI incompetence and corruption are everywhere these days, but believe me, they're not *that* stupid. And we know for a fact that Donald was tied up just like the others."

"You don't need to remind me. I'm the one who found him, remember?"

"I do. And I suppose, to be fair, we have to assume Van Gogh did *not* know for a fact that Donald was tied up the same way. But he had to believe the FBI wouldn't make such a mistake. So he assumes, rightly, as it turns out, that the ropes were the same. And what do you do with this assumption?"

Virginia frowned. "Thinking like Van Gogh now?"

"Right. The cops aren't just wrong about Donald. You've determined they've been led astray by something the general public knows nothing about."

"I'd start thinking the killer is somebody who knows about the ropes."

"Exactly! But who could that be?"

Virginia took a sip of tea. "I don't know. A cop?"

Jimmy grimaced. "Possibly, but very unlikely. In some movie about serial killers, maybe. But cops copying killers? That's the stuff of fiction, not the real world. No, I think you'd ask yourself a different question. *Who do I know that knows about my thing with the ropes?* That's not only a short list, but you'd have to know everybody on it."

"Like your friend Tristan?"

"Yes, Tristan knew. But he was in jail when Donald was killed. So it couldn't be him."

"And you think Dr. Nickles knew."

"I'd bet money on it. You had to see his face when I talked about the doll. He *knew*."

Virginia lifted the teapot and looked questioningly at Jimmy. He shook his head, then watched as the hot tea streamed into Virginia's cup.

"There could have been others," Virginia said, setting the teapot back on its trivet.

"Maybe," Jimmy agreed. "Only Van Gogh knows for sure. But what we do know is that he seems to have fixed his attention on the doctor. Singled him out—either because there weren't any others who knew or because he had other reasons to suspect him. We'll never know for sure. *But single him out he did.* And then he sicced me on him by driving Tristan to me. He wrote that letter to Tristan, knowing it would send him to me. Maybe he thought Tristan would actually show me the letter, I don't know. But if the name Deon Chevalier popped up in my dealings with Tristan—so soon after I saw your picture with my name on the back—Van Gogh had to know it would impel me to learn about their relationship. And it's a short step from Tristan's relationship with Deon to discovering Deon's with Nickles."

"That's a little . . . circuitous, don't you think?"

"That's a *lot* circuitous, you ask me. But it seems to have been how he did things. By indirection. Always with little feints and hints. Eddie Felch called him coy. *Sideways*, was how Tristan put it. So he sends me looking for you, he sends Tristan looking for me, and he hopes I'll pick up on the connection between the two of you—the connection being Van Gogh—and that I'll dig deep enough to find Nickles. Well, I did. The question is, what do we do now?"

Virginia turned to one side slightly, eyeing him strangely. "Let me get this straight. You think Nickles . . . picked up Donald, went back to my place with him, where he killed him, and then, knowing about the rope thing, tied him up to make it look like the killer was Van Gogh."

Jimmy nodded.

"It doesn't make sense," Virginia said. "I can see how he might know about Deon's ropes, but how would Nickles know Deon was Van Gogh? The police didn't, at that point. Nobody did."

"Nickles did. He knew the same way Tristan knew. From the weirdness of the guy. From the doll, with the missing ear. The same ear that was taken from each victim. He knew that they were tied up like the doll–that was public, all except the colors. *Tristan* had figured it out. He as much as admitted it to me. Why couldn't Nickles, who was privy to the same information and is a whole lot smarter than Tristan, believe me–why couldn't he figure it out, too?"

"And he just naturally assumed Van Gogh would tie up his real victims the same way?"

"Yes! Why not?"

"It seems pretty thin. To think that someone would plan a murder and try to make it look like Van Gogh's doing on the assumption they'd be tied up the same way as some doll in a closet? Because if the police were keeping it quiet, how could he be sure Van Gogh was using the colored ropes?"

"It wasn't as risky an assumption as you'd think," Jimmy said. "I went through all the press clippings when I started on this thing. The police were quite open about the fact that they were keeping something back about the way the victims were tied up. They just weren't saying what. The point is, given what he knew, Nickles was probably pretty comfortable assuming he knew what it was they were holding back. It was the color scheme."

"So why don't you take this to the police?"

"Take what?" Jimmy lifted his hands to show how empty they were. "This is a cleared case. Nobody's going to open it on a bunch of suspicions with no evidence."

"And if I do what you want in the act, that's going to change things?"

"Maybe not. But it might. Depending on how he reacts. If Agent Butler sees him, we might pique her interest. 'Cause I have to disagree with you about Donald's murder. It most likely was *not* planned, like Van Gogh's were. It was too rough, with the beating and all. I figure things got out of hand, and the doctor had to improvise. He must be slipping in his own shit by now. If we can get the FBI interested, it wouldn't be that hard to roll him up. He has a summer place down here, like you thought, just up the road in Truro—I checked with the registry on the way down. It wouldn't be hard to establish that he was here then. Maybe he left some physical evidence at your place that would show up in the forensic reports. All they'd need is a guy to match it to. Check his credit card purchases, his phone records. I'm telling you, I had the guy looking at his phone like it was a snake gonna bite him by the time I left. We just gotta give Agent Butler a reason to look. The question is, can you do your end?"

"Make the change in the act? No problem. But how do we get Nickles to show?"

"You do that, too."

There was dead air for a good fifteen seconds. Then, "How?"

"An invitation. In your fine, girlish hand. He knows you, after all. An invitation from you might do the trick. Maybe you could mention something about Donald?" He reached into his briefcase and retrieved a blank yellow pad. "We'll draft it together."

More silence as Jimmy laid the pad on the table and took out his pen. "'Dear Dr. Nickles.' Do I use a comma or a colon after that?"

Virginia appeared not to have heard him.

"Hey! You with me here?"

"A comma," Virginia said after a brief hesitation. "It's not a business letter."

"Good point. See?" He fired off a grin. "I need help with these points of etiquette." Looking down again, he tapped the pen against his teeth. "'Enclosed please find a complimentary ticket for Saturday night's performance—'"

"No. 'Please accept with my compliments.'"

"Good, good. What time does the show start?"

"Eight."

"'—a ticket for Saturday night's eight o'clock performance of

Where the Boys Are, at the Drooping Lizard in Provincetown. The show was one of Donald's favorites, and I'm sure–'"

"He wasn't that fond of it, actually."

Jimmy looked up in surprise. Virginia shrugged. "I'm sorry, but he wasn't. He thought drag shows were a throwback, something we should have outgrown once the mainstream began to take us seriously."

"Really?"

"Really. We just happened to differ over how seriously we were being taken. He wanted to assimilate. To pass, if you will. Me, I still want to get in their faces about it."

Jimmy considered this briefly. "Someday you can explain it to me. For now, can't we let the doctor think it was Donald's favorite?"

Virginia shrugged. Jimmy bent back to his work.

"'–and I'm sure he would have wanted you to be there for the special performance to honor his memory.' Is that laying it on too thick? What do you think?"

Virginia was eyeing him strangely again, like someone trying to place a snatch of song from long ago. "What are you getting at here?"

"Well," Jimmy said, looking down at what he'd written, "the guy has no reason to think I have anything to do with this show, right? At the same time, he has no reason to think that you have any idea that he had a . . . connection with Donald. Then, right after I rattle him about his relationship with Van Gogh, he gets a disturbing note from Donald's lover, who appears to know all about the two of them. Bound to make him curious, don't you think? And a little spooked, maybe?"

"Spooked enough to do what?"

"Respond to the invitation. To show up. Watch the show to see what you're talking about. Maybe even have a chat with you afterwards."

"Chat!" It was Virginia who looked spooked.

Jimmy raised both hands in a calming gesture. "In a controlled setting. Like in the bar downstairs. With me and Agent Butler close by–listening. Well, maybe not me, since he knows me. Just Butler, then. Anyway, we just put it in the invitation. How you'd like to meet him for a drink afterwards and talk."

"About what?"

"Leave that up in the air. Make him wonder."

Virginia nodded toward the legal pad. "Wouldn't any sensible person just throw it in the trash?"

"Maybe. But if he's all of a sudden worried that some Boston lawyer's taken an interest in his relationship with Van Gogh, he might want to know what this is all about—this strange request from someone who claims to know that he knew Donald. Maybe he'll want to find out why you're poking at him from an altogether different flank. Besides, there's no risk in it for him. He's just a guy who gets a free theater ticket with a cryptic note and shows up to see what all the mystery's about. Even gets to meet the star afterwards. Where's the risk in that? Especially if it gives him an opportunity to see what the hell this is all about?"

Virginia stared at him long and hard before smiling—sheepishly, it seemed to him—and shrugging once again. "You might be right. And what have *we* got to risk, after all?"

Jimmy beamed his agreement. They worked briskly at finishing up the draft invitation. Once the wording was agreed upon, he handed his pen to Virginia, who began handwriting a finished version on a sheet of stiff, personalized stationery while Jimmy escaped to relieve himself of some of the tea in the downstairs washroom.

As he washed his hands he spotted an old color photograph of Donald Gilfillen. It was snagged behind one of the bottom clasps that held the mirror to the door of the medicine chest. He examined the youthful face. Clean lines, he thought, along the jaw and cheekbones. A tiny vertical strip of blond through one otherwise brown eyebrow saved the face from a sterile symmetry. He couldn't help comparing the face to the older, puffy one that looked back at him from the mirror.

It's a good thing I'm straight. I never would have made it in this world.

Virginia hadn't quite finished when he returned. He sent more tea in the direction of his bladder while he waited. When the fair copy was finished, he looked it over, pronounced it acceptable, and handed it back to the scrivener. Virginia folded it once, smoothing the crease cleanly before slipping the note into a matching envelope. "How," Virginia asked before licking the envelope, "how should I address it?"

Jimmy followed its careful sealing while he considered the question. Flipping the envelope over, Virginia looked up at him inquiringly.

"Just 'Dr. Douglas Nickles,' I guess. I'll have it hand-delivered to his office in the morning."

Virginia complied, then handed him the sealed envelope. Jimmy held it by its edges, as you would a photograph, while he admired the handsome script and the heft of the quality paper.

"Who wouldn't take something like this seriously? Especially if it's hand-delivered?"

Virginia smiled encouragingly. "You want to get some dinner before you head back? I think it's my turn to feed you."

Jimmy checked his watch. "Sure. Why not? You wanna go to that same place—what was it called again?"

"Vaffanculo? No. Only when you're buying. Besides, I have a show to do later, so I don't have the time. I have some leftover fish stew, and some good bread. With a little salad we should be all right."

They were, too. It was a Portuguese stew, simple but spicy, with shrimp and scallops and linguica, its reheated surface strewn with fresh parsely Virginia deftly minced with a big chef's knife. Jimmy, who had missed lunch, downed it with relish, along with two bottles of Sam Adams. He was working on the last of these in the flagstone kitchen as they sat together and watched the darkness swallow the last of the October twilight out the windows. Virginia rinsed the knife under the tap and laid it in the draining basket before settling down to yet another cup of tea.

"How long," Jimmy asked, "since you quit drinking—if you don't mind me asking?"

"I don't mind. It'll be eight years next month. And no, I don't miss it."

Jimmy smiled. He hadn't intended to ask the question, but he accepted the answer. "Donald, too?" he asked.

"It's how we met, actually. At an AA meeting. Right here in Provincetown."

"You still go to those meetings?"

"Not as much as I used to, but yes, I still go. Couple times a week. It keeps me in balance, if you know what I mean."

"Sort of. I got an uncle's in the program."

"Then you know it's not exactly something you graduate from. I still need it." Virginia set the cup down and stared out the window. "Not the way I did at first, of course, when I was still losing arguments with inanimate objects–like pavement, lampposts, things like that. These days it's a way to keep order. I think of meetings as a breakwater against the squalor of my life. It's real easy to get deluged by all the crap in my own head. The meetings help me tell when I'm getting out of whack, and I can still do something about it."

Jimmy picked up his beer bottle and looked at it wonderingly. "But you keep beer in the house. It doesn't bother you to have it around? To serve it to people and watch them drink it in front of you?"

Virginia smiled at him. "It's left over from the party. I preferred women's drinks anyway, sweet ones like brandy Alexanders. No, seriously, it's no big deal. I just think through what would happen if I picked up, and I'm not even tempted. Believe me, I know exactly where it would take me. It's another reason I keep going to meetings. To keep that memory green–the memory of what it was like when I first limped in there."

Gloom seemed to settle over Virginia, who stared vacantly out the window for a moment. Jimmy caught a whiff of emotional ozone, signaling the gathering of a stormy and no doubt lugubrious drunkalog. He'd heard enough of them from his clients, the ones fresh out of rehab and trudging–for the moment, anyway–the happy road to sobriety because the other one led to the house of corrections. He wasn't sure how to head it off, so he tried to cut to the chase.

"I get that a *lot* in my line of work. Most of them can't see they got a problem until the judge is about to drop the hammer. So what was *your* hammer?"

Virginia chuffed amiably. "My 'hammer.' I like that. Nothing so dramatic, I'm afraid. No bust, no big breakup. I mean, people had been trying for years to get me to take a look at my drinking and drugging. But not me. Not on your life. Drinking wasn't my problem. My drinking was maybe *your* problem, but not mine. Mine was you. You and the other people trying to meddle in my miserable fucking life. You know what I mean?"

Jimmy nodded, though he wasn't sure he did.

"So like I said," Virginia continued, "in my case it was nothing very dramatic. I was experimenting with not drinking, which I used to do a couple times a year, just to prove I could quit anytime I want to—and in the process, clean myself up a bit. Maybe get the carbon out of my nervous system. Anyway, I'm at this friend's house and he offers me a beer and I think, well, yeah, I deserve a beer. I haven't had a drink in like fifteen days. So I do. Big deal. I ask for another. There aren't any. I know this 'cause I looked. I turn the place upside down, in fact. I go bullshit. Because I'm a guy who plans for contingencies, you know? I've never been in a one-beer situation before. I mean, what kind of an asshole offers you a beer when he only has one? One beer? If there's single beer in my fridge, it's safe. I mean, what the fuck *good* is one beer? Why would I ever drink *one beer*?

"So naturally I want to kill the son of a bitch—a feeling I duly impart to my improvident host. Impart? Hell, I scream it at him. And he's staring back at me like I'm Jack Nicholson in *The Shining* or something, lugging an ax through the topiary. And all of a sudden a light comes on: it's like, whoa, you may have a drinking problem here."

Jimmy felt an urge to take another sip of his Sam Adams. He opted to leave it there for the moment.

"Now, it's not as if this was a new experience or anything, this freaking out and watching friends look goggle-eyed at you. I've done a lot of really crazy shit. I mean, you're talking to a guy who once sent a note to his employer: 'Attempted suicide last night. Be in late tomorrow.' So I got a pretty high tolerance for personal craziness, as long as it's mine. But for some reason I'll never understand, this time I can see it clearly. It's right there in my friend's horrified look. And I go, *I got a serious problem here.* Two days later I go to AA, and it feels like I've just dropped about two hundred pounds."

"Is that what they call the grace of God?" Jimmy asked.

He watched Virginia's eyes roll skyward. "Please. That's your Recovery Channel talking. I don't know from Higher Powers and that whole God *shtick* in AA. I just know it helped me get my head on straight. So let's just say I was ready, that's all."

Jimmy said, "I thought it was kind a religious thing, AA."

"*Spiritual,* not religious. They say. But that's just the way they sugarcoat it for the hard bitten skeptics. Like me. To soften us up. You want to get driven bananas, you come to a meeting sometime where they talk about coincidence. You should hear them. 'There are no coincidences.' Make you gag."

Jimmy started to laugh. "I had a conversation just like this with my wife a couple days ago. About coincidences."

"Which side were you on?" Virginia asked warily.

"Yours."

"Oh, well then," said Virginia. "You should hear them go on about it in meetings. Because *everything* happens for a reason, you see. A guy has a bad day followed by a fleeting bit of good luck. Is it the odds evening out? No no no—no way. It's part of the 'Divine Plan.' My favorite one is the guy who's—listen to this—he's working his ass off down a manhole. It's freezing in there, and the guy busts himself on the nose with a pipe. Now, he's had it. He decides right then he's gonna drop the fuckin' tools, climb out of his hole, and get himself a drink at the package store he noticed when he climbed into the thing. And he starts up the ladder, too. So what happens? A car pulls up and straddles the manhole so he can't get out. He hollers and bangs on the frame until it pulls ahead. And who's driving the car? It's the guy's sponsor! You with me here?"

Jimmy is, but he's laughing.

"Now, the guy," Virginia continues, "he's just poleaxed by the quote-coincidence-unquote of all this. He decides to drink and somebody parks a car in his way, and it turns out it's the very person he's supposed to talk to when he feels like taking a drink. Well, this is just too much for him. It's 'God's will.' God kept him from drinking by steering his sponsor's car over his manhole. A coincidence, they'll tell you, is God's way of preserving his anonymity. Cute, don't you think? AA seeing its own reflection in the cosmos? Is that group narcissism or what?"

The question was apparently rhetorical, because Virginia didn't even slow down. "Now, does it occur to this guy that his sponsor was maybe in the neighborhood looking for him—which it turns out he was, by the way? Not. The whole thing's too *Twilight Zone* for such mundane explication. No, what we've got here is a Divine Plan. One more piece of compelling evidence that God's looking out for us recovering drunks."

Jimmy held up his hands to surrender the point, but Virginia paid no attention.

"Coincidences don't exist if you believe in science. Things happen for a reason—having to do with cause and effect and the laws of nature—well, maybe not at the subatomic level and all, not after Heisenberg. But anyway, they do *not* happen because some Benign Uncle has your personal well-being in mind. It's a matter of perspective. It has nothing to do with your consciousness of it. Consciousness is epiphenomenal anyway. And—"

"Epi–?"

"Epiphenomenal. Evolutionary developments that are the mere byproducts of something else. They perform no survival function. As in the ability to reflect on the nature of the universe and our place in it may be just pointless topspin on this big brain we're cursed with."

Jimmy stared at him. "Are you going to tell another one of those animal parables? About dolphins and shit? 'Cause if you are, I'm not–"

"No, no. You're missing the point here. The point is, shit happens because it happens. Period. And our place in it, yours and mine, has nothing to do with why it happens—except to the extent we might be a link in what caused it to happen or we are affected by it. But coincidence as miracle? Don't make me hurl. Because let's face it, that's what they're talking about, with this Divine Plan nonsense. To the extent coincidences are viewed as violations of the laws of nature, they don't exist. We use the word as a kind of shorthand to identify matters that appear to defy plausibility, something so unexpected it calls attention to itself. In a world of cause and effect, coincidence is always suspect. But the believers—they're like inverted conspiracy theorists, paranoids who put themselves at the center of things, to magnify their own importance.

"A Divine Plan. One devised by a loving, caring God—who'll never give you more than you can handle. You hear that all the time in AA. 'He'll never give you more than you can handle.' Well, shit, read the fucking newspaper. It's all *about* people who get way more than they can handle, for Christ's sake."

Jimmy thought of Phyllis for a moment, wondering if she was getting more than she—or he—could handle. He took another sip of beer.

"Where are we going with this?" he asked, feeling just a little nip of irritation all of a sudden.

Virginia smiled. "I guess I'm the only one going—and off on one of my rants. I tend to forget what AA did for me—and that I *do* see miracles, every time I go to a meeting. They're the people there, people who would have been in jail or insane or dead if AA didn't exist."

"My Irish grandmother used to say there's no such thing as a lousy miracle."

"Well, I can't argue with her. I walk sightless among miracles whenever I go to a meeting. That's the beauty of it. I can fume and rant, I can fail to live up to what I know is right, and no matter what happens, no matter how bad an asshole I've been during the day, I can look back on it and tell myself it was a successful day. Because I . . . didn't . . . drink."

Virginia was done now; Jimmy could sense it from the drop in energy. They smiled at one another. Virginia acted slightly embarrassed.

Jimmy felt oddly confused by it all. On the one hand, there was something of the performance in the . . . rant, whatever it was. As if it were a routine, a bit of business that had been pared from the show or something. Or maybe it was just a harangue vented too many times at too many AA meetings.

Yet on the other hand . . . well, he felt drawn to . . . okay, *her*—giving up on the pronoun at last. He felt vaguely protective, too. As if the forces of, yes, coincidence could overwhelm them all, and like Phyllis, Virginia was someone committed to his charge.

Jimmy shook his head to dismiss the thought. His Sam Adams was still sitting there unfinished a few minutes later when he climbed in the Taurus and headed back toward Boston.

CHAPTER TWENTY-FIVE

ALL EARS

Phyllis was asleep when he got home, and she was still sleeping when he slipped out of the house the next morning for his eight o'clock appointment. He got off the T at Government Center and trudged northward across the cement wastelands of City Hall Plaza. As if he needed to be reminded that winter was closing in on the city, gusts of cold wind lifted his open trench coat like a sail.

Jimmy entered the John F. Kennedy Federal Building, made it through security, and found his way to the cafeteria. The place was almost empty. After looking around for her in vain, he grabbed a glazed donut and filled a large Styrofoam cup with coffee and milk. He chose a small table far from any of the occupied ones. He was in the process of prying off the plastic lid when he heard her voice.

"Good morning, Mr. Morrissey."

Agent Butler smiled down at him from across the table. She wore a navy blue suit and a frilly white blouse. The freckles seemed to glow beneath the short blond bangs.

"Morning," he said, as she took the seat opposite him. "And please, it's Jimmy."

"Okay. You call me Eleanor."

"No breakfast?" he asked, bobbing his head toward the empty hands clasped before her.

She imitated the head bob, toward the donut on his plastic plate. "You call that breakfast?"

Jimmy grinned. "Fair enough," he said. "Just don't tell my wife."

"Your secret's safe with me."

"All of them?"

She paused, then smiled again. "All of them I'm not required to disclose."

"Fair enough again. But it was you, after all, who told me to call if I thought of anything. A tootle, I think you said."

"I did. I admit it. Still, I was surprised to hear from you. And I certainly never expected you to ask about reopening a closed case."

"How closed is it? I mean, everybody has to look at a cleared case sometime, don't they?"

She sighed. "Let me tell you about bureaucracies. And the Bureau, God bless it, is one, after all. A beleaguered one at the moment, in case you hadn't heard."

"I've heard."

"Well, from down here, where I sit, you don't get the sense there's much real direction at the top right now. So you end up with a kind of organizational lividity: blood collects in pools when there's nothing to circulate it. Well, one of the few bright pools is the Bureau's success in apprehending a certain serial killer, thus clearing a host of disturbing cases."

"Success? I thought you guys stumbled on Van Gogh when he botched his last murder—and then shot him when he waved an umbrella at you. If that's a success, we need to rethink a few things. A *lot* of things. Like why my donut doesn't count as breakfast."

She paused and gave him an odd smile before proceeding. "Is that the winsome persona you trot out in front of a jury?"

He grinned again. "Okay. It was a success. A righteous bust. And then I come along and want to take part of it away. Is that it?"

"That's it precisely. Imagine the joy in Mudville if I took them your theory. What little there is of one, based on what you told me on the phone."

"But I'm not asking you to sell them on my theory. I'm just ask-

ing you to test it out a bit. 'Cause all you'd need is a grand jury subpoena. You'd find the evidence to prove the link, I'm sure of it. This
guy? He's dirty, and he's scared. He'd crack like an old walnut if he
thought you were coming after him."

She picked up a plastic saltshaker and turned it about in her
hand.

"You say you got all this from the numbers on the back of that
photo?"

"That's where I started, yes. It's how I found Virginia–and
learned how Van Gogh got his hands on the picture."

"You're a resourceful guy."

"Well, isn't that why you guys came to me in the first place? No,
don't answer that."

She smiled again. "We came because we were going through
the motions on a wrap-up, that's all. Just massaging the file. We
never thought anything would come of it."

"I asked you not to tell me. How's the jovial Agent Ponsonby?"

"Back in Miami, where he belongs. Watching out for
Colombian drug lords and Pakistani terrorists. Look, what is it you
want from me on this? I admit you've done some good detecting–
thrown cockeyed, unfortunately, by wild inferential leaps. But as
I've tried to explain, I don't have a lot of latitude here. What do you
want?"

"Just two things. A little information and your company at the
Drooping Lizard tomorrow night." He smiled. "It'll be Friday night,
after all."

"I suppose you'd want me to keep that from your wife, too."

"No, I'll tell my wife. She understands me."

She smiled and shook her head.

"Okay . . . Jimmy. I'm not promising anything. Let's start with
the information you want. Bear in mind that our files are not exactly open to the public here. But if it will help both of us to understand what happened to Donald Gilfillen, maybe I can answer
some questions. Fire away. I'll let you know if you step on forbid-
den turf."

"How sure are you that Van Gogh is dead?"

She blinked at that one. "Quite sure, actually. We know that William Wolff is dead, obviously, and we have conclusive evidence that Wolff was Van Gogh."

"From the DNA in the semen?"

"Yes. Along with other evidence."

"In the case of every victim?"

"No. Not all of them. In three instances there was no semen found. We . . . aren't sure why."

"Which three?"

"The first two and . . ." She smiled. "And Donald Gilfillen."

"Does the Bureau have a theory on why that's the case?"

"Well, the team believes that Wolff used condoms when he raped his first two victims. Starting out careful. Then he stopped wearing a jacket because he was emboldened by his success or starting to lose his grip, take your pick. Maybe both."

"But Gilfillen? What happened there?"

"Gilfillen was a botched attempt, much like the last one, the one that got him caught. Gilfillen didn't ingest Seconal—we found no depressants of any kind in his system. Which may explain the manner of his death—blunt trauma to the head. It seems he wasn't drugged for some reason, and Wolff clubbed him to death instead of strangling him. Let's just say the evening did not go well."

"Yet he wore a condom?" Jimmy was incredulous.

"No. I'm not saying that. We figure, with all the confusion, he was not able to ejaculate."

Jimmy frowned. "But he *was* raped, wasn't he?"

"He had been penetrated anally, yes. But without a deposit to analyze, we can't be sure what with."

Jimmy realized he had not touched his donut. He left it that way. He tried to think through the implications of what Butler was telling him.

She interrupted him. "I know you want to believe that Donald Gilfillen was the victim of some 'copycat' killer. Believe me, Jimmy, that's Hollywood stuff. The simplest explanation is that Van Gogh screwed up and couldn't finish the job. There's no reason to go looking for more complicated explanations."

Jimmy looked at her. "Van Gogh thought so. Why else did he involve me in all this—first with the picture, then with the letter to Tristan? None of it makes sense otherwise."

"Jimmy, none of it makes sense, *period.* He was a crazy person. You can't build anything on such a person's motives. Listen, one of my first assignments was to transport a nice Midwestern housewife who helped her husband kill his sister. The two of them hacked her up and spent a whole day trying to feed her remains into a garbage disposal. They failed. It broke down. You want to know why— according to her? Because the sister was so evil, the disposal wouldn't swallow her. It just couldn't keep her down. It doesn't *have* to make sense."

"But it does! That's the point. Don't you see? You don't have to assume it's insane. If you follow the bread crumbs, as I did, they lead you to Nickles. Van Gogh didn't kill Donald Gilfillen, and he wants me to know that he knows who did."

Agent Butler steepled her fingers and regarded Jimmy. "You said all that on the phone yesterday. But I need more than that, Jimmy. Some discrepancy that can't be explained any other way. And you just don't have one."

The two of them sat in silence for a moment, hers respectful, Jimmy's gloomy.

"There has to be something," he muttered at last. "Are you telling me there's nothing that makes you wonder if Van Gogh is really responsible for all the murders attributed to him? *Nothing?*"

He almost missed it. How, for a second, her eyes skittered away from his.

"What?" he said softly, insistently. "Come on, Eleanor! There's something. I know it! What aren't you telling me?"

The look she gave him was opaque—as if, he thought, she was weighing her options. He waited her out.

"The one completely consistent thing he did," she said, finally, "was to collect the ears."

She paused. He prodded her. "Yeah?"

"He saved them, kept them in a tube. I don't know if you knew that."

"I knew that." How could he forget Eddie's sardonic simile: dried ears nestled together like Pringles Potato Chips?

"Well," she said, "he was one short."

Jimmy squinted at her, making an effort to contain his excitement.

"One of the ears was missing," she explained. "Or was never there. I don't know which. The point is, one ear is unaccounted for."

"Which means," he said, "one of the killings wasn't his."

"We don't know that."

Jimmy ignored her. He was grinning broadly again. "Which one? Did anybody ever figure out which one was missing?"

She looked at him as if he were a lunatic.

"No, no," he said. "I'm not suggesting somebody should have played mix and match. But the DNA! They could tell by comparing DNA, couldn't they?"

"Yes. Of course."

"Well, did they?"

She shook her head. "No. No one saw the need."

"Until now!" he said, triumph in his voice.

She shook her head again. "Jimmy. You'd have to have a lot more than you have now before they'd go to the trouble of matching all those ears–chemically or otherwise."

"But!" he said, with his index finger in the air. "You gotta admit it's pretty odd. That he should be missing one ear, this guy who's so compulsive about collecting and storing them. What are you saying, it like fell out of his pocket or something? Come on now, forget about convincing 'them.' Admit it. Doesn't it have *you* intrigued?"

She started to say something, then stopped, her eyes hard on his. Then she smiled. And he smiled back.

"Okay," she said. "So where is this Swooning Lizard?"

"*Drooping* Lizard. It's right on Commercial Street, a couple blocks west of the town hall. You can't miss it."

"And your plan is . . . ?"

"We meet there. Early, well before the show starts. There's a little balcony at the back, where you can sit unobserved and look down on the audience. If Nickles shows, we'll be able to see him from there and watch how he reacts."

"*If* he shows."

"That goes without saying. If he doesn't, I'm back to square one. Well, maybe not that far. Would you believe square three?"

He smiled, and she returned it.

She said, "You're trying not to let on, but you're excited by all this. Like it's this great big chess game, with real people as the pieces. And you think you've caught a glimpse of endgame. Am I right?"

Jimmy didn't know quite what to say this. He guessed he was a little excited. He just shrugged.

"Why don't you let it show?" she asked.

"You sound like my wife now."

"And what do you tell her?"

"That it's the Irish *omertà*."

She seemed to frown and smile at the same time. "I'm afraid to ask."

"It's our version of the Sicilian code of silence. You never rat out your feelings."

CHAPTER TWENTY-SIX

THE CANARY

T affy, you ravishing creature! What have you got for me on this fine Friday morning?"

She raised a monitory finger, her gaze directed somewhere slightly off to Jimmy's left.

"Whatever you say," she said—but she was speaking into the microphone that sprang like an errant bough from her headset, he realized after a moment's puzzlement. "I'll be sure to tell him as soon as he gets out of his closing. Is there anything else I can do for you, Mr. Previtt?"

She caught his eye now and rolled hers toward the ceiling.

"Yes, sir. I will. Bye now."

She rocked forward and punched a button, pulling off the headset with the other hand. She let it drop on the telephone console.

"Closing?" Jimmy frowned, his stomach sinking. "I got a closing this morning?"

"As far as Previtt's concerned, you do. 'Cause that's where I told him you were. You gotta talk to that man, Jimmy. He says he's going to the judge to get an order for that deposition. And for sanctions. He's pissed."

"Howie Previtt? Don't worry about him. We go way back. What about you? You get a hold of Connie Mook all right?"

She shot him an annoyed, sideways glance.

"Where do you *find* these guys? I get there, he's like sitting on a milk crate, half in the bag, with his coveralls unzipped partway to show off 'big, manly chest.'" She beat a fist against her breast like George of the Jungle. "And the stink! My Christ, the guy must get off on the smell of his own farts. No ventilation whatsoever. Some building inspector should make him keep a canary in a cage so you'd have a running chance when it stops singing. I mean, you light a match in that place? Kaboom!"

"And?"

"*And* I give him the papers, and the first thing he does is get grease on them—which he tries to rub off with an even greasier rag. And gets nowhere, of course. 'Not tonight, honey,' he says. Guy's got 'plans.' The dog track at Wonderland's my bet. But he'll do it tomorrow, he promises. Which I guess means today, sometime. If he's not too hungover. Tell me I should feel reassured by all this, Jimmy."

"You should be reassured by all this."

"Then why am I not having a warm, cozy feeling in the pit of my stomach?"

"Listen," he said, pulling Virginia's invitation from his briefcase. "Call Marathon Messenger and have this delivered to this guy's office. It needs to get there this morning. His office is over on Staniford, across from the Lindeman Center. Sixth floor. I forget the number. It's in the book."

Sighing, she took the envelope with one hand and gave him his messages with the other. As he walked toward his office, he fanned them out, sorting the slips like cards in a hand of whist. He shut the door behind him, then dropped the slips on the desk. He returned only one of the calls, and he didn't need the number.

"Hello."

"Hi, it's me."

"I didn't hear you come in," Phyllis said. "Or see you leave this morning."

"You must've been tired. How long did you sleep?"

"Too...long." He could picture her stretching, rolling her shoulders. "I feel groggy, and my back is killing me."

"Okay. You win. We'll get the new mattress."

"It's not that kind of back pain. Not like you slept the wrong way. More like, I don't know, like nerve pain, I guess."

"You ask the doctor about it?" He realized he was holding his breath. He let it out.

"About my backache?"

"You should call."

"All right, worrywart. I'll call. So how was Provincetown? Did you have your way with the lovely Virginia?"

"Hey. Don't be obnoxious. You stumble on one fetish, and you're all over me. It went fine. It's all set up for tomorrow night. Agent Butler will join me there."

"You're going there *again*? Tomorrow night? You're starting to make me jealous here, Jimbo. You sure you're not having an affair with this person?"

"Oh, right."

"I'm referring to the FBI lady now, not your transvestite."

He flattened out the tone of his voice. "Phyl. I'm fifty plus tax. I'm defanged and declawed. Women can *afford* to be nice to me. You know why? Because I present no danger. I am pathetically monogamous."

"You sell yourself short."

"That's because nobody's making a market. I don't have an adulterous bone in my body, and you know it. Well, maybe in my right hand, sometimes. But that's—"

He could hear her giggling.

"—about it."

"Don't," she said. "It makes my backache worse when I laugh. And let me husband my resentments. I get more life out of them that way."

"I gotta go down there, though."

"With the sexy Agent Butler?"

"Did I say she was sexy?"

"You didn't. Which is just my point. She is, though, isn't she?"

He paused.

"I knew it!"

"A little, I suppose. But–"

She was laughing at him again. "Enough. Are you going to tell me the master plan? The script?"

"Sure."

And he told her.

CHAPTER TWENTY-SEVEN

THE PLAY'S THE THING . . .

H ello, hello, hellooooo!" Virginia called out, then held out the microphone toward the audience–just as she had done the first night he had seen the show. As before, the audience roared back its welcome.

"Hello, hello, hellooooo!"

The house lights had gone down during the opening production number, so Jimmy was back from hiding behind Agent Butler and now seated beside her in the balcony's front row. Depending on the shifting stage lights, he could catch fleeting glimpses of the unsmiling visage of Dr. Nickles, who was seated in the near center of the audience–seated almost exactly, it occurred to Jimmy, where he himself had sat that first night. Maybe one or two rows farther back.

As planned, they had arrived early, Jimmy and Agent Butler, to claim seats in the balcony and watch for Nickles's arrival. They needn't have worried about seating; Virginia had arranged to have the seats reserved for them. The two of them sat there nervously for forty minutes, Jimmy intently watching out for Nickles, Butler seeming ill at ease with the rambunctious crowd. Not exactly knockoffs, he thought with a smile, of the recruits with whom she'd gone through training at the FBI Academy.

By 8:10, Jimmy was beginning to despair, trying to adjust to the reality that the note hadn't worked.

Then he saw the doctor languidly picking his way through the crowd.

Nickles settled on a seat and pulled off his windbreaker. When he turned around to drape it across the back of his chair, he scanned the room, then peered up toward the balcony. Jimmy ducked his head behind Butler.

"You see him?" he said. "Big guy hanging a blue coat and looking this way?"

"Yes," said Butler. "Good-looking guy."

"Tell me when he looks away."

He waited.

"Okay."

Jimmy sat up straight in his chair. Dr. Nickles was seated and facing front now.

Jimmy said, "I'm going to sit behind you until the show starts. He spots me, the whole thing goes bust."

"I'll save the seat," Butler said. She folded her jacket across Jimmy's empty chair and set her purse on top of it.

Jimmy had hunkered behind her until the house lights went down for good.

"He never looked back," Butler had whispered while the actors pranced through the production number.

"All the same," Jimmy said.

They watched the show. Virginia's opening routine was a replay of the one he'd seen, except for her descent into the audience, where her interaction with the crowd forced her to improvise. She went down the steps at something of an angle, with one hand raising slightly the skirt of her gown, the same turquoise number with its scoop neck and spaghetti straps. Throwing ad-libbed abuse before her like a jab, she bobbed and weaved through the tittering audience.

"Look!" Virginia shouted, pointing to a handsome young man in white shorts and a matching shirt. "Tennis whites!" She edged up to him and brushed one bare shoulder against his cheek.

"Abandon this brute, darling," she said with a dismissive toss of her head in the direction of his companion. "You and me, we'll hit the pro tour. Together we can bring new meaning to the term *mixed doubles.*"

At this, the young man's companion drew himself up and glowered down at Virginia with an air of feigned offense. Virginia shrank from the man. She clutched at her crotch with both hands and, looking down at them, began shrieking in the voice of the Wicked Witch of the East.

"Arrrgh! It's melting! It's melting!"

Straightening up now, she upbraided her audience. "You laugh? You think this is funny, just a fairy's threat? Well, read your classics, guys. Remember the wrath of Achilles? It wasn't over a woman, you know. I mean, the big hunk only sulked in his tent over a woman. No, what stirred his wrath, what brought him back to the battle, where he dished out the *real* slaughter–*that* was a man. Go look it up, you don't believe me. It was the death of Patrocles, his 'dear, dear friend.' Yeah, right–you know those Greeks. Well, *that* was what enraged Achilles. A *man*, sweetheart. Ask poor Hector, if you're still not convinced. He's the one Achilles took it out on, after all–and look how *he* ended up. Trust me honey: hell hath no fury like the wrath of a grieving queer."

Agent Butler was enjoying this, with the rest of the crowd, but Jimmy had his eye on Nickles, who–as far as he could tell from his angle, and in the semidarkness–appeared to be staring stone-faced at Virginia.

Beautiful, he thought. *This has got to be chewing him up.*

Jimmy fidgeted during the various routines that followed, the lip-synching impersonations alternating with Virginia's comic bits. He wished the lighting permitted a better view of Nickles's countenance, but he contented himself with waiting for the new wrinkle.

When it came at last, with Virginia making her appearance as the foul-mouthed magician, Jimmy twisted toward his right, scooting toward the edge of his seat in an effort to see around a man who momentarily blocked his view of Nickles. A clear sight line to Nickles's face, when the lighting illuminated it at all, was entirely dependent on the doctor's posture and that of the man beside him. Jimmy stifled his annoyance.

Virginia ran through her patter and performed a few card tricks before standing to one side for the rise of the curtain. It rose on the same two huge trunks, placed on end ten feet apart, their doors gaping. Virginia flicked the last few playing cards she was holding into the audience. They were still fluttering through the shafts of light when she turned with a grand gesture of welcome to Citronella Snowdrift, who was making her entrance from the right in the black-and-white costume of a French housemaid. She walked stiffly, with a correspondingly stiff smile, like an automaton. Looking pretty but lifeless—something from the display window of an FAO Schwarz for dirty old men.

Virginia was now brandishing a set of handcuffs. She stepped toward the lip of the stage, squatted in a ladylike way, knees to the side, and handed the cuffs to a woman in the front row.

"Try them on, dear. Just to show us they're real." She stood up again. "Don't worry. I have the key right here."

She held it out for the audience to see before handing it to the woman. "Try it. Make sure it works."

The woman complied. The key opened the handcuffs.

"Now cuff yourself to your mate, there," Virginia said, gesturing toward the woman's companion. "Oh, lighten up! Pretend it's a commitment ring. Expand your horizons, okay? They're not just a sexual aid."

Looking embarrassed, the woman fiddled about as she cuffed her left wrist to her partner's right. The two of them then held up their manacled arms in victory. The crowd applauded.

"Okay, okay," Virginia said impatiently. "So they work. Now unlock them and give them back. Save the consummation ceremony for later."

Giggling now, the woman fumbled at unlocking the cuffs. Once free, she handed them and the key to Virginia.

"You can assure all these people that they work? That they're real?" she asked.

Both young women nodded vigorously.

"Okay. Citronella, dear?" She turned toward the French maid, still standing midstage, equidistant between the two trunks, her doll's smile frozen. "Come, dear. Face away from the nice audience."

Citronella complied, and Virginia cuffed her hands behind her back. Slowly she spun her subject back around to face the audience again. Citronella dipped to offer a wooden, oddly demure curtsy.

"Now, watch this," Virginia said. And with a Frisbee-tossing motion, she flipped the key into the audience. Two young men scrambled for it, banging into one another in the process.

"Get a hold of yourselves, guys," Virginia said. "It's not a bridal bouquet."

Virginia took Citronella's elbow again and escorted her to the trunk on the left. After showing everyone that the handcuffs were securely clasped, she twirled Citronella around once more and backed her into the trunk.

"Say bye-bye, dear."

With doll-like movements, a bright-eyed Citronella mouthed the words, but no sound came.

Lip-synching must be a hard habit to break, Jimmy thought.

Virginia closed and latched the trunk door. She paced off the distance to the other, still-empty trunk, which she closed and latched as well. Then she sidled to a point midway between the two and spread her arms wide, palms out, chin up to peer up at the ceiling.

"*Introibo ad altari Dei,*" she intoned. "This is in memory of my beloved, Donald."

Whereupon she slowly brought her hands together, the palms still up, her head still raised.

When the edges of her hands touched, the hall went pitch-black.

Jimmy started counting. One Mississippi, two Mississippi . . . At the count of four the crowd started murmuring. When he reached eleven, a solitary spotlight came on, a cone of white light singling out Virginia in the darkness. Then two more, one on each of the trunks. Jimmy searched ravenously for a glimpse of Dr. Nickles, but with the only illumination focused elsewhere, he could make out nothing more than the man's shape in the semidarkness below.

Virginia unlatched the trunk Citronella had entered. She swung open the door to show it empty. Seemingly annoyed by the absence of any response from the crowd, she turned to them and wind-milled her hands in an impatient gesture, to incite applause. She got it, but there was no enthusiasm in it.

She shrugged her indifference and stepped over to the other trunk. After unlatching it, she stepped aside and swung open the door. Citronella was revealed. In a departure from the first show, she had not changed costumes. What caught the eye instead was the green cord that loosely bound her feet, and the white cord knotted around her bare neck. At Virginia's signal, she shuffled out of the trunk in tiny half steps permitted by the cord around her ankles. When Virginia spun her about to display her back to the audience, the handcuffs were gone. In their place was a red nylon cord that gleamed like wet blood in the smoky half-light.

The crowd seemed mystified, bemused even, by the peculiar manner in which the French maid was now bound. When Citronella and Virginia bowed to signal the end of the trick, they were greeted by tepid applause–dampened, Jimmy thought, as much by confusion as anything. The two performers took a step back when the curtain started to fall. The house was once again plunged into darkness, a briefer one this time, punctuated by heavy electric guitar chords that boomed through the room. An offstage voice asked the audience to welcome Bonnie Raitt, and the curtain rose again, this time revealing Yvette Bimbeaux with a guitar.

Jimmy followed none of Yvette's takeoff on Bonnie Raitt. He was looking frantically for Nickles. Looking in vain, he realized with some bitterness, for the doctor's chair was now empty. Somehow, during the brief darkness that separated Virginia's and Citronella's bows from Yvette's appearance, Nickles had made his departure.

"He's gone!" Jimmy hissed to Butler. "He ran out right after he saw the cords! As soon as it was dark. Did you see?"

"Shhh. No, I didn't see anything."

"Well, he's gone! Come on! Hurry!"

Jimmy kept his head down as he moved to the left, toward the stairs at the end of the row. A man behind him barked at him to stay down, but he ignored him, gesturing insistently for Butler to follow him.

He had to waste precious moments at the top of the stairs, waiting edgily to see if Butler was coming. She did, finally, and the two of them scrambled down the stairs and out the entrance of the little theater. They came to a stop on the landing, both of them peering down the steps and looking out into the dense crowd of passersby.

There was no sign of Nickles.

Jimmy hurried down the staircase. "Come on!" he called back to Butler. Butler complied, but too slowly for his liking. Jimmy rushed into the street, among the hundreds of ambling tourists and residents, looking both ways for some hint of Nickles. He was still craning his neck, first in one direction, then the other, when Butler came up to him.

"He's just gone, Jimmy. You'll never spot him in this crowd."

Jimmy sagged back against the front fender of a big beige Acura Legend parked beside the curb. He felt—he wasn't sure what he felt. A mixture of exultation and despair. The guy had bit, been spooked, and now he was gone. What was he to make of that?

"Jimmy," Butler said. "Relax, will you? You look like you're about to have a coronary or something."

"Did you see?" he demanded. "Do you see what this means?"

The look she gave him was pitying. "Means? Jimmy, it doesn't mean anything."

"What are you talking about? He showed up! He sat through the whole show, all the way up to the part where he saw the colored cords—and then he split the first chance he got, when the lights went down again. And you tell me that doesn't mean *anything?*"

"Mean what? That he didn't like the show? Who could blame him? Some grotesque skit dedicated to the mutilated victim of a killing right here in Provincetown—and then the girl reappears, bound hand and foot just like the dead guy? Jimmy, even to someone who knew nothing about the colors, that's gotta seem like—like what? Tasteless. A grotesque travesty. He's probably not the only one who walked out. I'm sure he's not the only one who considered it."

Jimmy gaped at her in disbelief.

"Jimmy, look. If I took this to my boss and asked for a grand jury, you know where I'd end up? Brownsville, Texas, that's where. Helping out on some immigration scam. There's nothing here, I tell you. That doctor's reaction was absolutely understandable. You were hoping he'd maybe display some consciousness of guilt? Well, I'm sorry: that reaction didn't evince one iota of guilt. More like common sense, if you ask me."

"So you're gonna give it up? Just like that?"

She lifted both hands, palms up. Helpless. "Come on. What do you want me to do with this, Jimmy?"

"What we planned, that's all. Check out the bar downstairs. See if he shows up for a drink with Virginia."

She stared at him, head tilted to one side. "You think he's coming *back*?"

"He could." Jimmy knew he was reaching. "Hey, it's what you came to do in the first place. What have you got to lose by hanging around another half hour or so? Look!"

He pointed up the stairway to the entryway landing, where the actors were gathered just outside the door. "The show's over now. It's ending just like it did the first time I saw it. The troupe greets the audience as they come out the door. So we're talking less than half an hour now. Stick around, okay?"

Butler looked at him, then softened.

"Half an hour," she said. "I'll be in the bar, watching for him."

Jimmy nodded. "I'll stay out of sight in case he does."

"I don't think you really need to worry about it."

"I'll be in that place over there." He nodded toward a tavern called the Green Parrot, directly across the street.

She turned away and ambled toward the glass-enclosed bar that occupied the first floor of the building. She had to circle around the stairway to reach the door.

Jimmy did as he'd promised, finding a table that gave him something of a view of the front of the Drooping Lizard. He ordered a Rolling Rock and kept watch. There was nothing to watch. Just people walking by in astonishing numbers. Little or no action visible at the Drooping Lizard.

Had he been wrong the whole time? Was Butler right—that you could infer nothing from someone's reaction to that stupid little tableau he'd convinced Virginia to stage? He supposed it *was* pretty grotesque. Transvestites luridly trussed up like Van Gogh's rape victims. Maybe he had let the weirdness of this whole morbid adventure get to him, let it warp his judgment and make him see links and hints that just weren't there. Maybe the photograph of Virginia Dentata had become a fetish after all. God knows, it had certainly obsessed him these past few days. And for what? For nothing? Was Nickles just a conflicted soul with a secret he wanted kept?

He was working on his second beer when he saw Butler emerge from the bar. Quickly, he dropped a ten on the table and hurried out the bar to meet her.

He caught up with her right where they had separated, almost an hour earlier: beside the Acura that was still parked in front of the Lizard. She smiled bleakly as she watched him cross the street and approach her.

"And?"

She shook her head. "Nothing. He didn't show. But I waited, like I promised. In fact, I lasted longer than Virginia did. Richard, I should say. He gave it up and went home about ten minutes ago."

He couldn't hide his disappointment. "That's it, then? Your cleared case stays cleared?"

She smiled again. "I'm sorry, Jimmy. It was stretch from the get-go, you know. I'm afraid there are no neat answers to this little puzzle you set for yourself."

"You really think I set it myself? It wasn't Van Gogh's doing after all?"

She tipped her head to one side. A gesture of annoyance, he thought. "Who knows, Jimmy? Obviously, some of it came from Van Gogh. He did get the picture and put your name on the back. Like I said, though, the guy was a nutcase. You keep wanting to make sense of what goes on in that whacko's head."

Jimmy sighed–a big, deep sigh. Of surrender, he realized. "Maybe I'm the nutcase. I was so sure."

"Well, if it makes you feel any better, so was Agent Ponsonby. He was sure you and Wolff had something going together."

"Ah," Jimmy said, his smile back now, "and you said he had no sense of humor."

They were smiling at one another again.

"Look," she said. "Another time. Under more pleasant circumstances. You give me a tootle. Okay?"

"Okay. But Virginia? She really left?"

"'Fraid so. So which way is your car? I ended up way down there, the west end lot by the boat launch, past the Coast Guard station." She nodded toward the west.

"I'm in the lot at the wharf," Jimmy said. "The other way."

"I'll say good night, then."

"Good night. Thanks for making the trip."

"Hey. I liked the show. And the company."

"Me too."

"And don't forget the tootle," she said, smiling again.

With that she turned away. Jimmy watched her stride west. It wasn't long before she was swallowed up by the crowd.

For a moment he didn't know what to do with himself, standing there alone in front of the Drooping Lizard on a busy Friday night in Provincetown. Despite the press of bodies, he seemed to see before him nothing but a flat, empty vista. Dull. Depressing. Desolate, even. All without the excitement of the mystery he had been pursuing with such vigor over the past days. Or that of the strange new world he had discovered through Virginia. Excited– isn't that what Butler had accused him of feeling? Well, scratch that. Not anymore. The zip seemed to have been sucked out of him by Nickles's disappearance and now Butler's departure. Even Virginia had gone home.

What did he have to go back to now? A mutinous Taffy. To the grumpy likes of Howard Previtt, wanting a deposition or a closing or a continuance. To his unvoicable dread about Phyllis.

He turned away and started walking east, in the direction of the wharf. With heavy feet. Halfway up the block he stopped. Turned around and looked back. For one more look at the Drooping Lizard–where his adventure had first taken its weird turn the night he'd scribbled the note to Virginia after the show.

The second floor theater area was dark now, imparting an air of dilapidation to the whole wooden structure. The stairway and landing were empty. The multicolored pennants strung from the line of heavy rope that served as a banister snapped desolately in the chilly evening air. There was life and light from the bar beneath it, but the second floor seemed as dead as an abandoned pier. Jimmy sighed, then turned away.

And froze.

Something had caught his eye. He turned around again in search of it. Yes, there it was. On the Acura where he and Butler had said their good nights.

It was a vanity plate.

It was a pretty simple one, though the owner must have had to do some fast talking to those torpid clerks at the registry of motor vehicles. Because none of the plate's characters was a number or a letter.

It used only a symbol. The symbol for cents. Five times, in fact:

$$\boxed{\text{¢ ¢ ¢ ¢ ¢}}$$

As Jimmy stared at the plate, the realization dawned in three easy jumps.

Five cents.

A nickel.

The car was Nickles's.

He was still here. And Virginia had gone home.

Jimmy started running.

CHAPTER TWENTY-EIGHT

MORE THAN YOU CAN HANDLE

Jimmy breasted the angry crowd for the first two blocks, fighting to make headway. Then he was able to turn left on Court Street, where the foot traffic thinned out. Gasping for breath already, he pushed on, running north now, until he reached Bradford, dodging the honking traffic as he crossed it. He headed east again, several more blocks, passed the Pilgrim Monument, and cut left, chugging up the hill on Windsor Street. The hill slowed him down considerably, his legs feeling dead and his breath coming in hot, ragged gasps.

Another block and he had to stop. Take a short breather. Like a winded basketball player, he leaned over and dug his hands into the tops of his well-padded hipbones.

Maybe Phyllis was right about his diet and lack of exercise.

He dug out his phone. He thought of trying to call Butler, but he had only an office number for her. She would have to wait. The phone was still off. He it turned on. It beeped that he had voice mail, but who cares? He ignored the signal, selecting instead the call log from the main menu. He thumbed through the list of his outgoing calls, hoping he would recognize Virginia's number when he saw it. Yes. The 487 prefix gave it away. He didn't know anybody else in this neck of the woods.

He pressed the button to ring the number and waited.

A busy signal.

Virginia was on the phone?

Or it was off the hook?

He was on the hoof again, running with renewed purpose. Still uphill, until he saw the outline of Virginia's bungalow.

The downstairs lights were on. Jimmy had to stop when he reached the steps to the front porch. The stitch in his side had become almost debilitating, and he needed desperately to catch his breath. He was working on the pain, kneading hard, when he heard shouts from the rear of the house.

He bounded up the steps and shoved his way through the front door. He was already through the foyer when the condition of the door finally registered.

It had been ajar.

The shouting was louder now. He could tell it was coming from the kitchen.

"You think you can get away with this? You want to fuck this thing up now, after all I've gone through?" It was the bullying, angry voice he recognized from the doctor's office, but super-charged. Jimmy hurried through the hallway toward the back of the house, then came to a stop in the arch over the entrance to the kitchen.

"If this is some kind of twisted shakedown—"

Nickles apparently heard or caught a glimpse of Jimmy in the doorway, for the doctor stopped now, staring over at him with shock. To Nickles's left, Virginia had her back to the sink, both hands gripping its porcelain flange as she cowered before the enraged doctor who towered over her. Even now, as she looked up to take in Jimmy's arrival, the expression on Virginia's face was one of outright terror.

"Oh boy," Jimmy wheezed, his chest heaving. "I just love being a jock."

Nickles's fury now seemed to run in new channels.

"You!" He turned to face Jimmy head-on. As the man moved rapidly toward him, Jimmy took a step backward. For some rea-

son—he suddenly realized in the ridiculous clarity of the moment—
it had never even occurred to him that the man might physically
threaten *him*. Well, he was now, and the big man, red-faced and
shaking, was almost upon him. It was as if the whole sequence of
events were taking place underwater, in some viscous medium that
slowed them both down, moving with comically retarded velocity.
He felt himself hunch involuntarily, in tiny increments, bracing for
a blow that seemed unavoidable, unstoppable. The only sound that
cut through the waterlogged unreality of it all was a scrabbling
noise from the sink area.

Nickles suddenly have a grunt of mild surprise, his eyes widen-
ing slightly as his forward progress halted. The look of surprise gave
way to one of puzzlement, the head cocking to one side—as if he
were trying to remember who this strange man was, the one who
had suddenly filled the doorway to intrude on his argument with
Virginia.

The doctor opened his mouth to speak. No sound emerged. For
an incongruous second, Jimmy recalled Citronella Snowdrift in her
maid's costume, mouthing her doll's good-bye before the trunk lid
swung shut.

Then, still in the slow motion of it all, Nickles sank to his knees.
The look he gave Jimmy was imploring—a man begging, it seemed—
until it struck him with preternatural lucidity that Nickles wasn't
seeing him at all, that he was focusing on nothing. His head twisted oddly to one side, another gesture mimicking surprise, before he
tumbled forward, his skull making a sickening sound as it hammered against the flagstone floor.

From the very middle of his back, dead center between the
shoulder blades, sprouted the wooden handle of Virginia's chef's
knife. A willow twitch, dowsing for the man's life's blood, which
now blackened his blue windbreaker. Because he had pitched forward from his knees, with his rump still somewhat elevated,
Nickles's right cheek lay pressed against the slate, distorting his features. His eyes were still open. His mouth was open, too, and a
small but bright dribble of blood puddled the floor around it.

Through his shock Jimmy became aware of a dull humming

sound. He looked up to see Virginia, right arm still in the air after driving the knife into Nickles's muscular back. Her fingers trembled, and the humming sound, he realized, was coming from her. It grew louder, higher in pitch, as the horror took complete control of her face. The hum modulated to a moan, a wail, and she slid down the front of the sink cabinet to sit slackly on the floor. With her trembling hands how resting on her thighs, she shook all over.

Jimmy rushed to her. Dropping to one knee, he laid his hands on hers, holding them firmly. Shaking them a little.

"It's over," he said. "He can't hurt you. It's all right now."

But as if to refute him, Nickles twitched spasmodically for a few seconds. Then he was still again.

Virginia's eyes were still on Nickles, and still so full of horror Jimmy found himself following her gaze, to the open eyes that stared off to one side of the kitchen, as if he were sighting along the floor to see that it was level.

Was he dead?

Jimmy scrambled back to Nickles's body on his hands and knees. The man's torso was still and unbreathing. He felt for a pulse—on the neck, on the wrist. He found none. He rolled away from the body, sitting on the floor with his back to the sink cabinet, right beside Virginia.

He groped for his cell phone, lost for a moment, then found it in his jacket pocket. It had never made it back to the clip when he hung up after trying to call Virginia. He punched in 911 and raised it to his ear.

"No!"

He stared at Virginia.

"No!" she said again. "Please! My God, my life is ruined!"

Slowly he lowered the phone. He could hear the voice of someone answering. He pushed the disconnect. He stared at Virginia again.

"What are you talking about? This is self-defense here."

"Are you crazy?" Virginia was shrieking at him now. "Look at him, for Christ's sake. He's stabbed in the back. *Look* at him! Do you think that looks like self-defense?"

Come to think of it, his vision of the dead doctor raised a better question: *was* it self-defense? No. Not technically. If she was defending anyone when she struck, it was Jimmy, not herself. The guy seemed to have fixed his wrath on Jimmy. Justifiable homicide, then? Probably. A trickier case to make, though—especially to an ambitious prosecutor who gets a whiff of the media's prurient interest. Because the press would eat this one up. *Drag Queen Offs Dead Lover's Rapist.*

Jimmy looked at Virginia. She was watching him the way a hungry dog watches a man eat a sandwich. Still shaking. Shattered.

Virginia was right. Win or lose, it would destroy her.

But not making the call? That could destroy *him.* He was a lawyer, after all. He couldn't just walk away from this. And what the hell else could she do anyway?

"The boat," Virginia said. From out of nowhere, as if following his train of thought.

He frowned at her.

"Donald had a boat," she said. "He kept it in back of his cottage. You know, that line of little saltboxes just west of town. The ones in all the pictures of Provincetown."

"A cottage?"

"Yes. He had it for years, since before we met. And he kept a boat there. It's just a little rowboat, but maybe we . . ."

She left the thought hanging there, uncompleted.

He completed it for her. "You want me to help you dump the goddamn body? Not just forget about calling it in, but actively conceal a homicide?"

She said nothing. Watched him.

Jimmy shook his head. "Sorry," he said as he hauled himself to his feet. "I never signed on for that. You gotta make the call. It'll work out. Won't be pleasant, but it'll work out."

"No, it won't. I know it."

She stared up at him from her sitting position on the floor. Again, he felt the urge to protect her, as he had after listening to her harangue about coincidence and Divine Plans. What was that riff she had run off about God never giving you more than you could handle? She wasn't buying it, he remembered that much. And whatever He was dishing out now, it was plainly more than she could handle.

Did that mean he would have to handle it for her?

No, wait. He needed to think this through more. Okay, truth be told, he wasn't all that hung up on his legal obligations here. First do no harm, right? If he had to hide a killer's body to protect the guy's victim—his victim twice over, in fact—well, Jimmy could live with that on his conscience. But not if it meant he would go to jail and lose his license to practice for doing so. How risky was it?

They could probably get Nickles out of the house and into a boat at this time of night without being seen. And there ought to be a way to see to it the body didn't pop up somewhere. But could Nickles's disappearance be traced back to them? Butler knew about their charade, about the invitation that brought him to Provincetown. So far as she knew, Nickles had shown up and then left. Whatever convinced him to show up hadn't been enough to make him stick around for the finale. But if he turned up missing . . . ? What would that set off in her thinking?

He smiled to himself. She might think he was right—that Nickles had been implicated in Gilfillen's death. That the show had spooked him, all right—spooked him into flying the coop. They might look for him, with an eye to questioning him about Donald's death, perhaps. But there was no reason for suspicion to alight on Jimmy or Virginia. If anything, all the evidence would point away, in another direction. Toward the missing doctor.

Jimmy's mind was whirring. Why not? The risky end was getting the body into the boat without being seen. If it was wrapped up and put in the trunk of the Taurus . . .

He made up his mind.

"Okay," he said, taking charge now. "I gotta get my car. Might take me fifteen minutes. While I'm doing that, I need you to pull some shit together. A rug—a big rug. One to wrap him up in. And some rope to tie it up. Any color, this time."

The look in her eyes cut off any attempt to make a joke of it.

"And a couple concrete blocks. Didn't I see some in your garden shed that time?"

She waited several seconds before nodding.

"Okay. Let's see. A couple flashlights. That should about do it. Can you get all that stuff together while I'm gone?"

She stiffened. "You mean you're going to leave me here alone? With him? With . . . *that*, stuck in him like that?"

She motioned toward Nickles with a barely detectable twitch of the head but kept her eyes on Jimmy. He looked over at the knife, its wooden handle still extruding from the man's back.

He gave a sigh of resignation and pulled himself to his feet.

"All right," he said. "We'll deal with the body first. Go find me a rug–preferably not one that could be traced to you. One big enough to wrap him up in."

Virginia eyed him with suspicion.

"Go on," he said, with a wave of his hand to get her moving. "I'll . . . take care of the knife. And empty his pockets in case the body is found after all."

She had to roll from her sitting position to her hands and knees before she could manage to pull herself to her feet. He helped with a hand at her elbow. She staggered as she moved toward the doorway. There she stopped, turning back to face him.

"Jimmy," she said, and waited until he had made eye contact.

She meant to thank him. He waved her off. "Just go on. Get the rug–and some rope."

When she had gone, and he was alone in the kitchen, he looked down at Nickles again. He straddled the big man, then sank to his knees, each one fetching up snug against the outside of one of the doctor's powerful thighs. He leaned forward to grasp the knife handle. As he did, he was jolted by a glimpse of his reflection in the floor-to-ceiling window to his left.

Leaning over the raised buttocks of Dr. Nickles from the rear.

Jesus Christ. I look like a goddamn rapist.

Van Gogh had a lot to answer for.

He leaned on the man's buttocks, pushing the body flat on the floor, then reached out again for the knife handle. Slowly and carefully, he tugged on it. Given the force with which the knife had been driven into the man's back, he was surprised by how easily it pulled out of him.

CHAPTER TWENTY-NINE

MY HERO

A bat-wing of cloud slid across the new moon, dousing what little light it had cast over them—as if drawing a curtain against what was taking place below. There were a few pinpoints gleaming along the shoreline toward the end of the peninsula, but otherwise the rowboat slopped along in near total darkness.

For this Jimmy was thankful. On the beach the half-light had played nasty tricks on him. Driftwood burls took on frightening shapes. The bladderwort grew monstrous, sprouting suckered tentacles to tangle about his feet. Even as they had struggled to load the rowboat in silence, their breath hung in the air like the guilty whispers of ghosts.

She sat in the stern, facing him, but he could not make out her expression for the darkness. He could tell only that she was erect and unmoving, with a hand on each gunwale.

He heard the creak of the oarlocks and the slap of the oars on the water. His rowing was clumsy and inefficient, his strokes so ill-matched the oars hacked bluntly at the water and threw stinging spray into his face. He was tired, too, the adrenaline long since drained away and fatigue flooding in to take its place. A little more, though. At least the return trip would be easier. He put his back into it.

"Here," he rasped when he felt he could go no farther. "This should do it."

He pulled in the oars and rested for a moment. The boat bobbed gently. He listened to the light chop of waves and the sound of his own labored breathing. He licked his lips and tasted the salt. Then, gripping both gunwales, he scrabbled aft toward her. He laid his hand on her right shoulder, felt the neck tendons flex in response.

"Turn around and face the rear," he said. "Then scooch over a bit so I can slip in beside you. We'll roll it off the stern."

"What about the blocks?" she asked as she slid to the port end of the bench.

He eased his legs over the bench. It was a tight fit, but soon they were seated side by side. He reached forward to touch the rolled carpet that lay crosswise at their feet.

"Can you lift the block on your side?" he asked. "Maybe we can set them on top of the rug and push everything off at once. Go ahead, try it."

He heard her grunt with the cement block. The boat suddenly pitched to starboard, and she dropped the block. He grabbed the near gunwale in an effort to steady her, then froze until the rocking slowed.

"Should I take that as a yes?" he asked. "Do you think you can do it?"

"Yes, I think so, but how do we—"

"Listen to me. If you can lift it, we're okay. First we pick up the carpet and push it back. Then we lift our blocks together and set them on the carpet next to the edge. Together. That way we won't have to worry about capsizing the goddamn boat. Then we can shove the whole mess off the stern and into the water. You got it?"

She said she got it. He reached down and felt his end of the rolled carpet. The ends were crimped tight with nylon rope—like a fancy tamale, it occurred to him, or a Tootsie Roll—and it was reassuring that the bundle was still snugly together. He slid his hands under it. He could sense her doing the same from her end. Even through the heavy Persian wool, pinched by taut coils of rope that formed a spiral girdle along the carpet's length, he could feel the unmistakable shape of a head and shoulder.

At least she had the lighter end.

As one, they raised the bundle and eased it aft, where it fetched up against the lip of the transom. He wedged his left knee under the center of the carpet to keep it from drooping. "Okay," he said, taking his hands away. "On three we hoist the blocks. You ready?"

"Yes."

"Okay, then. One . . . two . . . three!"

He had to restrain himself to make sure he didn't raise his faster than she could lift hers, and the boat pitched some with the shifting weight, but they managed to balance their blocks on top of the bundle. He held his breath as he waited to see if they would stay put. They did.

He said, "Check to make sure the rope through your block is still tied tight to the one around the rug. If it's not weighted down by both blocks, it might end up bobbing to the surface. Especially once it starts to bloat. From the gases."

"I didn't realize I was teamed up with such an expert."

"Shut up. Just check. Is it okay?" He felt the knots at his end. Still solid.

"Uh . . . yes."

"Then let's start pushing."

They pushed. Again, he tried to match his progress to hers. It wasn't easy with the blocks bearing down on the carpet, but they managed in the end to tip it off the stern. As he should have expected, the teetering bundle favored one end when it fell, and the boat, once relieved of its burden, pitched wildly in a cockeyed motion that was mostly fore and aft. He felt her clutch his arm, the fingers digging in painfully. Water pelted his face from the splash. Then the boat recovered its equilibrium. The two of them did, too.

As if on cue, the sliver-moon broke through again. He could just make out her face. She was smiling bleakly at him.

"My hero," she whispered hoarsely.

The sudden flush of his rage took him by surprise. It was all he could do not to heave her in after the son-of-a-bitch.

CHAPTER THIRTY

VICE VERSA

My hero, indeed.

Two hours later, Virginia's kitchen cleaned up at last and the trunk of the Taurus having passed his inspection, Jimmy was finally back on Route 6, headed for Boston. And wondering where it came from, that flare of almost unslakable rage he felt to hear her call him a hero. Maybe it was just the enormity of it all, and the realization that he had put so much at risk—his reputation, his law license, even his liberty—just to keep this neurotic cross-dresser from having to deal with the police. From dealing with authorities who, he knew, had every need and right to know what had happened in Virginia's crowded little kitchen. No, as he looked back on it now, it seemed nothing at all like heroism. More like a failing, a weakness.

But there was more to his reaction, something deeper and inaccessible. He didn't know what. He squinted into the darkness, past the tunnel cut by his headlights, and tried to shake it off. No, it was done. A fait accompli. There was nothing he could do about it now but see it through.

He checked his watch—2:16. No wonder he was so exhausted, up so late on top of everything he'd been through. If only, instead of facing a two-and-a-half-hour drive, he could just wish himself home, in his bed beside Phyllis . . .

Phyllis. He remembered the message that had come in on his cell phone. What if she was the one who had tried to reach him?

He reached across to the passenger seat to grab his jacket. It was still damp from his sweat and the salt spray. He groped blindly for the side pockets while keeping his eyes on the road. Finding one, he fished in it for the phone. He was briefly puzzled by the smooth object he felt there, then recognized it as Nickles's wallet. He had stuffed it there, along with the rest of the contents of the doctor's pockets, while Virginia fetched the rug. He would need to think about the best way to get rid of them.

He tugged the jacket about and found the other pocket. The phone was still in it.

He hated trying to do this when he drove, holding the phone and the wheel with one hand while seeking out the right buttons in the dark with the other, all while his eyes jumped back and forth between the phone and the road. After a couple of failed tries, he finally succeeded in entering the password to retrieve his messages.

There were two of them.

The first one had come in at 3:10 and sounded as if the caller was stuck inside the Callahan Tunnel. He could hear the rush of ambient traffic, its echo almost drowning out the caller's voice.

"Jimmy," said the voice. "It's Mook. Look, that thing you wanted us to do? Serve those papers? I mean, we did it all right, he's been served and all. At the guy's work site there, up on Savin Road. About twenty minutes ago. But it didn't go totally smooth, 's what I'm callin' to tell you. The guy got a hair across or something, and Phil had to handle him. No big deal or anything. The guy turns smart-ass when we tell him we're police officers. Says he's got a right to examine the shields, see the badge numbers, like. Couldn't have that, of course, so Phil shoves the guy up against his truck for bein' such a smart-ass. Didn't last more than a coupla seconds. You know, a knee to the balls, a shot to the kidney, and he's down on one knee and fresh out of curiosity. I mention it only 'cause when we left, he was shoutin' all kinds a' shit, 'bout how he was gonna report us to the Department and it was that bitch on the papers put us up to it. No big deal, like I said, but I thought you oughta know about it. Case anybody squawks, like. Call, you got any questions. I'll put the papers in the mail. See ya, guy."

"You idiot!" Jimmy shouted as he pushed the button to erase the message—and Mook himself, if he could. He tossed the phone on the other seat. Too furious even to think for a moment.

Taffy was right. The guy was a moron. A *lazy* moron. You know a guy's got a hard-on for authority. You've been told as much. You've been given his home address and told to serve him there. And you go to the place he *works!* Right in front of the guys he works with. And if that isn't humiliation enough, you go and work him over, too?

Jimmy was reaching for the phone again before his brain had finished making the next connection. He pulled over to the side of the road this time. Punched his way through the phone's directory. Found Taffy's home number. Entered it. He had to warn her.

He heard her voice, but it was on her machine.

"Have you or someone you love been injured in an accident? You may have a valuable claim against those responsible. Call the Law Offices of James A. Morrissey at six-one-seven, seven-eight-one, eight-seven-five-one. He'll fight for your rights. On the other hand, if you're perfectly healthy and reasonably sane leave me a message and I'll call you back. And remember . . . wait for the tone!"

Screwball. He was still waiting for the tone when he remembered she wasn't staying at home now anyway. She was down in Quincy—with Darvonne Something. And he didn't have the number.

After breaking the connection, Jimmy held his head in both hands, his elbows on the steering wheel.

What else?

The other message. He retrieved it.

"Jim. It's me." Jimmy felt his stomach lurch to hear her tone—flat, lifeless. "Call me when you pick this up, okay?"

He didn't bother erasing the message. He just disconnected and called home.

She didn't sound groggy when she answered, not like someone his call had awakened. Just tired. Real tired.

He said, "Hi, it's me." Holding the phone with both hands. "Are you okay?"

"Yes–well, no, actually. But one thing at a time. Where *are* you, anyway?"

"I'm . . . coming up on Wellfleet, I guess. On my way back. Phyl, what's going on?"

"It's Taffy," she said. "She's in the hospital. That boyfriend of hers? The one you–"

"Yes. What about him?"

"Well, he assaulted her. He was waiting for her when she left work. Beat her up real bad. George called me from the office. They've arrested the guy and everything, but she's in a pretty bad way, Jim. Nobody's saying it's life-threatening or anything, but George says it's not pretty. She may need reconstructive surgery."

"Aw, jeez." Some hero. "Where is she?"

"Boston City."

He squeezed the phone hard against his ear.

"And Jim?"

She waited for him.

"Yeah?"

"We have to talk, Jim. When you get in. It's not good."

He knew she had switched subjects–that she was not talking about Taffy now.

"I saw Dr. Bergman. About why I'm getting the back pain. I think she thinks the cancer is back."

Jimmy sat stock-still. As mute and lifeless as Citronella's automaton.

"You think she thinks?" he said finally, but there was little hope in the query. "What did she *say?*"

"Well, all she said was she needed wait for the test results. But the look on her face, Jim? It said it all."

He pressed his eyes shut for a second, then jerked them open again. No time for that.

He said, "Looks are just that, Phyl–looks. You gotta wait to see what the tests say. Phyl?"

"I'm here, Jim."

"I'll be there in an hour. Hour and a quarter, tops."

"Don't speed, Jim. You're no good to me wrapped around a bridge abutment."

"No, I won't speed."

"Love you, Jim."

"I love you, too, Phyl. More than I could ever tell you."

"You're sweet."

When she was gone, he dropped the phone on the seat and gripped the steering wheel with both hands. Hard. Way too hard, he realized, for the wheel was vibrating from the force of his grip and the shaking of his arms.

It was a little after four when Jimmy finally reached home. He found Phyllis asleep on the couch in the living room. She had her head on a sofa pillow and an afghan wrapped around her shoulders. He tiptoed upstairs; got out of his filthy clothes and showered; pulled on his bathrobe. Then he settled into the recliner across from her. Just sat there, watching her sleep—peacefully, it seemed to him—while he waited for the sun to rise. He listened as the old house made its night noises. And sometime during his vigil, despite everything—or maybe because of everything—he fell asleep, too.

They woke up about eight, Phyllis first, and had breakfast together. Well, coffee anyway; neither one of them could eat. They had their talk, too. Each of them sitting at opposite ends of the couch. Phyllis told him more of what she'd heard about Taffy from George Palmer's phone call. How she'd been attacked right there on Milk Street, pummeled, knocked down, kicked in the ribs and the head. Jimmy briefly entertained satisfying images of really setting the dogs on Rebstock, of letting Mook and Harney work their rough magic. Well, maybe not. But he'd see the guy go down, that was sure.

Fantasies of retribution were no defense when Phyllis began to fill him in on the details of her conversation with the oncologist. Jimmy was determined not to let her go coiling off into an emotional tailspin over what hadn't even been said yet, let alone confirmed. He reminded her of their deal.

"Deal?" she said, incredulity in her voice. "You mean our talk about adopting?"

He nodded, even while grasping at once that he'd sounded a wrong note.

"Oh, babe." Her face seemed to take on a look of indescribable sadness now—one for him, he realized, which made it worse. "That wasn't a deal, Jim. It was a fantasy. There's no way—"

"No," he said, even as he knew he was just going through the motions. "I promised you. That was the whole point. It was about how I was a lawyer, that I could—"

"Jim. Think about it for one second. No agency in the *world* is going to entrust a child to a woman with a history of breast cancer, at least not one as recent as mine. And I don't mean that silly business about how many breasts I have. The situation would be just too *unstable*—even without this latest . . . wrinkle. And a 'deal'?" She shook her head slowly. "Sometimes you don't have a clue, Jim. It wasn't about a deal. It was about us. How you understood—and were ready to do whatever. Even when there was nothing to do. That's what made it so sweet. So loving. And comforting, too."

Looking at her now, Jimmy felt he was the one who needed comforting. He didn't trust himself to try to speak.

"Come here," she said. She scooted across the space between them and snuggled up under his arm, tugging the afghan about her shoulders again. "Let's just let it alone for a little while. We'll talk about something else. Tell me how your script went down at the Drooping Lizard."

The Drooping Lizard? It sounded like a bizarre joke told eons ago, before the events that had rushed in on him since. He considered briefly how much he should tell her of his long night, how much of the weight to share given everything *she* had been through. A single look, taking in the expression on her face, told him he could hold nothing back.

So he told her. Everything. Dryly, mechanically, almost without affect. He faced front as he talked, checking her every once in while, watching her curl up into a little ball beneath her afghan, seeming to get smaller and more tightly hunched as she absorbed the full horror of it all.

"My God, Jim," she said—whispered hoarsely—when he'd finished. "How on earth could you *do* such a thing? Are you crazy? Do you know what could happen to you?"

"Yes, I know. I'm a lawyer, remember?"

"Apparently, you *don't* remember. You've jeopardized everything you have, everything you're supposed to uphold. And why?"

"You think I'm just cutting corners again, is that it? Playing loose with the rules to get something done. Like threatening Nickles or scamming some gangster's girlfriend?"

"Well, you're not exactly playing *tight* with the rules here, are you?"

Jimmy shrugged. "No, I'm not. You're right. But you had to see her, Phyl. The look on her face when she was sitting there looking at him. I mean, I didn't do this for *me*, you know."

She took her time considering this. "No," she said finally, "I don't suppose you did. It wasn't a selfish thing you did."

"I made a choice," he said. "A choice between two very unpleasant alternatives. Both of them came with terrible consequences."

She was quiet again. Then she said, "Okay, Jim," the sharpness gone from her voice now. "Let's call it an ethical dilemma, then. And you made your choice."

"It wasn't an easy one, I can tell you that."

"It must have been horrible," she said. "And then you come back to . . . *this*—and Taffy."

He smiled. "You think He's giving me more than I can handle?"

She frowned. "Who?"

He shook it off. "Nothing. It's just an expression of Virginia's. How people in AA meetings say God won't give you more than you can handle. She didn't believe it. Me either, I guess."

She said nothing for a moment. Then, "It's a statement about faith. If you've got it, the world seems that way. You have a place in it and you're cared for. If you don't . . . ?"

She flashed him a wintry smile and shrugged.

"And you?" he asked.

"I don't know, Jim. I really don't know. But you have to act *as if.* As *if* you lived in such a world. Where things happen for reasons that have something to do with you personally."

"Take it *personally?*"

"Yes."

"How the hell do you do that?"

She let out another deep breath. "You just do the next right thing, and hope it works out all right. The chips fall where they may. Otherwise, you're lost anyway, because we're the kind of creatures that tear ourselves to pieces if we *don't* do the right thing. Doing the next right thing is the only defense you have against the falling chips."

"Is this some shrink's way of saying virtue is its own reward?"

"I suppose. Sometimes its *only* reward."

"And what's vice then? Versa?"

"Maybe. Maybe not. But when you think about it, it's still the only option. The next right thing. Otherwise, you're lost."

At a little after ten he left to go visit Taffy. He promised to be back before noon. She said not to hurry; she wasn't going anywhere.

When he got back in the Taurus, he could smell the sour sweat off the jacket from the night before. He made a mental note to drop it off at the cleaners on the way back. He started the engine and backed out of the driveway and into Vinal Avenue. Phyllis was in the doorway now, waving for him to wait. She had the afghan under one arm and was making her way down the porch steps. Jimmy pulled the car over to the curb and lowered the passenger window. When she reached him, she leaned inside.

"Another thing. About Richard."

Jimmy was lost for a second and it must have showed, for she said, "That's exactly what I mean. His name is *Richard,* dammit. Richard Taub. Stop calling him Virginia. There *is* no Virginia. And he is not a *she.* I mean, of course gender is a social construct and all that, but *sex* isn't. The man *has* a penis, doesn't he?"

Jimmy blinked at her. "It's not something I really wanted to get into with . . . him."

"Well, don't forget it, that's all. That's probably what suckered you into helping him last night. It's the old Catholic schoolboy in you. The more you see him as a helpless little *female*, the more you're likely to fall for crap like that."

She smiled at him.

"Remember, Santa Claus: there is no Virginia."

CHAPTER THIRTY-ONE

SANDWICH BOARD

Jimmy always appreciated that hospitals painted lines on the floors to guide you to whatever wing or care unit you were seeking. Boston City Hospital was no exception, and Jimmy gratefully took the advice of the woman at the information desk. He followed the yellow line.

They ought to do this, Jimmy thought as trudged along, at the Board of Bar Overseers. When they impose discipline. They could have a red line for a meeting with a prosecutor. Yellow to get your a private admonition, maybe blue when you came to be publicly reprimanded by one of the Board members. And for a disciplinary hearing, from which disbarment might follow? Black, of course.

Black. Wasn't that the line that awaited him if what he'd done for Virginia ever came to light? He pushed the thought from his mind and kept walking.

When he reached the wing he wanted, the duty nurse pointed him to Room 4231. He peeked into the room. He saw an old woman on what looked like life support staring vacantly in his direction. Her breath wheezed and rattled. Confused, he was about to turn away when he noticed the curtain separating the woman's bed from another one next to the window. The outline of feet beneath bedclothes told him the other bed was also occupied.

He smiled gamely at the old woman as he sidled past the foot of her bed toward the one behind the curtain. He poked his head around it.

He wouldn't have recognized her. One eye was purple and swollen almost entirely shut, a butterfly bandage above it. The other was completely hidden by a large, cushionlike patch of gauze and tape. She had a livid bruise on her puffy right cheek, and her left arm was in a cast to her elbow.

The eye that wasn't patched was nothing more than a slit, and he couldn't tell if she was awake or not. He stood there, just his head and one shoulder on her side of the curtain, wondering whether to go or stay. He decided she was sleeping and started to pull away.

"Don't split on me now, Jimmy. You came this far."

The voice was thick and rheumy, as if she hadn't spoken in a while.

Jimmy stepped all the way in, past the curtain, and showed her an uncertain smile.

"Hey, Taff. You can forget the typing. If I ever go on television, I can feature you in one of my personal injury ads."

"Mmmph."

He wasn't sure how to translate that.

"Look, kiddo," he said softly, edging his way in between the curtain and the bed, "I'm real sorry about what happened. I thought those guys would keep him away from you. But you were right. Connie Mook is a moron."

"Smells, too."

He smiled. "You're a tough kid, Taffy. We'll get you over this little bump. And Rebstock? Forget him. His new residence will have no knobs on the inside of the doors, and you can't open Plexiglas windows. Seriously, he's gonna do real time, you watch. None of those picnics in the house of corrections. He's headed for Concord, I get my way. Maybe Walpole. I'm not without influential friends, you know."

"Like Mook?"

"Not all of them."

She was quiet for a moment.

"I get you anything? Water, maybe?"

She shook her head.

"They say I might lose the eye, you know. The bone around it is crushed, from where he kicked me."

"Aw, jeez, Taffy. I'm so sorry."

He felt stupid. Nothing to say.

She said, "They say you won't be able to tell the difference when they're finished. Except I wouldn't be able to see out of that side. But it might not come to that."

He chewed his lip and patted her hand.

"The house I grew up in," she said. "It wasn't pretty, you know. No white picket fences in East Boston—shit, not much white paint *any*where. A lot of jumbo jets coming in low overhead. And my old man. 'Cause you never knew, that's the whole point. You never knew what kind of mood he'd be in when he came home. We'd sit around, all of us kids and my mom, and we'd listen for the sound of his key in the lock. Trying to read the sound, then to read his face. And me, I'm being the good little girl. I'd hurry and get his drink ready for him, and he'd sit there and tell you how he'd *earned* that fucking drink. And you believed him. *Believe* me, you believed him."

"Taffy, you don't—"

"Shut up, Jimmy. Let me just say it, will ya? Okay?"

He said okay.

She said, "We'd all wait like the goddamn bomb squad to see if he'd explode. You couldn't ever figure out whether he would—or why, that was the worst of it. You never knew if it was 'cause he drank too much or he drank too little. Was it something you did or something you didn't do? The point is there was just no way to tell, you understand what I'm saying? But half the time, something, whatever it was, would set him off."

Jimmy spotted a tear on her cheek now. It had escaped from the unbandaged slit.

"Usually it was Mom he'd hit. But sometimes it was one of us. And you never knew. But you know what I *did* know, Jimmy?"

"What, Taff."

"I knew that when I got out of there, I would never let another man do that to me. *Never!* And I never did, either. Some guy tries to get rough with me, he's gone. You know that. You were there. If they wouldn't stay gone, I'd be on you to get an RO. I was never going back to what I grew up with. *Never.* You understand what I'm saying?"

Jimmy nodded. "Yes. I understand."

"Then how come, tell me this, how come I ended up with so many of these losers? Can you tell me that? What is it about me? Do I walk around wearing some kind of, like, psychic sandwich board, says, 'Come on guys, go ahead, take a shot'?"

Jimmy managed a hollow grin. "You could maybe cut down on the 'Fresh Kill' ads, you ask me."

She rolled her head toward the window.

Did I offend her?

"Taffy," he said, "you got so much going for you. You don't know the half of it. You're smart and you're tough and good-looking. And young. Jesus, there's a lot of good guys out there that can handle that. I promise you."

She remained silent.

"And I really am sorry about Mook. I thought I could finesse this–keep him away and you safe. Kind of the way I try to finesse everything, Phyllis would tell you. Tells *me*, anyway. I guess there's just some things you can't finesse. This was one of them. I seem to have bumped into a whole passel of them the last couple days."

She turned back to look at him–or so he assumed, at least. He still couldn't see her eye.

"You in some kind of trouble, Jimmy?"

"No, not really. Not what you could really call trouble. Just a few . . . *situations*, is all. I'll be okay. Will *you*?–that's today's question."

She nodded.

"Good girl," he said. "I'm relieved to hear it. I'm feeling a little vulnerable right now, if you wanna know the truth."

"Fuck your vulnerability. When I get outa here, we're gonna talk about my *new* job. Something a little more than your gal Friday."

Jimmy raised his eyebrows.

Oh, boy.

CHAPTER THIRTY-TWO

POST-IT

Boston City Hospital was not in the city's safest neighborhood, so Jimmy figured he had something to be grateful for when he found the Taurus still in the lot where he'd left it. With wheels, even. He unlocked it and lowered himself into the driver's seat. Sagged, more like. He closed his eyes, then straightened his neck back against the headrest, pressing hard, real hard.

What a fucking botch he'd made of everything. He didn't protect Taffy–the only thing she'd asked of him. You get a wild idea about a murder involving a transvestite, you enlist her in the hunt, and she ends up scarred for life in a horrible incident–which ends up involving you in what? Violating a crime scene, tampering with evidence, and who knows what all? Interfering with a corpse? He seemed vaguely to recall some statute prohibiting that. And then, while he was off on *that* little jag, he wasn't even available when his wife found out her cancer might be headed south on her. Way south, if the tests were bad.

What a guy.

He sniffed and made a face. Smells, too–bad as Mook, Taffy might say.

He looked over at his soiled jacket, the source of the odor. It was still lying there across the passenger seat.

Cleaners, he thought. Inanely.

He reached over and picked it up. Felt the lump that was Nickles's wallet. He looked around for a Dumpster as he shoved his hand in the pocket and emptied it. He dropped the coat on the floor and laid the wallet and the rest of the stuff on the seat beside him.

He checked out the wallet. Alligator, dyed burgandy. License. Credit cards. Hospital ID. He laid it down and picked up a money clip. Silver. Nice. It held several folded twenties, a five, two ones. No, he'd leave the bills. He was not the kind of ghoul that would loot a corpse. He dropped the money clip on top of the wallet.

It was folded in half, but he recognized at once the envelope that had borne Virginia's invitation to the show. Why did the guy carry it with him? A lurid memento of some kind?

Jimmy picked it up, unfolded the stiff, creamy paper. Opened the envelope and pulled out and unfolded the invitation itself, so neatly written in Virginia's hand. Turned it over. Nothing on the back. He shrugged, refolded it. Lifted the envelope again and started stuffing the note back into it.

He stopped. There was something else in the envelope.

He shook it out of the envelope. It was another piece of paper; a little slip, pale blue, and folded in half. When it was flattened out, he saw that it was a Post-it, a three-inch square. There was writing on it, too. Hurried and less neatly wrought than that on the invitation itself, but it was done, he was certain, in Virginia's hand.

Jimmy plucked his reading glasses out of his shirt pocket and put them on. He read the little note.

> D. Disregard all the hype and drama. Just come. Don't jump to conclusions. And *don't* call. I'll explain later.
>
> V.

Jimmy frowned down at the little note, then compared it to the writing on the invitation he and Virginia had drafted. The same hand, yes, and also done with the same pen. *His* pen, the one he had handed Virginia to use in making the fair copy. Which was done, for the most part, while he was in the bathroom, comparing his own physiognomy to Donald's.

It had to have happened then. She had jotted the little extra note while he was out of the room, then surreptitiously stuffed it into the envelope with the one they'd drafted together. He'd sat there and watched her seal the envelope, and still he'd missed it.

But then, she did magic tricks for a living.

But why? Nickles had shown up, yes, and evidently he *had* "jumped to conclusions" of some sort when he left the show. There was no questioning the rage that had hold of him in Virginia's kitchen. No, the anger was real—as real as Virginia's terror when she cowered before it.

He tried to reimagine the scene in the kitchen. Just what was it had Nickles been shouting? Something about a shakedown, he remembered that. There was another thing, too, though. An odd bit. So odd, in fact, he could remember the doctor's exact words.

You want to fuck this thing up now, after all I've gone through?

What "thing"? And why did he make it sound as if Virginia knew exactly what the "thing" was that was about to get fucked up?

Jimmy sat for a long time in the parked Taurus. Going through everything. Slowly, piece by piece, it started to come together for him. He saw at last that he had failed to ask the most important question of all—until it was too late.

Why would Nickles go around carrying lengths of colored nylon rope when he didn't have any expectation of using them?

CHAPTER THIRTY-THREE

HONEST JOHN

It was not surprising that it took more than a week before Jimmy got back down to Provincetown. A nightmare of a week, in retrospect. Dr. Bergman's tests confirmed the worst: the disease was back, having released noxious little seedlings into Phyllis's bloodstream and morphing into secondary bone cancer. Intense chemotherapy was indicated, including hormone-based treatments to slow further releases and some mysterious stuff called bisphosphonates to reduce bone destruction by inhibiting cancer cells already in place. For the pain in her back, should it worsen or (God forbid) pop up elsewhere, Dr. Bergman proposed a short course of radiotherapy, on an outpatient basis. Often, she assured them, a single treatment would do the trick, easing the pain in a matter of a week or two.

The prognosis? *Guarded* was the only word Jimmy took away from the esoteric disquisition that followed his question—and he could tell from the look on the doctor's face that, as always, she had chosen her words with great care. In Phyllis's presence he did his best to seem encouraged, but he took to sucking Altoids to get rid of the awful, coppery taste that seemed to have invaded his mouth.

Taffy underwent successful surgery to rebuild her left eye socket. The eye itself was lost. Even so, two days after the operation she seemed much like her old self, wondering aloud why she couldn't keep an array of glass eyes in different colors—as accessories, she said, to be popped in as she chose, depending on outfit and occasion and whim. Jimmy told her about W. C. Fields's role as a bartender named Honest John—was it in *Six of a Kind?* Every night he'd served a shot of booze and a glass of water to a man with a glass eye. The man would take out his glass eye and drop it in the water glass while he drank his whiskey. And one night, after the man had finished his drink and was headed for the door, the bartender had called out to remind him not to forget the eye.

"*Ever since then,*" Jimmy had quoted, in his best imitation of W. C. Fields's sonorous bray, "*they've called me Honest John.*"

Which set Taffy wondering if the eye was something she should mention in her personals.

Jimmy also had to scramble to catch up at the office. He finally produced his client for Previtt's deposition—an event of such stupefying tedium that Jimmy's own client took to kneeing him when he nodded off. The temp who filled in for Taffy was a hunched, sour matron beneath a brass-colored conk named Wanda—the temp, not the conk. She screened none of his calls—not even cold calls from stockbrokers—and one afternoon, when things got too slow for her taste, she decided to replace his handwritten Rolodex cards with typed ones, botching the spellings and phone numbers in the process.

It was Agent Butler's unexpected call that got him off the dime. Wondering if she had heard of Dr. Nickles's disappearance, Jimmy braced himself for the worst. But she just wanted to know how he was doing, she said. He told her his wife wasn't well and what had happened to Taffy. She told him she was sorry and wished everyone well. He found himself wishing he didn't have to deal with this over the phone: a visible shrug was a much simpler and—to his mind—more eloquent response than any words he could muster.

"I want you to know," she said after a brief silence between them, "that I had to file a three-oh-two about our little outing in Provincetown. It's required. You know what that is, a three-oh-two?"

"A field report."

"Yes. Raw stuff. Means absolutely nothing. I mention it only because when I did, I had to write out your theory, such as it is. And report how the drag show didn't pan out as you'd hoped. And setting it out on paper like that? Well, it made me think it through, step by step. And I finally figured out the flaw in it—why it's so wildly improbable that Gilfillen's death could have happened the way you said."

"And you're going to tell me, right?"

"Not if you don't want me to."

"Sure. Go ahead."

"It was the ropes. The very thing that made you so sure it was Nickles in the first place. Because your theory was that the killing was unplanned, some tussle that got out of hand. And then Nickles, drawing on his inside knowledge about Van Gogh, tries to make it look like one of his by tying him up with the colored ropes. Right?"

Jimmy knew exactly where she was going with this—he'd just been there himself—but he limited himself to acknowledging that she was right.

"Donald Gilfillen was killed between eleven P.M. and two A.M., according to the medical examiner. Where, I ask you, would Douglas Nickles find three pieces of rope—in three very distinctive colors, mind you—in the middle of the night? Can you answer me that? I mean, it's not like he would be carrying them with him, would he?"

No, Jimmy agreed, he probably wouldn't.

"Because that would require planning, preparation. Which isn't what you were postulating at all. This was a guy he picked up in a bar someplace, an impromptu tryst that went real bad. Not a premeditated murder. You're not suggesting premeditation here, are you?"

No, he wasn't. He admitted she was right. So conceived, his scenario had been—well, wildly improbable.

Jimmy tried to attend to the rest of the conversation, but his mind was wasn't on it. He encouraged her, mouthed phatic responses. He realized he'd been sitting on what he knew, and that he'd known it longer than he had been willing to acknowledge.

Well, he couldn't sit on it much longer. If he could put it together, why wouldn't Butler—especially once she began wondering why Nickles had gone missing so hard on the heels of their—what did she call it again? Their outing. An odd choice of words under the circumstances. All to test his wildly improbable theory.

After listening to her for a minute or two, Jimmy began to sense something else about Agent Butler.

She liked him.

Not there was anything like . . . *forward* about it. Just an amiability between the two of them. It surprised him. For days, he had felt anything but likable.

Always with the angles, Phyllis had said. The con. Or finesse, to use the more neutral term, the euphemism he had preferred with Taffy.

No, not likable. More like a bust, he figured—as a husband, a friend, a boss, a lawyer. As a human being.

He fought off the gloom and ended his conversation with Butler on what he hoped was a pleasant note. Promised her a tootle when things settled down again.

Depression settled over him after he replaced the receiver.

In his mind's eye he saw again the collection of buoys that had been suspended from the rafters in Virginia's garden shed. With their colored lines still attached to them.

He willed his funk away and drew himself to his feet. Checked his watch—10:10.

"Wanda!" he called out. "If there's anything on my calendar for the day, start canceling and rescheduling. I'm gonna be out."

CHAPTER THIRTY-FOUR

THE NEXT RIGHT THING

D o you think that's a good idea? I mean, so soon . . . after?"
Jimmy said, "Yes. There's loose ends that need to be
picked up."

"Loose ends?" Virginia repeated. No, check that—*Richard.*
Phyllis was right.

Richard sounded anxious now. "Did we overlook something?"

"I did, anyway. You don't have any plans to go out anywhere,
do you?"

Richard allowed as how he didn't. And it was Monday; there
was no show. He'd be around the house.

Jimmy snapped the cell phone onto the little clip on his belt.
He maneuvered the Taurus toward the ramp leading to the
Expressway, southbound.

It was a beautiful autumn day, brisk but not too cold. The
October leaves showed their full New England colors, some still on
the trees, others skittering about in gusts. The kind of day he should
be enjoying with Phyllis on the back porch or on a drive up to
Woodstock. Well, there were going to be a lot of those days, and
soon. Just let him get this piece done. Finish it off.

Jimmy pulled over on Windsor Street, directly across from the
bungalow. Richard, he noticed, was bending over the hood of a car,

a garden hose in his left hand and a gigantic sponge in the right. His sneakers were bumping up against a bucket of soapy water at his feet.

"It'll just rain," Jimmy called out as he walked up the drive. "That's why I never bother."

Richard paused in his swabbing and looked over his right shoulder at him.

"It depends on how long you want to keep it." He stood up straight and dropped the wet sponge into the pail, tossing the hose off to the side. "Me," he said, taking a step back to admire his handiwork as he wiped his hands, front and back, on the sides of his sweatshirt, "I want to hang on to this one. Might even have a burglar alarm installed."

"Are you kidding? That's a fucking Hyundai. Who would steal a Hyundai? It was a Yugo, now, I could understand it. You had one of them, and actually running still, you'd have something with real collector's value. But a Hyundai . . ."

"I was thinking," Richard said, head to one side. "I could get one of those Pat Buchanan car alarms. You know the one. Set it off and it starts blaring his speech to the '92 Republican convention— the one they said sounded better in the original German. I hear they sell like hotcakes up in Cambridge—and scare the shit out of car thieves."

Jimmy forced a smile. "Job's that boring, huh? It's got you working up new routines?"

"Whistle while you work," he said with a shrug and a bright little smile of his own. "Let's go inside. After you."

Jimmy led the way up the front porch and through the foyer. When he kept going straight, Richard touched his elbow. Jimmy stopped and looked back at him.

"Not the kitchen," Richard said. "The living room, okay?"

Jimmy tried to read his expression. "What's the matter? You got another room you can't use? A new spot to walk around?"

"Be nice."

They took seats in the living room, the same ones they'd sat in that first night, after the other party guests had gone home.

"Can I get you anything?"

Jimmy shook his head. "No. I just need to talk some things through. Get it clear in my head."

"Like what?"

"Like what happened to the murder weapon."

Richard winced visibly. "What's that, lawyer talk? You're calling it a murder now? The other night you said it was self-defense."

"I'm not talking about the knife." When he got no response he added, "I mean whatever was used to kill Donald."

Richard's wince turned to a look of puzzlement. "What—?"

"Because you were there. You had to be. That was the big hole in my theory, you see. I never stopped to ask myself why Nickles would just happen to be carrying bits of colored rope around with him. In case he lost his head and killed somebody? And then had to make it look like Van Gogh did it? Bah! Pretty stupid of me, wasn't it?"

Again he got no answer.

"I appreciate your reticence. One of us calling me stupid is enough. But I was. I was so . . . *into* that business of Nickles having inside information about Van Gogh—knowing the ropes, so to speak— that I overlooked the fact that my theory only made sense if there were *two* people involved. One who knew about the rope colors— that's Nickles—and one who knew where to find them when they suddenly became necessary. That was you. You had them in the garden shed, tied to the buoys you or Donald or somebody had salvaged. Nylon, God bless it, doesn't rot, so they were good as new. So when you and Nickles found yourselves with Donald's messy body on your hands, the two of you were able to pull it together. To find a way to convince the police—even the FBI—that he was just another one of Van Gogh's dead fags, and it would end there. How'm I doin' so far?"

Richard just stared at him.

"You think I'm crazy? Concocting another harebrained theory? Hey, I thought we were in agreement when Nickles showed up and he seemed ready to kill one or both of us for stumbling onto his secret. I mean, his behavior that night only makes sense if my original theory was at least *partly* on the right track. Why else would he be so bent out of shape by the show and end up screaming at both of us afterwards?

"But Agent Butler, she figured out that my theory didn't hold water. That unless it was a premeditated murder, Nickles would have had no way of coming up with the ropes he needed to stage his little misdirection in the middle of the night. No, it took two people. One with the secret knowledge and one with the ropes. You and Nickles."

Jimmy stuck two fingers in his shirt pocket and started fishing around. "Thing was, I didn't really need Agent Butler to explain it to me. She wasn't telling me anything new. She just made it crystal clear why my original theory couldn't work. Because I already had this."

He pulled the little blue note from his pocket. Richard's eyes flicked to it, then back to Jimmy's.

Jimmy said, "Too bad you displayed so much squeamishness at the sight of Nickles's body—and to this *day* I wonder how much of it was feigned. If *you'd* been the one to go through his pockets before we bundled him up for that ceremonious burial at sea? Well, then I never would have found your note. But I'm being unfair. Why would it ever occur to you that the man would bring it with him? You probably should have just called him, you know. But then again, I had just finished telling you how dangerous phone records could be, hadn't I? So you took your shot with the note. When I was in the john.

"Point is, I did find it. It told me the two of you had a history of some kind. You were telling him he should trust you. And you expected him to. To show up and do nothing. Let the goofy lawyer put on his silly show and lay his suspicions to rest.

"And that's not all it told me. Because when I put the note together with what went on in the kitchen, well, it just didn't make sense. What was that *thing* Nickles said you were about to fuck up? I thought it was a little odd when I heard him say it. Because I remember his exact words. '*You want to fuck this thing up now, after all I've gone through?*' What's 'this thing' was he talking about? I supposed at the time he was referring to his efforts to cover up Donald's murder. But the . . . locution was off, you know what I mean? It was odd, like I said. The way he put it made it sound like it was some kind of *joint* thing, something the two of you were involved in."

"You *are* crazy." Richard seemed to be engaging him now.

"I got a Rolodex full of people willing to second that–me with 'em, half the time. But that doesn't make me wrong about this. So let me try out my new theory. What I think *really* happened that night."

He shoved the little piece of paper back into his shirt pocket.

"It was a Sunday night. Like you told me, Donald was supposed to be in Boston that night, not on the Cape. But it's a Sunday night–there's no show. The Lizard is dark on Sundays and Mondays, right? So does it make sense–you're Donald now–that you'd troll for trade in some bar and bring him home on a night when your partner isn't working and you're not supposed to be in town anyway? Huh?"

Jimmy answered his own question. "Of course not. Because that's not what happened at all. It puts it backwards, in fact. It was *you* brought home the handbag. Isn't that the word you'd use to describe him? The hunky Dr. Nickles? And it's Donald who shows up unexpectedly, catches the two of you together. Unseemly melee ensues. For some reason, the big guy gets rough. And Donald ends up dead.

"What happens next? It's not that much of stretch. I've seen it myself. Same script, the whole performance. 'My life is ruined! Oh, what can we do?' And one of you–Nickles, since he knows about Van Gogh–comes up with the cord thing. Oh, if we only knew where to get some colored cords. No problem, says the lady. Right out back, in the shed. All kinds of 'em. Just tell me what color you want."

He watched Richard's eyes roll with disdain.

"Okay, okay. So it's a bit over the top. Maybe Nickles could've seen the ropes there himself. We haven't established how often he'd been to the house. Would that be so hard for the police to determine for themselves?"

Richard eyed him, slyly now. "If that's the case–that Nickles knew the ropes were in the shed–he could have seen them there on some earlier occasion with Donald, not me. You don't need my involvement to explain it."

"Fair enough," he agreed. "In fact, I spent quite a bit of time considering that very point. But the problem is, you see, I *have* your involvement. Right here." He clapped his right hand over his shirt pocket. "That's why you sent him the note. Why else would you send it?

"But send it you did. And my theory—my new, improved one, in the fancy box—it explains it. You were involved with Nickles in Donald's death. And your ruse with the ropes would have worked, too, if someone else hadn't entered the scene.

"Yes, Van Gogh. An unlikely figure, to be sure. But he doesn't appreciate being tarred with somebody else's messy brush. He develops his suspicions about the doctor. And he sets everything in motion. The photograph. Tristan.

"And me, in particular. Like a goddamn pinball. I wish I could say I'm proud of my part in it, but I'm not. Because somehow I let you pull me into your mess as well."

Jimmy sat back. He watched Richard for some sign, some indication that he was right. Despite the aura of certainty with which he had laid it out, he knew he had been stacking inferences, shaky ones at that, on top of one another to a ridiculous height.

And Richard gave nothing away. Just shook his head. A pitying gesture.

"I'm not even going to get into it with you," he said. "You seem to have this facility for twisting your theories to adapt to data that doesn't fit. I expect you'll just keep on doing it, no matter what I say."

"Don't need to," Jimmy said, with a tight smile. "Got it right this time. One of you killed him—I've been assuming it was Nickles, not you, but I'm not even sure of that. Because it occurred to me, knowing as I do what a convincing performer you are, that maybe you killed Nickles to shut him up. Not out of hysterical fear that he'd kill you or me. No, to keep him from blurting out what happened to Donald. That really *would* make it self-defense, wouldn't it?"

Richard gave him a tiny, dismissive shake of his head.

Jimmy said, "It's okay. I didn't really expect an answer. But answer me this, will you?"

He waited until he had Richard's complete attention again. "Which one of you cut off the ear? And who fucked the corpse?"

Richard's eyes widened. From what? Shock? Revulsion?

Jimmy said, "He *was* raped, after all—and after he was dead. Which makes sense, of course: all the others were. If you hope to pass him off as one of Van Gogh's victims, you strive for consistency. So *one* of you did. Which one? And with what? There was no semen, I'm told, but I guess that's understandable, given the circumstances."

Richard looked down now, shaking his head as he stared at his feet.

Jimmy pushed on. "You should have just dumped the body, you know. Like we did with Nickles. Instead of all the elaborate subterfuge. Of course, you'd have had a hell of a mess to clean up–nothing like Nickles. That was pretty clean. A little blood on a stone floor, that's about it. But still, I'll bet that occurred to you many times since. Especially after I showed up and started making trouble. No wonder you were so quick to hit on the idea of using Donald's boat. You'd probably been wishing for months that you'd used it to do away with Donald."

Richard shifted in his chair. When he looked up at Jimmy again, his eyes were shining. He said, "I loved him. I don't expect you to believe that."

"I don't know why not. I hear it all the time. Guys up for killing their wives? They always tell me how much they loved her. Never moves the jury, though–or the judge at sentencing."

"You're crazy," Richard said, slapping his palms on his knees. "But it really doesn't matter, does it? No one would ever believe a word of this."

Jimmy had to give him that one. "You may be right. Van Gogh's dead. Nickles sleeps with the fishes. How could they ever prove any of it?"

Richard was now standing now. "I think you should leave now," he said. He began to move toward the front door.

"On the other hand," Jimmy said as he stood up himself, "I could sure put you through hell in the process. 'My life is ruined?' Isn't that what you said? And what about your big break? You think Rosie O'Donnell would still want you when this becomes public?"

Richard stopped. He turned around to face Jimmy, a little smile tugging at one corner of his mouth. He said, "I wouldn't be the only one ruined. You'd have to explain your own role in all this. They'd never be able to touch me, but what about you? You'd be admitting to all kinds of wrongdoing, wouldn't you?"

Jimmy snorted. "You think I give a shit? Compared to everything I got on my plate right now, *you think I give a shit?*"

He walked past the man and toward the front door. He almost made it, too, before Richard stopped him with a question.

"What are you going to do?"

Jimmy turned back to look at Richard. In the fading light from the bay windows, Richard seemed suddenly older: fragile and defenseless. He felt the old protective impulse.

Then he recalled Phyllis's injunction: there was no Virginia.

But she was wrong. Because he had been there. He had known her. Cared about her, even liked her.

Jimmy shook his head once, hard.

"What'll I do? The next right thing, I guess. But you? What are you worried about? You'll be okay. You said it yourself. No matter what happens, at the end of the day you can always tell yourself you had a successful day–because you didn't drink."

He heard the screen door slap shut behind him as he descended the porch steps. Dry oak leaves carpeted the sidewalk, and his feet rustled through them on his way to the street. A breeze eddied some of them where the grass gave way to blacktop.

Winter coming. A long, hard one from the look of things.

He turned right and took four strides to reach the driver's door of the Taurus. He pulled the door open and paused, looking back for a moment at the little bungalow. He dropped his right hand and felt the cell phone against his side.

He wondered if he really would give Agent Butler a tootle.

The next right thing?

Whatever that was.

AFTERWORD

I have many people to thank for their assistance and kindness during the writing of this book.

Chris Johnson advised me regarding contact prints and other technical details of photographic reproduction. Tom Peisch and Tony Fugate helped me through some of the thickets of criminal law. Any lapses here are mine, not theirs.

Emily Schatzow and Charles Deutsch first suggested the notion of amalgamated film titles and even came up with most of the examples Joanne mentions here.

Neil Leifer allowed me to appropriate his own experience with identity theft and credit-card fraud—he was the victim of a scam remarkably like the one Tristan works on "Neil Leifer" in the book. Neil even had the good grace to let me use his name in the retelling.

Christine Casoli is the author of a personal ad I adapted here and ascribed to Taffy. I hasten to add that Taffy's character is not otherwise modeled on Christine's. As all who know her will attest, Christine is a model of probity and respectful decorum—not to mention a woman with a nationally acknowledged fashion sense that is nothing like Taffy's.

Because I must confess to being only marginally less ignorant about the gay community than Jimmy Morrissey, I went to some lengths not to blunder into giving offense. Some members of the community were kind enough to read all or parts of the manuscript with these concerns in mind. If any lingering insensitivity in this regard nonetheless disfigures the book, the tin ear is mine, not theirs—and I beg the reader's forgiveness.

Those interested in learning more about the history of cross-dressing, and the psychosocial responses it has evoked, are referred to Marjorie Garber's fascinating study, *Vested Interests: Cross-Dressing & Cultural Anxiety* (Routledge, 1991). In other respects, the reader will detect my large debt to Jacques Chailley, *The Magic Flute Unveiled: Esoteric Symbolism in Mozart's Masonic Opera* (Knopf, 1971).

Perhaps most notably, I wish to thank Kandi Kane (AKA Charlie Edwards-Hides), whose stage persona and theatrical troupe, Big-Boned Barbies (née Boys-R-Us), were models for Virginia Dentata and Where the Boys Are. While I appropriated the format of these acts into the novel, I am proud to say I only stole one of Kandi's jokes. I try to restrict myself to stealing only one of hers per book. Thank you, Kandi.

I owe a special debt of thanks to friends who gave me feedback on the manuscript: Richard Alfred, Ellen Braithwaite, Dan Crane, Steve Gallos, Lynn Goldsmith, Hon. Dermot Meagher, Rusty Russell, Steve Schaffran, Bradford Swing, Dvora Tager, Ruth Tager, and my mother, Evelyn Fredrickson. Again, I am grateful for the generous support of the Demo's Writers' Workshop and in particular its founding fellow, Samuel Shem. And I don't even know how to begin to express my gratitude to my tireless agents, Sam Pinkus and Gene Winick, or to my indulgent editors, Bob Gleason, Brian Callaghan, Eric Raab, and the eagle-eyed Sara Schwager.

Finally, and once again, thank you, Jolly and Zeke, for your love and support and patience.